PRAISE FOR LA… S

"Sexy, dark, and suspenseful. . . . Larissa Ione brings to life a riveting new world filled with sizzling sensuality, dark wit, and wicked hot demons. Larissa Ione is an exciting voice in paranormal romance."

—Lara Adrian, *New York Times* bestselling author

"Wicked . . . decadently sinful . . . prepare to be burned."

—Gena Showalter, *New York Times* bestselling author

"Dangerously erotic, wonderfully satisfying. . . . Ione knows how to make your heart race."

—Cheyenne McCray, *New York Times* bestselling author

"What a ride! Dark, sexy, and very intriguing, this book gripped me from start to finish. I can't wait to read the next in the series."

—Nalini Singh, *New York Tines* bestselling author

"Dark, dynamic, and dangerously seductive."

—Jaci Burton, *New York Times* bestselling author

"Very dark, very sexy, and very creative. Ione's Demonica series will have the most jaded paranormal fans perking up."

—Emma Holly, author of *Demon's Fire*

LARISSA IONE'S DEMONICA NOVELS

Pleasure Unbound
Desire Unchained
Passion Unleashed
Ecstasy Unveiled
Sin Undone
Eternity Embraced

LARISSA IONE

THE MOONBOUND CLAN VAMPIRES

Bound by Night

POCKET BOOKS
New York London Toronto Sydney New Delhi

Pocket Books
A Division of Simon & Schuster, Inc.
1230 Avenue of the Americas
New York, NY 10020

First Pocket Books paperback edition October 2013

POCKET and colophon are registered trademarks of Simon & Schuster, Inc.

For information about special discounts for bulk purchases, please contact Simon & Schuster Special Sales at 1-866-506-1949 or business@simonandschuster.com.

The Simon & Schuster Speakers Bureau can bring authors to your live event. For more information or to book an event, contact the Simon & Schuster Speakers Bureau at 1-866-248-3049 or visit our website at www.simonspeakers.com.

Designed by Leydiana Rodríguez-Ovalles

Manufactured in the United States of America

10 9 8 7 6 5 4 3 2 1

ISBN 978-1-4767-0017-5
ISBN 978-1-4767-0019-9 (ebook)

For my mom.
With this book, I finally get to explore a little of our
Native American heritage. I hope you're proud.
I love you.

Prologue

THE VAMPIRES WERE behaving weird today. Not that anyone believed Nicole when she told them. No, all the adults simply smiled, patted her on the head, and told her to go upstairs to play until her older brother arrived to take her to the zoo.

Half brother, she'd told them, and again, they'd smiled and shooed her away. She never reminded her mother about the half-brother thing, though. Chuck had a different mom, and although Nicole didn't understand what an "affair" was, talking about Chuck always brought up that word, and it made her mom and dad fight.

One of the household vampires, Anthony, grinned as he passed her in the foyer with a tray of decadent hors d'oeuvres, but something about his smile made goose bumps prickle her arms. Like all the servants, he'd always kept his eyes downcast—"secured his gaze," as her father called it—in the presence of humans, but not this time. This time, he looked at her the way her dad looked at the Thanksgiving turkey.

Barefoot and wearing the pink princess dress she

was never supposed to wear outside, she darted out the back door reserved for the servants and ran as fast as she could, squinting against the bright summer sunlight. She slipped unnoticed past the wet bar and the food-laden tables, through the crowds of people partying around the pool, until she reached the hedges designed to conceal the gardening shed and equipment. Laughter and the clinking of glasses followed her through the dense brush. She scurried like a little animal, not caring that the branches were scratching her skin and catching on her dress.

Panting, she crouched in the very spot where, just six months before, her vampire nanny had died, her unborn baby with her. Nicole shivered at the memory. She'd been so excited about Terese's baby. Terese had been the best nanny ever, always teaching Nicole new things, reading to her, asking her opinion on things as if Nicole were a grown-up. Terese would have been a great mommy to the baby. Secretly, Nicole had sometimes wished Terese were *her* mommy, too.

Tears stung Nicole's eyes as she reached up and wrapped her necklace around her fingers, bringing the ring Terese had given her to her lips.

It's a secret ring, Terese had said as she pressed it into her small hand. *You can hide things inside it. I want you to have it. And remember what I said. Be a good girl and a good adult. You'll have a lot of power someday. Use it well. I love you, Nikki.*

Terese had been killed half an hour later . . . by her own mate.

Riker.

The very name struck fear into Nicole's heart.

Terese had loved him, trusted him. And he'd driven a blade into her throat.

Nicole would never forget Terese's broken voice as she pleaded with him. She'd definitely never forget his face. His glittering silver eyes. His sandy hair that Terese said was silky-soft. His fangs that had been longer than Nicole's finger.

All of it haunted her nightmares.

"Nicole Michelle."

Nicole jumped at her father's angry voice. He stood a few feet away in the dappled shade from the huge oak tree, his lips pressed together in a forbidding line.

"How many times have I told you to stay away from the shed? It's not healthy for you to hang out here like a damned dog mourning the loss of his master. Terese was just a vampire. We got you a hamster *and* a new nanny. It's time to get over it."

"But I don't like my new nanny! Chelsea's grumpy, and she doesn't read to me before bed—"

"We didn't purchase her to be your best friend," he snapped. "And look what you've done to your dress. Your mother is going to have Chelsea spank you."

Terese would never have spanked Nicole. Hand shaking, Nicole automatically reached for the comfort of the ring Terese had given her, but in an instant, her father fisted the chain and yanked, snapping the necklace and sending the ring tumbling into the grass.

"Enough with the ring! You were supposed to throw it away. It's beneath you to wear a slave's jewelry. And frankly, it's disturbing." He flung the destroyed chain into the bushes. "Go to your room and—"

A shrill scream interrupted him. Maybe it was weird, but her first thought was that Daddy hated to be interrupted. Whoever did that would be in *big* trouble.

Her father spun around as another scream joined the first. And then another. And another, until suddenly, all Nicole could hear were cries for help and shrieks of terror.

"Stay here, Nicole." Her father turned to her for just a second, but in that moment, she saw something in his face she'd never seen in him before: fear. "Hide. No matter what happens, don't come out."

She nodded, but he was already gone, running for the main house. Frightened and confused, she wedged herself between the storage shed and a bush and listened to the screams and pleas, the groans, and the wet, horrible crunching sounds punctuated by maniacal laughter. On the ground, the ring Terese had given her lay in a tangle of trampled grass, and Nicole found that if she focused on the shiny oval ruby, she could pretend the noises all around her weren't real.

Suddenly, a huge foot came down on the ring. Too petrified to move, Nicole could only gasp when massive hands ripped her from her hiding place and hurled her against the supply-shed wall. She crumpled to the ground, pain tearing through her back, her hips, and her right leg. She tried to scramble to her feet, but her body wasn't working right.

Trembling, choking on a sob, she looked down at her thigh and the bloody end of bone protruding through mangled flesh. Her princess dress was grass- and bloodstained now. Even through her unimaginable agony and terror, her mind could form only one thought with any semblance of clarity: she would be in so much trouble for ruining her clothes.

"I've been looking for you, Nicole."

Through a haze of anguish and tears, she glanced up at the vampire looming over her. "B-Boris?" She cried out as her family's chef lifted her and once again slammed her against the shed, this time pinning her there. "Where's my daddy? I want my mommy. *Mommy!*"

"Call for her all you want," Boris said. "She's not coming." He touched her cheek with his finger, and a stab of icy terror shot straight to her heart. "I've fed you since you were old enough to eat solid foods, you spoiled little human. Now it's time for you to feed me." He took a deep breath, like he was smelling her. "I've always heard that children taste better than adults. Sweeter. Purer. Now I get to find out for myself." He grinned. "It's going to hurt, since I have no fangs."

Nicole tried to fight. Tried to kick, hit, scream. But Boris was strong, and she was a petrified eight-year-old girl with a broken leg. His dull teeth sank into her skin. Grinding, crushing sounds accompanied a storm of agony as he chewed into her throat. Liquid warmth streamed down her neck, and when she tried to scream, only a gurgling noise came out of her mouth.

Why was he doing this? Why would someone who had baked her cookies for after-school snacks and strawberry cakes for her birthdays want to hurt her so badly?

You can domesticate animals, but you can never trust them or know for sure that they won't bite. You can't override instinct, her father once said. *Vampires are animals that must always be harnessed. Remember that, Nicole.*

She hadn't believed him. But as her body went mercifully numb and her struggles weakened, she recalled what her father had said when she'd argued that their household vampires, like Boris and Terese, were kind and loyal.

Even cute, fluffy pet bunnies can bite.

Darkness closed in, and in the last second before she lost consciousness, Nicole wondered if bunny bites hurt as badly as vampire bites.

"GO FUCK YOURSELF."

Hunter, MoonBound clan's leader, leaned back in his chair and gave Riker an expectant look. "Go fuck yourself . . . ?" He made a *come on* gesture with his fingers. "Finish the sentence."

Riker rolled his eyes. "Go fuck yourself . . . *sir*."

Nodding his dark head in satisfaction, Hunter kicked his boots up onto the scarred oak conference table. "Better." He laced his fingers together over his abs, his deeply tanned skin making his white T-shirt seem even brighter. "Now, as I was saying before being told to do something anatomically impossible, if we can storm the Martin residence with enough of our warriors, we can take hostages. The humans will be forced to give Neriya back to us."

Another warrior seated at the table, Baddon, flipped a pen toward the ceiling. "Why don't we get ShadowSpawn to pony up some muscle to help?" Without looking, he snatched the pen out of the air. "It's *their* female we're trying to rescue."

"I already tried," Hunter said grimly. "They insist

that because Neriya was taken by the humans while in our care, we're responsible for getting her back, or they'll declare war on the eve of the new moon."

Katina, the clan's only senior-level female warrior, hissed. "That goes against every vampire custom and protocol there is. No one declares war so close to moon fever." She braced her elbows on the table and leaned forward, as if ready to launch herself at anyone who dared argue with her. She'd certainly done it before. That table had seen a number of brawls over the years. A few dents even belonged to Riker. "You know they wouldn't do it on the eve of the *full* moon, when the *males* need to feed."

"No clan would risk that," Baddon said. "But females mean little to ShadowSpawn except as breeders. They don't give a shit if the females miss a new-moon feeding."

"Fuck 'em," Katina spat. "Let them come. Our warriors are well trained and powerful. We'll give them the fight of their lives."

As much as Riker wanted to agree with her, the odds were in the enemy clan's favor. Not only did they outnumber MoonBound clan three to one, but ShadowSpawn had no code of ethics and made no distinction among males, females, and children when it came to killing in battle or otherwise. As ruthless and cold as Riker could be, even he had boundaries, and murdering noncombatant women and children was a hard line in the sand.

"Wendigo legend is based on ShadowSpawn," Hunter reminded them. "They're killers, cannibals who have destroyed clans up and down the West Coast.

Neriya was lost while she was a guest in our home. Make no mistake; if we don't return her to Shadow-Spawn, we'll feel their wrath. They're desperate to get her back."

Understandable. Vampire mortality rates during childbirth were dangerously high, and Neriya's rare ability to deliver babies safely made her precious among their people. Her gift was the reason she'd been with MoonBound in the first place. ShadowSpawn had allowed MoonBound to borrow her for a birth in exchange for weapons and a case of prepackaged human blood that Baddon had stolen from a delivery truck.

"I'm not afraid of them." Katina shifted, her leather jacket squeaking against the back of the chair. "Riker has prepared us for this. We can win, even if we have to scatter into the forest and fight like guerrillas until the end of time."

"Perhaps." Hunter's gaze went to the far wall of the conference room, where a painting depicting a bloody battle between two vampire clans hung next to other vampire and Native American artwork. "But our females and children will be dead. What will we have won?"

Riker had lost a female and a child, so he knew the answer to that.

And he wished like hell he didn't.

Hunter signaled to one of the clan's maidens, who brought over a tray laden with a leather flask, glasses, and a ceremonial pipe. Hunter waited until she left the room before saying, "Now, let's do the peace thing."

Peace? Riker was nowhere near ready to toast to a "good hunt" and smoke to "plentiful blood." Their clan was in danger from a rival vampire clan whose members were savage animals, and until the threat was over, Riker wasn't going to back off or play nice. Not even with the male who had led MoonBound clan for nearly two hundred years.

"Didn't you hear a word I said?" Riker whipped a dagger from his weapons harness and sank the blade into the table, where it vibrated as violently as the temper pulsing through his veins. "I don't give a shit if you're Supreme King Alpha Commander of the Known Universe. You're going to listen to me."

One ebony eyebrow climbed up Hunter's forehead, and the other three warriors stopped moving and breathing. All except Baddon, anyway. He traced one of the skull tats on his forearm and let out a soft *holy shit* whistle.

"Someone's feeling his oats today." Hunter folded his arms across his broad chest and studied Riker with deceptively calm, half-lidded eyes that were as black as his hair. "Why don't you make me listen? And then tell me why I shouldn't fire you as my second before I toss you into the pit for a month."

Summoning his military sniper training, Riker inhaled a slow, measured breath in order to steal a few precious seconds to set up his next shot. He'd stepped over the line by disrespecting Hunter in front of the senior warriors, and Riker would take his punishment like a good little vampire later. Right now, he had to knock some sense into his thick-headed clan leader.

"You're a great chief, Hunter," Riker said calmly. "But urban battle and covert ops are my specialty, and I'm telling you that in this case, a stealthy surgical strike is going to be more effective than numbers and brute force. If my plan for rescuing Neriya doesn't work, you can rally the clan for a larger assault, but you've got to let me do this my way. You've trusted me in charge of our warriors for more than thirty years, so trust me enough to handle this now. I can get her away from the humans who captured her. We'll return her to ShadowSpawn before they have a chance to come after us." Riker popped his dagger from the wood and sheathed it. "And you don't want to fire me because you'll be stuck dealing with Myne on your own. Which is also why you shouldn't drop me into the pit."

Hunter appeared to consider what he'd said. Although Riker was only half kidding about why Hunter shouldn't fire him or drop-kick him into the pit used for nonlethal punishments, there was some truth to what he'd said. Myne and Hunter, the only two pureblood male vampires besides Baddon in the clan, got along like two tomcats in a bag, and neither would admit that he needed the other.

"Where is the bastard, anyway?" Hunter asked, and Riker shrugged. Myne wasn't one to share his plans.

"Patrolling, probably. Not my day to watch him."

Jaggar, a male who had worked with the CIA before being turned into a vampire fifty years ago, cleared his throat. "Riker's right about stealth. I'd feel better if we had a whole team going in to rescue Neriya, but until we have more intel on her situation, it might be wise to let Riker go in the way he wants to."

"Especially with the increase in hunters and poachers lurking in the forest lately." Katina growled, her pearly fangs flashing in stark contrast with her brown skin. "A large group of vampires heading toward Seattle's billionaire district is a lot more likely to attract their attention than one or two of us."

Except for the sound of the cuckoo clock ticking on the wall behind Katina, there was silence as Hunter looked each of them in the eye. Finally, like a great cat rising from its jungle resting place, he dropped his feet onto the wood floor and unfurled to his full, impressive six-foot-seven height. Those who had been born vampires instead of turned into them were generally taller than most humans and turned vampires. They also got to keep their natural eye color, unlike turned vampires, whose eyes always became some shade of silver as their fangs grew in.

"I'll give Riker a shot at doing it his way." He jerked his head toward the door. "Out. Everyone but Riker. Fill in the other senior staff. We'll let the rest of the warriors know what's happening when we need to."

"What about general clan members?" Baddon asked. "Everyone is on edge."

"I'll speak at dinner. Assure everyone there's nothing to worry about for now." Hunter nodded at the door again. "Go."

Jaggar, Baddon, and Katina filed out, each shooting Riker a sympathetic glance as they went. Once the door closed, Riker got to his feet and moved away from the table, waiting for the dressing-down.

It came in the form of a right hook to the face.

Riker hit the wall hard enough to make the picture frames rattle.

"Don't disrespect me in front of the others again." Hunter glanced down at his knuckles. "Also? You have a hard face to match your hard head." No one went from pissed to playful in a split second the way Hunter did.

Tasting blood, Riker tested his jaw. Nothing broken or loose, but he'd feel it for a while. "You didn't learn that the first ten times you decked me?"

The truth was that Hunter had held back. Riker had never felt the full brunt of his chief's anger, but he'd seen it. If Hunter had wanted to, he could have shattered every bone in Riker's skull with a single blow.

Hunter gave a lazy shrug. "I'm a slow learner."

That was a load of crap. The ancient vampire came across as a laid-back, couldn't-give-a-shit slacker who liked video games, *Sports Illustrated*, and muscle cars, but he was a lot smarter than anyone who didn't know him gave him credit for. His calculating mind was blade-sharp, his smiles frequent, and his nature affable and calm, outwardly, at least. He'd never ruled with an iron fist—and he didn't need to. Respect for his leadership kept the clan running smoothly.

"You won't regret this," Riker assured him. "I can do it."

Doubt all but billowed from Hunter's pores as he lifted the ceremonial pipe from the tray. "If this were any other mission, I wouldn't be concerned. You know that."

"I know," Riker admitted. "But *you* know I'm right about this. I'm familiar with the Martin house. I've memorized the grounds. I've studied every detail of their security, both inside and outside the house."

"Studied?"

"Okay, stalked. But my point is—"

"I know what your point is. And I know how much your hatred for the Martins has eaten at you. Hatred makes you sloppy. Makes you focus so completely on revenge that you're blind to the dangers around you. Makes you—"

"Makes me determined to succeed."

Hunter put his back to the wall and propped one foot behind him, his pose casual, his expression as serious as Riker had ever seen it. "Your mate was a slave in the Martin household. How can you be sure you can do what needs to be done without that history coloring your actions? A pissed-off bear will run straight for the hunter with a gun."

"Because this is my home." Riker met his leader's gaze head-on. "This is my family. And if I screw up, I lose everything." He glanced over at the depiction of MoonBound's battle with the now-extinct CloudStrike clan. "We *all* lose everything."

TWO DAYS AFTER persuading Hunter to let him have his way, Riker stood on a ridge on the outskirts of Seattle, a cemetery at his back and, fittingly, a dead man at his feet.

Dead but not bleeding.

Riker had drained him of every last drop of blood—a fine vintage, aged about twenty-five years in the veins of a vampire hunter.

A rush of exhilaration flooded Riker's body, because nothing beat the high of taking down a hunter or poacher. Both were scum, just different subspecies of scum.

Tasty scum.

He touched the tip of his tongue to a fang as he looked down on the lights of the city that had propelled vampire slavery from a local phenomenon into a worldwide passion. Seattle's nightlife, which had exploded along with the population in the last twenty years, used to draw him; there was so much sport to be had in a thriving metropolis. But he no longer lived for fun. Couldn't remember the last time he'd had any.

No, life now was about revenge, just as Hunter had said.

As a vampire, he ate food daily, drank blood when he had to—and sometimes, like tonight, when he didn't.

"Hey, man, you ready to head back to the clan?"

"Not yet." Riker looked over at the vampire standing next to him. "It's time."

Myne's thick mane of pitch-black hair whipped at his temples as he shook his head. "You know I'm all for cutting through the humans like a tomahawk through snow, but—"

"But you think I'm stupid."

The slow roll of Myne's shoulder was a screaming *Hell yeah.*

"Humans tortured you for years. Defanged you. Were going to fucking *castrate* you." Riker eyed with admiration one of the few vampires who had escaped human slavery. It had been eighty years since humans had become aware of the existence of vampires, sixty since they'd enslaved them, and in that time, only a handful of lucky vampires had found freedom before the great uprising twenty years ago led to even stricter controls. Myne was one of the few to slip the slavery noose. "You slaughtered more humans in twenty-four hours than I have in my life. You kill people every chance you get. So tell me, how am I stupid?"

"Dude, I don't have enough fingers to count off all the ways."

"Ass," Riker muttered.

Myne regarded the glittering skyline in the distance, the streaking blurs from the headlights and taillights on the freeway. "You're stupid because you plan to do this on your own. I can't believe Hunter went along with your crazy plan." His mocha eyes shifted to Riker. "And how fucked-up is it that I actually agree with Hunter for once? We both think you're being an idiot. You need to rethink this."

"I'm not scrapping the mission. There's less risk of the clan being discovered if we do it my way."

If Riker acted alone, authorities would waste time scouring the city's trashy underbelly for him among the many lone vampires who lived there like cockroaches. But the more clan members he enlisted, the greater the chance that said authorities would realize they had an organized group on their hands. And soon after, the forest, usually left alone by the government, would be crawling not just with the usual hunters but also with Vampire Strike Force personnel—specialized law-enforcement agents whose mission it was to kill or capture every nonenslaved vampire on the planet.

Once VAST entered the picture, it wouldn't be long before someone from MoonBound was caught and tortured into revealing the clan's location. Although the entrances were concealed by both physical camouflage and magic put in place by the clan's mystic-keeper, Riker knew there was no such thing as completely secure. There was always a way to breach a wall, penetrate an enemy stronghold, and locate the hidden. Just one careless clue left behind by a clan member could lead VAST to the second-largest population of free vampires in the Pacific Northwest.

In the distance, a coyote yip-howled, and Myne listened, almost as if he understood the creature. He probably did. Myne had grown up with his Nez Perce tribe until he was a teen, and after that, he'd lived with animals for longer than he'd lived with people.

"What happens if you fail?" he asked.

"Then the clan goes with Plan B. Hunter's proposal." Which involved far more people, coordination, and risk.

"Shiiit." Myne kicked a stone off the ridge and watched it tumble down the rocky bank. "Let me help your sorry ass. With me, your insane scheme has a shot of success."

Riker grinned. "I knew you couldn't resist a challenge."

"So you were counting on my offer to help?"

"Yup."

"You could have just, you know, asked."

"Asked?" Riker snorted. "And turn in my male card?"

Riker ignored Myne's string of curses as he made his way down the embankment, moving toward the mansion he'd been staking out for the last week. Myne followed, his footsteps as light as a cat's despite his massive size. At six-foot-five and a born vampire, Myne was one of the tallest males in the clan, save Hunter. Not that Riker was short, but Myne seemed to enjoy flaunting his extra three inches and twenty pounds.

Riker would just smile and claim extra brains and an extra three inches on another part of his anatomy.

"So what's my job?" Myne dropped his hand to the dagger at his hip and skimmed his thumb along the hilt. "It better involve fighting."

"It does."

"And feeding?"

"If you want." Riker crouched behind a fir tree to avoid the sweep of a security spotlight sitting atop the mansion's north wall.

"And fucking?"

Riker shot Myne an *are you kidding me?* look over his shoulder. "Even if there was time for that, I didn't think you were into humans."

"I'll dive into any lake in a drought, man."

Myne was full of shit. He might be stuck in a perpetual sex drought, but Riker knew damned well the guy went for vampires. He'd gotten his fill of human sex a long time ago, and Riker only knew that because the guy had gotten so shitfaced once that his tongue had loosened. The next morning, Myne had been practically suicidal—and homicidal—over what he'd revealed, and Riker had probably saved both of their lives by lying to him, telling him that whatever Myne imagined he'd said had been all in his drunken head.

Thank God. Riker wasn't sure who would win in a contest of hand-to-hand, but he knew who'd win a fang free-for-all.

Myne's titanium chompers could rip limbs from bodies and heads from necks with the messy ease of a chain saw.

"So." Myne's fingers caressed the dagger hilt like a lover. The guy had carved it himself from the thigh bone of a poacher decades ago. The thing was so smooth from his touch that it practically shone in the moonlight. "What do we do first?"

Riker effortlessly leaped to the top of the twelve-foot stone fence that circled the mansion and surrounding grounds. "See the northwest fence corner? Where the stone is built up into the tree?" Riker peered into the branches. "That's a sniper station. Built after my mate died. We need to take the sniper out, or he'll smoke-check us before we get halfway across the lawn."

"Cool." Myne had always preferred a stealthy stalk-and-kill over a full-blown battle. Said it was a measure of skill and patience and a more honorable way to hunt an enemy. Riker figured dead was dead, but whatever. "You really think this Charles guy is just going to hand over a captive vampire because we tell him to?"

"Charles? No. That's why we're not bothering with that asshole." He scanned the property, taking one last inventory of the cameras, the dogs, and the security detail, all of which he'd been familiar with for two decades. "I'm after much more . . . sensitive . . . prey."

Myne landed in a crouch beside him, whisper-soft. "Who?"

Ahead, through one of the mansion's giant windows, a figure moved. A ginger-haired female. Tall. Curvy.

Enemy.

"Dr. Nicole Martin."

Riker felt Myne's eyes boring into him. "She's alive?"

"Apparently." A shiver of hatred slithered up Riker's spine. Until last week, when he'd seen a newspaper article glorifying the return of the Martin heir, he'd believed only one member of the godforsaken immediate family, Charles, was alive. "After the rest of the Martins were slaughtered in the rebellion, she was sent to Paris to live with her mother's relatives until she was old enough to work in Daedalus's French division as a vampire physiologist."

The mere mention of the infamous Seattle Slave Rebellion made Myne's voice degenerate into gravel. "And she's here now?"

Riker nodded at the female in the window. "Right there and all grown up. And if you're done jacking off your dagger, we'll go have a chat with her."

"You think she'll cooperate?"

Hell no. She was a Martin, after all, current CEO of the company that had revolutionized vampire slavery and used vampires like lab rodents to advance human medicine. Daedalus went through vampires like a slaughterhouse went through cattle, and Riker doubted the company held to any kind of "humane" standards.

"For her sake," Riker said slowly, "I hope so."

3

NICOLE MARTIN SHOULD never have left Paris. She hated the Seattle weather. Hated the family mansion.

Hated the vampires.

She would never have believed that the vampire situation could be so different here.

She tossed a Chinese-food container into the trash bin hard enough to send bits of rice flying and turned to the tele-screen on the obnoxiously decadent black-and-gold granite kitchen counter. Her towheaded half brother, Charles, stared at her from his desk at Daedalus Corporation's headquarters.

"You okay?" He gestured in the direction of her garbage can. "You subjected that poor takeout to some serious abuse."

"No, I'm not okay. I miss Paris." There. She'd said it. Pretending to be happy about returning to her childhood home was officially a big lie. "I miss my research lab. I miss my friends."

Sure, most of her friends had been of the casual kind, Europe's wealthy and powerful who only wanted what she—and Daedalus—could do for them, but she'd genuinely liked some of her colleagues. Plus, surrounding herself with people at all times kept her busy and kept the memories of her childhood at bay.

"You'll make new friends," Chuck assured her.

"Really?" She snorted. "I think it's more likely that after tomorrow, I'm going to be a pariah no one is going to want to look at, let alone invite to cocktail parties."

"Don't worry about the meeting." Like Nicole, he'd inherited his green eyes from their father, and they softened as he met her gaze. "The partners will get to the truth about what happened at the Minot facility."

A sting in her bottom lip was a sharp reminder that she was biting it. Bad habit, and one she'd been trying to break for years. *A lady doesn't fidget*, her mom used to say. Later, in private, Nicole's nanny Terese would tell her that Nicole was a child, and children could fidget all they wanted. The secret, she'd said, was to fidget productively.

Nicole reached past her medication bottles for the dwindling stack of paper on the counter, one of many she kept around the house.

"They don't want to get to the truth, Chuck. They want a scapegoat." She folded one corner of a sheet of paper and smoothed a crease into it. "Three dozen vampires from the Minot lab are dead. Ultimately, I'm responsible for everything my company does, and I'm going to get shipped off to Siberia for this."

If she was *lucky*, she'd get sent to the Siberia office. The other alternative, criminal prosecution, was also a possibility, thanks to groups like the Vampire Humane Society and Humans for the Advancement of Vampiric Entities, which had, in the last five years, forged huge inroads regarding the ethical treatment and disposal of domestic vampires.

"Don't think like that. You have a defense worked out." Chuck scribbled something on the notepad in front of him. "When you present your evidence, the board will have to give you the benefit of the doubt."

Uh-huh. Sure. The board had been looking for a way to get her out of the company for years. Her mother and father had been the brawn and brains behind the business they'd built from the ground up, but Nicole had merely inherited her position.

Even Chuck, whose illegitimacy hadn't allowed him a guaranteed place in their father's empire, had worked his way from the mailroom to chairman and then, finally, seven years ago, to CEO. The position had been temporary until Nicole was ready to take over, but she'd been happy to let him run the company, so he'd remained, and she'd settled into medical research.

Until two months ago, when she'd turned twenty-eight and legal clauses from her parents' wills and trusts kicked in, requiring her to rule the kingdom or lose everything. She hadn't wanted to drag her parents' names through the mud, so she hadn't fought the clauses and reluctantly moved back to Seattle to take over.

Understandably, there were now a lot of envious, bitter people sitting on the board of directors. At least Chuck had understood, and he'd returned to his prior chairman position with grace.

Nicole made a quick series of folds in the sheet of

paper, and the shape of a bird began to take form. "I should have asked for more help when I took over as CEO. Daedalus is too big, and my suggestions to sell off everything but the medical and scientific divisions haven't exactly been popular."

Chuck gave her a *no shit* look. "That's because you're asking that we keep the least profitable branches of the company and get rid of what our father founded the company on." His leather chair creaked as he shifted. "Acquiring, training, and selling vampire servants are the cornerstone of Daedalus. We make billions from supplying the public with vampires and all the accessories that go with them."

It took effort to not roll her eyes. "Oh, please. We make nearly as much from our scientific breakthroughs. Or haven't you noticed that people will practically sell their souls to stay young another fifty years or to heal from serious injuries faster or to be cured of cancer? We need to focus more fully on medical advancements. Let someone else handle the tasks that don't reflect positively on us."

"Like?"

"Like draining recently deceased humans to package and distribute their blood to vampire supply shops. Like conditioning and processing newly captured vampires before they're sent to a training facility." Nicole might hate vampires, but neutering, defanging, and torturing them until they broke didn't sit well with her.

"Look, Nicole," Chuck said, with a deep, long-suffering sigh. "I understand why you want to concentrate company efforts on the research side. I know how hard it is for you to live with your medical condition."

She ground her teeth at his bullshit soothing tone. Her ideas for the company were *not* about her medical issues. Her ideas were about helping people while getting away from the vampire trade. "But?"

Chuck braced his forearms on the desk and leaned closer to the screen, his expression a mask of concern. "But some Daedalus staff members think that's why you ordered the deaths of those vampires. To sabotage the company."

"What?" Her jaw dropped. "Are you kidding me?"

"Come on, sis. Like it's so ludicrous? You hate vampires."

"And that's reason enough to sabotage the company? You honestly believe I'd do that?"

"Of course not." He jammed his fingers through his two-hundred-dollar haircut, leaving messy grooves. "I'm just telling you what people are saying."

The intercom beeped, and the gate guard's voice droned. "Mr. Altrough is here to see you."

Dammit. "Let him in." She was going to need more paper.

Chuck tapped his Montblanc on the notepad. He'd never been able to sit still. Not that she had any room to judge. She had a house and an office full of origami art that spoke volumes about her inability to relax.

"You finally giving Roland a chance?" he asked.

Still irritated by Chuck's casual revelation that people inside the company believed her capable of such a despicable act, she snapped, "Not on your life. But he won't take no for an answer."

Nicole doubted that Roland Altrough, executive vice president in charge of Daedalus's Lifeblood Supply division—one of the divisions she wanted gone—would ever back off his pursuit of her. At least, not while she was in charge of Daedalus. Maybe there really was a bright side to being ousted from the company.

"Then why are you seeing him tonight?"

"Because besides you, he's the one person on my side in this mess."

One pale eyebrow cocked up. "So you think that if you sleep with Roland, he'll stay on your side?"

"I'm not sleeping with him. He's a pig." A handsome pig but a disgustingly misogynistic creature nonetheless.

Chuck grinned. "Smart girl." Behind him, a shadow approached, and Nicole's heart lurched. It was only Jonathan, Chuck's longtime servant, but she always had the same reaction. Twenty years had passed since her attack, yet she still got jumpy at the sight of a vampire.

As Jonathan placed a glass of bourbon on the desk, Nicole held her breath. Chuck shifted at the same time as the vampire pulled his hand away, and the glass tipped, sloshing amber liquid onto the papers.

With a snarl, Chuck shoved himself out of his chair and backhanded Jonathan hard enough to send the defanged vampire reeling into the wall.

"You clumsy shit!" When Jonathan scrambled to clean up the mess, Chuck struck him again, and Nicole sat, stunned. Chuck had always had a temper, but she'd never seen him attack anyone like that. Then again, they'd lived oceans apart for two decades, so things could have changed . . . but this much? He'd always been kind to her family's servants, especially

Terese, whom he'd sometimes brought extra blood as a treat. "Get the hell out. You can forget your ration this week."

The vampire's silver eyes flashed, but whether it was with disappointment or anger, she couldn't tell. After Jonathan slipped out of the room, Nicole found her voice.

"That was a little harsh, don't you think?"

Chuck looked at her as if she'd grown another head. "He's just a vampire."

"It was just a spilled drink," she shot back, still shocked by this side of her brother. How could this be the same person who had smuggled chocolates to Terese on her birthday? "Don't you worry that you're going to push him too far?"

"That's ridiculous. What happened to you—to *all* of us—can't happen again. We have better safeguards in place now." Chuck graced her with a look dripping with syrupy sympathy, the kind reserved for people with a phobia everyone else thought was stupid. "It was a long time ago. You need to get over it."

Get over it. He wasn't the one who'd barely survived a brutal attack that killed almost everyone she loved and left her with a rare medical condition that would eventually kill her. Right now, the meds developed by Daedalus scientists were helping to control the disease ravaging her organs, but eventually, she'd grow resistant. Then she'd have a lot of misery to look forward to until she finally died in agony.

So, yeah, *get over it* wasn't an option.

"Attacks on humans by their servants still happen," she pointed out, although, granted, rebellion wasn't that common. Microchip implants that could be activated by special remote wrist devices kept vampires in fear for their health and were much more effective than the old-style collars that only kept vampires from crossing barriers.

But if the Vampire Humane Society had anything to say about it, the new devices would soon be outlawed. Nicole shivered, once again wishing she was still in Paris, where groups like the VHS weren't tolerated, and vampire slaves were an extravagance reserved only for the wealthiest of the wealthy.

"Don't worry, Nikki. My servants wouldn't dare lay a hand on me or my family."

Nicole's father had probably believed the same thing, until a vampire decapitated him and left his head mounted on a newel post only a few feet from where Nicole now stood.

You believed Terese would never harm you.

Nicole still believed that. The vampire had been like a big sister to Nicole, spending time with her when her mother couldn't, teaching her things her tutors wouldn't. Terese's gentleness and the ring Nicole now wore on her right hand were what Nicole clung to when she needed to be reminded that not all vampires were monsters.

But then she remembered that Terese had died at the hands of another vampire. A vampire she'd trusted with all her heart. Nicole hadn't seen much that day, but what she *had* seen—a blade at Terese's throat, held there by her mate as Terese pleaded and cried—was seared into Nicole's brain. Terese, so birdlike and fragile, was certainly no match for the much larger male whose growl had frightened Nicole so badly she'd wet herself.

The scene replayed itself over and over in Nicole's nightmares. Sometimes in those dreams, Nicole tried to overpower Riker and save Terese. Sometimes Nicole managed to scream, something she hadn't done in real life. But the end result was always the same. Terese would die, and usually, Riker killed Nicole, too.

With his teeth.

Swallowing against bloody nightmares and the too-vivid real-life memories, Nicole hovered her finger over the end button on the tele-screen. "I gotta go, Chuck. Roland is going to help me review my presentation to the board."

Chuck nodded. "Don't stay up too late. Get some rest. And for God's sake, be on time tomorrow. You need every minute you can get if the board is going to rule at one o'clock sharp whether you're there or not."

As if she needed the reminder that the trajectory of her entire career was going to be determined one hour after lunch, when everyone on the board was full of food and liquor. *Jesus.* She was facing an absolute catastrophe. This wasn't the job she would have chosen for herself, especially not after dedicating her life to becoming an expert in vampire physiology. But the inherited duty had been thrust upon her, and she'd always prided herself on being the best at whatever she did. Even if what she did wasn't what she wanted to do.

Failing her parents' company, especially after the tragedy that had killed them, would be devastating.

"Night, Chuck." Nicole clicked off the comm unit and started toward the grand living room. She'd been here almost two months, but she still took the long route, avoiding the dining area where her mother had "passed away."

Passed away. The words everyone but Nicole used for what happened sounded so . . . polite, when there'd been nothing polite about it. Elise Martin had had her throat brutally ripped out, but only after she had to endure unspeakable torture at the hands of her assailants.

The front door creaked open, and Nicole made a mental note to say something to Roland about letting himself in so casually. She'd let it go this long because he'd lived here as the caretaker for years while Nicole was in France, but now that she was back, he needed to learn to knock.

"I'll be right there, Roland," she called out.

"No, Nicole—" Roland's strangled voice broke off, and a sudden lump of foreboding plummeted to her belly.

She rounded the corner, skidding to a shocked halt. The lump leaped into her throat, strangling her, cutting off her scream before it even started.

A black-haired male who was clearly a vampire—with gleaming metal fangs—was holding Roland against his chest, one massive arm wrapped around Roland's neck. Roland's eyes were wild, his struggles almost comically futile.

But that wasn't what stopped her cold. No, what froze her all the way to her marrow was the monster standing beside him.

Funny how Boris wasn't the monster who came alive in her scariest night terrors. No, the title of Nightmare King belonged to the male looming like a death sentence in front of her, a gorgeous sandy-haired vampire in worn, bloodstained jeans and a loaded weapons harness beneath a long leather coat. A male named Riker who, twenty years ago, had killed Terese.

His own mate.

The murder in his cool silver gaze said he was about to do the same to Nicole.

A cold rush of fear coursed through her, destroying two decades of therapy in a matter of heartbeats.

"Fucking animals," Roland rasped. "Slavery is too good for your filthy kind."

The dagger-fanged vampire grinned, and Nicole watched in horror as, with a jerk of his head and a spray of blood, the vampire ripped out Roland's throat with his teeth.

Oh, dear Lord, please, no. Not again. A soundless cry escaped from her lips as she wheeled around. Terror made her clumsy, and she slammed her hip into a spindly Elizabethan table, sending a priceless Tang bowl filled with Nicole's origami flowers crashing to the floor. She made it four steps before a heavy body hit her like a truck and sent her sprawling on the floor. The jarring impact expelled the air from her lungs in an agonizing burst.

"Don't bite her!" The male voice boomed, and the vampire on top of her, his teeth shredding her turtleneck, cursed.

"Aw, come on, Riker." The memory of being not bitten but *chewed* made Nicole tremble violently as fangs scraped across the scars Boris had left on her throat. "I wasn't going to kill her. Just taste."

"Not now." Riker barked something that sounded like "She's mine," and the male on top of her cursed again.

"You got a reprieve, human." Ginsu-Fang's softly spoken words against the shell of her ear were more menacing at a whisper than if he'd snarled. "*Temporary* reprieve."

With agonizing slowness, he pushed off her. Before she could even think about trying to run again, a hand clamped down on her wrist and yanked her to her feet. Nicole tried to wrench away, but with just one hand, Riker managed to hold her still.

"Give me the vampire named Neriya, and I'll let you live."

Neriya?

Riker swung his powerful body into hers and shook her hard enough to rattle her teeth. "Did you hear me? Give me the female."

Ginsu-Fang slipped silently to the window, but Nicole kept her attention on the vampire holding her tightly. "I-I don't know what you're talking about," she croaked.

Riker's silver eyes, which gave him away as a turned vampire instead of a rare born one, flashed like razor blades. "Daedalus captured her two weeks ago. I want her. *Now*."

His voice, warped with rage, turned her insides to liquid. Despite what he'd said, there was no doubt he was going to kill her regardless. None at all.

But Nicole still had no idea what he was talking

about. "I don't know where she is." Her voice was shaking as much as she was. "How do you even know Daedalus has her?"

"It doesn't matter how we know." His fury blistered the very air around them, and she braced for a blow. Instead, he growled, "Find her."

"Find her?" she echoed. How was she supposed to do that? As far as she knew, all vampires brought in from the wild were tagged with new designations, so Neriya's name wouldn't be on file. Tracking her down was going to take time, which was something Nicole doubted she had much of.

"Yes," he said slowly, as if she were a child. "Find her."

"Why? Who is she? Your new mate? Are you going to kill her?" Nicole blurted before she could stop her runaway mouth. She had a terrible habit of saying dumb things when she was afraid or nervous.

Riker blinked as if taken aback, but he recovered quickly, his face shuttering. "Why the fuck would I want to rescue a vampire just to kill her? And why do you keep asking questions? I told you what to do. Do it."

Bluff. "I'll need to go to my office. I'll have access to computer files there."

"How stupid do you think we are? Your offices are crawling with security." Riker squeezed her arm to that wire-fine line between mere discomfort and pain. "You'll do it from here."

Indignation at his order pierced her bubble of fear, and she squared her shoulders in defiance. "I don't negotiate with vampires who break into my house and kill my friends."

Riker smiled, the coldest smile she'd ever seen, which was saying something, since, as CEO of a multinational conglomerate, she swam with grinning sharks on a daily basis.

"See, that's where you're wrong. This isn't a negotiation. You cooperate or you die. It's that simple."

The other vampire appeared at Riker's side. "If you're going to torture her into giving us what we want, you might want to do it somewhere else. Our secret is out. Two armed males approaching from ten o'clock."

"They won't be alone," Riker said.

Myne's long fingers found the hilt of the dagger at his hip, and a deep, rumbling purr pumped from his chest, which was still wet with Roland's blood. "Bring 'em on."

He relishes this. What a bastard. And what the *hell* was up with his fangs?

"My fangs?" Ginsu asked, and she realized she'd spoken out loud. "What, do I have something in them? Yo, Rike. Do I have a piece of that Roland dude in my teeth?"

Abruptly, *stupidly* enraged, Nicole lunged, but Riker caught her before she could punch Ginsu in the mouth.

"Last chance, Nicole," he warned. "Call off the guards, and make the calls, or you're coming with us."

As if her body suddenly remembered she was in grave danger, a fresh shudder of fear wracked her. Her options were limited, and the few she had sucked. If she went with Riker and Ginsu, she'd probably die. Then again, if she assured the guards that everything was okay, Riker and his steak-knife-toothed friend would likely kill her after she made the calls anyway.

So her choices came down to death . . . or death. That left her with choosing the timing, and maybe the method, of her demise. The vampires would kill her after she finished with the phone calls, but maybe if she went with them, she could use the travel time to plot a way to signal for help or find an opportunity to use the one weapon she had for an escape.

Riker's eyes flared at the same time she tasted blood. Dammit, she was biting her lip again. In front of a vampire. Might as well ring the damned dinner bell.

"Human," Riker snapped. "Call off the guards."

"Go to hell," she said, with a lot more calm than she felt. But if she was going to die, she was going to go down fighting the way she hadn't been able to when she was a child.

"You first." He gripped her chin roughly in his palm and held her face up so she was forced to look at him. And then . . .

Blackness.

FUCK.

Never before had Riker's favorite four-letter word been so appropriate. Because *fuck*, they were *fucked*.

He caught Nicole as she slumped against him, a victim of his hypnotic ability. Given how terrified she'd been, he'd expected her to capitulate to his demands and make things easy. But no, nothing could ever be that easy for him, could it?

"Man, I wish I had your hypno-talent," Myne said as he moved swiftly to one of the windows. "Handy for feeding."

Riker barked out a laugh. "You wouldn't use it. You like your food to fight back."

"Adrenaline adds a pleasantly piquant note to the blood," Myne said in an obnoxious French accent, as if he were a food critic describing a tasty menu item at his favorite restaurant. "Also, six more dudes are approaching from the main gate."

Myne wheeled around in a blur; his speed made a mockery of most vampires' already enhanced movement. Being a born vampire instead of a turned one came with a shit-ton of perks.

"We can slip out the back. There's a row of hedges that'll keep us in the shadows." Riker had often taken advantage of the area designed to conceal the gardeners' equipment when he used to sneak onto the property to visit his mate.

Myne glowered at the woman in Riker's arms. "I don't like this. She'll slow us down." He paused, probably hearing the guards' shouts outside. "Leave her. We can work over the other Martin."

Bad idea. The minute word got out about Riker and Myne's break-in, Charles Martin would ramp up security measures and take every precaution to avoid a similar incident. No, it was Nicole or nothing.

"We won't be able to get close to the bastard." Riker hefted Nicole more securely against his shoulder as Myne palmed two long blades from the sheaths on his back.

"Would have been a lot simpler if she'd cooperated," Myne muttered, putting his spine to a wall to peer between the slats of a window blind.

Riker'd give Myne that one. Now they had to evade the authorities while hauling an unconscious human through the forest. Assuming they didn't get hunted down and executed in front of TV cameras, that still left them having to take the human to the clan's headquarters. Had everything gone as planned and Nicole cooperated, VAST would still have been sent after the vampires who broke into the Martin mansion, but kidnapping one of the most prominent people on the planet was going to launch them into a whole new level of manhunt.

"We don't have a choice," Riker said. "If we don't get Neriya back—"

"Then we rain hell down on ShadowSpawn before they know we failed and come after us."

Attacking ShadowSpawn clan before they knew what hit them would give MoonBound a distinct advantage, but eventually, the enemy's sheer numbers and utter lack of ethics would result in MoonBound's destruction. Riker would never risk that.

No, Nicole was the key to MoonBound's survival, so she was going with Riker and Myne. One less human in the world, especially a Martin, would only be a good thing.

Myne brought up the rear as Riker hauled ass to the back of the mansion and took the old servants' passage to the south entrance. The dust on the scuffed wooden floor spoke of months, if not years, of disuse, and the door Riker had seen his mate disappear through too many times had been chained closed from the inside. Myne tugged on the lock. The thing snapped with a loud crack, and they slipped out into the night.

The hedges were manicured to perfection as if frozen in time. Memories clawed at him as they ducked between the shrubs, and he made a point of not looking at the spot where Terese had taken her last breath. The scene had been too well preserved, and although he knew it was impossible, he didn't want to risk seeing his mate's blood splashed on leaves or pooled in the grass.

Using the landscape and shadows as cover, they made their way toward the stone security wall. Three rottweiler guard dogs merely watched as Riker and Myne broke out of the hedges and jogged across the expansive lawn. Riker had zapped them with his hypnotic gift on the way in. They'd love him forever now, which was cool, because he liked dogs.

They'd made it just more than halfway before nearly a dozen humans in black-and-red Vampire Strike Force uniforms flanked them. Riker assessed the enemy in an instant, and if Myne's lopsided grin was any indication, he had, too. These were first responders, their weapons deadly but average.

"Put. The human. Down." A male with a blond high-and-tight cut that made his head look like a toilet brush broke away from the pack, easing forward in a smooth crouch. "Do it now, or I blow your head off."

Complying slowly, Riker set Nicole on the ground. As he straightened, he cut a *let's do it* glance at Myne. In an instant, Myne was in motion. He took down Toilet Brush and another dude before Riker could land his first blow.

Oh, but when he did, the sound of the VAST officer's jaw breaking was like a stiff shot of bourbon. The officer flew backward, his weapon flipping into the air. Riker snagged it one-handed and whirled, jamming the butt of the rifle into the gut of another asshole who made the mistake of trying to use a shock stick on him.

Spinning, he laid out another guy with a boot to the chest, but as Riker landed, he took a blow to the kidney, followed by a sweeping kick to the back of his knee. He grunted as he hit the ground, narrowly avoiding a shot from the VAST guy's AE-47 rifle. One bullet from that particular Daedalus weapon modification would torture its victim for hours as it delivered a series of powerful electric shocks through the body, burning organs and flesh. Vampires had a fifty-fifty shot of surviving. Humans had nil.

Riker shoved his palm into the guy's throat and watched with satisfaction as the human went down, futilely gasping for air through his crushed windpipe. A sudden spray of blood splashed on the lawn in front of Riker, and he glanced over to see Myne standing over the decapitated body of one of the agents, his fangs buried deep in another's throat.

The remaining humans either were dead or wouldn't be recovering anytime soon.

"Come on." Riker scanned the horizon for more humans, but so far, so good. "The next wave will be here any minute." And they'd have better training, deadlier weapons, and greater numbers.

Nicole lay where he'd put her, still unconscious, her long strawberry-blond locks spilling over the grass like blood, her bottom lip swollen from biting it. He gathered her in his arms, aware that he hadn't held a female this way since his mate. But Terese had been smaller. Lighter. Much more fragile. And where Terese had smelled of rose water, Nicole's warm skin carried a hint of crisp pears.

What. The. Hell. Why in the world was he comparing the two? They were opposites. Human and vampire. Tall and petite. Evil slaver and innocent victim.

"Hunter's going to kill you," Myne said as he fell in next to Riker.

"He's not going to kill me."

"But he'll lecture you with Hunterisms. 'A dead buffalo can't cross the plains,' or some shit. You might as well be dead." Myne wiped one of his blades clean on his pants before sheathing it. "You know the rules. No humans at headquarters who aren't food."

"Who says we aren't going to eat her?" Riker gave him a sideways glance. "And since when do you care about vampire laws?"

Myne's gaze raked Nicole, contempt—and hunger—gleaming in his eyes. "Since I decided I don't want to see you dead over some lowlife human." Riker cocked an eyebrow, and Myne snorted. "That wasn't a declaration of love or anything. The clan needs you. You're one of their best fighters."

Their best fighters. Riker didn't miss the way Myne didn't include himself as a member of the clan, even after decades of living among them, fighting beside them.

The woman moaned, a delicate noise that should have tugged at the one heartstring Riker had left. Sure, it was frayed, barely hanging on, but what remained sometimes vibrated with a faint sympathetic echo of times past.

Times when he'd had a mate, a child on the way, and hope for a future.

But thanks to Nicole's family, he now had none of these, so not even her whimpers could conjure a shred of sympathy from Riker.

With a sudden, angry growl, he leaped onto the fence. Nicole shifted, burrowing her face into his neck so her cold nose prodded his skin. Of course she'd be chilly—he'd taken her out of her warm house and into the freezing late-fall temperatures, and she was wearing only a cream turtleneck and gray slacks with chunky-heeled dress boots. Not that he felt bad. Not when she stood for everything he hated about humans. Hell, given her youthful appearance, she was probably using one of her company's products, an antiaging serum called "vampire juice" that her scientists had developed to extend human life spans.

Unfortunately, the process *took away* centuries from vampire life spans.

How many vampires had lost their lives to "juice" extraction? Not to mention to decades of experimentation before the antiaging therapy had been perfected.

Riker could feel his rage mounting again. He hated humans. With the passing of his human brother ten years ago at the age of seventy-six, he'd lost his last connection with humanity. And the human race had lost their last decent member.

But if he was honest with himself, he could admit that vampires weren't exactly a race of sweet kittens, either.

He allowed himself a grim smile as he carried Nicole off the grounds and into the forest, because she was going to learn firsthand about juice extraction. And he planned to be the one to show her.

5

HANGOVERS SUCKED.

Groaning, Nicole rolled onto her back. She didn't even attempt to contain a wince at the aches in her joints and the throbbing in her head. Maybe it was time to lay off the gin and tonics for good. She didn't indulge often, but when she did, she often forgot that a mere two drinks could put her on her butt.

A heavy hand came down on her shoulder, and she groaned again. Last time she'd felt this crappy—after a company party celebrating her return to the United States—it had been Chuck who'd found her. And who had teased her mercilessly for weeks.

"Wake up, sleepyhead."

"Screw you." She shrugged away from his grip, squeezing her lids tight to shut out any light that would launch her straight into Migraineville. Chuck had thought it was funny to turn on every light in her house before shaking her out of a dead sleep on the couch.

A horrifying thought wormed its way through the hangover haze: he'd also brought one of his servants with him. Chuck didn't go anywhere without a vampire to wait on him hand and foot.

Dammit. She'd sworn to never again be caught in a vulnerable state with a vampire around. She'd told him they weren't allowed in her house, and if he went against her wishes, she'd assign him to the farthest reaches of nowhere, in one of their one-man-team sales offices.

That was assuming Daedalus's board didn't hand her over to the authorities or find a way to boot her out of the company.

"You'd better not have a damned vampire with you," she muttered.

She swore the air temperature dropped ten degrees. "Honey," came the husky, southern-accented female voice, "I have an entire army of vampires with me."

Pain forgotten, Nicole snapped her eyes open. The blurry image of a woman's face hovered in front of hers. Beyond her head, pinpricks of light shimmered from what appeared to be a ceiling made of stone and . . . roots? She blinked, bringing a little focus to her vision. The woman peered down at her, her dark skin creating indistinct lines in the background, which was definitely composed of stone, roots, and what looked like packed earth.

Maybe this was a dream.

The rock jamming into her spine said otherwise. But how had she gotten here?

Riker.

The break-in at her mansion came back to her in vivid 3-D—her terror at the sight of Riker, the feel of

Ginsu's fangs scraping her neck, and the masculine, smoky scent of Riker's skin.

"Where . . ." She swallowed, grimacing at the raw scrape of her voice on her throat. "Where am I? Who are you?"

One black eyebrow popped up. "Aw, you can't even guess?" A smile joined the amused cant of the woman's eyebrow. "You're in a vampire stronghold. And I'm a vampire. Basically, you human scum," she said, her smile widening to reveal glistening, deadly sharp fangs, "you're in your worst nightmare."

THE PIERCING SCREAM caught Nicole off guard, drilling into her head with laserlike intensity until it felt as if her brain would explode. Only when the vampire slapped Nicole hard enough to roll her onto her side did she realize that the scream had come from her own throat.

The female leaned close, her eyes glinting like silver fishing lures caught in the sunlight. "I have a bizarre condition that makes me go into murderous rages when I hear screaming," she whispered. "So don't."

Nicole nodded, swallowing the fresh scream that had built in her lungs.

"Katina." A familiar male voice froze Nicole to the cold ground. "I'll take it from here."

The female vampire inclined her head sharply and stood with effortless, sinewy grace. "She's all yours, Rike." Katina pegged Nicole with a look so full of hunger that she should be drooling. "But when it's time to eat her, share the wealth. The skank looks like she has rich blood."

Skank? Nicole planted her palms on the hard-packed dirt floor and sat up. "You have no idea, you bitch." Probably not the brightest thing to say in this situation, but then, Chuck often teased that the default mode for Nicole's tact switch was set to off.

Riker went down on his haunches in front of her, and her heart skipped a beat. Maybe two. He was as imposing as he'd been at the mansion and as huge as she'd remembered as a child. Always before, when she'd thought about him, she'd wondered if her memory had exaggerated, if maybe her small size had made him seem bigger.

But no, if anything, he was larger than she'd remembered, an intimidating figure clad in jeans, a black T-shirt, and a black leather jacket that didn't do enough to conceal the weapons stashed on his body. Worse, he was even more handsome, and how twisted and sick was it that she thought anything about this bastard was attractive? He was a vampire. One who had killed his own *mate.*

Yet she couldn't deny his savage beauty, his chiseled cheekbones and full, crimson lips. Sterling eyes framed by thick lashes a few shades darker than his messy blond hair. A jaw as strong and sharp as a knife blade . . . or a vampire's fang.

"I'd be careful about slinging around insults if I were you," he said. "Can't think of many that can't be thrown right back in your face."

Nicole could think of several. *Bloodsucking fiend. Fanged monster. Every dentist's nightmare.* It was probably best to engage her tact switch, though. Chuck would be proud.

"Where are we?" She peeled her gaze away from him long enough to scan the surroundings. "What is this place?"

Now that she was sitting up and the blur in her vision had cleared, she could see that her initial impression was correct. She was in some sort of underground chamber. Faint light streamed through the tiny barred window in the door, allowing her a chilling view of chains and shackles secured to slabs of stone in the wall. But what truly freaked her out were the rows of skulls, some human, some vampire, high up on one wall.

"You're at my clan's headquarters." Riker flicked his tongue over a fang and grinned at her involuntary flinch. "In what we affectionately call the prey room."

Terror tightened around Nicole's chest like a steel band. Breathing became a luxury as fear put a stranglehold on both her lungs and her memories. This was like something straight out of a horror movie, and while she'd expected nothing less from vampires, seeing it firsthand chilled her to her bones.

Calm down. Remember that vampires are as afraid of you as you are of them. The words of her therapist came back to her in a rush, easing her anxiety but only a little. Riker didn't strike her as being afraid in the least. But then, she'd dedicated her life to learning about vampire physiology, not psychology, so maybe she should trust what her therapist had said. Plant some doubt into him. Some fear. Maybe at that point, she could regain a measure of control.

And if worse came to worst, she had a weapon.

Clearing her throat, she shoved herself to her feet. Riker rose with her, much more gracefully.

"I don't think you know who I am."

"Really." He folded his thick arms across his chest. "Enlighten me."

She lifted her chin to look him directly in the eye. "Since you broke into my house, you must know I'm a member of one of the most powerful families in the world." His expression remained impassive, but she didn't falter. Even before she'd taken over at Daedalus, she'd still been involved with the company, and she'd earned her stripes in boardrooms full of stone-faced executives and shark-eyed lawyers. "But you made a fatal mistake, because I'm also the CEO of Daedalus Corporation. If the authorities aren't aware that I'm gone already, they will be shortly, and I promise, very soon you'll have the weight of every law-enforcement agency on top of you. Not to mention VAST and, most likely, every private bounty hunter my brother can hire."

Riker might as well have yawned, he looked so bored. "I'm shaking in my human-skin boots."

Son of a— Had he just said *human*-skin? She looked down at his brown leather work boots. "Are those really . . ." She couldn't finish the sentence.

"Made of the soft, supple skin of a human orphan I stole from the loving arms of a caregiver?" When she nodded, he laughed. "The fact that you believe we're such monsters says a lot about you."

Right. Because the fact that he and his friend broke into her house, murdered her colleague, and kidnapped her didn't lend any credence to the monster thing. "So prove me wrong. Let me go."

"After you arrange for Neriya's release."

"Call me skeptical, but I somehow doubt you'll

just let me go my own way." Casually, she rubbed her ruby ring against her thigh, taking comfort in its weight . . . and in the weapon concealed inside. "And I swear to you, I won't go down easy."

His gaze dropped to her neck. Automatically, she reached up, as if covering her throat would prevent him from sinking his teeth into it. "Maybe I like a challenge," he drawled.

"Let me have one of those knives strapped to your chest, and I'll show you a challenge."

The light of battle flared in his eyes, and a sinister smile curved his lips. "Do your best, human." He whipped a dagger from a sheath and pressed it into her palm. "This should be fun."

"Fun?" Shaky legs barely supported her as she backed away from him. "I don't stand a chance against you."

"Then why did you ask for the knife?"

With a macabre sense of satisfaction, she put it to her throat, to the scarred skin where Boris had chewed through her flesh. "Because I'd rather die than let any one of you touch me."

As true as that was, driving a blade into her own jugular was a last resort. She'd simply needed the dagger so she'd have a weapon against other vampires after she took him down.

The amusement fell off his face, and he barked out a nasty curse. "Don't. Don't do that."

"Why not? You're going to kill me anyway, right?" She would *not* die at the hands of a vampire. They'd tried to kill her once; they wouldn't succeed the second time.

Riker held out his hand. "Give me the knife. Now."

Again, he hadn't answered her question. Again, she made a suggestion for a vacation spot. "Go to hell."

"I can take it away before you can blink, female."

She pressed inward, until the sting of the blade let her know she'd broken skin. A warm drop of blood rolled down her neck, but oddly, the lingering pinch energized her. For the first time since she'd been grabbed, she had a measure of control, even if the control was merely over her own pain.

Or her own life.

Riker's body went taut, a subtle sign she comprehended too late. Then he was there, fist around the blade. Startled, she jerked, driving the tip of the knife deeper into her throat. "You stupid human!"

With a snarl, Riker wrenched the knife away and shoved her against the wall. The blade clattered to the ground, but the fangs jutting from Riker's gums were just as sharp and probably far more lethal.

Nicole's therapist was a huge fool if she thought vampires were more afraid of humans than humans were of them. Dr. Bhatia was so fired.

Riker's gaze shifted down. To her throat.

Then his mouth shifted down. To her throat.

Boris's face flashed in front of her eyes, and panic squeezed her heart in a cold fist. Like she had so many years ago, she tried to fight, but Riker held her easily, pinned to the wall with his weight. As his lips closed over her skin, she stopped breathing and waited for the rip of his teeth.

Instead, there was only a warm sweep of his tongue

and, with it, the most bizarre and disturbing sense of pleasure.

Vampires could release a chemical through their saliva that created a euphoric feeling in their victims, but she doubted Riker would use it on her. And even if he did, given her background, how could she possibly feel even the slightest amount of pleasure? Self-loathing gurgled up inside her like a storm sewer after a torrential rain.

But her disgust didn't stop the odd tingle of awareness that spread from where Riker's tongue soothed her laceration to every part of her body that touched his. Everyone said that vampires were inherently sexual creatures, dangerously seductive even when they weren't trying. Hell, a special market existed for vampire sex slaves, which Nicole had never understood.

Until now.

Now she got it. But she wished she didn't.

On her wrists, Riker's fingers were callused, his skin hot. Vampires ran three to five degrees warmer than humans, and she felt the difference in body temperature with every blistering stroke of his tongue and every point of skin-to-skin contact.

Why was he being so . . . well, she wouldn't call it gentle, exactly, but he could be causing her a lot of pain.

Vampires are crafty. They're predators that play with their food. They feed on blood, pain, and fear.

One of her father's many lectures rang in her ears, and she started to tremble. Riker wasn't hurting her at the moment, but he would. The way Boris had so easily hurt her after years of being kind to her.

A slow roll of anxiety threatened to smother her.

She drew a deep, calming breath, desperate to keep her head clear.

Think. Hard to do when there was a vampire licking you.

Think. Her bottom lip stung. She was biting it again.

Think, dammit! She needed a weapon, a . . . *duh*. The ring. How could she have taken leave of her senses so easily? Other than the fact that a vampire was licking her. And then there was the distraction of her tingling breasts and an odd ache starting low in her pelvis.

Jesus, if Riker was ever captured by hunters, he'd be tagged for the sex market, for sure. Too bad he hadn't been caught a long time ago, because if he had, maybe Terese would still be alive.

The thought was enough to hurtle Nicole back to her senses, and as she ran her thumb over the cool metal ring, she thought about how ironic it was that Riker was going to be taken down by his own mate's jewelry.

Smiling, Nicole wedged her fingernail under the ruby lid's latch.

This is for you, Terese.

SIXTY SECONDS AGO, rage and pain had twisted through Riker, so intertwined that he couldn't separate them. The stupid human had put a blade to her own throat. Why did this keep happening to him? Why were females so damned eager to kill themselves?

Fuck it all, this one wasn't going to die. Not until he was ready.

So he'd put his mouth over the scarred skin of her throat with the noble intention of sealing the wound. But the moment he tasted her, a jolt of sheer, burning bliss streaked all the way to his groin.

Full. Stop.

He hadn't felt much in the way of a sexual stir from feeding in decades, let alone with a female he despised. A human female, at that.

He froze, his body tense as a trip wire, but his heart was pitching a fit against his rib cage. His fangs throbbed in time to the pulse in his swelling cock as both body parts made it clear how much they wanted to sink deep into warm, wet flesh.

"Stop," Nicole whispered in his ear. "Please, stop."

Her voice quivered, and shame formed a knot in his belly. He'd never worried about his victims before, but then, he usually brought down his prey quickly, taking pride in a swift, silent kill few of his kind could match. It was a special-forces skill left over from his military days and amplified by vampire speed, strength, and supertuned senses.

His prey rarely had time to know the sour taste of fright. When they did, it was because he'd wanted them to.

This was different. Nicole had been in a prolonged state of fear and would be until they got Neriya back. She might be the CEO of the most reprehensible company on the planet, and she might be complicit in crimes against his people, but he'd never been the type of male who reveled in a female's fear.

Even if it was deserved.

He shoved himself away with deliberate, measured composure, as if backing off was entirely his idea. Nicole's wide peridot eyes kicked him right in the gut, but he steeled himself, summoning his inner hardass.

He didn't have to reach very far for it.

"There. You're healed. No thanks necessary." He licked his lips, savoring the last rich, silky drop of her blood. Unlike most of the humans he fed on, she tasted of health and a hint of fine wine. He wanted more. "Don't try that again. You die when I say you die. Help us, and you'll avoid that fate."

"You're going to be hanged and staked for this." Her fingers fluttered up to her throat, scarred by some sort of heinous injury, to trace the thin crimson line that had been bleeding a moment ago.

"Aren't you a ray of sunshine." He breathed deep, measuring her fear level by scent. She was afraid but not as much as he'd expected. "What happened to your throat?"

The sour note of fear spiked. "Why do you want to know?"

The ring on her right hand glinted with little crimson sparkles as she covered her neck with her palm. Her scars forgotten, he snared her hand, bringing it—and the ruby ring decorating one of her fingers—so close he caught a metallic whiff of gold.

"Let me go." Nicole struggled against his hold, but he squeezed her wrist as tight as his lungs felt. He could barely breathe, barely speak.

"Where did you get that ring?"

"It's mine."

His blood, already vibrating with the heat of unwanted arousal, began to boil with anger. *"Where did you get it?"*

A glint of pure, unadulterated hatred sparked in her eyes. "From. Your. Mate." She hurled the words at him like weapons, and like an expert marksman, she hit every one of his vulnerable spots with sniper precision.

With a snarl, he wrapped his fingers around the throat he'd just healed. "Did you take it from her while she was alive, or did you loot it off her corpse?" Rage made his voice warble, which only made him angrier. "Did you even wait for her body to get cold before you stripped her of everything she loved?"

"How dare you!" Nicole spat. "How can you talk about love, when you're the one who killed her?"

He blinked in disbelief. "How dare *I*? *Your family* killed her the day they put her in chains and forced her to wait on your despicable asses hand and foot."

"And that," she said, "is why I don't believe for a second that you're ever going to set me free. You plan to take your revenge on me, don't you?"

Her voice was as flat as his was furious. It should have been a clue. He shouldn't have been surprised when she flipped the hinged lid on the ring and jammed her hand in front of his nose.

When she blew a powdery substance into his face, he could only utter a single curse before he was gasping for breath and stumbling backward in an uncoordinated tangle of his own feet.

"That was for Terese, you murdering bastard."

For his mate? Why? Through blurry eyes, he saw Nicole swipe the dagger off the ground and tuck it into her waistband.

"What . . ." He inhaled, coughed, doubled over in agony. Someone had replaced the air with fire. Holy fuck, he was breathing napalm. "What . . . did you . . . do?"

"Boric acid." Her reply was muffled. Or maybe the ringing in his ears was dampening outside sounds.

"Bitch." He dropped to the ground like a sack of rocks, his lungs burning, his vision developing spots that swirled around her as she crouched next to him.

"I'm not done. See, boric acid is lethal to vampires. My company, the one you hate so much, figured it out. *I* figured it out after analyzing why your kind can't use firearms. I'm sure you're aware that gunshot residue and propellant destroy your lungs. It made me wonder what else would do that." Damn, but she sounded like she was enjoying this. "We're starting to put acid-delivery devices out on the market so that soon, humans everywhere will have their own handy-dandy vampire pepper sprays." She leaned in, so close and personal he felt her warm breath whispering across the shell of his ear. "In forty-eight hours, you'll be dead, and it's no less than you deserve."

He'd laugh if his lungs weren't burning as hot as the surface of the sun. Forty-eight hours? That was nothing. He'd been dead for twenty years already.

RIKER'S CLAN'S HOME was like a maze. Or, more accurately, like a warren. A series of dimly lit tunnels and caverns skirted what appeared to be a massive complex of dwellings, all carved out of dirt, stone, and a framework of tree roots. The closer Nicole got to what she guessed was the center, the more finished, clean, and bright the tunnels became.

How had they built this? How did they have electricity? They'd even decorated. When she'd first escaped the cell, the paths leading from it had been bare, simple dirt and rough-carved stone. But as she scurried through the passages, the stone became smoother, the walls dotted with carved wooden or leather art or paintings in a variety of styles, mostly Native American. The pounded dirt floor became inlaid with cobblestones, and once, Nicole peeked over a carved wooden railing into what appeared to be an elegant, if basic, common room with colored floor tiles that formed a giant dream catcher.

The sophistication of the place stunned her. By

most accounts, vampires were supposed to be instinctive, base creatures that, if not cared for and trained by humans, lived like animals. Nicole had never been convinced that vampires were so primitive, but her arguments with her college instructors, colleagues, and peers had been met with either scoffing and derision or accusations of being a "filthy sympathizer."

She couldn't wait to rub this in their faces. Assuming she got out of here alive, anyway. She just hoped Riker remained in the boric-acid stupor for at least half an hour. The chances of her getting caught were already astronomically high, but if he came out of it before she escaped, she might as well schedule her funeral.

She kept to the shadows and crevices as best she could, instinctively moving along uphill paths and staying far away from the few vamps she saw and definitely avoiding eye contact. Even if a vampire didn't sense the fact that she was human, she had a feeling everyone knew everyone else in this community, and a stranger would stick out like a neon sign.

Heart pounding so hard she was sure every vampire in the place could hear it, she followed a cool draft of fresh air around a corner and bumped so hard into someone that she *oof*ed and careened into the earthen wall. The person she'd collided with, a small female wearing cutoff Daisy Duke denim shorts and an orange wool sweater, slammed against a log support beam. The *crack* of the girl's skull on the hard wood reverberated through the tunnel.

Nicole watched in horror as the other female crumpled to the ground, blood streaming from her temple.

"Shit," Nicole breathed. She hurried over to the

girl and crouched next to her. "Are you okay?" She dug into her pants pocket for a tissue. "Just hold still, and let me put some pressure on that wound."

For a long heartbeat, the girl, who must have been no more than sixteen, didn't move or even open her eyes. And in that brief moment, as Nicole pressed the tissue against the wound, she realized she was trying to help a vampire. While trying to escape from these same vampires.

Stupid.

The girl's eyes popped open. Confusion lurked in the silver-gray depths. Then, in a wild flailing of limbs, she scrambled to her feet and stared at Nicole like a cat eyeing a mouse.

Oh, God. Nicole was dead.

Very slowly, with her feet rooted to the ground as if she were part of the warren's structure, Nicole stood. Her fingers trembled as she casually reached behind her for the dagger she'd taken from Riker.

"Human?" The female got right up in Nicole's face, apparently oblivious to the fact that she had a tissue stuck to her temple. "You have candy?"

Nicole's hand froze on the dagger's hilt. "I—what?"

The vampire's broad smile revealed a perfect, gleaming set of fangs. "I like chocolate. And hard candies. Riker brings me candy sometimes. You know Riker? He likes chocolate, too." In an abrupt shift of mood, she reached up to wrap her orange-streaked brown ponytail around her fist, a pout turning down the corners of her mouth. "Hunter says candy is no good for my teeth. It's always blood, blood, blood. All the time, blood." She stomped her bare foot like a petulant child. "I *hate* blood."

Well, *that* could only be good news.

"So," the vampire said brightly. "You have candy for Lucy?"

It was pretty clear the vampire wasn't playing with a full deck, but that didn't mean she wasn't as dangerous as a vampire who held all the cards. Best to be nice and see what Nicole could learn.

"Lucy? Is that your name?"

Lucy nodded. "Who are you? Humans aren't allowed here. Not never." She appeared to think about what she'd just said. "Well, only for food." She wrinkled her nose. "Blood. Yuck. Do you have candy?"

Right. Okay, she could work this. "I'm sorry, Lucy, no candy. But I can get some if you tell me how to get out of here."

Lucy's eyes narrowed. "Are you tricking me? Humans aren't allowed to leave."

Raised voices echoed from somewhere in the maze of tunnels, and Nicole's pulse went into overdrive. "I can't get you candy if I don't get out."

"Humans aren't allowed to leave," she repeated with such conviction that Nicole's heart sank. "Hunter would kill them. But you helped me. I can help you get candy." Lucy clapped her hands, and guilt pricked Nicole's conscience at Lucy's pure, ecstatic joy. "I can show you a way out."

"Lucy, I don't want anyone to see me leave. Is that possible?"

"Uh-huh." She cocked her head to study Nicole

for a moment. "I don't want Hunter to kill you. So you can see my secret entrance."

Smiling, Nicole gently plucked the tissue from Lucy's temple. "I'd like that. I don't want Hunter to kill me, either."

Lucy immediately ducked into a darkened, dusty hallway and led Nicole through a series of tunnels that grew progressively smaller and less used, until Nicole felt like Alice down the rabbit hole. Damned good thing she wasn't claustrophobic, because they were eventually crawling in pitch blackness. Rocks bruised her knees, and her hair kept catching on dangling roots, but they finally broke out of the tunnel and into a thick copse of prickly bushes.

Nicole stood, grateful for the fresh—but cold—air and weak afternoon sunlight that permeated the green canopy overhead. She'd been inside the vampire compound all night and for most of the day. Damn, she was going to need food and meds soon.

Lucy stood up next to her. "You bring me candy now?"

"I'll do my best." A gust of wind rattled the tree branches and pierced the thin fabric of Nicole's torn turtleneck. Shivering, she surveyed the landscape. "Lucy, do you know which way I need to go to get to the nearest city?"

Lucy pointed at a pile of rocks in the distance. "Follow the river."

"I appreciate this." Nicole touched the vampire's arm lightly, part gesture of thanks, part apology for lying about the candy.

Lucy leaped at her so fast that by the time Nicole could open her mouth to scream, Lucy was engulfing her in a rib-crushing hug. “I like helping. I don’t get to help much ’cause I always mess up.” She pulled away, her lean frame going rigid, alertness screaming from every pore, reminding Nicole that Lucy might have the mind of a child, but she was still a vampire capable of things humans could only dream of. “You better go. I think you better go quick.”

Oh, shit. “Why?”

“Because I hear trouble.” Lucy’s expression became pinched with worry. “Shouts. Calls to capture the human. They’re hunting for you, Candy Lady. Run.” Lucy pushed Nicole in the direction she’d indicated. “Run as fast as you can. I hate blood.”

7

RIKER BURST OUT of the clan's main entrance, Hunter and Myne on his heels.

"She's mine," he snarled. "When we get her, she's fucking *mine*."

He inhaled a breath that burned but was nothing like what he'd felt in the prey room. But how long would that last? Did he have forty-eight hours of excruciating pain to look forward to? And how the everliving *fuck* had Nicole gotten Terese's ring?

Myne sniffed the air, doing his bloodhound thing. "I'm not catching her scent." Frustration laced his tone. Myne hated failing at anything he considered Born Vampire 101. "Which way do you want me to go?"

"South," Riker said. "If she's looking for an easy path, that's where she'll go." Total bullshit. The thinning forest to the south would make sense for a runner, but the city was to the west, and if Nicole had any sense of direction, she'd head that way. Which meant no one but Riker was taking that route. "I'll roll west."

Hunter spoke up. "You're sure you're okay? No one gets the drop on you like that."

"I appreciate the humiliating reminder, Chief," Riker drawled. "But yeah, I'm fine."

If Hunter knew Nicole had dosed Riker with a lethal agent, he'd drag Riker to Grant, their mad-scientist-slash-closest-thing-they-had-to-a-doctor and chain Riker down if he had to. All Hunter and Myne knew was that she'd knocked him out somehow, and that's how it was going to stay.

Hunter probably saw through Riker's BS, but he didn't press. "I'll get a couple of your teams together to go wide on a search, and I'll have everyone in the clan scouring the warren."

There were miles of tunnels where Nicole could hide, but Riker's gut said she was in the forest. "She's out here."

Hunter's obsidian eyes narrowed to slits. "You fed from her? You can track her?"

Nicole's heady wine flavor lingered on his tongue, but a large amount of ingested blood was needed to track the donor. "I didn't feed, but I tasted enough to get a general feel for her."

The leather thong around Hunter's temples held his midnight hair out of his eyes, emphasizing his Cherokee ancestry as he inclined his head in acknowledgment. "Good hunting."

Riker took off, his adrenaline surging hotly through his veins. He loved a good chase and takedown, and this one was going to be especially gratifying.

He smelled her before he saw her, two miles from clan headquarters. Her pear-and-ginger scent made his mouth water . . . until he caught more scents. Human. Male. At least ten. And from the unwashed stench of them, they were poachers, the worst kind of vampire-killing scum.

He went balls to the wall in a massive burst of speed, leaping fallen logs and cornering hard by pushing off trees. Nicole was ahead, making enough noise to alert a deaf man to her presence.

A flash of strawberry-blond hair between a pair of firs put Riker at thirty yards from his prey. But the stink of a couple of poachers came from maybe a hundred. They were close. Too close.

He sprinted the final distance, catching Nicole as she tried to navigate a gully lined by thick ferns and gnarled berry bushes.

"Riker." She gasped as he swept her up and over the gully, taking them both to the forest floor on the other side.

"Disappointed to see me alive?" He rolled with her, pushing her beneath him as a bullet sailed over their heads. "You might get your wish soon enough."

"What the—"

"Poachers." A spark of hope lit her pretty wide greens, but he was about to dash it. "Chill, Sunshine. They'll only chop *me* up for body parts. If I'm lucky, I'll be dead when they start. But you? It'll be a while before they put you down."

"But I'm human." Her dry swallow made the wound he'd sealed on her throat writhe. "I'll tell them who I am. That they'll get a reward if they return me safely."

"You can try that tactic." He yanked her to her feet and dragged her behind a massive tree. "But more likely, they'll say they found you dead and ransom your body. What they're doing is illegal, and they won't want you alive to tell anyone what they did to you or what they were out here for."

"I don't believe you," she ground out.

Two shots rang out at the same moment that three men in camouflage burst from the brush. Nicole, the slippery minx, took advantage and wrenched away from him to dart toward them.

"Nicole, no!"

Riker ducked the swing of a machete, only to be nearly laid out by a baseball bat from behind. The blow smashed into his lower back, knocking him off balance. Gnashing his teeth against the pain, he palmed two daggers and struck out at the nearest poacher with a devastating one-two slice that took both sides of the man's neck down to the spine. As the human's spasming body hit the ground, Riker dodged more gunfire in an effort to catch Nicole, who had tripped and was scrambling to her feet.

"Help me!" Nicole reached for a burly, black-bearded dude who held an ax like a lumberjack.

Lumberjack's smile was psychotic, as if he'd just struck gold and was going to take out everyone who knew about it. He put out his hand . . . and slammed his fist into Nicole's face.

Riker snarled, his anger sparking to insanely dangerous levels. With a roar, he dived into Lumberjack, not caring that several other assholes were closing in. His focus had narrowed to a needle-thin pinpoint that would only end in the ax-wielding poacher's bloody death.

The man grunted as he hit the ground with Riker

on top of him. Riker plowed his fist into the human's throat, but as he reared up to deliver the death blow, pain lanced Riker's chest, nearly as intense as what he'd experienced back at the den. Exhaling on a curse, he looked down at the hilt of a throwing knife vibrating between his ribs.

Riker spared the thrower a glance, judged him to be a lesser threat than the poacher beneath him, and prepared to finish him off. In a single powerful motion, Riker drilled his fist through Lumberjack's breastbone and ripped his beating heart from his chest.

"Riker!"

Nicole's breathless shout for help came from a distance. Riker burst to his feet, barely avoiding a crossbow bolt aimed at his head and another chop of a machete.

"Enough with the fucking machete!" Twisting, he ripped the blade from his attacker's hands and spun, turning the machete into a blender that sliced into two men. Both fell. One wasn't going to get up. The other would be lucky if he ever ate solid food again.

Holding his ribs, Riker lurched in the direction Nicole had gone. Slowed by his injury but still faster than the humans, he loped through the woods. As he closed in on the asshole chasing Nicole, he wrapped his blood-slick fingers around the hilt of the knife in his chest and yanked the blade free. The poacher was nearly on her when Riker pitched the weapon into the bastard's spine, dropping him like a rock.

Riker didn't have time to stop. A hail of gunfire rained down on them, chewing up leaves, tree trunks, and clumps of dirt.

"Son of a—!" He grabbed Nicole by the hand. "Come on." He half dragged, half carried her through the forest at a blind, desperate run in the general direction of their only hope: caves.

There was a series of caves to the north, built and later abandoned by one of the first colonies of vampires in the area. Now they served as both overgrown lairs for wild animals and temporary hideouts for any vampire needing a place to evade enemies, be those human or other vampires.

"You were right," Nicole said between labored breaths. "They weren't going to help me."

She sounded so surprised. Must suck to learn that some humans were worse than vampires. "No shit."

A bullet exploded into a tree just inches from Riker's head. A split second later, another blasted apart a tree branch, and splinters ripped into his jaw and neck.

He dived into Nicole, and they both tumbled down an incline, skidding over dead leaves and banging into dead branches and mossy rocks. At the base of the trench, he pulled her to her feet, hating the fear in her eyes.

"We'll be okay," he whispered. "I promise."

He didn't stop to think that they were in this position because of her. He just hauled ass with her through the forest, listening as the hunters fell back and, finally, were no longer on their trail. The bastards were tenacious, though, and they'd keep hunting, call in reinforcements, and form a net to catch them.

"Where are we going?" Nicole asked, her voice low and hushed, punctuated by exhaustion.

"To a safe place." He eased them to a stop and

gave her a second to catch her breath. Gave himself a second to rein in the burning in his upper body. He couldn't tell if the lava pouring through his chest cavity was from the stab wound or the acid Nicole had dosed him with, but it was getting worse. They needed to get to the caves before he passed out and made it easy for the poachers to butcher him into dozens of different pieces. "I'll carry you from here." At her questioning look, he added, "The people hunting us are experts at what they do. They'll be looking for two sets of tracks." He eyed the landscape, mapping out a route in his head. "And I can move faster than you can, even carrying your weight."

She glared. "You don't have to make it sound like I weigh five hundred pounds."

No, she definitely didn't weigh that. She was tall and muscular, probably a little self-conscious about her size, but he'd always liked a woman who didn't look like she'd break in half in a strong wind—the way his mate had.

"Let's go." Roughly, he hauled her over his shoulder and leaped a fifteen-foot gully, landing feather-soft on a fallen log.

Nicole squeaked in surprise but wisely kept quiet as he forged his way through the wilderness. He used his ninety years combined of Army and vampire experience to leave minimal evidence of their passing, but he had to waste precious time making sure his blood didn't leave a trail. They moved more slowly than he'd have liked, and by the time they reached the system of caves, his various minor cuts and scrapes had healed, but his lungs and ribs were screaming in agony.

He scaled a rocky ledge and slipped through a narrow cave entrance concealed by boulders and brush. Once inside the dark, dank cavern, he eased Nicole to the ground and caught her when she stumbled backward on wobbly legs.

"You okay?" An ugly bruise was spreading from her cheek to her temple. Frowning, he put his fingers to the swollen flesh around her eye, hoping nothing was broken.

She jerked away from him. "I'll have a black eye soon, but it could have been worse."

He dropped his hand, strangely offended by her reaction, even though he'd expected nothing else. "Yeah. You could have been poisoned with boric acid and then stabbed."

Dead silence. She probably didn't realize he could see her in the pitch blackness, and the sudden guilt in her expression was a surprise. Guess she didn't think she'd be around to watch her victim die.

"Look," she finally said. "What would you have done if someone had kidnapped you from your house, put you in a cell, and threatened to torture and kill you?"

"Do you even hear yourself? Humans have been doing that to vampires for decades." He didn't bother waiting for a reply.

He strode through the darkness as easily as if the place was wired for lights and pushed aside a recliner-sized rock that concealed a recess loaded with supplies. His arms shook with the effort, which had been far more work than he'd have liked. His injuries were draining him fast. Too fast.

"What are you doing?"

He lifted a burlap sack out of the hole and returned to Nicole, his gait faltering for the last couple of feet. Not good.

"We might be here for a little while." He dug matches and candles from the bag and lit one. Nicole looked around the cavern, blinking as her eyes adjusted to the flickering light.

"You stay here often?"

"Let's just say that we have a lot of hideouts." He plucked a first-aid kit from the bag. "You never know when some asshole is going to try to poach or enslave you."

She flushed. "I didn't realize . . ." She trailed off, rubbing her arms.

"You didn't realize what? That we live our lives looking over our shoulders? Or that we're smart enough to be prepared when humans hunt us? Or that your precious humans aren't always the good guys?" He tossed a blanket and a bottle of water at her and dug a roll of gauze out of the first-aid kit. "Don't try anything stupid. The poachers are going to be swarming the area."

"So we're just going to sit here? For how long?"

"Until I say it's safe or until I'm dead. Whichever comes first." He shrugged out of his coat, trying to keep the pained winces at a minimum. "I don't suppose there's an antidote for the poison you gave me."

"It's available through our labs. If you can get me to the Norwalk research facility on the west side of Seattle—"

"You'll save me?" He snorted. Which hurt. "I think

it's more likely I'll be captured and either experimented on or gelded, defanged, and turned into a slave. Probably yours."

His fingers found the buckle to his weapons harness, but his right arm wasn't working right. Pain speared him from his biceps to his knuckles with every movement, and to his utter humiliation, he kept fumbling the leather strap and the buckle. Finally, when his muscles turned to water, he dropped his hands, hating himself for admitting defeat.

Then Nicole shocked the shit out of him by leaning over to unbuckle the harness. Her strong, slender hands eased the straps from his shoulders, and his cheeks heated when she helped him out of his bloody T-shirt. He didn't like that he needed her help, but he wasn't so full of pride that he'd refuse it.

"I don't have vampire servants," she said quietly.

"Really." She averted her gaze, and something occurred to him. "It's not because you think slavery is wrong, is it? The reason you don't have a slave is that you hate vampires so much."

"I admit I don't harbor any love for vampires." She handed him the gauze he'd dug out of the first-aid kit. "But I've never supported slavery. Believe it or not, there are people trying to end vampire ownership."

Vampire *ownership*. Sounded so . . . pleasant. He'd have laughed, but merely breathing was becoming an effort. "That's a damned joke. Those groups want slavery to end, but they also want to make sure every vampire is either confined or destroyed. Slavery is wrong, but vampires are too dangerous to be loose in the world, isn't that right?" He tore a strip of gauze off the roll and packed his wound. Why was it still bleeding so badly? It should have been halfway healed by now. "But even those groups are few and far between. You humans love slavery."

"How can you say that?" Nicole scooted closer and groped around in the first-aid box. "You're painting everyone with the same brush."

"Humans have been obsessed with slavery since the beginning of time," he said tiredly. "Any group a majority views as inferior—animals, other humans of different race, sex, or religion—has either been persecuted, hunted, exploited, or turned into workhorses. When you discovered the existence of vampires, no longer human but able to perform as well as humans, we were your guilt-free dream slaves."

"Maybe." Nicole's long, graceful fingers measured out a length of medical tape, and he had a sudden, unbidden image of her using those fingers on sensitive parts of his body. Clearly, blood loss was making him delirious. "But there have always been other humans fighting for human and animal . . . and vampire . . . rights."

"And what have you done . . . ?" He trailed off, a sudden blurring of his vision and a light-headed spinning in his head whisking away his concentration. What had they been talking about? The gauze Riker held to his chest grew sticky and wet. Every breath was like breathing water.

"Dammit." Nicole leaped across the distance separating them and lifted his palm from the wound. "Riker? I'm going to need you to lie down."

She sounded so authoritative. So strong. He'd

think it was hot if he didn't hate her. And if he wasn't about to bleed to death.

As if his body was in tune with his thoughts, the scent of his own blood became overpowering, and a trickle of warmth began to stream down his torso.

"Know this, human. I will die before I allow myself to be taken." Suddenly, every breath was a firestorm of pain. He gasped, choked on his own blood. "Looks . . . like that . . . might happen."

"You're not going to die." She didn't sound very convincing. Hell, she'd probably slit his throat the second he lost consciousness.

He sagged against her, felt her easing him backward. "If poachers find us . . ." He inhaled a raspy breath, trying to find the words to tell her about the tunnel leading to another exit at the back of the cave. Instead, agony ripped him apart.

He felt her hands on his shoulders. "Riker. Stay awake."

Yeah, that wasn't going to happen. "I know . . . you hate us." Desperate to convey his urgency, he searched blindly for her hand. When he found it, he squeezed, and for the briefest moment, he took comfort in the fact that she squeezed back. "But please . . . when you get back . . . let Neriya go."

The pain took him.

NICOLE'S CHEST WAS tight as Riker went limp and passed out. He'd suffered what appeared to be a deep puncture wound between his fourth and fifth ribs, but it took a lot more than that to put down a vampire. The problem couldn't be the boric acid; she'd lied about that. Oh, she'd dosed him with it, and it *was* lethal to vampires, but she'd only given him enough to lay him up for a few miserable days.

His medical condition wasn't her concern, though. Her only concern was getting home alive, and with him incapacitated, she had a shot at it.

She hurried to the cave entrance, pausing in the early-evening shadows thrown by the surrounding trees and rocks. How far would she make it in the dark, especially given her lack of appropriate clothing? Even if she didn't die of exposure, night was the domain of vampires, and clearly, these woods were crawling with them. If not them, hunters and poachers.

The memory of being chased by the men, some of whom had fangs and other body parts hanging from their belts and necks, sent a chill up her spine.

They'll only chop me *up for body parts. If I'm lucky, I'll be dead when they start. But you? It'll be a while before they put you down.*

Riker's matter-of-fact words put a damper on her eagerness to leave. Maybe she should wait until morning.

She cut a tentative glance over her shoulder. Riker lay on the ground, drenched in darkness, a pool of blood spreading around him. Vampires could lose far more blood than humans and still recover, but it usually took massive trauma to lose that much. With the rapid way vampire blood clotted and wounds sealed, even the loss of a limb or a severed artery rarely resulted in death. But Riker wasn't clotting.

So what? He kidnapped you, threatened to kill you, and . . . saved you from poachers.

Snort. He'd saved her from poachers so he could kill her himself after he got what he wanted.

Neriya.

Who was she? Why did Riker want her so badly that he'd begged Nicole to release her if he died? He'd actually been desperate enough to use the word *please.* She had to wonder how hard that had been for him.

A howl broke in the distance. A wolf, maybe? Another howl joined the first, this one much closer, and Nicole's heart skipped a beat. Bad enough that she was stuck in the middle of the wilderness with vampires and poachers. Now she had hungry wolves to worry about.

What if the howls weren't wolves? What if that was how the poachers signaled one another? Yet another howl, this one so close she jumped, rang through the forest. Oh, God, she wasn't going to make it even a mile before someone or some*thing* caught her.

Reluctantly, she turned back to Riker. Lying there unconscious and with a trickle of blood streaming from the corner of his mouth, he still managed to strike fear into her heart, but without him, she didn't stand a chance.

Calling herself all kinds of crazy, she crossed the distance between them and crouched to light another candle. Under the cast of the flickering light, she peeled back the soaked gauze covering Riker's wound. Blood and air sucked in and bubbled out of the puncture with every labored breath. This was not good, and the situation became a lot more *not good* when she slid her gaze upward. His trachea had cranked hard to the left side of his neck, flanked on either side by distended veins that bulged up from under the skin. Dropping her ear to his chest, she cursed. The diminished breath sounds in his right lung confirmed her suspicions.

Tension pneumothorax.

Her vampire-physiology schooling had included medical classes, and Riker's signs and symptoms were straight from the basic trauma manual. Under normal circumstances, a vampire could survive, but there was nothing normal about these circumstances, not when Riker's natural healing ability was being compromised by the acid she'd dosed him with.

Hastily, she rummaged through the first-aid kit, cursing at the contents. She wasn't a medical doctor, but with her knowledge of vampire anatomy, she figured she could perform a minor operation if she had to.

But not with gauze, dull scissors, and tweezers.

Shoving the first-aid kit aside, she dug into the bag of remaining supplies. Water, protein bars, a pad of sticky notes, more candles, and a blanket that might come in handy later, but they weren't going to help with Riker's out-of-control bleeding now.

Which left her with no choice but to handle the boric-acid poisoning.

Closing her eyes, she flipped through mental files pertaining to the development of the antivampire powder—basically, mace for fanged people—and the cure. Although the highly concentrated boric-acid powder was now in use by both private citizens and law enforcement, Nicole had, only days ago, signed off on large-scale production of the antidote for distribution to the public.

She remembered that day clearly, because a few hours later, she'd been informed that dozens of vampires had been executed in the very lab where the antidote had been perfected, supposedly on her orders.

It had been sunny outside. She'd been planning the company Christmas party, even though it was still months away. She'd even made a teeny origami Christmas tree.

And then Chuck had burst into her office to show her the video of the vampires being dosed with boric acid and left to die in writhing agony in their cells.

Nicole had thrown up in the garbage can next to her desk. When she'd finally stopped heaving, she'd gone on a rampage that included firing most of the staff at the Minot lab facility. Then she'd been forced to hire them all back when Chuck shoved a signed execution directive under her nose.

The signature had been hers. It didn't matter that she swore she hadn't signed the order. What mattered was that suddenly, she'd had her eyes opened to a reality she hadn't wanted to face. How many vampire test subjects had suffered in Daedalus labs in order for her company to profit from the weapon she'd used on Riker? How many vampires had died horrible, excruciating deaths?

Nicole had dedicated her life to saving humanity from the vampire scourge. But right now, as she looked at Riker, helpless on the ground, and thought about Lucy, who only wanted candy, not blood, Nicole couldn't work up any pride in what she'd done.

Riker gasped, spitting blood onto the cave floor, and she shoved her shame into a box to be explored later. She couldn't be responsible for killing him. Not with a Daedalus weapon, anyway.

So the antidote . . . She bit her lip, her brain working a million miles an hour. A large percentage of the cure contained calcium carbonate as a neutralizing agent. Calcium carbonate was often used in antacids. A frisson of hope shot through her, and she dug through the first-aid kit again, hoping like hell that vampires used Tums.

Nothing. *Dammit.* She stared at the candles while her mind spun like a centrifuge. In the background, Riker's breathing grew more labored. He had a couple of hours at the most.

One of the candles flickered, spitting a drop of wax down the side of the white pillar.

Ash.

Son of a bitch, of course!

"Hold on, vampire." She darted to the cave entrance, hesitating only a second to listen for the poachers before creeping out into the twilight to gather an armful of twigs, sticks, and rotted wood.

She hurried back inside, but her heart sank at the sound of Riker's uneven respirations filling the cave with an ominous death rattle. He didn't have much time.

Adrenaline and fear made her hands shake as she used the wood and a candle to start a fire that was no larger than the burning end of a match.

"Come on," she urged the tiny flame, but it seemed the fire had its own *slow* agenda.

Dammit. Had this been any other situation, she'd have burned the sticky notes, too. But vampires were so sensitive to chemical vapors that even minute quantities of the chemicals used to process paper could further damage Riker's already compromised lungs.

Forcing herself to stay positive, she turned to check on Riker just as he hissed in pain, lips peeled back to expose fangs streaked with his own blood. His mouth twisted in a silent snarl, and instinctively, she leaped backward, her heart thundering in her chest. *Jesus.* Even hovering near death he was terrifying.

But he *was* hovering near death, and as he settled down with a low moan, she got her anxiety under control.

He might be a vampire, but right now, he needed help. She inched closer to him, her fingers flexing as if eager to touch him. He'd been gruff with her, threatening, a little rough, even. But he hadn't harmed her . . . yet. She couldn't help but wonder why, given that he seemed hell-bent on blaming her for every wrong done to vampires, including the death of his mate.

And what was up with that, anyway? Why would he blame her family for that incident, when *he* was the one who had driven the blade through Terese's throat?

Something wasn't adding up, and Nicole hated secrets, hated unknowns. Even as a child, she'd wanted answers to everything, had loved Nancy Drew and wanted to grow up to be a private detective.

Terese's death and the slave rebellion changed all of that.

Riker groaned, his big body shuddering. His misery skinned her alive. It didn't matter what he was or what he'd done. He was hurting, and it was her fault. A strange sensation, one she hadn't felt in twenty years, coursed through her veins and straight into her heart: true compassion for a vampire.

"Damn you," she muttered. "I'm sure you'd just as soon eat me as look at me, and here I am feeling sorry for you."

Very gently, she placed her palm on his sternum, feeling his chest rise and fall in a halting rhythm. His heartbeat was strong, but his skin was chalky and hot. Shifting, she put her fingers to his throat and winced at the bounding pulse. A low, pained moan vibrated all the way up her arm and once again crept into her heart.

She glanced over at the small fire. "I'll be right back." She had no idea if he could hear her, or if he even cared that she'd be back, but for some silly reason, she wanted him to know he wasn't alone.

Cursing herself for a fool who was probably saving the life of her own murderer, she tore open a packet of alcohol swabs and tossed the contents. The fire hadn't even come close to burning all the plant matter, but she used a stick to scrape up what little ashen cinders she could get into the little foil packet. Next, she dusted off a flat rock and dumped the warm ash onto it. With another rock, she ground the would-be medicine into a fine powder.

She returned to Riker, cradling the pulverized ash in her palm. "Hey." She eased down next to him and tilted his head up. "I'm going to need you to breathe this in."

He thrashed, slamming his arm into hers and dumping half of the precious ash out of her hand. She tried again, with similar results and what would no doubt be a knot on her elbow later.

"I guess we do this the hard way," she muttered.

She straddled his broad chest, using her thighs to hold him still. The moment he exhaled, she gripped the back of his head and lifted it until his nose was in her palm. When he tried to squirm away, she held harder.

"Riker, settle down, okay? I need you to inhale for me."

She wasn't sure if he heard, but he sucked in a huge breath, the rush of air sounding like it had come from someone who had been holding his breath underwater for an hour. Ash shot into his mouth and nostrils, and then he was coughing, bucking under her, and clawing at his throat. For a split second, his eyes opened. Misery and accusation whirled in the silver depths, gutting her.

"Easy, vampire." She pulled his hands away from

his neck and held them against his chest. He was strong, though, and she had to plaster the weight of her body on his to ease his struggle and keep him from tearing at his own skin. "I know it hurts, but the ash is working."

She hoped. God, she hoped. If she'd made things worse, she'd never forgive herself.

Gradually, he stopped fighting, but he kept hold of her hands, even when she tried to extricate herself from his grip. Between her thighs, he was hot, his body so wide she figured she'd feel the tug of tightness in the morning.

Dear God, what would sex with him be like, if just holding him still gave her muscle strains? And why in the world would her mind go there?

Maybe because there was some truth to all of the talk about vampires being supersexual creatures. A friend of hers had once said that the ugliest man on earth would be hot if he had fangs. And if he had the extremely toned body that came as standard issue on all vampires. Daedalus was still trying to figure out the biology behind *that*.

Had Riker always been cut like a superhero—or super*villain*—or had he been molded into one by the turning process?

Either way, she had Supervamp beneath her, his bare chest under her palms . . . when only hours ago he'd wanted to kill her. And she'd nearly killed him.

With a light, faltering touch, she skimmed her hands over his rock-hard abs and up to his shoulders, telling herself this was part of a medical exam, but when she reached his left bicep and found the tattoo there, all pretense went out the window. She was flat-out curious about his body. Oh, she'd studied vampires in class and lab settings, but this time, her focus was more personal. This time, she wanted to learn about the individual vampire, not the species as a whole.

Beneath her fingers, the tattoo seemed to pulse as she traced the curved lines of the sideways crescent moon circled by a serpent. The design was simple but elegant, and she wondered what the meaning behind it was.

"MoonBound," Riker rasped. "It's our symbol."

Startled, she jerked as if she'd been burned and peered into his eyes. The dull, tarnished silver reminded her how close to death he'd been. "Thank God," she breathed. "You're okay."

"How?"

"I neutralized the effects of the boric acid with calcium carbonate. Ash," she explained. "Now that your body doesn't have to fight the toxins, it can heal the other wounds." She grabbed a bottle of water from the bag of supplies next to her and held it to his lips. "Drink."

He took greedy, long gulps, draining the bottle in a matter of seconds. Once finished, he closed his eyes, perhaps in relief. His hand squeezed hers . . . in gratitude? Flustered, she remained frozen, even when he moved his hand to her thigh. He seemed to have no problem breathing now, his chest rising in a steady rhythm, but *she* had stopped taking in air the moment he touched her leg.

She struggled to catch her breath as his hand drifted up to her hip. Then higher, easing along her waist and rib cage, and when his thumb brushed the side of her breast on its trek north, she finally sucked in a cool, desperate rush of air.

His fingers slid over her collarbone, finding her throat. The pad of one finger scraping her scars brought an involuntary flinch. Riker's eyes popped open. No longer dull, they shone with an eerie light, all marble gravestone under the full moon.

For what seemed like hours, she stared, mesmerized. It wasn't until she tried to swallow—and couldn't—that she realized he'd wrapped his hand around her throat with a viselike grip.

Firmly but gently, he pulled her so close that the heat of his breath fanned her cheeks. "Why," he growled. "Why did you save me?"

She was beginning to wonder the same thing. "Because I'm not the killer you seem to think I am." *And if I have any hope of surviving the poachers, it's with you.*

In an instant, he flipped her and came down on top of her, his heavy body flush against hers, his hand still on her throat, his hips pressing down between her legs.

"What I think," he said in a deep, guttural voice, "is that you're going to regret not letting me die."

BETWEEN NICOLE'S LONG legs was the last place Riker thought he'd be today. Of course, he hadn't thought he'd be poisoned, stabbed, or shot at, either. The day was full of surprises, and it was only early evening. There was still time for a meteor to land on top of him or some shit.

Nicole lay beneath him, her throat throbbing under his palm. To her credit, she wasn't freaking out. If anything, she seemed annoyed.

"Well?" he asked.

"Well, what? Do I regret not letting you die? You'd love for me to say yes, wouldn't you? All your preconceptions about me would be confirmed." Scowling, she flattened her palms against his chest and shoved.

Amused by her pathetic efforts to dislodge him, he grinned. "Not by a long shot. I have a *lot* of assumptions about you. Few are flattering."

"You are such a dick." She struggled like a rabbit caught in a snare, but he controlled her easily, sinking more of his weight onto her smaller frame.

Big mistake. He might not like her, but he hadn't

been in this position with a female in decades, and his body didn't care what he thought about her. All it cared about was how her curves fit against his hard muscles and how her pelvis was rocking against his. It also had immense appreciation for the way her magnificent breasts rubbed against his bare chest.

He slid one hand to her butt to hold her still, but all he accomplished was putting her sex in direct contact with his. He also discovered that her ass was rock-hard and a nice handful.

"Stop that," he ground out.

"Screw you." She bucked harder, and he hissed at the blatantly sexual motion. Behind the fly of his jeans, his rapidly swelling cock rubbed against her smooth slacks, creating a blistering friction that made him light-headed with sudden need.

"I mean it, Nicole." His sexed-up voice was gravelly, rusty from disuse. "Stop thrashing."

She sank her nails into his chest and tried to push again, but the little pinches of pain only added to the soaring pleasure as lust surged through him, hot and potent.

"Or what?" Almost before the words were out of her mouth, it became very clear to her what was going on. He saw it in the way her expression went slack and her skin flushed pink, felt it in the sudden taut set of her muscles. "Oh," she breathed.

God, she was a study of female perfection right now, with her hair fanned out in a messy pool on the ground, her panting breaths, her full lips open and glistening. She looked like a woman who needed a mattress, a lot less clothing, and a male willing to use every dirty trick in the book to make her mindless with ecstasy.

Braced on one elbow, he eased his hand around to the back of her slender neck to where her spine met her skull. With one swift thrust of his fingers into that spot, he could kill her before she knew what happened.

Or he could stroke the soft skin and thread his fingers through her silky hair.

This was stupid. It was completely crazy and inappropriate that his body was responding to her at all, let alone with a powerful rush of desire that had him dipping his head toward that perfect mouth. He wondered how she'd taste, wondered if her kisses were as sweet as the decadent nectar in her veins. The very thought made his body burn.

Without thinking, he brushed his lips across hers. Beneath him, Nicole stiffened, and when he did it again, this time with an even lighter touch, she let out a gasp. Under his thumb, her pulse ticked madly, and the scent of her anger and fear blended with a subtle note of arousal.

Instantly, his body burned hotter. He needed more. Much more.

He sealed his mouth over hers, groaning as he tasted his first female since Terese's death. Her lips parted slightly, and the warm, wet recess of her mouth drew him deep. She was soft all over but firm enough in the right places for him to know instinctively that she could take him at his roughest. His wildest.

He shuddered at the direction his thoughts had taken. They couldn't do this. He'd never been the type to have sex with a female he didn't like, no matter how hot she was or how much she revved him up.

Growling with frustration, he kissed her harder, which made no sense, and he knew it. Or maybe it did. The kiss was punishing, brutal, because, dammit, it was her fault he was between her legs in the first place.

Nicole's breasts pressed into his bare chest as he shifted, moving against her in a primitive surge that made them both moan.

More. He gripped her hip and tucked her more firmly under him.

More. He dragged his mouth along her jaw. She smelled so good, so feminine. He moved his mouth to her neck, and instantly, she went taut and recoiled.

Right. He was a vampire. Worth about as much as a stray dog. And this stray dog was humping her leg. She must be mortified.

Fucking humiliating. He shoved himself off her, averting his gaze so she wouldn't see the color change in his eyes that signified arousal. She was too aware of his desire as it was, and he was an idiot for letting it go as far as it had.

With a curse, he grabbed up his ruined shirt. It was bloody, dirty, and torn to shit. It wasn't wearable, but he put it to good use while he waited for his heart rate and breathing to return to pre-hump-the-enemy levels.

After splashing the shirt with the bottle of water, he wiped the dried blood from his chest. His wound had nearly healed. Another couple of days, and there wouldn't even be a scar.

The scrape of Nicole's chunky-heeled boots echoed

through the cavern as she came to her feet. "Um . . ." She cleared her throat, because, yeah, this was all kinds of awkward. "Do you need blood? You know, to replenish what you lost?"

Yup, he did. He was operating at about half strength right now, but hell if he was going to tell her that.

"Don't worry, Sunshine. I won't sink my big, bad fangs into your pretty little throat." He shrugged into his weapons harness. "Not until you get Neriya back, anyway."

That particular threat was getting old, but right now, he needed to get his brain functional again, and that would require thinking about something other than sinking anything of his into anything of Nicole's.

Her huff told him she was just as tired of the threat hanging over her head. "Why is she so important to you, anyway? Who is she?"

Riker didn't owe her an explanation, but what the hell. They didn't have anything else to do while they hung out in the cave except talk. Besides, maybe if she understood the importance of getting Neriya away from the humans, Nicole would be more willing to cooperate.

"I'm sure you're aware that the vampire race suffers from a low birthrate, and when a female does get pregnant, the birth can be extremely complicated and dangerous."

Nicole moved around in front of him. He wished she hadn't. Even though she was dragging her fingers through her messy locks in an attempt to tame them, she still looked like she'd just gotten out of bed after a tumble with a man, and he definitely didn't need to be picturing her on a mattress. Or with a man.

Or with him.

"One in four deliveries results in the death of either the mother or the child or both," she said, sounding like she was reading straight from some *Vampires for Dummies* book. "I know."

"Well, Sunshine Smartypants, all vampires develop special abilities at some point in their lives, depending on if they're born or turned. One of the rarest abilities is also the most precious. We call it *usdida*." Crouching, he gathered the first-aid supplies and tried to stuff them back into the box. They appeared to have multiplied. "Basically, people with this gift can ease labor and deliver babies safely. No one knows how it works, just that very rarely does a child or a mother die when a midwife with *usdida* is present." What the hell—seriously, did bandages breed? Frustrated, he forced the kit lid closed. "Neriya is a midwife from another clan. We arranged to have her present for a birth, but on our way to return her, our team was attacked by hunters, and she was taken."

"What makes you think my company has her?" Nicole asked.

He glanced up at her, a little surprised at the lack of defensiveness in the question. "Because a warrior who survived the attack reported hearing the hunters mention having a buyer at Daedalus lined up."

There was a long pause, as if Nicole was gathering her thoughts. Finally, she shook her head. "That's impossible. We don't have people out gathering vampires for us. It's illegal for anyone but federally sanctioned hunters to capture wild vampires."

Wild vampires. As opposed to domesticated slave vampires, he supposed.

"So you're saying my warrior is a liar."

"I just think he's mistaken," she said, like a perfect little diplomat.

He ground his molars so hard his jaw ached. "Baddon doesn't make mistakes."

"I see." Arctic air practically swirled around her. No doubt, she didn't believe him and was sure her fabulous company was completely misunderstood. "In any case, I can understand why you're desperate to get Neriya back."

"You have no idea." He shoved himself to his feet with a little more force than was necessary. "Her clan, ShadowSpawn, has given us until the new moon to return her. If we don't, they'll destroy us down to the last child."

Nicole's mouth fell open. Closed. Open again. Finally, she simply turned away. "There's so much more to your people than anyone knows."

"Shocking, isn't it, how we have feelings and families and we even celebrate holidays." He wished she'd turn around so he could gauge her reaction, but he'd have to settle for listening to the beat of her heart as it sped up or slowed down . . . or skipped a beat the way it had a moment ago. "But you know what ruins our families? Our holidays?" He let the answer fly like a right cross. *"People like your family."*

Nicole wheeled around so suddenly he actually stepped back. "I'm not defending what humans have done to you," she said fiercely. "But my family was good to our servants."

"Servants? My mate wasn't a *servant.* She was a slave. You can't even say it, can you?" Loathing bil-

lowed up inside him, raw and hot, as two decades of festering wound tore open, spilling fresh pain. "Your family ripped her from our home and turned her into a damned nanny to a snot-nosed kid who grew up to hate vampires."

"I loved Terese!" Nicole took an aggressive step toward him, her hands fisted at her sides. "She was like a sister to me. She cared about me."

"*I* cared about her," he shot back. "You took her away from me. From the people she loved."

"Yes," she said, her voice as caustic as the acid she'd nearly killed him with. "Your mate loved you so much that she tried to abort your baby. Twice."

It had been a long time—decades, really—since Riker had been sucker-punched. Now it all came back to him . . . the moment of stunned confusion, the pain that left him reeling, the sudden absence of breath that made the lungs tighten into shriveled husks.

With a few words that came out of left field, Nicole had laid him out like no blow ever had. He couldn't think. Couldn't speak.

All he could do was walk, zombielike, out into the night.

NICOLE FELT LIKE a heinous bitch. She was starting to understand Riker's bitterness toward her and her family and toward humans in general, but she was so protective of Terese, and he'd completely dismissed how Nicole had felt about the vampire.

And she still wasn't sure what happened the night Terese died. All Nicole knew was that she'd heard his angry voice and had seen him holding a knife to Terese's neck while she pleaded with him. The memory still cut deep, still had the power to reduce her to tears sometimes.

"Please, Riker. Don't do this. Please."

The male vampire had Terese pressed against the shed, his hand covering hers, and both of their hands were wrapped around the hilt of a dagger that was digging into Terese's throat. Tears dripped down Terese's cheeks as she pleaded with him. A single drop of blood welled on her skin where the knife blade rested.

Nicole searched her brain for a way to stop that vampire from hurting Terese, but Nicole was so little, and he was so . . . huge. She tried to scream, but only a squeak came out, and for a heart-stopping moment, Riker shifted his gaze in her direction. Terror froze her to the ground. Could he see her?

She couldn't move. Couldn't breathe. It wasn't until he turned back to Terese that Nicole was able to scramble from her hiding place in the bushes and make a break for the stables. Legs pumping as fast as they would go, she burst into the horse barn, where Uncle Paul was saddling a polo pony for her cousin Ted.

"Help! Uncle Paul!" She paused to catch her breath. "A wild vampire. At the shed. He's going to kill Terese. Help her!"

Uncle Paul hit an alarm on the wall. A siren screeched, and the horses went crazy. "Stay here," he told her and Ted. He grabbed a pitchfork and raced out the door.

She never saw him alive again.

Hours later, her father found her and Ted crouched in the hayloft. Someone came to get Ted, but her father stayed with her, holding her against his chest as he broke the news that Uncle Paul had been killed, and so had Terese. The vampire who murdered them both had gotten away.

Nicole's heart banged painfully against her ribs at the memory, and a dizzying wave of nausea made her sway. She'd wanted revenge on Riker for so long, and now that she had him in her grasp, she'd saved his life. And then she'd honed all her stored-up anger into a razor-sharp verbal blade and had sunk it into his heart as deep as she could get it.

The pain in his eyes when she told him about the attempted abortions had been raw and real, and with a clarity she couldn't explain, she was sure that even if he had been responsible for Terese's death, he was as haunted by it as Nicole was.

Now she had to clean up this mess she'd just made. She was still a little dizzy as she exited the cave, and she welcomed the brisk, cool air when it hit her face. A fine mist fell from a low, featureless cloud layer that swallowed the tops of the trees, but Riker didn't seem to notice the droplets of water clinging to his hair and skin. He was crouched on his heels, forearms draped across his knees, head bowed.

"Riker—"

"Was what you said true? Did Terese try to abort the baby?"

She closed her eyes, but doing so didn't shut out the shame. "I don't think—"

"Tell me." His voice cracked like thunder, and she knew there would be no arguing with his command.

"Yes," she said softly.

"How?"

"Does it matter?" she whispered, hating herself for bringing it up in the first place. "Why are you torturing yourself like this?"

"Maybe I like pain." He spoke from between clenched teeth, his jaw muscles twitching furiously as he ground his molars hard. "How?"

The wind whipped her hair against her cold cheeks, but the sting was nothing compared with what Riker must be feeling.

"The first time, she drank a tea of tansy and pennyroyal oil. My father was furious." Nicole had pleaded with him not to hurt Terese, but that hadn't been his intention. He'd chained Terese to a bed until she swore to behave. And she had . . . for three weeks. "The second time, she threw herself down a flight of stairs." Nicole had seen it happen, but she'd lied to her father, telling him it was an accident.

Riker raked his hands over his face before pressing the heels of his palms into his eyes and going utterly still.

"I'm so sorry," she murmured. "It was cruel of me to bring it up. I shouldn't have gone there."

Very slowly, Riker's head came up, but he didn't look in her direction. His hollow gaze was focused on the distance. "Is this a joke?"

"Is what a joke?"

"Your apology. Humans don't care about being cruel to vampires."

Ouch. "I could say the same thing about vampires and cruelty to humans," she said, resisting the urge to stroke her fingers over the scar on her neck, "but I know Terese cared about me. My apology is genuine, Riker. I don't know what happened between you on the day Terese died, but I believe you loved her, and I'm sorry I said what I did."

"Really." His voice dripped with contempt. "And what makes you believe I loved Terese?"

Her cheeks heated at the memories. "I saw you," she said quietly. "Sometimes when you'd sneak onto the property to be with her . . . I'd see you."

Still crouching, he pivoted and leveled a probing stare at her. "What, exactly, did you see?"

Oh, God, talk about awkward. "Um . . . at the time . . . I mean, I was just a kid—"

"What?" he barked. "What. Did. You. See?"

Your mouth on hers. Your hands roving tenderly over her arms, her stomach, her breasts.

Those images had stayed with Nicole, becoming more meaningful as she matured. He'd been so very careful with Terese, which was why her death was such a shock, such a mystery.

"Just kissing. Touching," she said, sounding stupidly girly and breathless. "Only once." All the times after that when Nicole had seen them together, Terese had been pregnant, and the stolen moments with Riker had been tense.

Nicole chewed her lower lip, wanting to ask the question she'd held on to for twenty years, but now that she could, she wasn't sure the answer would do anything besides devastate her. She spit it out before she could change her mind.

"How did she die, Riker? What happened that day?"

As if she'd just lit his fuse, he burst to his feet, fangs bared. "She was a fucking slave! That's what happened! She was so damned miserable that she took her own life. Is that what you wanted to know? I went that day to break her out of there, but she wouldn't go."

Nicole stared blankly, unable to process what he'd just said. "I don't understand," she said, shaking her head. "If you were there to rescue her, why did she kill herself?"

"Because your family destroyed her, Nicole. All she wanted at the end was to die."

"But why wouldn't she have gone with you?" This was crazy. He was lying. "She could have been with you and the baby."

Swallowing, the tendons in his neck standing out

starkly under his skin, he turned away. "She hated the baby, and she didn't see a future for us."

"Why not?"

"Because the baby wasn't mine." His words, sharp and edged with hatred, cut like an icy blade. "It belonged to your father."

YOU LYING BASTARD." Her face stricken and pale as a corpse, Nicole backed away from Riker, her steps wobbly. "I don't know what kind of game you're playing, but I know damned well that humans and vampires can't breed."

Riker shoved his hand through his damp hair. "I didn't mean that your father was the baby's sire. I meant that it belonged to him. He created it. He wanted it for experiments or a breeding program or some shit. I don't know."

"Experiments. A breeding program." Nicole's voice was utterly flat. Steamrolled of all emotion except doubt. "You're saying that Terese was impregnated in a lab?"

"Impregnated is the polite, clinical way to put it."

Riker looked out at the forest, hoping there were no hunters around, but at this point, he was feeling reckless, maybe even a little hopeful that he could release some tension with a good fight. Terese had never been a strong person, and being sold into slavery had weakened her even more. Then she'd disappeared for eight months . . . eight months in which he'd gone crazy, trying to find out where she was, if she'd been sold to another family, if she'd been killed. No one knew.

And then, one day, she was back at the mansion, heavily pregnant. At first, he'd been thrilled, assuming it had happened during one of their rare trysts. A boy, she'd said. But the thrill soon faded as he discovered that the female who used to be Terese was gone. The new Terese had two settings: angry and emotionless.

But the good news was that the Martins had exchanged her lethal perimeter-control collar with one that would cause only a mild shock and unconsciousness if she crossed the invisible property barrier. Riker finally had a way of getting her out of there without killing her.

"I'm taking you home today. Myne, Baddon, and Katina are waiting behind the wall."

"It's too dangerous. I won't let you do it." Terese's hands slipped under his jacket. "I won't let you die for me." She brought a dagger, lifted from his harness, to her throat.

The warrior in him, the male who despised weakness and never stopped fighting, got really fucking pissed. "Dammit, female, what are you doing?" He wrapped his fingers around her hand. "I'm not worried about the danger, and I don't plan to die. I'm taking you, and that's final."

A single drop of blood formed where the tip of the blade made a dimple in her pale skin. "Please, Riker. Don't do this. Please."

"We've got it figured out, Terese. We can do this. We have to. You're due any day now, and I won't let our son be born here."

Terese stared blankly. "It's not your baby, Rike." There was no emotion in her words. It was as if she was reading lines from a book she didn't even like.

It was Riker's turn to stare, his brain having trouble processing what she'd just said. Finally, he managed to utter a few stunted, croaked words.

"Not mine? Whose?"

"I don't know his name."

Riker shook his head, still unable to think through the cobwebs. "You fucked someone else? Was that where you were this whole time? With him?"

"I was locked inside a Daedalus lab." Her gaze went somewhere he couldn't follow, and he wasn't sure he wanted to. "There was a male in a cell. They put me in it with him."

A slow burn started low in his belly. "And you . . ."

"I was restrained."

Emotion consumed him . . . rage that Terese had been abused that way, self-loathing that he hadn't been able to protect her, and sorrow that the child he'd been wanting so desperately wasn't his.

*But her confession explained so much, and as he looked down at her swollen belly, he knew that what she needed right now wasn't an explosion of fury that would terrify her. She needed comfort and reassurance, and he needed her and the baby—*his *baby, dammit—to be okay.*

"Listen to me, Terese. Everything will be all right. I promise you. We'll raise the baby as mine. I will be his father, and no one has to know."

"I can't!" she cried. "Don't you see that I can't do this? I don't want this monster inside me. I don't want the memories in my head." She gave him a small, sad smile that chilled him for a reason he couldn't pin down. "I've never been strong,

not like you. You deserve better than to be saddled with me. You always have."

"That's not true," he croaked. "Our match wasn't of our choosing, but I never regretted it."

"That's because you're a good, decent male who doesn't go back on his word. You made a commitment, and you kept it. But I release you from it now." She pushed the tip of the blade deeper into her skin. "Please. Do it for me."

"No! How can you ask that?" He squeezed her hand in an attempt to pull the knife away, but she didn't budge. "Dammit, Terese, we can do this. I'll get you out of here. Once you're home, you'll see that it'll all work out."

Then he saw it in her eyes, something that had been there for weeks but that he'd denied with all his heart: lifelessness. She'd lost the will to live. She was dead before he'd even arrived on the Martin property.

"Riker?" Nicole's hand came down on his shoulder. He wanted to shrug away from her touch, but his body wouldn't obey. "That day . . . the day she died, I heard her beg you for something."

Bitterness welled up like acid, scorching his throat and putting a caustic edge on his words. "She begged me to not risk my life to rescue her. And then she begged me to kill her." He'd been angry at her weakness, and now remorse threatened to eat him alive. He could have handled things so differently. "When I wouldn't, she did it herself. I think I could have talked her down or overpowered her, but a siren went off."

Terese had panicked at the sound of the alarm and raised voices, and while Riker was distracted, she'd plunged the blade into her throat.

He didn't see Nicole stiffen, but he felt it. "It wasn't your fault."

It *was* his fault, but he wasn't going to shoulder the entire blame for Terese's death. "No, it was yours."

An odd, pained sound came from Nicole. "I—what makes you say that?"

"Because she wouldn't have felt the need to kill herself if your family hadn't made her a slave, treated her like a lab rat, and forced a pregnancy on her."

Silence. Then some shuffling. A moment later, Nicole pressed something into his hand.

"I know you don't believe me, but I loved Terese, and I know she loved me. She gave that to me the day she died, but I think . . . I think it belongs to you."

Nicole started back toward the cave entrance, her hair damp and clinging to her neck and slumped shoulders. She looked as defeated as he felt.

Exhaling on a curse, he glanced down at his hand.

Lying in his palm was Terese's ring.

NICOLE WAS SHAKING so hard that she stumbled as she approached the cave entrance. The ground came at her, but then Riker was there, hauling her up with his arms around her waist. She found her balance, but Riker didn't release her, his grip sure but surprisingly—no, *astonishingly*—tender.

"Are you okay?" he asked gruffly.

For some reason, she couldn't find her voice, could merely nod. As if he didn't believe her, he stepped back and scanned her from head to toe, his gaze lingering a little too long on her neck. Damn her and her self-consciousness, she reached up to cover the scarring.

Riker covered her hand with his and gently moved it aside. "What happened?"

A shudder ran through her. When he'd asked before, she hadn't answered. She didn't want to talk about it, but Riker had just opened himself up about Terese, a trauma that was surely far worse than hers.

"Vampire," she murmured.

Frowning, he skimmed the pad of one finger over her neck, and an unexpected pleasant sensation ran through her. "That's a lot of damage."

"He was a . . ." She started to say that Boris was a servant, but Riker was right. Boris was a slave. Still, she couldn't quite get the word past her lips. "He'd been defanged."

Riker's eyes flared, and she expected another blast of bitterness. "It must have been brutal." When she didn't reply, because she didn't even have the words for how brutal it had been, he asked, "Did it happen during the slave rebellion?"

"Yes." The memory, combined with the churning in her stomach that was only getting worse, sparked sudden anger. "No doubt you wish I'd been killed."

"You were a child. You didn't deserve what that vampire did to you." He smoothed his finger over the skin of her throat. "My clan adopted rules of engagement a long time ago, and killing children goes against every one of them."

Her anger flagged, and she glanced away, overwhelmed by everything that had happened since being kidnapped from her home. She'd learned more about vampires in the last twenty-four hours than in her entire twenty-eight years of life. And she was considered an expert in her field.

What a joke.

"What's the matter?" When she said nothing, he hooked a finger under her chin and lifted her face so their gazes locked. "You don't believe me?"

"It's not that." She took a deep, shuddering breath. "It's just . . ."

"Just what?"

"I was raised to think vampires were soulless monsters. Creatures that needed to be kept under strict control or they'd kill everything they could lay their hands on. And then I was told you'd killed Terese and my uncle, and after that came the slave rebellion."

The memory of being attacked got all tangled with the way Riker was touching her, and her heart stuttered, as if it was having difficulty deciding between fight and flight. Someone really needed to add *freeze* to the instinctive response options to stress. *Fight, flight, or freeze.*

"You said you loved Terese."

"I did. And that's the wrench in this whole mess. I thought she was a fluke. The cat that likes mice or the retriever that doesn't fetch." She swallowed. "And now . . ." Now she was seeing life from the other side. The way she'd been raised, capped off by the slave rebellion that had taken her parents, her cousins, and her friends and had nearly killed her, had left her with blinders over her eyes.

Now the blinders had been ripped off, and her

new experiences and new knowledge were making her head spin.

Another wave of nausea washed over her, and she wobbled. So maybe the spinning head was about more than sensory overload. About more than stress or exhaustion or fear. She needed her meds. Riker caught her again, but this time, he swept her up and carried her deep inside the cave.

"What's going on, Nicole?"

She supposed the truth wouldn't hurt, and at this point, denial would only make her look stupid.

"I have a medical condition that causes imbalances in iron and blood-sugar levels." He set her down, but when her feet hit the dirt, her legs wouldn't support her. Very carefully, he lowered her to the ground.

Then he shocked her by sinking down in front of her. He made himself comfortable with one leg propped up and his arm draped over his knee like they were getting ready to enjoy a picnic. "Do you need to eat?"

"Food would help. But what I really need is medication." Or a blood transfusion, which was a very temporary measure and would only prolong the inevitable.

He stared at her, the calculation in his shimmering eyes making her squirm. "Let me guess." Skepticism dripped from his words. "Your medication is at your house, and if you don't get it, you'll die."

"Yes. Not right away but eventually."

"Insulin?"

She shook her head. "It's an antiviral drug developed specifically for me, although there are a couple of other known cases of *vampiridae* that are being treated with the same drug."

"*Vampiridae*?"

"I contracted the vampire virus when I was bitten."

"Then why aren't you a vampire?"

She turned her left hand over, revealing the round pencil-eraser-sized scar on her wrist. "Because I'd been immunized against the orally contracted form of the virus."

Vampires carried two forms of the virus, but humans were immunized only against the virus that was transmitted by saliva. No company had yet developed anything that would defend against the more powerful strain of the virus vampires carried in their blood. Daedalus was working on it, and Chuck claimed they were close, but trial results were, so far, not as satisfactory as the FDA would like.

"The immunization kept me from turning, but it didn't stop the virus from attacking my body." Closing her eyes, she slumped against the cave wall. "No one knows why it happens, but in cases like mine, the virus creates dangerously high levels of iron that shut down the pancreas before shutting down other organs."

He cursed. "Can I do anything?"

"I could use some food and water."

"Hold on." She hadn't expected him actually to do anything, but he fetched the duffel full of supplies. "Here," he said as he handed her a wrapped protein bar. "It's not a hot meal, but it's better than nothing."

"Thank you." Gratefully, she took the food he offered. As long as she kept hydrated and kept her blood sugar as level as possible, she could go without the medication for a couple of weeks, until the iron in her blood and organs built up to lethal levels.

But no need to worry, she thought. She'd probably be dead long before she had a chance to die from her disease. Some vampire was likely going to rid her of the iron-in-her-blood problem. And the blood-in-her-veins problem.

She took a bite and tried to pretend it didn't taste like a bird's nest. Without thinking, she offered the bar to Riker, who blinked in surprise.

"It's yours," he said, shaking his head.

"You must know what they taste like," she muttered.

"Hey," he said, his tone light, almost teasing. "I gave you the best of the two flavors." He jerked his thumb over at the survival kit. "The other one is Peanut Butter Sawdust."

She laughed, thankful for a moment of levity, no matter how brief it might be.

"Eat." He started toward the cave entrance. "There's more water in the bag, too."

"Where are you going?" She hated herself for the alarm in her voice, hated herself more for relaxing when he halted at the entrance and gave her a reassuring look.

"I'm going to patrol the area. I want to make sure no one is close." His voice went low, soothing. "I won't go far, and I won't be gone long."

Yesterday his words would have been threatening. Today they were comforting, which was messed up. Here she was, relieved that her kidnapper was going to return. Worse, he was probably planning to take her back to his clan to be tortured or something.

No longer hungry, she forced herself to choke down the protein bar. When Riker hadn't returned by the time she finished, she downed a bottle of water and dug the pad of sticky notes out of the bag. Although her eyes were burning with the need to sleep, she made two tiny origami birds and a flower. As she started another flower, Riker strode through the entrance. The sight of him, moving with confident, easy strides, the weapons harness molded perfectly to his muscular bare chest, sent a wave of both unease and hot, feminine appreciation rippling through her. He could just as easily kill her as protect her.

Hurt her as kiss her.

Bite her as caress her.

Suddenly, the chilly cave felt a lot warmer.

As Riker sauntered toward her, the heat cranked up even more. "What are you doing?"

"Doing?"

He gestured to her paper figures. Flustered and embarrassed, she tried to sweep the creations into the bag, but he crouched down and captured a bird.

"They're silly things I make sometimes." She shrugged dismissively. "Terese taught me."

"Terese taught you origami?"

"She taught me to focus my fidgeting."

Riker studied the tiny bird in his palm. "So this is a nervous thing?"

Nervous didn't quite cover it. Stressed out beyond belief? Yeah, that. "You've never been nervous in your life, have you?"

"Vampires can be nervous," he said. "And afraid." He settled down next to her and ran his finger over the bird's angular head, almost as if it were alive. The sight of such a rock-hard warrior carefully stroking something so fragile filled her with an odd sense of warmth, as if something inside her was melting. "And I wasn't always a vampire, you know."

"Your eyes do give you away." Sliding a covert glance at him, she wondered what color his eyes had been before he was turned.

"Blue," he murmured.

"I almost believe you can read minds."

The amused tilt of his mouth drew her gaze. He really did have perfect, lush lips made to please a woman, and her own lips tingled in remembrance of the kiss they'd shared. She still couldn't believe it had happened. She'd read once that intense situations made people bond quickly and behave in ways they normally wouldn't, and while she wasn't sure about the bonding thing, the rest was spot-on.

Because never in a million years would she have thought she'd kiss a vampire.

"I know people," Riker said. "You said you're a researcher. That means you're curious. So . . . blue."

She didn't like that a vampire had read her so well. She also didn't like that she now knew what color his eyes would be when he was intensely aroused, which was the one time a turned vampire's eyes reverted to their natural color. But even then, the color would be enhanced with an intense, erotic glow said to render the opposite sex powerless to resist.

"Wait . . . so why, when you were on top of me . . ." She paused, desperately seeking words to make this less awkward, but all she could do was think about how her face was on fire with mortification.

"Why didn't my eyes change color?" His gaze snapped up to hers, a cruel glint reflecting off the silver surface. Suddenly, the cave was cold again. "I guess I wasn't that turned on."

She was both relieved and insulted. Definitely irritated. She snatched the paper bird away from him and shoved it into the bag.

"Do I have time to get some rest?"

"You have all night."

Yawning, she settled back against the cave wall. She didn't need all night. Just a few minutes of sleep would do . . .

"NICOLE."

Riker's hushed voice pierced the darkness.

"Nicole." She felt herself being shaken. "We have to go. Someone is coming through the rear entrance."

Groggy, disoriented, she opened her eyes. "What?"

"You fell asleep. You've been out for hours." He didn't wait for her to wake up. In an instant, she was in his arms, and they were darting into the early-morning light at the front of the cave.

She wrapped her arms around his neck, holding on for dear life as he leaped off the ledge and hit the ground at a dead run. He moved silently, his powerful strides barely touching the ground. Branches slapped at them, but mostly, everything was a blur until, miles later, he jerked to a halt and set her on her feet.

"Do you hear that?"

"No," she whispered, her voice sounding strangled

to her own ears. “Poachers?” The very word knotted her gut with dread.

“I wish.”

Vampires burst from out of the forest, and if Riker’s expression was anything to go by, these weren’t the good guys.

SIX MASSIVE VAMPIRES surrounded Riker and Nicole, bodies laden with an extra fifty pounds of weapons each. Blood in various stages of drying was spattered on their fatigue-style clothes, and the stench of death clung to them like a leech. They looked hungry but not for food.

For killing.

This was one of those times Riker missed the feel of cold steel in his hands, the sexy curve of a trigger under his finger, the sure weight of an automatic weapon that would take out all of these assholes in seconds. Riker didn't miss being a human, but he definitely missed the guns.

Riker glanced over at Nicole, silently cursing the flush of alarm in her cheeks. From a situational standpoint, showing fear to ShadowSpawn warriors was like slitting your wrists while swimming with a school of sharks.

From a personal standpoint, Riker didn't like to see Nicole afraid, and *that* was something he didn't want to dwell on.

"Fane." Riker moved toward the leader of the group of newcomers, a turned vampire with a New Jersey accent, at least a dozen piercings, and an uneven bleached-blond Mohawk.

Fane broke away from the pack to meet him. "Worm."

Riker stopped a foot away from the other vampire. "I always forget how much I hate ShadowSpawn until I see one of you assholes."

"And I always forget how useless MoonBound clan is to the Vampire Nation until I see one of you," Fane growled.

"Now that we've exchanged greetings," Riker said, "why don't you tell me why you're here?"

Fane's silver eyes gleamed as they shifted to Nicole, and Riker bristled. "First, tell us who your human morsel is."

Riker put himself between Fane and Nicole. "That's none of your business."

"You know the law," Fane said, as if Riker were a mewling baby vampire who needed lessons in interclan treaties and directives. "Unless you claim her as *apish-wa*, she's fair game for any vampire."

An intense, foreign instinct rose in a volcanic rush, overwhelming rational thought. The idea that Fane—or any male—would sink his fangs and cock into Nicole's tender flesh steamed Riker's blood. Then his blood damn near boiled out of his veins when Fane inched toward Nicole, his eyes as bright as a cat's before it pounces on a mouse.

"The human is *apish-wa*. Mine." Riker took Nicole by the arm and tugged her close. He could feel her flustered gaze boring into him, and he hoped she was smart enough to play along. "Touch her, and I'll strangle you with your own intestines."

"Of course." Fane inclined his head in a civil nod. Damned ShadowSpawn might have no problem slaughtering women and children in the course of war, but they respected property. Most vampires did. Probably because they had so little of it.

Satisfied that Nicole was safe—for the moment, anyway—Riker released her. But he remained so close that her body heat warmed his skin. "Now, why are you here?"

"We came to see if you'd gotten Neriya back." Otto, a ShadowSpawn warrior covered in gang and prison tats from his human days, stepped forward. "Poachers ambushed us about halfway to your headquarters."

"Ambushed?" Riker snorted. "So much for the infamous ShadowSpawn stealth, eh?"

"Fuck off," Fane spat. "We took 'em out. And we got a bonus."

Otto jerked his head toward the forest. "The poachers had one of your females strung up like a fox in a snare, all jerking around and dislocating limbs."

Oh, shit. "Who?"

"Your simpleton."

Riker's stomach clenched. "Lucy?" Next to him, Nicole inhaled a sharp breath.

"Do you have so many simpletons in your clan that you have to ask?" Fane's warriors laughed at that.

"Easier to ask how many of their clan *aren't* fucking retards," one of them said.

"Enough," Riker snapped. "Where is Lucy?"

Fane's upper lip curled, and Riker hoped the ring piercing in it hurt. "We have her. Tell Hunter we'll hold on to her until you return Neriya."

"We told you we'd get her back," Riker bit out. "You don't need Lucy as leverage. We gave you our word."

"The word of a MoonBound warrior is no better than the word of a human," Fane said.

"Be careful," Riker warned. "You're calling a chief and a pureblood vampire a liar."

A shadow of shame flickered in Fane's expression but was quickly replaced by a superior sneer. "I know turned vampires who are worth ten born vampires."

"And I know that Hunter is worth more than all of you combined." Riker got nose-to-nose with Fane. "We *will* have Neriya returned to you by the deadline, and if Lucy has so much as a scratch on her body, every one of your scouting party is going to pay."

Fane grinned, turned away, and strode off. His warriors joined him, and they melted into the forest.

Next to Riker, Nicole made a quiet sound of relief. He turned to her, expecting to find residual terror in her eyes. Instead, she was staring in the direction Fane had gone.

"That vampire," she said firmly, "is a jackass."

He barked out a laugh. "Look at that," he said, starting off in the opposite direction. "Something we agree on."

A FULL TEN minutes of traipsing through the forest had passed before Nicole gathered her thoughts enough to speak beyond calling Fane a jackass.

"What's *apish-wa*?" she asked.

"A blood whore." She nearly tripped over a broken branch that Riker had nimbly avoided. "Watch where you're going," he said, as if she had been *trying* to fall on her face.

"You called me a blood whore?"

"Not just *any* blood whore." He sounded mildly insulted. "A *personal* blood whore whom, by vampire law, no one can drink from without permission."

"Oh," she said dryly. "That makes it better."

"Did you want me to share with them?" He forged ahead, blazing a trail through the thick brush. "They're probably within hearing distance if we shout."

She glared at his back and decided not to respond to his sarcasm. "Where are we going, anyway?"

"To my clan."

She'd had a feeling he'd say that. So now what? Did she go with him, or did she try to run away? Not that she'd get far. Even if she got past the hunters and poachers, she wouldn't get past Riker.

Besides, after the night in the cave, her hatred for him was waning. She didn't trust him, certainly. But she was starting to understand him and why he and his clan would go to such great lengths to save Neriya. Wouldn't she do the same if the roles were reversed and his clan had captured someone she cared about?

Still, the idea of going back to the clan made her heart sink.

"The prey room again," she whispered to herself, but Riker stopped, his boots crunching on old pine needles.

"I'm taking you to our lab. You can hang out with

Grant. He's our resident scientist. A little insane but mostly harmless. Given your background, I'm thinking you'll be more comfortable there."

Stunned, she opened her mouth to thank him, but he threw his hand out, stopping her in her tracks. Except for the flare of his nostrils, he'd frozen solid, and chills ran up her spine. *What now?* Another enemy clan? More poachers? A bear?

At this point, she'd be happy to see a bear. She was rapidly learning that four-legged animals were far less frightening than those on two legs.

Very slowly, Riker looked up. Nicole followed his gaze and barely suppressed a startled squeak. Above them, crouching on a thick tree branch, was a woman. Her crossbow sights were trained on Riker, but where the woman was looking, Nicole had no idea. Her eyes were hidden behind wraparound sunglasses, the camouflage-painted frames matching her skintight garb, which made her nearly invisible against the backdrop of trees and moss.

The woman didn't move a muscle until Riker started walking again. Even then, the woman dipped her head a mere fraction of an inch, but it was just enough for Nicole to catch a glimpse of silver-blond hair tucked under a black stocking cap.

When they were out of crossbow range—Nicole hoped—she tapped Riker on the shoulder. It was like tapping on a marble statue. "Who was that?"

"Sabbat. She's a hunter."

She lifted her brows at him. "You seem pretty nonchalant about a human who hunts your kind."

Riker lifted her across a narrow but deep stream.

"If she'd been hunting us, we'd have died before we knew she was there."

"How . . . comforting." What was comforting was his hands on her waist, holding her steady as he effortlessly lowered her on the far side of the water. When he released her, the warmth of his touch remained like a brand, and she had to resist the urge to smooth her fingers over the tingly sensation.

Nicole Martin, you're an idiot.

His lips quirked into the barest semblance of a smile. "Sabbat only takes out problem vampires."

"Problem vampires?"

Riker ducked a branch and then held it out of the way for her. He was being far more gentlemanly than he'd been yesterday. "Vampires your government has issued execution orders for."

Just last week, a local news station had reported that hunters were looking for a vampire who had fallen into bloodlust. She wondered if Sabbat was one of those hired to handle the situation.

"And you're okay with that?"

He shrugged, the stacked layers of muscle in his bare back shifting under the weapons harness. Nicole had never been attracted to warrior types, let alone vampire warrior types, but something about him had made her normal tastes in men go haywire.

"If a vampire is out of control and drawing attention to us, we want him or her gone," he said, with another shrug of those magnificent shoulders. "Hell, we do it ourselves if we can. Sabbat goes after the worst of the worst, and as long as it stays that way, we don't give her trouble."

"Yeah, well, I think she needs to go after the jackass," Nicole muttered as she brushed a pine needle off her cheek.

"I'd pay to see that." Riker's head swiveled back and forth as they walked, his keen gaze seeming to take in everything around them at once. Nicole tried to do the same, but if she looked away from the ground for more than three seconds, she tripped. Riker sighed, but he didn't look back at her. "Are you having trouble walking?"

She clawed at a spiderweb stuck in her hair. "Excuse me for not having your super-duper vampire reflexes."

"It's not just vampire reflexes. I spent several years training in the military."

Interesting. "When?"

"Are you asking how old I am?" he asked, amusement pitching his already deep voice even lower.

"I guess."

He cast a glance at her from over his shoulder. God, he was handsome when he wasn't scowling at her, and she shivered in feminine appreciation. "How old do you think I am?"

Turned vampires aged very slowly, nearly ten times more slowly than humans. Born vampires aged similarly to humans until they reached maturity, and then they aged even more slowly than turned vampires. Determining age was nearly impossible in both cases.

"If you were human, I'd say late twenties."

"I was twenty-nine when I was turned sixty years ago."

"Wow. You're a geezer." She suppressed a smile at the dirty look he gave her. "How did it happen?"

Sudden tension turned the supple muscles in his back to stone. "My Army unit was sent to Spokane for a joint operation with the Air Force. At least, we thought it was a joint operation. We found out too late that we were there to be turned into vampires."

Nicole stumbled over a root. Only Riker's catlike reflexes kept her from falling on her face. As he held her by her upper arms, steadying her against him, she swallowed. She knew this story from history classes.

"That's when the use of vampires by the military became illegal," she said. "There was some sort of accident at the base. The base commander and several of his staff were killed by rogue vampires—"

"Not rogues!" he snapped. "Created. We were created, and we broke free. The history you learned? It was fiction." His eyes had become hard-edged blades that challenged her to deny his version of events. "They wanted supersoldiers. What they got was a pissed-off bunch of vampire soldiers who knew exactly how to strike back."

He still hadn't released her, but she didn't fight him, kept her voice low and nonconfrontational. "How many of you escaped?"

"Out of thirty of us, I only know of seven who made it out alive. My two best friends died. One didn't survive the turn. The other got away with me. We made our way to Seattle, where MoonBound found us. But Steve . . . he was never the same. He was violent. Insane. Eventually, he didn't even recognize me anymore."

One out of a hundred vampires came out of their turn with their wires crossed, but so far, no one in the scientific community had determined why that was.

She palmed Riker's cheek, an automatic response that made no sense, but neither of them fought it. The contact, tentative as it was, grounded them in the here and now and pushed the past back where it belonged.

"I'm so sorry, Riker." She skimmed her thumb over the sharp outline of his cheekbone. He watched her warily, his nostrils flaring. "And before you accuse me of lying, I want you to know that I'm sorry about Lucy, too."

"You know her?" His wariness lingered, but at least he wasn't angry anymore. "How?"

Nicole paused. She didn't want to throw Lucy under the bus, but at this point, keeping secrets from Riker was only going to cause more distrust. "She helped me escape."

"Let me guess. A secret tunnel?" When she didn't answer, he cursed and stepped back. "I thought we found all of her passages. She's like a damned gopher." He looked up at a hawk sailing overhead, waiting until it disappeared in the treetops to ask, "Why did she help you?"

"I sort of knocked her over. It was an accident," she added when Riker shot her a troubled look. "She was bleeding, and I helped her." She thought about Lucy's request and hoped the vampires who had taken her would treat her to something sweet. "And let's just say I owe her some chocolate."

She was surprised to see a genuinely fond smile

playing on his lips, almost paternal. "She's got a way of getting what she wants."

"Was she always—"

"Simple?"

Taken aback by his curt, defensive tone, Nicole paused before saying, "I was going to ask if she was always so enthusiastic about candy."

"Sorry." Riker scrubbed his hand over his face. "I'm a little protective of her. We all are."

"How long has she been with your clan?"

"About ten years." He started moving again, his long legs eating up ground and forcing her to almost jog to keep up. "Katina found her in an alley. She was living like a rat in the sewers, doing her best to avoid humans and feeding on bums and drug addicts. We have no idea how she got there, when she was turned, how old she is . . . nothing. She won't talk about her past."

How horrible. "Who takes care of her?"

He glanced over his shoulder at her like she'd just asked the dumbest question in the history of dumb questions. "We all do."

Of course they did. Judging by what Nicole knew about MoonBound so far, clan members were family. Really, she wasn't seeing anything different from how humans lived.

Aside from diet. Which was a pretty big deal.

But still, they took care of their own and found compassion even for the children of adults they hated. Terese had taken care of Nicole as if she were Terese's own child. She'd gone above and beyond what had been required of her even after everything humans had done to her.

Now it was time for Nicole to give back, to take the compassion Terese had taught her and use it to help the people Terese had cared about.

"Riker?" She seized his wrist and jerked him to a halt.

He swung around, his gaze hooded. Unreadable. So much distrust, and she couldn't blame him. "Yeah?"

Squaring her shoulders, she said firmly, "Take me to your clan. Let's get Neriya and Lucy back."

HUNTER NEEDED TO get his head out of his ass.

At least, that was what the two drop-dead-gorgeous sisters, Danneca and Tena, were telling him. Problem was, he couldn't concentrate on the naked females, and it didn't seem to matter how much they touched him or touched themselves. His head—the one on his shoulders—was not in the game.

No, right now, his game was poker, and if he wasn't careful, ShadowSpawn was going to realize that Moon Bound had a shitty hand.

"C'mon, Hunter." Tena sat up on the pallet, letting the plush fur coverlets fall to her hips. Her firm, high breasts, the opposite of her sister's fuller, heavier ones, were a stark reminder of why he was here.

This wasn't about sex for the sake of pleasure; it was about sex to make baby vampires. Danneca had given birth three years ago, but the boy had died two days after his first birthday, leaving her heartbroken and the entire clan saddened. Children were rare for vampires, rarer still if the male wasn't a born vampire or hadn't imprinted on the female. Hell, that was an understatement. Hunter had been sowing his seed for more than two centuries, and only three females had gotten with child.

Two females had died during childbirth, his son and daughter with them. The third female had survived, but the child, a boy, hadn't. Since then, he'd sworn to always have a midwife available, even if the midwife had to be borrowed from another clan because fucking poachers had killed MoonBound's.

The memory brought a growl up from deep inside Hunter's chest. He'd found the human poachers and torn them apart. Afterward, he'd burned their trophies—vampire fangs, organs, blood, and bones earmarked for sale on the black market.

Human scum.

Danneca swung her legs off the pallet and stood, her voluptuous body drawing his gaze. She wasn't as pretty as her sister, but her curvy figure and quick mind more than made up for it.

"Come to bed," she said, holding out her hand. "We'll even help you out of those jeans."

He looked down at the unbuttoned fly, behind which was a tool he put to frequent use but which didn't want to play today. He couldn't even care enough to be humiliated, and when a pounding on the door sent both females scurrying under the covers, he breathed a sigh of relief.

"Hunt." Riker's deep voice boomed from behind the heavy oak door. "We have trouble."

"What else is new?" he muttered. He scooped up the females' robes and tossed them to the bed. "Sorry, girls, we'll have to do this another time. Let yourselves out the back way."

Hunter shoved open the bedroom door, not bothering to throw on a shirt or shoes. Riker was in the office, shirtless, his body streaked with dirt, his jeans torn and bloody. In other words, it was business as usual for a guy who mixed it up with poachers and hunters whenever he could. What *wasn't* business as usual was how Riker was splashing whiskey into two highball glasses. Rike was more of a beer guy.

"No, really," Hunter said wryly, "help yourself."

Riker tossed back the contents of one of the glasses and poured another. "Thanks."

Hunter ambled over and snagged the second glass off the desk. He had a hunch he'd need it. "So what's the trouble?" He swirled the liquor, letting the heady fumes scour away the lingering softer scent of the females. "Tell me you caught the human."

"Of course I did." Riker shoved his hand through his hair. "I also ran into a ShadowSpawn scout party. They have Lucy."

An instant, hot rage sizzled through Hunter's veins. Lucy might have the body of a teen and enough years on her to be an adult ten times over, but she had the wits and innocence of a child. He squeezed the glass so hard a crack popped under his palm. If anyone touched a hair on her head, Hunter would skin the bastard alive and leave the body to the scavengers.

"And?" he ground out.

"And they won't give her back until their midwife is returned."

"Son of a . . . *fuck*." Hunter hurled his glass at the wall, shattering it into a million pieces that *clink*ed on the floor as they fell. He gave himself to the count of three to calm down and stop wasting energy on impotent fury. He was a leader, and whether he liked it or not, he had to act like one. "Did the human give you any problems?"

"Nothing I couldn't handle, and I got some interesting intel from her. New vampire weapon made of boric acid. Turns out that if we breathe it, we melt from the inside and explode."

Hunter stared. "Seriously?"

"No," Riker said with a shrug. "But it feels like it. It kills, and trust me, it's some nasty shit."

Just when Hunter thought humans couldn't sink any lower. He really needed to stop underestimating their knack for cruelty. "I'll call the senior warriors together. You can go over everything at the meeting. Where's the human right now?"

"I left her in the lab with Grant. She's got a doctorate in vampire physiology. Figured Grant might want to pick her brains."

"When he's done, I want her," Hunter said, and he didn't like the way Riker stiffened. "Don't get attached, Rike. When we've gotten what we want from her, you need to get rid of her."

"Kill her, you mean."

"We're not in the habit of letting humans live. She's seen too much. You know that." He didn't give the other male a chance to either argue or agree. "I changed my mind about waiting until Grant's done.

Take ten to clean up, and then let's go see your little vampire expert."

"DID YOU KNOW that the black walnut tree is the only plant that cannibalizes other plants?"

Nicole blinked at the vampire standing across the lab counter from her. "Um . . . no."

"That's because it's not true." The salt-and-pepper-haired male Riker had introduced as Grant lowered his head and peered through a microscope lens at a clear drop of liquid. "They can kill many species of plants within up to eighty feet, but they don't cannibalize."

She rubbed her arms and wondered where the thermostat was. The surprisingly sophisticated lab was freezing. "Then why did you say it?"

"Say what?"

"About the walnut tree."

Grant looked up, confusion flashing in his pewter eyes. "I didn't talk about a walnut tree."

How did this guy run a lab? Riker had warned her, but *ugh*. "So Riker said you were a microbiologist before you were turned."

"Yes." He moved over to a hematology analyzer and checked the readout. How did vampires get equipment like that, anyway? He even wore a white lab coat, although the professional appearance was ruined by a crimson tank top that clung to every honed muscle and butt-defining orange-and-black Oregon State University sweats. In college, he must have been the poster boy for sexy geeks. "And it was a *black* walnut tree."

He might be handsome as hell, but he wasn't the easiest guy to talk to. "Where did you work?"

"At Daedalus. Their Albuquerque facility."

She drew a sharp breath. Was he aware that Daedalus was her company? "That's the main blood-packaging plant." The general consensus within Daedalus was that only the weirdos and people the company wanted out of the way worked at the facility. Nicknamed Dracula Diner, the plant was where blood, drained from the corpses of deceased humans, was sent to be processed and bottled as vampire food.

By law, all humans in the United States must donate their blood after death. Organ donation was still a matter of choice. Nicole had always thought it was strange that humans were required to feed vampires but not to save the lives of fellow humans.

Grant glanced over his shoulder at her. "You know of the Dracula Diner?"

Intimately. "I, uh, work for Daedalus, too."

"Ah. Horrible people."

Well, this was awkward. "Did you think they were horrible when you were human and working for them?"

His smile was as chilly as the room and way too fangy for her liking. Not at all like when Riker smiled. His fangs were sort of . . . *don't think it. Do. Not. Think. It.* Riker's fangs were *not* sexy.

"Of course I didn't think that. I was a brainwashed fool with my own vampire slave." Grant measured a small amount of reddish liquid with a dropper and added it to a test tube containing white powder. "I met the CEO once. William Martin. Fawned all over him like he was a rock star or something. Practically pissed myself like a puppy welcoming his master home. Now I'd like to rip out his heart with my teeth."

"Someone beat you to it," she said, hoping Grant didn't notice the hitch in her voice.

"He's dead? Ah, yes, I remember now. Him and his entire family." He shrugged. "I hope they died in agony."

Bastard. "I'm sure they did."

Grant's broad grin gave him boyish dimples and softened his square jaw. "You think?" After a moment, he frowned a little. "Though someone recently mentioned a daughter who survived. There's still hope that one of us will kill her."

So this was what it felt like to be a mouse in a python tank. "Everyone needs a dream, I guess."

"Agreed." He positively beamed. "Humans are usually worth only the price of their blood. But I like you."

"Um . . . thanks?" She eyed the layout of the equipment in front of him as he poured a quarter of the contents of a blue liquid into a flask half full of pink liquid. "What are you doing, anyway?"

He held the now purplish mixture up to the light. "I'm mixing Kool-Aid flavors to find the best-tasting combination."

She arched an eyebrow. Kool-Aid? He definitely wasn't firing on all cylinders. Did his clan shove him into this lab to keep him out of the way? She wandered around, stopping at a corkboard covered with papers about vampire physiology, equations scribbled on index cards, and a photo of two male vampires, one blond and backed up against a tree, the other pressed against him, his reddish-brown hair falling forward to frame them both as their foreheads touched.

The intimacy of the photo took her breath away. She'd never been in a position like that, had never experienced a secret moment that defined a relationship as something to be treasured. She'd had lovers, but she'd never *loved*. Not like that.

"What's this?"

Grant wandered over. "Ah, Takis and Aiden." He touched his finger to the photo. "They're gay."

"Yeah, I guessed that."

He sighed. "Once a month, they have to feed from females. You know about that, I assume?"

"Of course," she replied. "On the eve of every full moon, male vampires must feed from female vampires, and on the new moon, the opposite takes place."

"Exactly. I'm trying to find a way around that for them."

She'd never considered the problems homosexual vampires would face. "I've hypothesized that the feeding is a biological imperative, sort of heat cycles for both sexes. Because vampires don't conceive easily or often, it's like a way to make sure vampires get together."

He nodded. "Most vampires mate during the feeding. The opposite sex's blood is an aphrodisiac to vampires. Aiden and Takis would prefer to spend the nights of the full moon together instead of with females."

"The most obvious solution would be to package female blood and let them drink it that way on the full moon."

Grant's lip curled in disgust. "The way humans feed their vampire slaves?"

It was possible that this could get more awkward, but she didn't see how. "Yeah. Like that."

A hiss sifted out from between his teeth. "Humiliating. No one feeds that way by choice. Human blood from little packages is one thing. Vampire blood in juice boxes is another." He turned to her, his deep-set eyes shadowed with irritation. "Have you ever seen vampires after they've fed from damned juice boxes of moon blood? Have you witnessed the hour of misery afterward as their bodies cramp from a lack of sexual release? Self-gratification only helps so much."

Yes, she'd seen their misery, which was why Daedalus now recommended that humans keep at least two slaves, one of each sex, or that they arrange for a partner once a month for a single slave. Packaged vampire blood kept them healthy, but without a sexual partner, recovery was much slower.

An unbidden image of Riker feeding from a female vampire flashed in her head. He was naked, his muscular body moving against the female in powerful surges. Did he have a regular partner, or did he feed from a variety of females? And why the hell did she care?

She cleared her throat. "We've found that a biological reaction takes place during the full- and new-moon feedings that, when combined with intercourse, causes a slight change in the body chemistry of both the male and the female, making conception far more likely than with intercourse at any other time of the month."

"Yes! Finally, someone who gets it." Grant threw up his hands. "That's what I've found as well. The key, I believe, is in the hormones and pheromones, which explains why, even if a vampire feeds from a vampire of the opposite sex during a moon phase and then has sex with a human, it doesn't completely alleviate the pain."

She studied the board. "Have you tried isolating the VR-2 enzyme? I've seen preliminary lab results that suggest giving extra VR-2 with a moon feeding can reduce the discomfort in males."

"Tried that." Grant sighed. "But the quantities required to cut the discomfort even by half cause undesirable side effects."

"Like what?"

"Uncontrollable rage and bloodlust. Aiden nearly killed Takis after a strong dose."

Interesting. Two years ago, she'd written a paper about the causes of irreversible bloodlust among vampires, and she'd theorized that the VR-2 enzyme might be responsible, although she didn't know exactly how. Now she wondered if, perhaps, an unnatural buildup from feeding could play a part.

"Do you mind if I look through your notes sometime?" she asked, and then chastised herself for being a fool. She and Grant weren't colleagues. She didn't work here or live here, and he wanted Nicole Martin dead.

"Only if you share some of your knowledge with me," Grant said.

"Deal," she agreed, but she doubted they'd get the opportunity to do either. "Now I'm wondering if the VR-2 enzyme might have something to do with the way some vampires come out of the turning half-insane."

Grant gave her a strange look. "Some things can't be explained by science."

"I'm surprised to hear you say that, being a scientist."

He jammed his hands in his lab coat's pockets. "A couple of decades ago, I'd have agreed. But I've seen things since being turned that defy science."

She didn't know about the *defy science* thing, but since being kidnapped by Riker she'd experienced things that defied belief. Like kissing not just a vampire, but the very vampire who had haunted her nightmares for years. Worse, something inside her wanted to do it again, to see if it would be as good the second time as it was the first.

Yup. Defied belief.

Giving herself a mental shake, she jumped back into the conversation. "It would help if we knew the exact origins of the vampire species. We think the first case of vampirism started around four hundred years ago, here in America, but we don't know where the virus came from, if it was originally airborne—"

Grant took a sip of his purple concoction and grimaced. "You know the vampire legend of their origins, yes?"

"Yes, but the legend is ridiculous."

"Is it?"

He had to be kidding. "Two Native American tribal chiefs kill each other, and then a crow and a raven fight over their bodies, spilling their blood into the men, who afterward rise that night as undead? Um, yes. Ridiculous."

"Some vampires agree with you. Mostly the turned ones. There are also rumors of demons creating the first vampires, but if they are so much as whispered inside these walls, Hunter will shut them down with rare temper."

She smiled politely. "When I see demon DNA, I'll believe it. Until then, I'm going with the natural-virus theory. If something supernatural was the cause, we'd see vampires with unexplained abilities. Instead of vampires with enhanced natural abilities, like super-speed, we'd see pyrokinesis. Teleportation. Telekinesis. Shape-shifting."

"Ah. But how many *born* vampires have you studied? They have rarer and more powerful abilities than turned vampires. Imagine what gifts the oldest, purest vampires must possess. And there have always been rumors of vampires who can do all of the supernatural abilities you mentioned."

"Rumors. There are also people who believe the earth is flat. People will always believe in things that don't make sense." She skimmed her fingers over the microscope like it was an old friend. "And there are scientific explanations about why that is, as well."

"You remind me so much of me." He sighed. "I hope Hunter doesn't kill you."

Er, yeah. She hoped so, too.

The door banged open, and her heart stuttered as Riker entered with another vampire.

The new vampire, a tall, broad male with an amazing mane of blue-black hair, strolled toward her. He was dressed like Riker, in jeans and a T-shirt, but that was where the similarities ended.

His ebony gaze marked him as a born vampire, and, like so many borns, his Native American ancestry was obvious in his bronze skin and the powerful, chiseled bone structure of select prairie tribes. An aura of ancient energy practically vibrated off him, and she'd bet her entire company that he was either an original vampire—one of the first humans who contracted the virus—or from a first- or second-generation mating. God, how she'd love to study him. Question him. Get some insight into their mysterious origins that had stumped scientists since vampires were first discovered.

The raven and crow story was just too ludicrous. Almost as ludicrous as the demon theory.

"You're Dr. Nicole Martin." It wasn't a question. Hell, it sounded like a threat. How could something as simple as her name sound like he'd said, *You're dead*.

Anxiety dried her mouth to dust. "I am. Nicole, I mean." *Wow. Way to babble.*

Grant rounded on her, knocking tubes of Kool-Aid all over the counter and floor. "You're a fucking *Martin*?"

She casually inched closer to Riker. "I'm the surviving daughter you want to kill."

"Huh." Grant went back to his project, righting test tubes and wiping up spilled liquid.

Okaaay. So not the reaction she'd been expecting. He was the most unpredictable person she'd ever met.

"Say the same thing to me," the new vampire rumbled, "and you'll get a much different response." He smiled, revealing fangs that were twice as large as Riker's. Those things would *hurt*. "We need to talk."

"Who are you?" She looked to Riker for help, but the vampire who had confided in her about his mate and child, who had saved her from poachers and handled her with such care, was gone, replaced by a stone-faced hardass with cold eyes.

"He's our chief." Riker's tone was all business, and disappointment cut deep. She wanted the Riker from earlier. With that Riker, she'd felt almost comfortable. This one frightened her nearly as much as he had when he'd kidnapped her from her home. "Name's Hunter."

Hunter stepped into her, so close she could smell smoky whiskey on his breath, and panic fluttered in her belly. He was blocking her view of Riker, using his size to intimidate her. It worked. She felt small. Trapped. And excruciatingly aware of how disheveled and dirty she was.

"Riker has told you why we need you?"

This guy didn't strike her as the type to mess around, and she wasn't naive enough to think that any friendly inroads she'd made with Riker would extend to the clan leader. She had to be careful if she wanted to make it out of this alive.

Craning her neck, she met his steady gaze. "I've already agreed to do everything in my power to find and release the female vampire you think my company is holding."

"We don't think," he growled. "We know."

It was probably stupid of her, but she was still clinging to the tiniest speck of hope that they were wrong, that Daedalus hadn't been skirting laws to acquire vampires.

"I said I'd help," she repeated.

"She's already helped," Grant chimed in. "She seems to have an advanced working knowledge of our biology. Can I have her when you're done? We don't have to kill her right away, do we?"

She let out a ridiculous mousy squeak. "You know,

I'm standing right here while you casually discuss my death."

Riker moved into her line of vision, and she wasn't ashamed to admit to herself that she was relieved. "No one is going to die."

An unreadable look passed between Hunter and Riker, and a sudden, tangible tension crackled in the air.

"Look," she said quickly, hoping to defuse the friction, "I want to get Neriya back and make sure Lucy is safe. I'll do whatever it takes, I promise." Figuring she had little to lose, she adopted her best CEO voice. "But here's the thing. You need me, so I'd like a little assurance that you'll release me when it's done."

Nicole was pretty certain Hunter would refuse. So she was totally shocked when he stepped back and said, "You have my word. Riker will take care of you. Speaking of which, Rike, while you were showering, I had a chamber prepared for her. Down the hall from yours."

For one glorious moment, relief gave Nicole a new lease on life. Hopefully a chamber of her own meant a shower and a bed.

Then she glanced over at Riker.

He looked both troubled and pissed, and once again, she wondered just how long she had left to live.

RIKER WILL TAKE *care of you.*

Yeah, Riker knew exactly what Hunter meant. *Taking care of* humans had never been a problem for Riker before. And it shouldn't be a problem now. But son of a bitch, Nicole had gotten under his skin.

She'd saved his life, shown vulnerability and remorse over Terese's death, and charmed him with her odd origami habit. And in return, like an idiot, he'd told this female things he'd never told anyone. No one in the clan knew that the baby Terese had carried wasn't his. No one knew she'd killed herself.

Somehow, despite all the trouble Nicole had caused him, he'd confided in her. He'd laughed with her. And he'd gotten hard for her.

"Are we done here?" Riker asked Hunter.

Hunter gave an almost imperceptible nod and swung around to Grant, letting Riker know he was dismissed. "Nicole," he said, almost as an afterthought and in a cheerful voice that made Riker's hair stand on end, "I look forward to having a more . . . in-depth session with you."

Before she could reply, Riker took her by the arm and hauled her out of there. She went willingly. Eagerly, really.

"Thanks." Her boots thumped softly on the stone floor as they walked down the hall, her slender legs in perfect sync with his long strides. "Things were kind of tense back there."

Kind of? Hunter was in one of the worst moods Riker had ever seen. Oh, he'd seen Hunter angrier, in full-blown, unreachable rages. But this was Hunter at his worst—or best, depending on which side you were on. The cold fury that started with Neriya's abduction and ended with Lucy's kidnapping was gathering deep inside him. It was the kind that rolled over everyone, including those he cared about.

Riker did *not* want to be in his path.

He steered the conversation away from his clan chief. "Did Grant bother you?"

"Not really. You were right about him—moments of confusion punctuated by spurts of lucidity." Her hair, full of soft waves, brushed her shredded turtleneck as she shook her head. The wild, windblown bob looked good on her. Much better than the severe, straight, hairsprayed-to-hell way she'd had it when he took her from her mansion. "It was your chief. Intense guy."

So much for his attempt to not discuss Hunter. "Talk about your moments of confusion and spurts of lucidity."

"Seriously?" She rubbed her arms, and he made a mental note to get her some warmer clothes. He also made a mental note to stop staring at her breasts when she did that. "He's unbalanced, too?"

He waited to speak until a trio of females passed them in the hallway. "Some might say so, but nah, he's the sanest male I know. He just has a tendency not to take things as seriously as some think he should."

"Some. Like you?"

She'd hit that stake on the head. For a human, she was pretty astute. He didn't answer that, though; clan business was none of hers.

"How are you feeling?" He didn't like that she still hadn't regained all the color she'd lost when she'd gotten ill in the cave. "Is there anything specific I can get you to eat or drink that'll help your condition?"

"Oh, um, yes." She stepped toward him to avoid being flattened by two males tossing a football as they ran through the passage.

"Hey, assholes!" Riker barked. "We have a common room for that. Not to mention a million acres of forest." As the guys sheepishly offered apologies, Riker turned back to Nicole. "Go on. What can I get for you?"

"Low-iron, low-carb foods. As the iron builds in my blood, my pancreas is going to get wacky with the insulin." She chewed her lip a little. "There are other issues that the medication handles, but they'll take a lot longer to kill me."

This was a complication they didn't need. The sooner they got Neriya, the sooner . . . what? The sooner Nicole would be released so she could use the knowledge she'd gained to destroy them? Or the sooner they'd kill her to protect themselves?

Fuck. This was a lose-lose situation. He thought back to his military days and all the no-win situations he'd been thrust into. Somehow he'd come out of them alive. But not everyone had. No-win scenarios always resulted in someone's death.

Like Jesse and Steve, both of whom he'd been close with since basic training. They'd all been together when they'd walked into the building at Fairchild Air Force Base for what he'd believed would be a briefing. Instead, they'd been sedated with drugged water and fed to vampires. Riker would never forget the next couple of weeks of torment as his body changed, his muscles, bones, and organs altering painfully fast. Gnawing hunger had nearly torn him apart as he threw up everything he'd been given to eat. The first bag of blood someone had thrown into his cell had been the best thing he'd ever tasted.

Until he threw that up, too.

But the worst . . . the worst had been finding Jesse dead on the floor, his body cold and contorted in agony. He hadn't survived the turning, and Riker's sorrow had been magnified by the fact that Steve had survived, but he wasn't himself. Vicious and angry, Steve had been almost uncontrollable, 'roid rage times a million.

A year later, he'd died, too.

At Hunter's hand.

"Riker?" Nicole tapped on his shoulder. "You okay?"

Right. They'd been talking about her diet. "I'll get one of our cooks on it," he said brusquely.

"You have cooks?"

"Everyone here has a job. Just like humans. And we eat normal food. Just like humans." Shrugging off her startled glance at his abrupt reply, he guided her to his quarters and pushed open the heavy wood door. "Welcome to my den."

He wasn't sure why he was welcoming her as if he was bringing home a date. Hell, he hadn't brought a female here for anything but the full-moon feeding since his mate died. Even then, he sent the females on their way afterward, while he went through the misery of the lack-of-sex cramps by himself. His regular blood partner of late, Benet, had been open about her willingness to sleep with him, but every time he thought he could go through with it, his interest—and his cock—flagged the moment she touched him intimately.

Inexplicable irritation made him grind his molars as he strode through the doorway and turned to Nicole, who remained in the hall, lower lip trapped between her teeth.

"You waiting for a different kind of invitation? Because they'll get less polite."

Nicole entered cautiously, as if she expected to step into a bear trap. "This is your place?" She glanced around, gaze landing on the rustic furniture, the handmade sofa and dining table, the small kitchen off to the right, and the doorway to the bedroom. "I didn't expect . . . I don't know . . . a home."

The irritation veered to anger. "No doubt you thought we'd live in dirt holes lined with leaves, like wild animals."

She inhaled sharply. "It's not that. It's just that I didn't expect such modern conveniences."

"No? What do they teach you in your vampire courses? That we cook over fires made by rubbing two sticks together? That we use dishes made of human skulls?"

A soft pink blush spread across her cheeks as she

turned away, and yep, he was right on target. Although, truthfully, there were clans like that. With the help of human sympathizers, some clans had built permanent habitats, villages like this one, with all the trappings of modern human society, including electricity, phones, and even vehicles. Others clung to the old ways, living in the forests or city sewers with only loose ties to any particular territory. Still others were loners, scrounging out a life however and wherever they could.

Nicole looked down at her feet as if ashamed, but when she looked up, there was fire in the green of her eyes. "I'm sorry I've had a mistaken view of how you live. I'm sorry I expect the worst from you. But you know, you're doing the same thing to me."

As much as he liked the way her temper stirred his blood, he didn't like what she'd said. She was dead wrong.

"No, it's not the same thing." He shed his jacket and tossed it over the back of a chair. "Your family owns my kind. Your family literally built a business from our blood and created the vampire industry. You're the CEO of a company that's responsible for more vampire deaths than all the others combined. A company that killed my mate. So no, it's not the same thing."

Instead of responding right away, she wandered around the room, touching his aircraft prints, running her hands over the guns mounted on the walls. He could no longer fire them, but being a sniper was in his blood, and he doubted that would ever change.

Nicole's hand skimmed along the barrel of his M-16, and abruptly, his body hardened and his skin grew clammy. His cock stirred as she caressed the cold steel he himself had handled with such care, and he nearly groaned when she took the trigger between her forefinger and thumb, testing the gentle curve. Christ, what a turn-on. Terese wouldn't go near his collection of weapons.

He drifted closer to her, drawn by Nicole's curiosity, her strength, her beauty, and the glow of life that radiated from her. Whatever else he might think about her, she was a survivor, and that was a turn-on all by itself.

"When I was little," she murmured, "I overheard one of our servants talking about his home. At the time, it didn't make an impact, but I guess now I can see what he was talking about. He lived like this, I think." She started toward the bedroom, and that fast, his lust veered to panic.

Leaping in front of her, he slammed the door to the bedroom closed. At her blink of surprise, he growled, "That room is off-limits."

She sniffed. "I'm happier about that than you can imagine." Her expression shuttered, she crossed her arms over her chest, closing herself off to him. Why that irritated him, he had no idea. "Why are we here, anyway?"

Cursing, he swiped his cell phone off the desk. "You're going to call your company, and you're going to arrange an exchange. Neriya for you."

"Gladly." She snatched the phone, and he wondered if she suspected at all that he was lying.

NICOLE DIALED CHUCK'S number with trembling fingers. Her brother would get her out of this mess, and if she could just explain to the board why she'd missed the meeting—

"Charles Martin speaking."

"Chuck!" Nicole turned away from Riker, who was watching her like an eagle. Such an apt comparison, given that both were striking. Formidable. And deadly. "Oh, my God, it's good to hear your voice."

"Nicole?" There was a crash and a curse on the other end of the line, probably Chuck jumping up from his desk chair and knocking crap over. "Shit, Nicole, is that really you? Where are you? Are you okay? Roland's dead, but there was no sign of you. Where are you?" he repeated, clearly rattled.

She took a deep, bracing breath. Hearing his voice was a soothing balm to her seriously frayed nerves. "I'm fine. I'm being held—"

Riker snared her arm in a vicious hold and shook his head, a warning to not reveal anything that might hint of her location. She jerked away from him. She didn't know where she was, anyway.

"I'm being held by vampires."

"You're what?" Chuck roared. "Where?"

She slid a covert glance at Riker. "I can't tell you that." She was so lost in these woods that she'd never in a million years be able to find her way back to the clan stronghold. "I need you to arrange to have a female vampire named Neriya set free. She was taken from the forest outside Seattle two weeks ago by bounty hunters."

"You know it's illegal for individuals or companies to capture wild vampires." Chuck's voice had gone flat. Lifeless. Guilty as hell.

Chuck was well aware that Daedalus had gone outside the law to acquire vampires. Doing so would be faster and cheaper, and it would bypass regulations regarding the number of vampires allowed in specific spaces—not to mention directives regarding their treatment.

"Yes," she said sickly, disappointment in her brother putting a cold knot in her belly, "I do. But apparently, Daedalus doesn't."

She could practically feel the anger steaming off Chuck. "How do you know we have her?"

"Because one of the vampires who was with her heard a hunter say he had a buyer from Daedalus lined up. So she's got to be at one of our facilities."

"Please," he scoffed. "You believe a fucking scumbag vampire? You're smarter than that."

She went taut at her brother's nasty words and condescending tone. "I have my reasons for believing this, so please, just check on it for me."

He uttered a nasty curse under his breath. "Hold on."

She waited, listening to Chuck type furiously on his computer's keyboard.

"Got it," he said. "Feral number eight-two-six was sent to the South Seattle B-lab."

She frowned. Besides the main corporate offices in downtown Seattle, there were nearly a dozen Daedalus holdings around the city, from laboratories and training centers to manufacturing plants and vampire-holding kennels, but she didn't know about a lab on the south side. "B-lab? What is that?"

There was a long pause, and the longer she waited, the more her stomach churned. And the more agitated Riker became. She heard the *clink* of ice in a glass and then the pour of liquid.

"Nicole, you haven't been back for long—"

"What. Is. It?"

Chuck's voice went low. Almost to a whisper. "It's a research facility. Top secret. Only a handful of people know about it."

"And why is that?" When he paused again, she repeated the question, sharper this time.

"Come on, Nikki. You know how those vampire-rights freaks get. We don't need them up our asses because we aren't giving those poor, helpless vampires cable TV in their cages or some shit."

She couldn't believe what Chuck was saying. "Bullshit. It's because we're running the facility outside the confines of the law, isn't it?" She cursed at his lack of response. Which, really, was an answer. "Why wasn't I told about it?"

Chuck's pauses were really starting to piss her off. Finally, he said, "Plausible deniability."

Jesus. What were they doing in that place? "I need you to get Neriya out of there." She looked over at Riker, who was watching her like he expected her to drop clues to her whereabouts or maybe just shout for help outright. "Now."

"Nicole . . . that won't be possible."

"Why not?"

"The partners won't allow it," Chuck said, impatience leaking into his voice. Yes, it must be such a burden for her to ask for something as simple as releasing an illegally obtained vampire.

"What do you mean, they won't allow it?" she snapped. "They have no choice. I'm giving an order."

"That's the thing. You don't give orders anymore. You missed the meeting, Nicole."

Unbelievable. "I missed the meeting *because I was kidnapped*. I think, given the circumstances, my inability to attend a board meeting can be overlooked."

"It's too late. They enacted code twelve-point-two-nine of the company bylaws."

She swallowed. Hard. Her father had made sure his offspring retained full control in the event of his death . . . unless said offspring was incompetent or unable to fulfill his or her role as CEO. In which case, after a board hearing, the CEO could be stripped of that position, and his or her company shares would go to the next in line to inherit.

Which, in this case, was Chuck.

"So . . . you're in charge now?"

His answer was a long time coming. "Yes."

Anger lit her like a fuse, but right now, she was more concerned about her survival than her company.

"Then you can get the vampire out of the facility yourself, in order to make the trade for me."

"I'm sorry, Nicole. I can't."

Her mind spun at his incomprehensible answer. "You're in control of the company. You can do whatever you want!"

"That's where you're wrong. This is a legal matter now. If I help you, I'll risk the company and jail time."

Her legs turned to rubber beneath her, and she sagged onto Riker's couch. "I don't understand. Why is this a legal issue?"

Again, there was a long, tense pause. Finally, Chuck said firmly, "Because the VHS somehow got hold of the video documenting the vampire deaths you signed off on, and it's now on every news channel on the planet. Public outrage has grown. It's a small minority, but they're loud. They're calling for your arrest on charges of cruelty and inappropriate execution." She heard more *clink*ing of ice in a glass and the gurgle of another liquor pour. "I'm sure it'll blow over. The majority of the population doesn't care about a couple dozen dead bloodsuckers. The board thinks that as long as you aren't in charge of the company anymore, the VHS will be satisfied. But that means you need to stay out of sight. At least, until we announce your kidnapping."

They hadn't done that yet? "You can't be serious. Chuck, you have to get me out of here!"

"Nikki, I'm sorry. This is killing me, but I don't know what I can do. Most of the board doesn't know about the lab, let alone how we've been procuring vampires. If they find out—"

"The entire company will be at risk, and everyone involved, including you, will go to jail."

"Yes," he whispered.

Her heart sank. Dear God, she was screwed. He was going to let the vampires keep her. "Dammit, you've got to do something. You have to—"

Riker swiped the phone from her. "Listen to me, you human scum. You have twelve hours to get Neriya back to us, or your sister dies."

Nicole sucked in a shocked breath, her heart squeezing painfully. She'd known she wasn't exactly a guest here, but she thought she and Riker had an understanding that would at least make him a little hesitant to kill her.

He didn't even have the courtesy to look her in the eye as he waited for her brother to reply. After a long moment, he quietly closed the phone.

"Well? What did he say?"

"He said he loves you." Riker swore, and her heart stopped completely. "And he's sorry."

CHARLES MARTIN WAS a piece of shit. Oh, he'd said he loved Nicole. He'd said he was sorry.

But it was all a load of crap. If Riker were in Chuck's position, he'd stop at nothing to save someone he cared about. He'd spent months searching for Terese after she'd been captured. After he'd located her at the Martin estate, he'd spent months planning to free her. Then he'd spent another eight months searching for her again when she disappeared, only to return pregnant.

Chuck's words were hollow, and Nicole knew it, too.

The devastation in her expression, her mottled cheeks, her liquid eyes, spun Riker off balance as she sat there, staring at the phone in his hand.

"He was stalling," she said. "He had to be. He'll come up with a plan." She looked up at Riker as if trying to convince him that her brother wasn't an asshole. "He will. I would. I'd do everything in my power to save him, even if it meant jail. I wouldn't let him die. He won't let me die—"

"Hey." He cut off her rambling before she went into a full-blown panic attack. "You're not going to die. I was bluffing about killing you, Nicole. Your brother might be bluffing, too," he said, although he suspected that wasn't the case.

She rubbed her arms again, and he felt like a heel for letting her get chilled. "But if he doesn't come through, I'm screwed. *We're* screwed."

He didn't like the way she'd said that, both because it meant that Neriya was in jeopardy and because it also implied that they were in this together. Which he supposed they were. He just didn't like it.

"It's not over." He snagged the black hoodie jacket hanging next to the door. "It's your company. If Chuck can't help, you still have power."

"I've been fired," she said, her voice so devoid of emotion that he couldn't get a read on her. "Daedalus is apparently no longer my company."

"Fired?" He draped the jacket over her shoulders and carefully freed her red-blond hair from under the collar. His hand lingered longer than what was appropriate, but damn, her hair was so soft, so silky, and it looked good against the black leather. She gave him a fragile but grateful smile, and he returned the smile like a kid with a crush. His heart even hammered in a crazy rhythm. He was a dolt. A big, vampire dolt. "Fired for what?"

Shivering as if he'd stripped her of clothing instead of giving her more, she looked down at her lap. "For slaughtering dozens of vampires in a lab."

His heart hammered harder, this time for a different reason. Just when he'd thought Nicole was a different kind of Martin—and a different kind of *human*—she hit him with this.

"And you killed them . . . why?" He spoke through clenched teeth.

"I didn't," she said in a breathless rush. "Yes, I mean, the vampires were killed, but *I* didn't order their deaths."

"Then why are they blaming you?"

"Because my signature is on the execution order." She lifted her gaze, the bold challenge in her eyes daring him to call into question her reasoning for signing the order.

Which was how he knew there was more to the story. Just forty-eight hours ago, he'd have believed she'd murdered dozens of vampires with no more thought than a butcher gave a cow. But now he wasn't so sure. No, strike that. He was sure. The Nicole who had saved Terese's ring and who had been so outraged at Lucy's capture wouldn't casually send dozens of vampires to their deaths.

"So what did the order say?" Putting a lid on his inner drill sergeant, he sat on the arm of the recliner, doing his best to come across as nonthreatening. Right now, he needed her cooperation, and her asshole brother had unintentionally given Riker a golden opportunity to swoop in and be the good guy. "Why were they killed?"

"Apparently, the lab where they were being kept was over capacity."

"They were murdered because the morons who work for you were too stupid to count?"

"That about sums it up." She got up off the couch and stared at the wall, as if she was as lost in his quarters as she'd been in the forest.

He wondered what she'd do if he came up behind her and folded her into his arms. His desire to comfort her was beginning to become a regular thing, wasn't it? What was it Myne liked to say? *Never dust off your give-a-shit. If you do, you keep having to use it.*

"Nicole?"

"Hmm?"

"Why did you sign the execution order?"

"I didn't." Tugging the jacket closed tight at the front with one hand, she started to pace. "My signature is on the paper, but I don't know how it got there." Frustration seeped into her voice. "I've stayed up so many nights going over it in my head, trying to figure out how the hell it happened. But ultimately, it doesn't matter. Even if someone else had signed the order, I was in charge of the company at the time, so the buck stops with me."

It was a command principle he knew well. Being a leader came with perks, whether that meant a lot of money, a lot of power, or a lot of fame. But it also came with a lot of risks. A single incident, even involving someone far down on the command chain, could end careers and ruin a lot of lives. The fact that Nicole was willing to take responsibility spoke volumes about her character, and he found himself softening toward her even more.

He'd done far more than dust off his give-a-shit. He'd polished it to a flawless shine the way he'd polished his combat boots and weapons so long ago.

Dumbass.

Nicole pivoted suddenly and made a beeline to his desk. She grabbed a pen and a pad of paper and started sketching a series of lines.

"What are you doing?" She didn't reply, just kept scratching furiously on the pad, her messy mop of hair hiding her face.

Without thinking, he stood and brushed a silky strand back behind her ear. The tips of his finger skimmed her cheekbone, her soft skin. She turned, and God, when her eyes met his, it was as if there was nothing between them. Nothing holding him back from tugging her hard against him and doing what he'd wanted to do to her in the cave.

His heart thundered behind his ribs, pounding painfully hard and fast. His intense response to her shocked him. She was the enemy. This was so wrong.

The argument was weak, and he knew it. Nicole might not be a friend, or even a neutral party, but she wasn't the enemy.

He drifted closer. Tension bloomed in the span of space between them, heavy and hot, like a summer storm brewing on the horizon. She swallowed, and instinctively, his gaze flicked to her throat.

Nicole flinched, and in less time than it took to squeeze off a rifle round, the tension snapped. So awkwardly that Riker felt sorry for her, Nicole inched away and returned to her sketches with a shaky hand. More desires bubbled up inside him, feelings he hadn't felt since Terese was alive.

His parents had always believed he'd grow up to be a doctor or some kind of teacher, so his enlistment in the Army had been a stunner for them. Delta had literally beaten most of the compassion out of him, and then decades of fighting humans as a vampire had sucked out the rest.

Until Terese.

With her, a harsh word or a raised voice would make her withdraw at best. At worst, she'd turn into a sobbing, trembling ball on the floor. The qualities his parents had admired in him had slowly surfaced again, only to be crushed and buried even deeper than before when Terese died.

Now, it seemed, they were creeping back into his life like a team of poachers. How long would it be before his rogue emotions took him down for good?

Nicole's scribbles started to form a pattern. A building with landscaping around the property, fences, gates . . . He tapped the paper. "That's one of your labs."

She nodded. "A few years ago, my uncle showed me the basic plans for all of the offices, processing plants, and research facilities so he could explain how the security worked. Daedalus designed all the labs to be nearly identical so employees, equipment, and security could be easily interchangeable." She labeled a room with the word *MEDICAL*, another with *STAFF*, and another with *UNKNOWN*. "Chuck told me Neriya was being held at what he called the B-lab. There's no reason to think that its design is different from any other Daedalus lab. I'm sure I can get in through the main entrance if word hasn't gotten out about my dismissal from the company."

"What are you talking about?"

"I'm talking about saving Neriya." She looked at him like he was a complete idiot. "Isn't that the point of all of this? If I can get inside, I might be able to bluff my way out with her."

Whoa. Was she really contemplating breaking into her own lab, or was this a trick to escape? "Let's slow down for a minute and think."

"Think?" She shook her head. "I've thought about it. We need to do this now, before my firing and kidnapping become common knowledge."

His gut told him her offer was genuine, but there were other considerations. "We can't do anything for a couple of days. The full moon is tomorrow. Starting today, no one is allowed to leave unless it's to patrol for enemies."

As if she didn't hear a word, Nicole went back to sketching with an almost obsessive intensity, her nonstop chatter heightening the insanity. "I'll go at night, when most of the staff is gone. The lower-level security people will be even less likely to know about my situation." The paper filled up with lines and barely legible words. "Neriya will probably be in the room over here—"

He grabbed her hand to still the craziness. "Will you stop?"

"What? No." She peeled his hand away and hunched over her sketch again. "We can do this. We can get in—"

"Dammit, Nicole, *stop*." He palmed her shoulders and dragged her around to face him. "We need to look at this from all angles."

"We don't have time. *I* don't have time. This is my fault. I have to fix it before more vampires die." The tremor in her voice socked him right in the heart. "Before *I* die." She tried to pull away, to go back to the notepad. The harder he held on, the harder she struggled, until she was fighting him, beating her fists against his chest and making sounds that were somewhere between mewls and sobs.

"Nicole." She didn't seem to hear. "Nicole." He captured her wrists, but that only made her use her whole body as one big fist as she rammed herself against him. "Nicole!"

Nothing.

So he did the only thing he could to stop her struggles.

He kissed her.

RIKER'S LIPS WERE firm, his body hard, his tongue demanding as he backed Nicole against the desk. Her rear hit the edge, leaving her slightly off balance and clinging to his shoulders to steady herself.

She'd wanted this, had wondered how she'd react. Wondered if she'd hate it or like it. Wondered if she'd be disgusted or relieved that he felt the same fierce, magnetic pull she felt.

And now she knew. She liked it.

And that scared her.

The smart thing to do would be to push him away. But in a matter of minutes, she'd lost everything, from her company to her hope of returning to a normal life after this ordeal was over. *If* it ever was over. Right now, all she had to cling to was the male kissing her senseless.

Riker roughly wedged his hips between her legs, forcing them open as he wrapped his hands around her waist and lifted her onto the table. His palms slid up her rib cage, his thumbs brushing the swells of her breasts just firmly enough to send delicious shocks through her body.

Again, she considered stopping this before it went too far. The thought made a hysterical laugh start to bubble up in her throat, because the truth was that this had already gone too far. And yet, as his tongue tangled with hers, she was sure they hadn't gone far *enough*.

"Shit," he breathed against her lips. "I've been wanting to do this since I first tasted you in the prey room."

The reminder that he'd tossed her into a cold, dank dungeon and then scared her to death should have put a damper on things, but it didn't. She was so stressed out, so tired of not knowing if she was going to live or die—she couldn't help but embrace these few precious moments of forgetting the hell that was her life and remembering what it was like to actually live.

Boldly, she ran her hands up Riker's arms, letting her fingers map the rough scars and thick veins that wound around his biceps. His muscles flexed and twitched under her touch, and when she grew even bolder, shifting her palms to his pecs, a low rumble of approval rolled through his magnificent chest.

"You feel good." His voice was a husky purr. "You're so beautiful." He kissed a trail to her ear and captured her lobe between his teeth.

"Mmm . . . yes." She gasped, both shocked and pleased by how something as simple as a nibble charged her up. She arched into him, and he answered enthusiastically, rubbing his arousal against her. She was going to do this with him, wasn't she?

She was going to have sex with a vampire.

She waited for a panic attack to overwhelm her. Waited for her brain to kick in and give her a million reasons why she couldn't do this. Waited for all of her insecurities and prejudices to rise up and give her excuses to stop this thing from happening.

While she waited, Riker's mouth did wicked things to her ear, and his hands . . . oh, God, his hands . . . they eased under her shirt, one at the small of her back, his fingers resting just below her waistband, the other sliding upward to her breasts.

There was no point in waiting for any of those things that might stop her. All her life, she'd been expected to do what was required to secure her family's legacy. She'd been raised and groomed to do one thing: run Daedalus. No one, including herself, had ever taken into account her dreams and desires, and even her focus on vampire physiology had been considered a nice little hobby by everyone but her.

But now, just this once, she was going to do something selfish. Something reckless. If she regretted it, she'd deal. So much of her life had been out of her control that she was actually excited to have a regret that was purely her own.

Riker's hand cupped her breast, and even through the fabric of her bra, his heat scorched her. She gasped as his thumb rasped across her nipple, and as if the sound were a trigger, Riker growled and surged against her. He kissed her in a desperate, hard meeting of mouths, and then his lips were on her throat and his fangs were scraping her skin . . . and his growl turned hungry.

For a split second, anxiety turned her lungs to stone. But no, she wasn't going to let a single, brutal act from her past undo the progress she'd made over the years, not to mention the greater understanding of vampires that she'd gained in just the last few days.

She stopped thinking and clung even tighter to Riker . . . until she realized he had gone taut.

"Riker?"

He extricated himself from the tangle of their bodies, and without looking at her, he said, "You need to go."

"What?" Baffled, her body practically shaking with unquenched desire, she grabbed his arm to pull him back. "Why?"

"Because this isn't going to work. Not if you can't handle what I am."

"Why don't you let *me* decide what I can and can't handle?"

Very slowly, his lips peeled away from his teeth, exposing those massive fangs. "And this is something you can handle?"

Despite the fact that she was so turned on she was about to burst out of her skin, she met his gaze steadily. "Yes."

"Yeah?" He inhaled, breathing deep. "Then why can I smell your nervousness? Why can I hear your heart beating like a hummingbird's?"

"Maybe it's because I'm all worked up, you dense vampire!" When he snorted, she sighed. "Riker, what's going on between us?"

"Nothing."

"That wasn't nothing."

He laughed darkly. "Well, it wasn't *something*. And hell, I'm pretty sure we wouldn't get much farther, anyway."

She had no idea what he meant by that, but she

still felt like she'd been punched in the gut, just the way she had at Chuck's inability to get her out of this mess. "I don't know about you, but I don't make out with random men for no reason."

"So what are you saying? That you're looking for a mate, a white picket fence, and two-point-five kids? I can't give you that."

"Of course not. Have I said or done anything that would make you think that?" Feeling suddenly cold, she shoved her arms into the jacket he'd given her. "I just like to know where I stand in a relationship."

"So you like labels. You want to label what we just did? Because the best I can do is call it a mistake. It's definitely not a *relationship*."

A mistake? Her chest emptied of any warm feelings she'd had toward him and became an icy, hollow void. "I see. I suppose I'll file it under research, then."

"Research?"

"I'm a scientist," she said briskly. "I know the physiology behind vampire mating habits, but I've never experienced it. Thank you for giving me some insight into why humans are obsessed with vampire sex slaves. I'm not sure I understand what the big deal is, but then, we didn't get very far, did we?" Straightening her clothing, she strode to the door. "I think I'll go to my room now." Not that she knew where it was, but she was reasonably certain someone would see to it that she found it. "Let me know when I can be of help in getting Neriya released."

She threw open the door, and immediately, two tall females came out of nowhere to escort her down the hall to her assigned quarters.

• • •

I'M NOT SURE I understand what the big deal is?

Riker wasn't sure if he should be insulted or angry, but he was definitely a lit fuse. He had to get out of this room. Heck, he needed to get out of headquarters. He didn't want to be under the same roof as Nicole right now. He'd lied about nothing going on between them, because there was definitely something there.

Something fiery and intense that made him feel more alive than he'd felt in decades.

A pounding at his door startled him. *Nicole.* Like a kid on Christmas Day, he hurried to the door—and found Myne standing on the other side, dressed in black from head to toe, his big body laden with weapons. It was probably for the best, but Nicole was much easier on the eyes.

"Can Riker come out to play?" Myne asked.

"Depends." Riker narrowed his eyes at his friend. Myne often had a skewed view on what was fun. "What are we playing?"

"Poach the Poachers."

Cool. Riker liked that game. Loser had to take over the winner's clan duties for a day, which meant doing laundry, cleaning the kitchen, dressing game . . . whatever the winner was tasked with doing. So far, Riker was ahead of Myne by one win, and it was driving Myne crazy.

They'd been engaged in friendly competition almost since the day Riker had found Myne lying on a riverbank, his naked body riddled with bullets. Myne had been so close to death that Riker had leveled a dagger over his heart with the intention of putting him out of his misery, but that was before Myne moaned, revealing gaping holes in his gums where his fangs used to be.

In a rare moment of compassion, Riker had fed him his own blood right there beside the river. Human blood would have been better, but there was never a scumbag poacher around when you needed one.

Hauling the six-foot-five vampire back to the clan's headquarters while trying to keep him alive hadn't been easy, but Riker had been determined to save the guy. No one should go through what he had and not live for revenge.

It had taken Myne a week to recover enough to speak, and when he had, his story of escape from human captivity had shaken everyone in the clan. The story about how he'd gotten his name had done more than shake them. It had rocked them all and reinforced every prejudice they'd ever felt about humans.

"What's your name?" Riker, perched on a stool next to the other male's bed, drew the cup of human blood away from his lips and waited for him to speak.

"Myne." It was the first word he'd spoken since arriving at the clan.

"Odd name." Riker reached for the small pitcher of blood on the bedside table and refilled the cup. "What's it mean?"

Myne's lip curled into a silent snarl. "That's what the man who bought me called me. 'You're mine, you fucking cur. That's your name from now on. Myne.' "

Jesus. *Riker fumbled the cup, splashing crimson fluid all over the floor. "You don't have to worry about that anymore. You're safe here."*

"No one is safe."

Forcing himself to stay calm, when what he wanted to do was hunt down the fucker who had so cruelly named Myne, Riker went at it from another angle. "What was your birth name?"

In an explosion of movement, Myne levered himself up and clamped his hand around Riker's throat. "The humans took everything from me," he rasped. "My clan. My brother. My fangs. My name. Until I get all of that back, you'll call me Myne."

"You got it, buddy," Riker choked out. "Now, do you mind letting me get some air?"

As if he'd used every drop of energy he'd had to sit up, Myne collapsed onto the pillow, panting, his eyes glazed over. "I . . . owe you."

Myne had passed out, not waking again for two more days. They'd become fast friends after that, but they'd never spoken about his name again. Myne rarely talked about his past at all, and when he did, information came out in bits and pieces, and he never answered questions.

Riker gestured for Myne to enter. "Have poachers been sighted nearby?"

"No, but Baddon and Aiden found what they suspect to be a trap. We're going to check it out. If we don't do it tonight, we'll lose our chance."

With the full moon tomorrow, all external affairs needed to be handled before every male in the clan got wound up with the feeding frenzy.

Riker nudged open his weapons closet with his foot. "What's the trap?"

"An injured human in a gully."

Taking homeless humans off the streets and leaving them, bleeding and injured, in the woods was an oldie but a goodie for poachers. Healthy, experienced vampires wouldn't fall for it, but there were a lot of vampires who either didn't know any better or were starving and saw an injured human as an easy meal. This close to the moon phase, vampires were even more careless.

"I'm in." Riker shrugged into his weapons harness and started loading his pockets with all the fun, sharp toys necessary for this particular game. "Extra points for poachers wearing jewelry?" Poacher jewelry was usually made of vampire body parts.

Myne grinned. "You know it. Ten extra points for nailing the leader."

"Excellent." Riker clapped Myne on the back as he strode out of the room. "I need to work off a little steam, anyway."

Somehow, though, Riker had a feeling that no matter how much steam he worked off, it wouldn't be enough to get his mind off Nicole.

THE HUNT WAS a success. Overnight, two vampire poachers had been eliminated and two poachers eaten . . . poachers who had been after different quarry: deer.

Riker and Myne had heard the shot, and they'd found a couple of drunk humans laughing over the body of a dying deer they'd shot out of season. The two bastards didn't even have the decency to put the poor animal out of its misery.

They'd made a fine meal. And the deer, humanely dispatched, would make a fine meal for the clan. Riker and Myne had left the deer poachers alive, since it was doubtful they'd report the attack on them, given their illegal activity. The vampire poachers, however, had been drained and left on the forest floor for the scavengers.

What hadn't been successful was Riker's attempt to get Nicole off his mind. Making matters worse, the pull of the full moon, now nearly upon them, wreaked havoc with his hormones, and whenever he did think about Nicole—which was always—she was naked.

Kissing him. Licking him. Putting those full lips on every sensitive spot on his body.

Snarling at himself, he started toward his quarters after delivering the deer to the kitchen. But somehow he found himself at the lab.

Might have something to do with the fact that since he'd entered headquarters, three people had told him Nicole was with Grant. As if Riker was her keeper or jealous boyfriend or some shit.

And here he was, hand on the doorknob and feeling like a jealous boyfriend.

The second he opened the door, he knew he'd made a huge mistake.

The two females assigned to watch Nicole acknowledged Riker with a nod before going back to propping themselves against the doorframe. He acknowledged them and then zoomed in on the human standing next to Grant, her shoulder brushing his as she reached out to pin a card to the bulletin board on the wall.

A deep, primitive urge to beat Grant to a pulp and drag Nicole off to his quarters made Riker forcibly lock his joints to prevent his body from firing off before he'd even pulled the trigger.

Grant turned to Nicole and smiled, and even from the doorway, Riker felt the male's moon hunger radiating off him. Normally, humans weren't the target of a moon-starved vampire. But sometimes when the hunger struck, mistakes happened. Eventually, the vampire would realize his error, but by then, it could be too late.

Riker didn't want any male taking Nicole by accident.

And that, he realized, included himself.

Clenching his hands into tight fists, he backed out of the room, trusting Katina and Zara to get Nicole out of there before Grant fell to the moon hunger. He all but sprinted to his quarters, stopping for a moment at the gym to order one of his newly blooded warriors, Gaelan, to get a message to Benet immediately.

The knock at the door didn't come soon enough. Or maybe it came too soon.

Benet strode into Riker's place, her long red hair pulled into a high ponytail to expose her neck, the way she always wore it for him. And, as usual, her brightly colored jeans—turquoise today—hugged every curve, and her black V-neck top revealed plenty of throat for him to sink his teeth into.

Not that he ever had, and as she started for the sofa in preparation to sit so he could take her wrist, he grabbed her arm, halting her in mid-stride.

"Riker?" Her husky voice wrapped around him like an embrace. Wrapped around him like Nicole's arms had when he'd kissed her in this very room.

Benet even sounded like Nicole, and now all he could think about was Nicole's sweet flavor. Her fresh scent. Her soft skin.

His fangs throbbed, pulsing to the beat of the blood in Benet's veins.

He pushed her against the wall and covered her body with his as he put his lips against her warm neck. "I need you," he said roughly. He needed Nicole so badly.

"This is different," she whispered, but he barely heard, let alone cared. All he knew was an all-consuming hunger, as if he'd missed several moon feedings in a row and was on the verge of starvation and bloodlust.

The glands behind his fangs tingled as he put his tongue to them, releasing fluid that would ease penetration and provide intense pleasure.

"Now." Nicole—no, Benet—rolled her hips against him and cranked her head to the side in a double invitation. Sex and blood. She'd give him both.

With a growl, he struck, sinking his canines into her tender flesh.

"Yes," she moaned. "*Yes*."

Nicole—had to be Nicole—wrapped one slim leg around his waist and rocked into his erection, her movements growing more frenzied with each pull he took on her vein. Warm, wet blood poured down his throat, firing his need for her even more.

"Take me, Riker," she whispered.

He intended to, and God help any fool who interrupted.

THE CLAN WAS a very strange place on the day of the full moon.

Nicole had spent the day in Grant's lab after a fitful night in the room she'd been locked inside, and while everyone had been cordial, they'd also been . . . intense. Even Grant, who had been so squirrelly the day before, had been serious, startling her with sudden growls and even the odd purr.

The purring happened when she got close to him. When they accidentally touched, Grant purred louder, and his gaze would drop to her throat.

She made a conscious effort to keep her distance.

The two male guards she'd started out with in the morning had been replaced by females as the day wore on, including the scary Katina chick who had threatened her in the prey room. But there had been no sign of Riker, which disappointed Nicole more than she cared to admit.

He doesn't want anything from you. You mean nothing to him. Less than nothing. He didn't even want your blood in the cave when he needed to feed.

Yeah, he'd made his feelings perfectly clear last night. Nicole had no right to be upset, but dammit, she'd laid herself out for him, thinking they at least shared a mutual attraction. And he'd turned her away without a second thought.

"Whatcha doin'?"

Nicole jumped at the sound of the scary Katina chick's voice right behind her. "It would be very helpful if you guys would stomp your feet when you walk," Nicole muttered.

"But then we couldn't scare you." Katina eased next to her. "What's in that vial?"

Nicole followed Katina's gaze. "The green one? That's Kool-Aid. Lime, I think."

"Why?"

"You'll have to ask Dr. Frankenstein."

Katina laughed, a deep, melodic sound that was as beautiful as she herself was. "I dare you to call Grant that to his face."

"I already did." She sighed.

"What did he do?"

Nicole rolled up the sleeves of the black-and-blue flannel shirt she'd picked out of the bag of clothes Katina had brought her last night. She figured she might as well color coordinate with the bruise on her face. At least the swelling had gone down.

She was truly grateful for the clothes, though. Even the ones that didn't fit so well. Like the two-sizes-too-big flannel shirt. Okay, so maybe the yellow granny underwear wasn't the most awesome thing ever, but the jeans she'd selected were perfect. She even liked the worn hole in the butt. The hole was the only way the yellow granny panties would ever look sexy.

"He called me Dinner à la O-Positive."

Katina laughed again. "Pretty cool how he can determine your blood type by smell, huh? Most of us can't do that."

"Cool is not the word I'd use," Nicole said as she pulled a tray of vials close, "but we'll go with it."

Katina flipped her thick black braid over her shoulder. The vampire had fabulous hair. "Did you know each type tastes different?"

"No, I didn't." Nicole squeezed a dropper full of liquid from one of the vials onto a microscope slide.

"It's true. You Os are lame. Too metallic-tasting. My favorite is B-positive. There's a spicy aftertaste I love." She frowned. "It's so rare, though."

"You need to be eating Asian people." Nicole checked on Grant's whereabouts—far across the room, thank God. "Asians have the highest percentage of B-positive blood."

"Really?"

Nicole's stomach turned when she realized she had just offered up an entire ethnic group of people on a platter. She might as well draw up a menu for all the blood types and people who shared them and distribute the menus to vampires who wanted to know how to find their favorite flavors.

"Um . . . can you pretend I didn't say that?"

"Nope. I'm so taking a trip to Chinatown tomorrow." Katina playfully slugged Nicole in the shoulder, and it was all Nicole could do to keep from rubbing her arm and crying like a baby. "You know, I'm glad we didn't eat you that first day. I think I'll ask Hunter if we can keep you."

Keep her. Like a stray dog or a captured wild bird . . . or a vampire slave. With every passing hour, Nicole became more and more ashamed of her race.

"How do you know so much about blood, anyway?" Katina asked.

"My specialty is vampire physiology," she said, happy to talk about something she actually enjoyed. "To know how vampires work, I need to know how humans work. Vampires are dependent on humans to live, which means I need to know everything I can about blood and how it affects vampires. Blood type can play a huge role in everything from the vampire origins to how vampires breed, mature, get diseases . . . The possibilities are endless, especially when we apply what we've learned about vampires to human medicine. It's fascinating. I even discovered a way to use the vampire rac1b2 protein to cure ovarian cancer in humans."

Silence.

Nicole took a deep breath. "Aaaand . . . I've just reminded you of why I'm here and why you hate me, haven't I?"

"Yup."

Katina stepped back, folded her arms over her breasts, and scowled. The knives sheathed all over her curvy body suddenly looked bigger. The other female by the door, Zara, ran her tongue over her fangs.

It occurred to Nicole that female vampires were scarier than males.

Bending her head, Nicole peered into the microscope. What she saw sent a thrill of excitement through her. "Grant? The cell expanded." She tweaked the magnification and grinned. "It's three times its normal size! We did it. I think we might have found the cause of bloodlust. I mean, we need more tests, but you were right about that enzyme. Grant?"

She turned, and her heart nearly stopped. Grant was hunched over, gripping a table so hard that cracks were starting to work their way out from his palm. Reddish glints lit up his eyes as they flitted between her and Katina and the other female.

"Nicole," Katina murmured, "come here. Walk slowly." The female snapped her fingers at Grant, drawing his attention. "Take one of *us*, Grant. Nicole is human."

Shit. This was the moon fever in action. Nicole slid a fat folder off the desk and inched toward Katina. "Shouldn't he have planned for this?"

"He did," Katina said, her voice barely above a whisper. "Zara is his usual partner. But sometimes he gets confused. It happens to us all every once in a while. Just happens to him more. Probably on account of him being not right in the head."

There was a blur of white streaking through the lab, and then Zara was on her back on a table. Grant's body covered her, his fists tangled in her chestnut hair, his teeth deep in her throat.

Nicole had seen vampires feed before, but in controlled settings, like labs. Once, in Paris, she'd been at a full-moon soiree thrown by some of the wealthiest people in France, and the entertainment had included a chained male vampire feeding from a chained female vampire. The raw violence and sex set against the backdrop of the luxurious decor and the elegantly dressed crowd had been shocking. Nicole hadn't been able to tear her eyes away. Much like now.

"Whew," Katina breathed. "I really did not want to be fed on tonight. And I definitely didn't want to sleep with him. Mad scientists aren't my thing."

Nicole's voice was as unsteady as her legs. "So you don't have a regular partner?"

Katina tugged Nicole toward the door, forcing her to look away from Grant, who had started to claw at Zara's jeans. "There are almost twice as many females as males here, so a lot of us don't have regular partners."

"What happens on the new moon?" Clutching the file against her chest, Nicole glanced back at the couple, who were frantically tearing at their clothes, their bodies writhing against each other. "I'd think that would cause trouble."

"It does. Some males feed two females, but most of us have to take turns and go a month between feedings. Makes for a lot of grumpy females one day a month." She nudged Nicole with her elbow as they walked through the cavern of halls. "Talk about your PMS. We call it VMS."

"VMS?"

Katina waggled her brow. "Vampire mean streak."

Well, that sounded less than pleasant. Most likely for everyone around the VMS vampire.

The halls were mostly empty, but a few females appeared here and there, until they reached Nicole's room, where a new female guard had been stationed. Katina took her place on the opposite side of the doorway, and Nicole entered her quarters.

Someone had been here while she was in the lab. More neatly folded clothes had been left on the couch, and piles of food and bottles of water covered the plain but sturdy coffee table. It had to be Riker's work.

He might have kicked her out of his place, but he'd remembered to send her the things she needed. Despite the disaster that was last night and his disappearance today, the clothes and food made her smile as she sank onto the couch and opened the file she'd swiped from the lab.

She nibbled on broccoli spears and ranch dip as she thumbed through the pages of Grant's notes on the cases of bloodlust he'd seen and the methods he'd used to treat them. The results were discouraging: fully 70 percent of the vampires he'd tended to had succumbed to either the disease or the treatment. Now, with her new knowledge of the VR-2 enzyme's role in bloodlust, she could see why the treatments that failed did so. What she didn't understand was why some of Grant's methods had worked at all.

There were too many variables and too many unknowns. Nothing that linked the survivors stood out.

She flipped through more pages, stopping when one particular name caught her eye.

Riker.

Grant's notes were scribbled on the page in his loopy, thick script as he described Riker being brought into his lab by four warriors, his limbs bound, his mouth gagged.

It was the day Terese had died.

The warriors who'd brought him in had outlined what had happened at the mansion, that at some point during the battle on the grounds, Riker had become uncontrollable, a killing machine who wouldn't listen to reason. They'd had to subdue him in order to escape the VAST team that had swarmed the property.

Riker had attacked and drained several humans. One of the warriors, Myne, had noticed the change in Riker after he'd killed an "overweight bald man who reeked of rot."

Uncle Paul. Nicole had, on occasion, heard the household vampires say that her uncle smelled of decaying flesh or ripe garbage. Nicole had never smelled anything, and to her knowledge, no human had. Only later, as an adult going through her family medical history, had she learned that Uncle Paul had suffered from lung cancer. He'd have died within a couple of months if he hadn't been drained to death the day Terese died.

She inhaled sharply. *Cancer.*

In the lab, she and Grant had injected a human protein associated with cancer development into normal vampire cells, and then they'd introduced the VR-2 enzyme, resulting in massive, almost instant growth. They'd theorized that the growth inhibited a vampire's ability to process the enzyme, causing madness and bloodlust.

What if the common denominator was cancer in the humans vampires fed on? And if that was the case, she could develop a serum to counter the protein and force the cells to shrink.

So excited about the possibilities that she was practically hyperventilating, she leaped from the couch. She had to tell Grant. No, he was busy. *Riker!* He'd want to know, especially since he'd almost died of bloodlust.

Without thinking, she darted out of the room and was instantly flanked by the two female security goons.

"Where do you think you're going?" Katina called out.

"I have to see Riker."

The two females didn't say anything, merely let Nicole jog down the hall to Riker's quarters. She tapped on the door. A sharp, high-pitched bark came from inside. "Come in."

She pushed open the door. And came to a shocked halt.

Riker had a sleek, fiery-haired female pinned to the wall, his teeth buried in her throat. Both were fully clothed, but the female was riding him as if she were naked, panting, whimpering in ecstasy. And that was when Nicole realized that the female had been the one Nicole heard tell her to "Come in." Except that hadn't been what she said.

I'm coming.

Inexplicable hurt and anger pierced Nicole in the heart, as sharp as one of Riker's cruel-edged blades. A choked squeak escaped her, and Riker's head whipped around. His eyes glowed an intense, bright blue, and his fangs, twice their normal size, dripped with blood. A low, pumping growl bubbled up from deep in his chest as he held her, utterly frozen, with his gaze.

The room shrank. Closed in on her the way the prey room had.

She had to get out of here. Mind overloaded with erotic images of Riker with the sultry female, Nicole stumbled backward through the doorway.

Then she ran like hell to her room.

THE PREY WAS on the run.

His heart pounding like he'd been giving chase for hours, Riker tore himself away from Benet and started for the door.

"Wait." Benet's breathy command stopped him, but he didn't turn around. "I'm here. I'm willing. I've been willing for years. But you want the human?"

Riker clenched his teeth as he tried to force out a lie, but the *no* wouldn't come. The soft tap of Benet's feet drew close, and then her satin lips were on his ear.

"This is the first time since Terese's death that you've shown interest in a female." She dragged her mouth to his throat, to the spot she always fed from. "Go," she whispered. "Get her."

She didn't have to say it twice. In the back of his mind, he made a note to thank her, but the rest of his brain was swamped with a need he couldn't control, and he shot out of his quarters with the single-minded purpose of a wolf tracking a female in heat.

So he really wasn't happy to see his buddy in the hall,

blocking his path. Riker slammed into Myne, knocking him out of the way.

"Dude." Myne caught Riker's shoulder and swung him around. "What the fuck?"

Riker let out a furious snarl and introduced his friend's spine to the wall. "Don't. Just. Don't."

Myne's smoky eyes flashed. "You need to feed, man. You're jacked."

"I already fed," Riker ground out.

Myne raked his gaze over Riker, nostrils flaring as he took in Riker's scent. "Ah, shit." Myne's voice went low. "Come on, buddy. Let's grab a bottle of rum and hit the game room."

Rum and the game room? On any other night, Riker would have taken Myne up on shots and some poker or pool but not now. Not while he was high on blood and riding the moon fever like it was his personal bitch. There was a dark, barely restrained lust lurking just below the surface of his civility, a living thing that had been clawing at him for years, waiting to get out.

Nicole had unlatched its cage, and it wanted to thank her.

"No." Riker shoved away from Myne.

"Dammit," Myne snapped, and this time when he tried to stop Riker, his face got intimate with Riker's fist. The crack echoed through the halls, followed by Myne's growl. "You stupid fuck. No good can come of you screwing the human." Myne put the back of his hand to his mouth and came away with blood. "You've been moping about Terese's death for twenty years, and it's a *human* who drags you out of it?"

"Shut up."

Never one to follow orders, Myne pressed on. "She's not just a human, you dipshit. She's a human who *owned* Terese. You're really going to stick your dick in that?"

Riker hissed. "You don't know what the hell you're talking about." His voice throbbed with anger. "Go find your pain-loving female, and give her a good dose of misery. Or is she with someone else this month?" Like Myne, Riker didn't ease up now that he'd struck a sore spot. Why go for the pain when you could go for the kill? "What are you going to do when her father finds her a suitable male to mate with? What then? What female is going to be eager to take your particular brand of affection? No one here will have you."

The brief flash of hurt and surprise in Myne's eyes shamed Riker, but Myne recovered quickly, his expression hardening into stone. "Don't come crying to me later when you're ridden with guilt and regret." Myne shoved past Riker and disappeared down the hall.

Dammit. Now lust *and* anger were ripping through his veins and spinning him off his axis. Only one thing would set him right again, and that soft, feminine thing was in a room down the hall.

He didn't even remember getting there. When Katina moved to intercept, all it took was a scowl, and she moved aside.

He found Nicole in the bedroom.

She jumped off the bed, where she'd been sitting with a piece of paper, hands frantically folding out some sort of animal shape.

"Get out," she rasped.

He prowled toward her. "After."

"After what?" She swept up a glass of water off her nightstand and hurled it at his head. He stepped easily aside but didn't avoid the water that splashed on his back when the glass shattered on the wall. "After you yell at me some more?"

"No," he said darkly. "After we finish what we started."

NICOLE'S HEART WAS pounding out of her chest. Riker stood there, his body radiating a combustible mixture of danger and lust, his fangs glistening behind parted lips.

Lips that had been on some skanky vampire's throat while she arched against him, her legs locked around his waist.

Nicole had no right to be jealous. Hell, she didn't even have a reason. They might have inexplicable physical chemistry, but there wasn't anything emotional between them. Nothing. She didn't even like Riker.

Liar.

"There's nothing to finish."

"Nothing to finish? You wondered why sex with a vampire was such a big deal. I'm going to show you." He moved toward her, slowly, like a cat sneaking up on a bird. "Stamina." He stepped closer. "Multiple orgasms." Closer, and her mouth went dry. "Flexibility." Closer. Her skin flushed hot. "Strength." Closer. Her stomach did a flip-flop. "The ability to sense heat so we know what parts of the body are the most sensitive at the right time." Closer. A throbbing ache started low in her pelvis. "The ability to hear the slightest change in the tempo of your pulse so we know exactly how every stroke, kiss, and lick affects you."

Oh. Dear. Lord.

Wetness bloomed between her thighs, and then he was in front of her, his hands on her shoulders, his mouth on hers. A needy, masculine sound rattled inside his chest as he rolled his pelvis into her belly. The rigid length behind the fly of his jeans was a *big* clue to what he thought they needed to finish, and she had to swallow a groan.

"You shouldn't have come back to my place," he murmured against her lips.

No, she shouldn't have. "Sorry. Did I ruin the mood for you and your girlfriend?"

He slipped one arm behind her waist to haul her even more firmly against him. "Not my girlfriend."

"My apologies. She's a casual screw, then."

He took her bottom lip between his teeth, then soothed the spot with his tongue. "We've never had sex."

Oh. Huh. As much as she liked that answer, she still had the image of them dry-humping in her head. "So I interrupted your first time."

"I didn't want her. I feed from her. That's all."

She shoved him away and stepped aside. "Really? Because you two were about thirty seconds from being a lot more than blood buddies."

"I'll be damned." A blatantly triumphant male smile lit up his expression. "You're jealous."

"I am not." Yes, she was. "I'm . . . confused. I'm so freaking . . . I don't know!"

He regarded her the way someone might look at a rabid animal. "I don't understand."

She rounded on him. "You wouldn't, you giant ass." To be honest, she didn't understand, either. But that didn't stop her from putting several days' worth of fear and stress on the table. "I'm scared, okay? I'm lost. I don't know where I am, and everyone here looks at me like they want to eat me or torture me. Maybe both. I want to go home, but then I don't want to go home because everything I thought I knew is one big lie. The people I trusted have turned against me, and even my own brother is afraid to help me." She paused to take a breath, fresh fuel for her tirade. "I should hate you, but instead, I'm attracted to you, which is beyond twisted, especially since I know that after I get Neriya back, I'm probably going to die." She dashed away tears with the back of her hand. "So forgive me if I'm a little emotionally unstable right now." She sniffed. "Ass."

"I'm not going to kill you, Nicole. I promise."

"Maybe not you, but come on. I'm not stupid. Your clan can't let me live. I know too much."

"I won't let that happen." He framed her face in his hands and bored his gaze into hers. "Listen to me. You're not going to die. Let's get Neriya and go from there."

She nodded, and very slowly, the atmosphere around them shifted from anger and confusion to an electric sensuality she couldn't ignore. She licked her lips, and his gaze dropped to her mouth, focused on her tongue. In agonizingly slow motion, he lowered his head until there was only a hairsbreadth of space between them.

"I want you, Nicole."

"Ten minutes ago, you were with another female," she pointed out, hating that she sounded so petty and sullen.

"Because I had to be. But I didn't want her. Not this way."

"This way?"

One corner of his made-for-sin mouth tipped up as he brushed his lips across hers. "This way," he whispered.

His lips were warm, the kiss lingering, until she went up on her toes to take more. As if that was the invitation he was waiting for, he swept her up, and with his vampire speed, he laid her on the bed.

Still kissing her, he stretched out alongside her and palmed her butt to bring her against him. This felt so strange but so good, and when he slid his hand up under her shirt, she arched to give him easier access. He dragged his mouth along her jaw, his warm breath caressing her skin.

With expert skill, he unhooked her bra and slid his hand around to cup her breast. Her breath came in a hot rush at his intimate touch, and then it didn't come at all when he reared back to pull off her shirt and bra. His own shirt didn't fare well, the sound of tearing threads filling the room as he ripped it off. He was magnificent in his urgency, the cords in his neck straining, the muscles in his arms flexing and rippling with power she'd witnessed several times now.

"I'm not going to ask if you're ready for this." His voice was rough, his movements rougher as he tugged off her jeans, leaving her in only the horrid granny panties. "I know you are. I can smell your desire." His fingers delved between her legs to stroke the damp cotton, and they both groaned. "I can feel it." He prowled up her body, his expression leaving no doubt about his intent. "But if you want to stop, tell me now."

Stop? Was he crazy? In answer, she wound her arms around his neck and pulled him down to her, taking a kiss from him. He tasted like dark chocolate, with a metallic bite of—

He tasted like that skanky vampire he'd been sucking on.

Raw, scorching jealousy and possessiveness lashed at her. A few days ago, she'd have spent time analyzing the emotions, but she wasn't that person anymore. She wasn't in a safe, controlled environment. She was in the wilderness with people who embraced their instincts and remembered their primitive roots. The wildness had permeated her mind, body, and heart. For the first time, she was going to embrace her instincts, too.

She gripped him hard, digging her nails into his neck. Scoring him. Marking him.

He hissed and ground his erection into her hip. Oh, but that wasn't good enough. While he thrust his tongue into her mouth, she wedged her hand between their bodies and yanked open his jeans. His hard length sprang free, and when she took it in her fist, the animal noise he made sent a shiver of dark anticipation through her.

He rose above her, his back arching as she stroked him. She was captivated by the fierce ecstasy in his expression, his slightly parted lips that glistened with her kiss and displayed a hint of ivory fang. When she'd started to think fangs were sexy, she had no idea, but she suddenly wanted them to glide over her body, delivering tiny pricks of pleasure as they went.

As if he'd read her mind, Riker fell forward and took her breast in his mouth. He bit her lightly, then laved the area with his tongue, circling her sensitive flesh and moving inward until he reached her nipple. The very tip of his tongue flicked back and forth, teasing her so deliciously. His palm drifted over her belly and slipped under her panties. She parted her thighs, eager for his touch.

He didn't disappoint. His fingers delved between her folds, and she cried out at the tender brush of one fingertip over her clit.

"You're so wet," he said against her breast. "So silky." He dipped one finger inside her, and she cried out again, already so close to orgasm that she wanted to weep. "I want to taste you."

Good God, yes. Oral sex had never been her favorite thing in the world, and truth be told, she'd always shied away from it. Too intimate. Too embarrassing. But suddenly, she couldn't deny Riker this; suddenly, she wanted it.

Riker moved down her body, kissing and licking, stoking the fire inside her into an inferno. When he settled himself between her legs, his massive shoulders spreading her thighs impossibly wide, she was sure he'd feel the heat blasting off her.

He didn't remove her underwear. He closed his mouth over the fabric and licked. The feel of his firm tongue pushing the cotton against her was like nothing she'd experienced before, and she reveled in the almost-there tease, rocking her hips upward to meet his mouth.

"That's it," he growled. "Take what you want."

"I want to come," she growled back.

Tunneling his fingers under the elastic, he pulled the panties aside and licked her again, this time flesh on flesh. She jerked at the intensity of the contact, and when he dipped his tongue inside her, she nearly arched off the mattress.

He wasn't gentle as he lapped at her, using his tongue as an erotic weapon that made her body writhe so violently that he had to hold her in place with a firm grip on her hips. Dizzying pleasure ricocheted through her, and when she heard the sound of tearing fabric, she knew he was as far gone as she was.

He lunged against her, thrusting his tongue deep. It swirled and stroked, taking her so high she thought she might pass out. She was at the very edge of orgasm, hovering on a blade's edge, but he denied her, skillfully bringing her down for just a heartbeat before working her up again.

"Please," she rasped. "I—"

She cut off at his sudden change of tactic. A quick lick up her center, and then she felt the most curious, smooth caress over her clit. His head moved from side to side as her pleasure climbed higher, and that's when she realized he was using the length of one fang to stroke her. The knowledge sent her over the edge and right into the most intense, mind-blowing climax of her life. It hadn't even ended when Riker covered her with his body and plunged inside her.

She came again, even though he wasn't moving,

was hovering over her, watching her with that menacing, predatory gaze.

"Multiple orgasms," he said in a guttural whisper. "That's what the fluid from our fangs does. Makes everything it touches extra . . . sensitive." He drove his point home by slipping his hand between them and flicking the tip of his finger over her swollen knot of nerves. Yet another orgasm struck with the intensity of lightning, short-circuiting her entire nervous system with pleasure.

She clawed at his back, encouraging him to get on with it. She had to see him come. Had to see this hardened, battle-scarred vampire lose himself to the ultimate pleasure.

Pleasure *she* would give.

A low, rough sound burst from his chest, and then he was pumping wildly, slamming his hips into hers, and shoving her up the mattress with each powerful thrust. A fine sheen of sweat formed on his skin, making his ropy veins stand out starkly on top of quivering muscles. The sounds of sex filled the room, the slap of flesh, the panting breaths, the wet slide of his shaft in her core.

Ecstasy built again, and oh, how easily he did this to her. She struggled to breathe through the waves that came hotter and faster with his increasingly frenzied thrusts. He churned above her, teeth bared, tendons straining. Flames of pure bliss licked through her veins and gathered at her core until she couldn't stand it anymore, and she locked her legs around his back so hard he grunted.

She lifted her hips to take him so deep he was

forced to adjust his position and grind against her in massive, undulating surges.

"Yes!" she cried. "Oh . . . *yes*!"

She convulsed in a rush of exhilaration and pleasure that expanded outward from her center and coalesced in a mind-blowing release. The joy of the moment was more than physical; it was emotional on a level she'd never experienced before. Nothing had ever felt so right. So perfect.

Her body clenched around Riker, bucking and writhing. It was only as she came down, her panting breaths filling the room, that she realized he wasn't moving. He'd gone still, his thick arms trembling on either side of her, his gaze dark with pain.

19

RIKER COULDN'T BELIEVE this. How the hell could he be in bed with a beautiful female and not be able to get his body to cross the line of ultimate pleasure? He was hard as a rock, his balls tight, his cock throbbing with the need to come, and yet he couldn't quite get there.

"Riker?" Nicole breathed. "What is it? What's wrong?" She shifted, squeezing her hot, silky core around him, and he hissed.

"I can't. Fuck, I can't." Shoving his fists into the mattress, he pushed himself off her on trembling arms. When she sat up and reached out, he lurched to his feet.

"What is it? I mean, it's, um, obvious you *can*."

He stood there like a pathetic dolt, his chest heaving, his skin coated in a glistening sheen of sweat. Between his legs, his sex stood erect, shiny with her desire and swollen with his.

"I can't," he repeated, this time with a frustrated, angry edge.

"Come here." She reached for him again, but he spun away, swiping his wadded jeans off the floor.

"It's not happening."

The mattress creaked. "I thought that when a mate dies, the imprint is destroyed."

He swung around. "What do you know about imprinting?"

"I know it happens to male vampires but not females. I know a male vampire can only imprint on vampires, not humans. And I know imprinting doesn't happen by choice, but we don't know what makes a particular female imprintable for a particular male."

"Imprintable?"

She sniffed. "It's a valid word in this case." She tucked her hair behind her ear, but if she was trying to tame it, she'd failed. She had the most gorgeous, sexy bed head ever. "The bond also means you can only have sex with the female you imprinted on, but I thought that link broke when the female died."

"It's not a bond," he muttered. "A bond implies that two parties are involved."

She rolled her eyes. "But it's supposed to dissolve when the female dies, right?"

"Let it go, Nicole." He tugged on his pants. "And males *can* have sex with females other than the one they imprinted on. They just don't usually want to. The link is so powerful that if a male imprints on a female he hates, he'll usually fall for her in time." He gripped the zipper tab and cursed when the zipper stuck. "Guess they don't teach you everything in your vampire anatomy classes, huh?" It was a low blow, but she didn't seem fazed.

"I just want to understand."

"You don't need to."

She threw up her hands in disgust. "So that's it? You break into my room like a madman, convince me that you want me, and then get me off while you hold on to your precious control? Is this a joke? A way to humiliate me?" She snatched up her own jeans and shoved her feet into them.

He stared. Stared more when she bent over to pick up her bra. "Why would I want to humiliate you?"

"Maybe because I'm a lowly human? Maybe because you hate me? I have no idea. But what else am I supposed to think? If your imprint will still allow you to have sex with me, why did you stop?"

If anything, the fact that he'd wanted her *despite* the fact that she was human was a rebuttal to her argument. "I'm not imprinted."

"So it *does* break with the death of a mate." He turned away, but she grabbed his arm and forced him back to her. "Right?"

"Yes."

"But?"

Shame and self-loathing made his skin tighten. "But I never imprinted on Terese," he snapped. "It was just one more way in which I failed her."

Nicole blinked. "So this is about Terese? How have you managed to have sex with anyone else, then?"

He shook his head, feeling abruptly deflated. "I haven't been with anyone in a long time."

"How long?"

He really wished she'd stop with these probing questions. "Long enough."

"Long enough that what? You forgot how to do it?" She tugged on the flannel shirt that nearly swallowed her but somehow looked good on her. Maybe because it brought to mind images of her wearing one of his shirts . . . with nothing on underneath. "Because I have to say, you handled yourself pretty well a few minutes ago."

He smiled, his ego getting a nice stroke. His cock jumped as if feeling left out of the stroking. "Trust me, I remember how."

"Then what's going on?"

His face heated. "I haven't touched another female, except to feed, since Terese died."

Her sharp inhale humiliated him even more. "That's . . . wow. Twenty years."

"Thanks for doing the math."

There was a long pause. Finally, she said quietly, "You really loved her, didn't you?"

Tilting his head back, he squeezed his eyes shut and searched his brain for an answer to that. But the dark recesses of his mind offered only silence.

"Yeah." But he hadn't loved her enough to keep her safe or keep her alive.

"I'm sorry." She sank down on the edge of the mattress. "How long were you mated before . . ."

"Before she killed herself," he finished bitterly. "Five years. But it wasn't a love match."

"How did you meet?"

"Jesus, is this an interview for *Vampire Times*, or what?" When Nicole crossed her arms over her chest and gave him an expectant stare, he sighed. "It wasn't a meet as much as it was a battle." He threw on his shirt. "She was from DreamDevour, a clan in California. They were taking her to mate with ShadowSpawn's leader. We ran into them on the edge of our territory, and a fight broke out. At the time, ShadowSpawn had far fewer numbers, and we were at war with them. They'd just killed the mate of one of our warriors, and Hunter figured what better revenge than to take one of theirs, especially a high-ranking female who was supposed to go to their leader."

"And you stepped up to the plate?"

"It was my idea. We'd captured her during the battle with DreamDevour, and Hunter wanted to hold her indefinitely, force both clans to bargain for the best deal. My idea was to mate her to someone in the clan and make an ally out of DreamDevour while sticking it to ShadowSpawn. Hunter figured that since it was my idea, I got to take the bullet for the team."

"And Terese was willing to mate with you?"

He snorted. "She had no desire to be mated to anyone from ShadowSpawn, let alone the male she was promised to." The bastard was a sadistic, brutal son of a bitch who reportedly whipped one of his daughters nearly to death. "But I terrified her, too. At first, anyway."

He'd never forgive himself for that. He'd been angry at the turn of events that had given him a mate he didn't want, and while he never took it out on her, he hadn't given her any reason not to be afraid.

"Obviously, she came around."

"We both did." He paced the length of the room, wishing he were outside, where he could open up and run for miles before the postfeed cramping started up. "She was really timid, like a fawn that lost its mother. I had to learn to tone it down around her. I think that between her trying to please me and me trying to keep her calm and safe, we grew close." Close, but like friends, not lovers. He turned to Nicole. "You said you loved her. You must have spent a lot of time with her."

"I did." Nicole smiled fondly. "If it's any consolation, she was treated well."

Treated so well that she killed herself. He resisted the urge to point that out again. Nicole had a child's view of Terese's life, and Riker had done enough to destroy her world already.

"Riker . . ." Nicole rubbed her thighs, and he wondered if she'd be folding origami birds if there were more paper nearby. "I still don't understand why this happened between us. And then didn't happen."

He didn't really understand, either. But for the last twenty years, he'd been unable to bring himself to sleep with any female. Terese's death had left him empty inside. Cold. There was far more to it than grief, but he'd never been able to dig deep enough into himself to figure it out, mainly because it had never mattered to him before.

Or maybe because he didn't want to face the ugly truth.

He hadn't loved Terese the way he should have, and she'd paid the price for his neglect.

"Let's just forget about it, Nicole."

"Really?" she said softly. "Are you really going to forget about it? Because the way I see it, we just did something that brought a whole lot of crap to the surface, and unless you deal with it—"

"Don't pull some psych shit on me." He shot a deliberate glance at her throat. "How much did therapy help *you*?"

She swallowed.

"Exactly."

"Don't be an ass." She tucked her legs under her on the bed. "You know what helped? Crazily enough, being here has helped me more than twenty years of therapy."

"Glad we could be of assistance," he said dryly.

"What did I say about not being an ass?" She huffed. "At some point during these last few days, I opened myself up to learning about vampires from your point of view. I let you in, Riker."

"I'm sure you'll regret that eventually." Clearly, he wasn't listening to her complaints about being an ass.

"I'll never regret it," she snapped. "Because somehow I feel like I've finally healed."

"What are you saying? That if I open myself up, climb into bed with you, I'll magically get better? I'll forget how your family destroyed someone I cared about, someone I was charged with protecting?"

"Yes," she said, her voice dripping with sarcasm. "That's exactly what I'm saying. In fact, let's try sex again." She leaped to her feet and tore open her jeans. "Maybe my magic vagina will cure you of all the traumatic acts my family has inflicted on you."

"Dammit." He snared her wrists to stop her from stripping. "Nothing you do will ever make me forget that."

Fury blazed in her eyes, so full of green fire he expected to find scorch marks on his skin. "You know, I've learned that not all vampires are the same. So why can't you open your eyes and see that not all humans are the same, either? Oh, wait—you *can*, you just don't *want* to. You'd rather hold on to your hatred and make everyone around you put up with your bitterness and guilt."

"You know nothing about me or the people around me," he bit out. "You've known me a few days, and you're an expert on my life?"

"Am I wrong?" she shot back. "Or do you wield your venom like a weapon, poisoning everything around you?"

Her swipe at him hit so close to home that it was almost a physical blow. His temper swelled, fed by his own self-hatred, which had been encapsulated by hardened layers of denial. Now the capsule had cracked, leaking toxic anger that Nicole didn't deserve but was going to feel the brunt of anyway.

"You have a death wish, don't you, human?" He surged closer to her once more, tempted to take her by the shoulders and shake some sense into her. The kind of sense that would teach her to never taunt a vampire. To never *tempt* a vampire.

She lifted her chin stubbornly. "You said you wouldn't kill me."

"And you believed me?" He bared his fangs for emphasis. "Me, a vampire?"

She cringed, almost imperceptibly, but he also caught a whiff of anxiety, so yeah, she wasn't 100 percent sure she was safe, and he felt like a fucking heel.

He'd come here to satisfy a primal urge for a female who had captivated him from the moment he touched her, but even as those raging hormones rushed through his body, he'd calmed in her presence. She'd admitted to being frightened and confused, lost in both her world and his, and all he'd wanted to do was to comfort her. Now he'd made her feel trapped again, like nothing more than a sheep awaiting slaughter in a pen.

He drew in a breath, hoping oxygen would clear his head and magically give him the right words for this situation.

Apparently, neither magic air nor magic vaginas existed.

There was a pounding on the door, followed by Hunter slamming it open and crossing to the bedroom in a matter of a heartbeat. He stood in the doorway, his gaze sweeping from the messy bed to their disheveled clothing, and Riker knew he was in for a first-class dress-down later.

Awesome. Because it wasn't enough to have Myne up his ass about his involvement with Nicole.

"There's something you need to see," Hunter said grimly.

Riker shifted his weight, crunching a shard of broken glass beneath his foot. "Give me a few."

"Now," Hunter countered. "Both of you."

If there was anything Riker knew how to do, it was take orders, even if he didn't like them. In sullen silence, he and Nicole followed Hunter to his office, where his television was on, the picture paused. He punched a button on the remote, and a reporter standing in front of Daedalus's headquarters started speaking.

"Dr. Nicole Martin, billionaire heiress and CEO of

Daedalus Corporation, is still missing after being brutally kidnapped by vampires, igniting a cry from some to eradicate vampires once and for all, and counter-protests by the Vampire Humane Society demanding freedom for vampires that Daedalus has played a large role in capturing."

The camera panned to a woman holding a sign that said *VAMPIRES ARE PEOPLE, TOO*. "Nicole Martin got what she deserved!" the lady yelled. "You reap what you sow. Free the vampires!"

A man across the street shot the VHS chick the finger and then shouted, "Vampires are abominations! They must be destroyed, or this kind of thing will keep happening."

The reporter's too-perfect face came back on, and Riker wondered if the guy had been the recipient of antiaging vampire juice. Riker would love to drain the *human* juice right out of the man.

"Charles Martin, Dr. Martin's brother, has sworn to stop at nothing to find her."

Yeah, right, Riker thought. But next to him, a faint smile trembled on Nicole's lips, relief that her brother intended to come through for her. But as she'd pointed out before, she wasn't stupid. She must know, deep down, that her jackass of a brother wasn't going to lift a finger to help her.

Charles came on the screen, and a dozen microphones were shoved in his face. "The evil creatures that did this to my beloved sister will be caught and executed. We've learned that these vampires escaped from one of our South Seattle facilities after being set free by vampire activists. Consider these creatures to be very, very dangerous, which was why they were locked up in the first place."

Riker frowned. "We didn't escape from the facility. What the hell is he talking about?"

Charles continued. "As a precaution, and to prevent incidents like this from happening in the future, we will close down the facility, which was a vampire rehabilitation center, and all vampires will be destroyed. We now know that it's far too dangerous to give these animals the benefit of the doubt."

"Oh, my God." Nicole's voice trembled. "He's lying to cover up for whatever is going on at the B-lab he mentioned. I'll bet he knows there's going to be an attempt to rescue Neriya, and he wants to make sure we don't even have a chance."

"Fuck," Hunter snapped. "How long do you think we have?"

Charles looked directly into the camera, as if he'd heard Hunter. "Effective tomorrow."

20

NICOLE STOOD IN the bright, early-morning sunshine outside the Daedalus lab grounds, Riker at her side. The sunglasses on her face were borrowed from Katina, the top borrowed from Benet, whom Nicole felt bad about thinking was a skank. The sneakers were actually new, given to her by a female named Caris, who had shyly handed them over with a quiet whisper of "Good luck."

Nicole hadn't the heart to say that it was Neriya and Riker who needed the luck, because truly, they were the ones Nicole was putting in danger with this plan.

"I hope to hell this works." Riker, dressed in jeans and an olive-drab long-sleeved T-shirt under a matching trench coat that concealed weapons, slid her a sideways glance.

"It will." She tugged the jacket of Riker's that she'd failed to return more tightly around her. "It has to."

Riker studied the building looming before them with detached calculation. They hadn't spoken about what had happened in her room, and now, she supposed, there was no point. The chances that both of them would come out of this intact were pretty slim. He could be caught and killed, and she could be arrested for any number of offenses. If not for the deaths of the vampires in the lab she was responsible for, then for breaking into the lab in front of her and conspiring with vampires to do it.

Then there was the uncertainty of her fate if, by some miracle, this *did* all go down without a hitch.

"We won't kill you," Riker said, and there went his mind-reading thing he claimed not to have again.

"I know," she said, and she meant it. Riker wouldn't let anyone harm her. "But you can't let me go free, either."

"True. But we can keep you with us. You'll be safe."

Katina had said something similar. Nicole smiled sadly. "Keep me. Like a pet. Or a slave."

His head whipped around, and although she couldn't see his eyes through his sunglasses, she felt the weight of his burning stare. His jaw was clenched so tight she was surprised she didn't hear the crack of teeth.

"I don't think I can live like that," she murmured.

Then you'll know how all the captive vampires feel. She could practically hear Riker speak the words, even if he had the decency not to say them out loud.

"Before we go inside, I just want to say that I'm sorry for everything my family has put you and your people through." She started walking, not wanting him either to reply with some lame *it's okay* bullshit that wasn't true or to cast her apology back in her face by accusing her of *too little, too late.*

He walked with her, a silent shadow at her side. She sensed that he wanted to say something, but she was thankful that he kept quiet, his demeanor shifting from sort of affable to deadly, focused warrior the closer they got to the building.

As suspected, entering wasn't a problem. The security guy at the front desk knew her and was aware of her kidnapping, and he was so relieved that she'd "escaped, thanks to the Good Samaritan hunter" accompanying her, that he let them inside without question.

"You should have let me eat him," Riker muttered as they hurried to the area where she was certain Neriya would be held.

"Right," she drawled, "because a severely anemic, unconscious security guard wouldn't have attracted attention at all." Then again, if the guard was doing his job, he'd be calling his supervisor right now to report her unannounced and irregular arrival. Maybe she should have let Riker eat him.

She picked up her pace, checking each door as they passed to orient herself. All Daedalus labs were of the same design, but the contents of each room varied according to what the main purpose of the lab was.

"I think it's the door ahead on the right. The big red one."

"I'll take point." The commanding tone in Riker's voice both annoyed her and sent a shiver of feminine appreciation through her. "You—"

A soft puff of air whispered across Nicole's cheek, followed by Riker's grunt. She spun as he yanked a dart out of his neck and stumbled into the wall.

"Riker!" She started toward him but froze as half

a dozen men popped out from doorways and hallways, weapons trained on them both.

"Hello, sis." Chuck stepped out from behind a big security guy. "I've been waiting for you."

There was a sting in her arm and then . . . nothing.

"NICOLE. HEY, SLEEPYHEAD, wake up."

Nicole woke to Chuck's voice, bright lights, and a headache the size of Europe. An awful snarl rattled every cell in her body, but where it was coming from, she had no idea. A thick strap across her forehead kept her from looking anywhere but at the ceiling.

Chuck's face appeared in front of her as he crouched down, and she realized she was lying on the floor inside one of the cells meant to hold vampires.

"What . . ." She swallowed, wincing at the dry roughness in her throat. After months spent in a hospital recovering from Boris's attack, she knew the feeling all too well; she'd been intubated and extubated. "What's going on? What are you doing?"

"I'm protecting Daedalus, just like I've done for the last twenty years."

"What are you talking about?" She tried again to move, but shackles pinned her arms and legs to the floor. "Where's Riker?"

"Subject fifteen-seventy-two, you mean?" That horrid snarl sounded again, and with sickness, she realized it was coming from *subject fifteen-seventy-two*. "I'll let you see him after you answer a question." A lock of hair fell over his eyes as he cocked his head, and he shoved it away with a vicious swipe of his hand. "Did he force you to come here, or are you working with them?"

Nicole's head spun. This was all so bizarre. Chaining her to the floor? To what end? Was this some sort of game? A prank? If so, it wasn't fun *or* funny.

She hedged, seeking his angle. "You know how much I've always hated vampires. Why would I work with them?"

"Because they're masters of seduction, Nikki. Liars with pretty words." He straightened, looming imperiously over her. "Look how they tricked you when you were a kid. They made you love them. Made you believe they cared about you. They don't. All they want is to eat us. They'll even murder their own kind." He started to pace, the *clack* of his shoes on the floor so annoyingly loud. "There's a simple truth we try to keep from the simple human population: that vampires are the top of the food chain. If we ever let their numbers get out of control, humans could face extinction. What we do here at Daedalus ensures that the human race keeps the vampires in check."

"Why are you telling me all of this?" He was spouting propaganda that she knew well. "I've heard it all before, same as you."

"Yes, but I've never tried to protect the vampire who kidnapped me. The vampire who murdered his own mate." Chuck's cheeks were mottled with anger. "Did you know that? Did you know this vampire behind me is the one who killed your nanny? Who butchered Terese?"

Taken aback by his sudden rage, she stared. Why did he care so much about Terese's death? What was the point of this? And how on God's green earth could this be the brother she'd followed around like a puppy and worshipped as a child? Granted, she hadn't seen much of him over the last twenty years, but they'd communicated frequently via teleconferencing, and he'd flown to Paris once a year to see her. Nothing he'd said or done during any of those times had made her think he'd gone off the rails.

She was beginning to lose hope that this was a prank.

"Well?" he prompted, impatience turning his voice guttural.

"Riker didn't kill Terese."

"Of course he told you that, but you saw it yourself." Chuck's patronizing smile made her want to scream. "So your denial tells me that either you're suffering from Stockholm syndrome or you've switched sides. Which is it, sister?"

She tried again to free herself, but her futile struggles only heightened her awareness that she was in a lot of trouble. *Stay calm. He's your brother. He won't hurt you.*

Maybe not, but he could hurt Riker, and she had no doubt he would.

"I'd be happy to discuss all of this at home." She cleared her throat and conjured her *I'm the boss* voice. "Release me."

"You don't run Daedalus anymore, so you don't give the orders. I do."

The first stirrings of true fear welled up at his words, his matter-of-fact tone. "Why don't you just get to the point of all of this?"

"Oh, Nikki." He sighed. "You're making this really difficult."

She was making this difficult? "I'm the one strapped to a floor for no reason I can figure out, so can you tell me what the hell is going on?"

"What's going on?" Chuck crouched beside her again. "I'm taking what rightfully should have been mine. I'm our father's eldest. It was *my* mother he loved, not the whore who trapped him with her family's wealth and connections. Your mother was nothing but a means to an end to him. The company should have passed to me, not you. I worked my way up and learned every nuance of the business. I know how many employees we have at each facility. I know how much the company spends on air travel every year. I know what kind of damn fertilizer is put on the lawn outside the Phoenix facility. *You* inherited Daedalus without paying your dues. You're clueless about how it works. This company is mine."

Nicole's mind whirled as she tried to puzzle out where this was going. Clearly, he was bitter about how he'd grown up, but if it was the company he wanted, he had it. So why was all of this necessary?

"Chuck, the company is yours now. The board kicked me out—"

"They changed their minds!" Leaping up, he crunched his foot into her ribs. Through disbelief that her brother had physically harmed her and pain that made her ears ring, she heard Riker's roar of rage, followed by threats that involved Riker putting Chuck's organs in places they shouldn't be. "Your kidnapping drummed up a shitload of sympathy for you. The board wants you back so they can play up your ordeal to the public and shine the spotlight on Daedalus."

Keep him calm. "I'll refuse to come back," she said in a rush. "I'll sign everything over to you. Just let me go."

"I can't." He scrubbed his hand over his face, and for the first time, she saw how tired he looked. His bloodshot eyes, identical to hers, sat like dull stones in their sunken sockets, and a five o'clock shadow darkened his puffy cheeks. "Don't you see that I can't?"

A panicky sensation began to wrap around her, squeezing her aching ribs. If he couldn't let her go . . . dear Lord, what did he plan to do with her?

"What happened to you, Chuck?" she whispered. "Why do you hate me so much?"

"Oh, Nicole," he whispered back. "Have you been listening at all? I've always loved you. You were sort of a dopey kid, but I felt sorry for you."

"You felt sorry for me? Why? I had everything you didn't."

"Except for a good mother," he said. "Your mother was a neglectful piece of crap. Terese took better care of you."

Nicole wanted to argue, but he was right. Well, she wouldn't have called her mother a piece of crap, but she definitely hadn't been PTA and Girl Scouts mom material.

"So you felt sorry for me." She could barely spit out the words; her body throbbed. But she had to keep pressing him, had to buy time to plan her next move. "When did that turn to hate?"

"I don't hate you. That's what's so hard about this." She heard a loud bang that sounded like a fist hitting a wall. "I love you, but you had everything I should have had. Our father should have divorced your bitch of a mother and married mine. Instead, I grew up in a shack across town until I was twelve and he finally decided to claim me as his. And that only happened because your mom couldn't have any more children and he was desperate to have a boy to carry on the family name."

Again, she couldn't form an argument. Her own thoughts on the matter had traveled that same route on occasion, and for years, she'd harbored guilt over how Chuck had grown up and been treated by both her mother and their father.

"Nikki, I loved you until the day you came back from France and took over a company you knew nothing about."

She wanted to tell him he was wrong, that she'd learned the ins and outs of running a corporation, that she'd understood what Daedalus was all about. She'd thought running the company would be more about managing day-to-day operations, handling publicity, and doing paperwork. She'd been content to stay on the fringes of the inner workings. Or maybe *content* wasn't the right word. Maybe she'd been happy to remain blind to what was truly going on inside the company her parents had built.

So in a way, he was right. She'd known nothing about the company, and the truth now just made her sick.

"If you'd just resigned like you were supposed to after the lab-deaths scandal, none of this would be happening."

Like she was supposed to? She inhaled as an unimaginable thought came to her. "Oh, my God, you were the one who signed the death warrants. You set me up, didn't you?"

"You left me no choice."

Flabbergasted, she couldn't even speak for a moment. When she finally found her voice, it was so full of anguish that even Chuck flinched. "How could you? My God, Chuck, you're my *brother*."

He brushed his knuckle over her cheek the way he used to do when she was little. The reminder of how close they'd been pained her. "You wanted to dismantle the company I've put my soul into. Your ideas to sell off entire divisions pissed off the board. Everyone was looking to me to rein you in. I had to do something. I wanted the company to send you to our Siberian post. You'd have been out of the way but still alive. I didn't want *this*, I swear."

A chill shot up her spine. "This? What is *this*?"

Chuck stood and shook his head sadly, as if this was all out of his control. "This," he said, "is a clinical trial."

"A what?"

"Clinical trial," he said slowly, as if she were an idiot. "Well, not technically. We don't have government approval, and obviously, we're bypassing the 'informed consent' portion of the test, but if it'll make you feel any better, this will help a lot of people in the future. Your sacrifice won't go to waste."

Her *sacrifice*? What kind of insane *trial* was this?

Using his foot, he hit the latch on the head restraint, and with a snarl, she whipped her head to the side in a frenzied bid to take a bite out of him. She didn't care that all she'd get would be a mouthful of leather. She wanted to hurt him the way he'd hurt her.

Her teeth barely scraped his shoe, and then he was gone, the cell door closing behind him with an ominous metallic *clank*.

Finally able to look at more than the sterile white ceiling, she craned her neck in Riker's direction. Her heart squeezed painfully tight at the sight of him hanging from chains on the wall. Dried blood plastered his tawny hair to his forehead, and fresh blood dripped from raw wounds on his wrists, where the shackles had bitten deep. His silver eyes were molten with hatred.

"Chuck." She peered up at him through the thick glass window that separated the chamber she and Riker were in from the main room. "You don't have to do this. We can work this out—"

"Too late." Chuck hit a button on the wall next to the door, and her remaining restraints popped loose. "While you've been busy trying to sell off Daedalus bit by bit, I've made progress on the new antivampirism vaccine. But government bureaucrats aren't convinced it's safe, and they won't give us the go-ahead to use convicted felons as test subjects."

Of course they wouldn't. The government wasn't as concerned about the blood-borne form of the virus as they had been about the saliva-borne form. Infection via contact with a vampire's blood was rare and, according to many lawmakers, not a pressing problem.

"I know how much you care about your work," Chuck continued, "so I figured that if we have to get you out of the way, at least you'll be making a contribution to humanity. I injected you with our vaccine, and now we'll see how effective it is."

She staggered to her feet, her aching bones and

stiff muscles making her clumsy. How long had she been out? "What if it works and I don't turn into a vampire or die during the transformation? What then? You'll have to kill me to keep me quiet. Are you prepared to do that?"

Chuck had the decency to flush and look away. "Let's cross that bridge when we come to it."

"Dammit, Chuck!" she shouted. "You can't do this. You don't want—"

"What I want," Chuck cut in, "is for that vampire behind you to do his best to turn you." He reached over and hit another button.

Riker's restraints snapped open, and he crashed to the floor. He was only down for a second before he leaped up, teeth bared and spitting blood.

"Fuck you," he snarled. "I'm not doing it."

Chuck smiled grimly. "I thought you'd say that, *Riker*." He pivoted around and disappeared around the corner.

"Asshole." Riker rushed to Nicole, angling his body between her and the door as his strong, warm hands came down on her shoulders. "Are you okay?"

"Yes," she lied. She was so not okay. *This* was not okay. Her brother—*half* brother—had lost his mind, and she'd put herself and Riker in terrible danger. "What about you?" He was bruised and battered, and while his wrists had stopped bleeding, they could use some antiseptic and bandages.

"I'll live." Riker glared in the direction Chuck had gone. "But if I get my hands on your brother, he won't be so lucky."

She didn't bother to defend Chuck or ask Riker

for lenience. What Chuck had done—was doing—was indefensible.

Chuck came back into view and stopped at another chamber. With a jerk of his wrist, he drew up the blind, revealing a naked, battered female strapped, facedown and spread-eagle, on some sort of metal contraption. Inside the room was a barred door, but what it led to Nicole wasn't sure. She'd never seen the design in any of the blueprints she'd studied.

"Neriya," Riker croaked. "You evil *bastard*."

"This is our breeding chamber," Chuck said as he punched a numerical code into a keypad on the wall. The door *whoosh*ed open, and when he entered, Nicole found out what was behind the barred door.

A mountain of male vampire attacked the gate, his growls and snarls like nothing she'd ever heard. He was as nude as the female, his body a mass of old and fresh scars, but it was his eyes that made Nicole gasp. They were brown, not silver, which meant he was a born vampire, but it wasn't the color that caught her attention; it was the pure, raw insanity that glowed like embers in them.

And they were focused not on Chuck but on the female. Nicole had to swallow against the bile that burned in her throat.

Dear God, it wasn't a *breeding* chamber. It was a rape chamber.

Chuck freed Neriya from the contraption and dragged her out of the room, holding the barely conscious female so Nicole and Riker would be forced to take in the full horror of Neriya's condition.

Her pale skin was marred by bruises, abrasions, and

numerous vampire bite marks. Dried blood clung to her lips and chin, and Nicole realized with sickening clarity that she'd had her fangs extracted.

"You sick son of a bitch," Nicole said, her voice hoarse with rage. "Who knows about this? How many board members are involved?"

"Only a handful," Chuck said, so calmly he could have been discussing his favorite red wine. "Roland wanted to tell you about it. Before you started talking about selling off his division. And before your new vampire friends killed him."

Dark, oily despair slithered through her at the magnitude of all this betrayal. "How long?" she croaked. "How many years has this been going on?"

"It was our father who developed the breeding program," Chuck said, and Nicole remembered Riker telling her something similar at the cave. "Your beloved nanny was one of his first test subjects."

At those words, Riker lost it. Completely, utterly lost it. He hit the glass with a full body slam, his roar of hatred and rage echoing through the chamber with such force that Nicole's ears hurt.

Chuck dragged Neriya to what Nicole recognized as an industrial-sized refrigerator. "Nicole, get your vampire friend to calm down and turn you." He shoved Neriya inside the icy fridge. "Do it, or she dies. And I promise it won't be quick and painless."

RIKER COULD BARELY see through the anger that formed a crimson veil over his vision. When Chuck came out of the refrigerator, his self-satisfied smirk made Riker swear to rip him from limb to limb. What he'd done to Neriya and to Nicole made Riker want to do the tearing of limbs very, very slowly, over a period of days. Maybe weeks. Hell, if Riker could keep the fucker alive long enough, months.

The human would also pay extra for Terese's treatment. Riker had suspected abuse, but the reality was far, far worse than he'd imagined. How many times had she been strapped to that contraption? How badly had that brutal male hurt her?

"You've got an hour," Chuck said. "Nicole takes blood first. We've found that the rate of infection is slightly higher if the vampire gives blood to the human before feeding rather than the other way around."

Chuck disappeared through a door at the rear of the gymnasium-sized chamber Riker hadn't been able to see when he'd been hanging from chains. Now the giant room appeared to contain dozens of small cells like the one he and Nicole were in, plus some sort of large cage near the center. There was movement from within, but Riker couldn't tell what it was.

"That son of a bitch." Nicole's voice was stricken, her expression equally so, as she gazed in the direction Chuck had gone. "I'm sorry, Riker. God, I'm so sorry."

"I know," he said. "But let's not worry about that now. We need to get out of here."

She slammed the side of her fist into the window, and the resulting warbling sound reverberated around the room in an almost musical wave. "These cells are built to neutralize most vampire abilities, so unless you have a laser-vision superpower we didn't know about that can burn a hole in the Plexiglas, we're screwed."

Well, she'd just explained why he hadn't been able to use his hypnotic ability on Chuck while the asshole was stringing him up in shackles. "Sweetheart, I've been screwed many times, and trust me, this doesn't even come close to being the worst of them." She shot him a dark look, no doubt thinking of their encounter in her room when he *wasn't* screwed, and he clarified. "When I was in the military. I spent a lot of time pinned down in burnt-out buildings and on mountain ridges. There's always a way out."

"Then what do you suggest?"

He scanned the area, noted the cameras mounted in dozens of spots on the walls and ceiling. "Do you think he's watching?"

"Probably." She glanced at the twenty-four-hour clock on the wall in the main chamber. "It's the middle of the night, so except for a guard, he'd be the only one." She rubbed her ribs where Chuck had kicked her, the bastard.

"I still can't believe this is happening." Riker didn't have that problem. Humans were capable of anything. Nicole turned to him, her eyes haunted, her face pale and etched with desperation. "You've got to try to turn me."

He shot a middle-finger salute at one of the cameras. Yeah, yeah, real mature. "Not an option."

"It's the only way to save Neriya."

"You know he's not going to release her."

"No, but maybe he won't kill her," she said, looking so troubled and disgusted that he had to fight the urge to take her in his arms. No way was he going to give Chuck a means to hurt them both. Better if he believed they were enemies. "The longer she stays alive, the more time we have to figure a way out of this."

"I'm not going to turn you."

She studied the equipment in the outer chamber. "I hate to even say this after everything Daedalus has done, but the company *has* had great success with its medical applications. The vaccine Chuck injected me with should work."

"And if it doesn't? You had complications from the first vaccine. What if something similar happens with this new one? Are you prepared to spend the rest of your life being what you hate the most?"

There was a long pause. "What I hate the most isn't vampires."

Her gaze slid up to his, and the devastation in her eyes rocked him to the core. He suddenly didn't want to know what she hated the most, but he had a feeling she was looking inward rather than out.

He hated seeing her in pain, and the irony wasn't lost on him, since for two decades, all he'd wanted was to see everyone in the Martin family suffer. But now that he was here with a Martin who was suffering inside her own facility where vampires had been tortured and killed, he felt no sense of vindication. Nicole wasn't the monster he'd believed, and again, he had to fight the urge to comfort her. Protect her.

How could he sink his fangs into those scars on her throat, knowing how much a vampire had hurt her? "I swore I wouldn't bite you."

"And I swore I'd do whatever it took to rescue Neriya," she said firmly.

Shit. This was a no-win situation if he'd ever been in one. They weren't going to get out of here unscathed, but he was determined that they *would* get out. Not a win, exactly, but not a loss. At this point, he'd take a draw. And he *hated* draws.

Nicole blew out a long breath. "This is my fault, Riker. I need to do something to help."

As much as he loathed seeing Nicole in agony, he loved how fierce she was when she was trying to make things right.

"You know how you can help?" He angled himself so the cameras wouldn't miss what was coming next. "You can die."

"Excuse me?"

Savagely, he wrapped his fist in her hair and wrenched her head so his mouth rested against her ear. "I'll try to turn you," he murmured, "but I'm going to make it look brutal. Your brother thinks I'm an animal, so I'll give him what he expects. Then you need to play drained."

"He'll come for me to keep you from killing me," she whispered.

"Exactly." He snarled, hoping to hell Chuck was watching, because he didn't like doing this. If he was going to take Nicole's blood, he wanted it to be intimate, pleasurable. Maybe it was foolish, but he suddenly wanted to erase the memory of the vicious attack on her as a child, to show her that a vampire's bite didn't have to be an instrument of pain. He might not be able to make it an especially enjoyable experience, but he could at least make sure she didn't suffer more than she already had. "It won't hurt, Nicole. I promise. But I need you to struggle and scream like it does."

"No." She shoved against him. Unprepared for her sudden movement, he released her, and she scrambled backward. "No!" she shouted. "I don't care about Neriya enough to do this." She looked into a camera. "Chuck, let me out. Please!"

Good girl. Riker almost smiled. She should have been an actress. In a flash, he lunged at her, catching her around the shoulders even as he bit into his wrist and released a stream of blood. She struggled as he jammed his arm against her mouth. She shook her head, fought hard enough to score him with her nails.

This killed him. Under all that determination, he scented her anxiety as blood filled her mouth and dripped down her chin. She wasn't swallowing; self-preservation and instinct had likely kicked in, overriding her brain.

Come on, Sunshine, you can do this. He loosened his grip a little, hoping to ease the feeling of being trapped, and her struggles lessened.

She swallowed, and a single tear rolled down her cheek. Relief and sorrow knotted in his chest. He'd never turned a human, never even thought about it, let alone done it against the victim's will. Oh, Nicole was willing, but it wasn't because she *wanted* it. She was being forced by her brother, and Riker was the weapon of choice, the gun held by the crazy person.

Pulling back his wrist, he licked the wound to seal it, tasting Nicole on his skin. God, what he wouldn't have given to make this a special, tender moment. Cursing silently, he touched the tip of his tongue to the backs of his fangs, releasing the liquid agent that both turned pain to pleasure and injected an almost instant high.

"I'm so sorry," he murmured against her neck.

Her entire body trembled as he sank his teeth into her tender throat. She stiffened, gasping at the invasion of his fangs into her body, but within the span of a heartbeat, pleasure made her groan.

Fight me, dammit. He cleared his throat softly, a prod that worked, because suddenly, she screamed and kicked, and as her blood flowed over his tongue, he began to drown in self-loathing.

Because as much as he hated this situation they were in, he found himself loving every moment of having Nicole in his arms and in his body.

JUST A WEEK ago, no one could ever have convinced Nicole that she would enjoy the feel of a vampire's fangs buried in her throat. Now she had to keep reminding herself to struggle against Riker, when all she wanted to do was melt into the warmth of his touch, and even his bite.

The taste of his blood still lingered on her tongue, but her stomach hadn't rebelled. In fact, she felt a little drugged, even relaxed. Her initial struggles hadn't been feigned; her instinctive panic had been far too real. But now . . . now she had to make a conscious effort to fight him.

After what seemed like seconds, he withdrew his fangs, but he kept his mouth over the punctures, licking, making the sucking motions for her brother's benefit. *Half* brother. And now she couldn't consider him even that. If she turned into a vampire, she was going to kill him. If she died, she was going to haunt him.

"Weaken your struggles gradually," Riker murmured against her skin. "In about sixty seconds, stop struggling and play passed-out."

She obeyed, slapping him weakly instead of punching. She kicked but in less frequent intervals, until she finally stopped . . . but threw in a few twitches for fun.

I hope you're watching this, Chuck. I hope you lose a lot of sleep, you bastard.

"Don't kill her!" Chuck's shout blared over the din of her own thoughts, making her even angrier. The mere sound of his voice irritated her. Had he always had that whiny, nasally tone that made everything he said come across like a complaint?

Riker tucked her close. "No matter what happens, stay still," he whispered.

Her gut rolled. The next instant, Riker grunted and jerked, and she knew he'd been struck by a shock dart.

"Get back," Chuck warned, and a moment later, Riker let out another pained grunt.

Nicole cracked her eyelids just enough to see Riker stiffen and collapse onto the concrete in a sprawl of flailing limbs. It took every ounce of self-restraint she had to remain limp and unmoving, when all she wanted to do was leap to her feet and help him.

She heard the sound of flesh-on-flesh strikes; Chuck was beating Riker.

Don't cry . . . don't cry . . .

By some miracle, she managed to keep her lids squeezed tight and not shed a tear. An endless minute later, she felt herself being lifted, and she risked another peek to see Chuck slamming the chamber door, locking an unconscious Riker inside.

Chuck plopped her unceremoniously onto an exam table and put his fingers to her throat, feeling for a pulse. "Nicole?"

She lifted her lids. "Surprise, asshole."

Chuck's eyes widened in disbelief. Lifting her leg in a powerful surge, she bashed him in the face with her knee. Blood spurted, and he fell back with a shout, clutching his nose. "Bitch!" He came at her, but she dodged his fist and rolled onto the floor.

She hit the tiles hard. Pain speared her hip and shoulder. Flailing like a marionette having a seizure, she made it to her feet, but Chuck nailed her with a kick to the back of the knee, and she spun into an instrument tray. Her fingers found a scalpel.

She didn't hesitate.

Spinning in an uncoordinated circle, she swung the blade, catching Chuck in the neck. The wound was barely a scratch, but Chuck screamed like he was dying, grabbed his throat, and staggered toward an exit.

"Nicole! Hurry!" Riker's strangled shout drew her attention away from her fleeing brother. She bolted to the chamber, where thick jets of fog were spewing from holes in the ceiling. Her heart nearly stopped.

Boric-acid gas. The dozens of vampires Chuck had killed using her "order" had died that way, suffering in gas chambers, all caught on video.

Hands shaking so hard she was barely able to work the control panel by the chamber door, she punched buttons, cutting off the gas and unlocking the door. Riker burst out of the room, gasping for breath.

"I know where they keep the antidote." She ran across the room to a glass cabinet and swept boxes of meds, vials, and first-aid items onto the floor, desperate to find the container marked as . . . yes, right there! She raced back to Riker, who was slumped against the wall, struggling to breathe.

"This . . . sucks."

"The gas is highly concentrated." She measured five CCs of antidote into a syringe. "It's ten times the strength of the powder I used on you. You'll need an injection and a nasal application. Hold still." She plunged the needle into his shoulder and pushed the medicine into his muscles. When the syringe was empty, she tossed it to the ground and broke open an ampoule of powder. "Sniff hard." She put the little glass container up to his nose and inhaled with him, as if that would help.

Almost instantly, he stood up straighter, and his color went from ashen to tan. "Better."

"It'll take about an hour for all the symptoms to disappear, but we can't wait. We've got to get out of here. Chuck will send the police and VAST." She shot a glance at the supply closet. "But first, we're destroying this lab."

AS RIKER CAUGHT his breath, Nicole kicked open a locked file drawer and loaded a plastic garbage bag with thick files. When the drawer was empty, she hit the meds cabinet next and swept dozens of pill bottles and vials into the open bag. Moving quickly, she left the stuffed bag next to the exit and then began hauling gallon-sized jugs out of a closet.

"I'll start a fire with these," she said, "but if there are any vampires in these chambers, we need to free them first."

She darted to the cage in the center of the room, where a scrawny, gangly male vampire, a teen by Riker's estimation, huddled inside. He wore only a pair of loose navy sweatpants and a stained white T-shirt that showed way too many ribs through the thin fabric.

Still feeling like he was breathing fire, Riker blocked her. "I'll do it. We don't know how he'll react. Stand back."

Bracing himself for a launch attack, Riker opened the door. The kid inside shrank against the wall, the acrid scent of his terror coming off him in waves.

"We won't hurt you," Nicole said, but the kid just stared with wide, crystal-blue eyes, his thin body shaking so hard his teeth chattered.

Fuck. They didn't have time for this. "Come on, kid. We're rescuing you." When the male didn't move, Riker snared him by the arm and dragged him out of the cage.

"No!" the kid shouted. "No!" He wriggled like a spitting-mad kitten and tried to claw his way back inside the cage.

"Hey," Nicole said softly. "It's okay—"

The kid's croaked "Help" cut her off.

"Shit," Riker muttered as he wrapped his arms around the kid's body to stop his struggles. The boy rocked his dark head back and caught Riker in the mouth hard enough to make his ears ring. Too bad his hypnotic ability only worked on humans and some animals. "Got sedatives around here?"

Nicole dashed to the cabinet where she'd gotten the boric-acid antidote and spent a few precious moments locating a sedative and measuring it out into a syringe.

"Jesus," she muttered as she injected the kid. "Do they even feed him?"

The boy immediately settled down enough that Riker could prop him against the wall and leave him. "Start the fire," Riker said. "I'll get Neriya and handle any other vampires."

An alarm blared, and *shit*, their time had run out. Riker put on a burst of speed and tore open the refrigerator door. Cold air stung his cheeks as he darted inside . . . and found a chamber of horrors.

Dead vampires hung from hooks in neat rows,

and body parts sat in metal bins or were wrapped in plastic and stacked neatly on shelves. Riker had seen a lot of gore in his life, had witnessed atrocities that still haunted him to this day. But this . . . this was worse than anything he'd ever encountered.

Save your mental trauma for later.

Shoving the gruesome scene to the back of his mind, he searched for Neriya. When he found her, hanging at the back of the fridge with her throat slit, the boiling of his blood countered the freezing temperatures. Rage and hatred and horror mixed like volatile chemicals that threatened to tear him apart and take down everything around him.

He'd failed.

The room spun and closed in around him as the reality of the situation crushed him in its cold, dead fist. His mission to rescue Neriya had met with disaster, and now, not only was a valuable, gifted female dead, but his clan was doomed to war.

War and, likely, extinction.

"Riker, hurry!"

With the icy deliberation of someone with nothing left to lose, he strode out of the meat locker and checked the remaining chambers. Empty. All except the conjoined breeding chamber where the naked male watched them, his gaze glued to Nicole. In a few strides, Riker was inside the vampire's cell. The male, no more a vampire than a corpse was a living person, crouched, his fangs dripping with drool.

Behind Riker, Nicole splashed something on the floors and walls, and the harsh reek of chemicals burned his nostrils.

"It was you, wasn't it?" he asked the creature. "My mate was put into a cell with you."

The only reply was a bloodthirsty growl. Riker should hate the vampire, should want to rip him apart with his bare hands for what he'd done to Terese and countless other females. Instead, Riker felt only pity. This male was as much a victim of Daedalus's cruelty as Terese had been.

With lightning speed, he slipped behind the vampire and snapped his neck. When he stepped out of the cell, he found Nicole staring at him.

"You killed him."

"I put him out of his misery." The kid was still sitting where Riker had left him, his eyes glazed. Maybe it would be best to put him down, too.

"Don't even think about it," Nicole snapped. "Where's Neriya?"

"Dead."

Nicole fumbled the lighter in her hand but caught it before it hit the floor. When she looked up, her eyes were liquid with regret. But they both knew there was no time for mourning or useless apologies.

"Pick up the kid." She flicked the lighter mechanism and lit the corner of a paper as he threw the skinny male over his shoulder.

With one last look around, she dropped the flaming sheet and grabbed the garbage bag full of files. The place went up in a flash. Searing heat licked at their backs as they fled the building through a rear exit.

Once outside, Nicole stopped on a grassy knoll at the edge of the property. The clan's beat-up Jeep was parked within sight, but Nicole didn't even look in its direction. Despite the blare of sirens bearing down on them, she very slowly swung around and stared at the flames engulfing the lab. He expected to see grief in her face. Or pain. Or even anger. Anything but what he saw reflecting in her eyes.

Acceptance.

Nicole had just willfully destroyed part of her life, and now she was watching the remains burn to ash. Her strength humbled him, and when she finally turned her back to the crumbling skeleton that had belonged to her family, she did it with a finality that astonished him.

They didn't look back again.

NICOLE WASN'T SURE how far they'd run with Riker carrying the kid over his shoulder after they parked the Jeep on property discreetly owned by MoonBound. But every time she faltered, tripping over branches or stumbling from exhaustion, Riker would catch her. It hadn't taken long for VAST to swarm the forest, and the sounds of pursuit kept her moving. Now, with the shouting voices practically upon them, her panic made her even clumsier.

"It's okay," Riker said, steadying her with a hand around her biceps. "Clan warriors are attacking our pursuers."

She sucked in a panting breath. "You could have told me earlier."

"Didn't want to ruin the surprise."

"In the future, keep in mind that I don't like surprises," she muttered.

They continued on, thankfully at a slower pace, and

after a few minutes, the boy came around, his groggy gaze unfocused and confused.

"Hey, kid," Riker said. "We're almost home." He lowered the boy to the ground.

Standing, the male was at least six feet tall, but he probably weighed no more than Nicole. His shaggy black hair fell in a mop to his jaw, and he had to push it out of his face to see. He wobbled as he looked around, his eyes wide, his mouth hanging open.

"Where are we?" The boy's strained voice was barely audible. "What *is* this?"

"We're in the forest outside of Seattle," Riker said. "We're safe. The humans can't touch you here."

The boy backed away from them in a panicked scramble, and when he bumped into a tree trunk, he yelped and leaped away as if he'd been bitten. He sucked air in huge gulps, his gaze darting everywhere at once, as if he was looking for somewhere to run.

"You're okay," she said, in a low, steady voice. He reminded Nicole of a stray kitten she'd once coaxed out from underneath a bush. "You're safe now. Where are you from?"

The question seemed to stump him. "From?"

"Yes." Reaching out, she took his hand. It was cold and bony, and her heart broke. "Where did you live before you were captured by humans? Where's home?"

The boy frowned. "The lab is my home."

"Are you saying you were born there?" Riker asked, incredulous.

A crow cawed nearby, and the kid gave a start. "I-I was born in a human house. But the lab is all I remember."

The lab was all he knew? *Jesus.* "Where are your parents?"

"I don't know who my sire is." The boy's voice was so quiet she had to strain to hear. "My mother is dead."

Nicole wanted to hug him. Losing a parent was awful enough, but then to be raised in a lab . . . She couldn't even begin to imagine that kind of nightmare. "Did she die during childbirth? How did Daedalus get you?"

"She was a servant. A wild vampire broke onto the grounds and killed her. Humans cut me out of her belly before I died." He gave her such an honest, innocent look that her eyes stung. "They saved me."

Good God, he was actually grateful for how Daedalus had treated him. She cut a glance at Riker . . . and gooseflesh erupted from her scalp to her toes.

Riker had lost all the color in his face and was staring at the boy, his jaw clenched, his throat working on swallow after swallow. Something was very, very wrong.

"Riker?"

He didn't acknowledge that she'd spoken. He kept his gaze fixed on the boy. "How old are you, kid?" The boy blinked, as if not understanding the question. "How old?" Riker barked.

The boy made a noise of distress and shrank away from them both, lifting one skinny arm over his face.

"Nice," she snapped at Riker. "Well done." She eased close to the kid again, speaking in soothing tones. "We're not going to hurt you. I promise. You can tell us. When were you born?"

The boy eyed Riker warily. "The lab people do tests on me every June. They say it's my birthday. Last time, there were a lot of tests because they said it was twenty years."

"Oh, God." Riker's voice grew constricted. "Terese . . . she died twenty years ago last June."

It took several moments for Nicole to process what Riker was saying, and when she did, she clamped her hand over her mouth in stunned silence. This gaunt vampire kid, who looked to be no more than sixteen or seventeen, was Terese's son.

Nicole studied his face, mapped the curve of his jaw, the color of his eyes, and even the shape of his lips. He'd inherited it all from his mother.

Riker was still staring, shell-shocked and maybe a little apprehensive and lost. Nicole had to pull herself together to help him. To help them both.

She squeezed the boy's hand. "What's your name?"

"Subject One."

"That's what they call you?"

He nodded.

Nicole's gut crash-landed in her feet, and she was very glad when Riker swore, several nasty, choice words that perfectly expressed her feelings right now.

"Riker?" She moderated her voice, going for calm and quiet, knowing her next question was a sensitive one, and it could go over very, very badly. "What was Terese going to name the baby?"

"I wanted Sebastien," he croaked. "Bastien, after my brother." Riker stood still as a blade, his eyes closed. As the breeze picked up and ruffled his hair and the leaves overhead, he lifted his lids and gave Nicole the briefest nod of permission.

Memories of Terese swirled in Nicole's head. She

remembered Terese's gentleness, her warm embraces, her soft voice. She remembered a woman who had made more of an impact on Nicole's life than her own mother had. The pain of losing Terese had stayed with Nicole, but now it was as if a piece of her was back. No matter how horribly wrong today had gone, something good had come out of it.

Nicole's eyes stung as she took both of the boy's hands in hers and smiled. "From now on, you'll be known as Bastien. Is that okay?"

He tested the name on his tongue, saying it over and over until he finally gave her a fragile smile. "I think it's okay."

23

SHIT.

Of all the millions of words that could be running through Riker's head right now, *shit* was the one that kept repeating itself over and over. Somehow he'd kept the presence of mind to take Nicole and Bastien—*holy shit, Bastien*—straight to the clan's lab to have them checked out before he lost his shit.

Yeah, there was a whole lot of shit going on.

So while Nicole and Bastien—*unfuckingbelievable*—were getting a medical once-over, Riker was jogging down the hallway leading to Hunter's chambers as if his feet were on fire. He'd needed to get away from Bastien, to outrun his own feelings.

His own guilt.

Already he regretted the way he'd treated Bastien. He'd yelled at the poor kid, then stared at him, speechless. He'd been immobilized by shock, rendered helpless by his own disbelief. He'd let Nicole comfort the boy while Riker tried to untie himself from the knot of emotions that had been strangling him.

Had Bastien even understood what Nicole and

Riker had been talking about? Did Bastien know that he was, for all intents and purposes, Riker's son?

Shit. The next conversation with the boy was going to be fun. *Hi, I'm your father. Well, sort of. An insane monster is really who sired you. And the humans lied when they told you your mother was killed by a vampire. She killed herself because she hated you. And then I left you to be raised in a lab like a rat in a cage. Good talk, son. We'll toss around a ball or something later.*

Riker stumbled as emotion overcame him. He should have been there. He shouldn't have just assumed the baby died with Terese. He'd missed what should have been twenty happy years with Bastien. Missed his first steps. His first words. The boy could have grown up safe and wanted, with a father who loved him. Instead, he'd grown up inside a box in a sterile, cold laboratory.

Footsteps rang out in the distance. Riker pulled himself together before someone saw him in the middle of a breakdown and jogged the rest of the way to Hunter's chamber. He burst through the heavy double doors and wasn't surprised to see the chief standing in the middle of the room, hands clasped behind his back and an expectant look on his face. Behind him, a Mario Bros. game had been paused on the Nintendo.

"From the look on your face, I'm guessing things didn't go well," he said, his deep voice echoing off the walls.

"Neriya is dead."

Hunter's jaw clenched. "Shit."

"Word of the day," Riker muttered.

"What about the human?" Hunter's nonuse of Nicole's name was intentional, Riker was sure, but he didn't take the bait.

"She's with Grant. She grabbed some files from the Daedalus lab before we burned the building down."

One dark eyebrow cocked. "And she allowed you to do that?"

"It was her idea." God, she'd been magnificent. Calm and efficient. She was a warrior, as full of heart as any vampire Riker had fought side by side with in battle. Which brought him to the next subject. "But there's a complication."

"Of course there is."

"Her bastard of a brother forced me to try to turn her with my blood. He immunized her against it, but it was a test dose."

Hunter's gaze raked Riker from head to toe, as if trying to assess how Riker felt about this news. He wished his leader luck, because he wasn't sure about it himself.

"So you're saying she could turn."

"Yeah." Riker eyed the wet bar, wondering how many bottles of whiskey he could drink before Hunter stopped him. "There's more."

Hunter held up his hand. "Wait." Swiftly, he moved to the bar and splashed two fingers of bourbon into a glass. "You look like you need this."

Riker took the glass gratefully. For a long moment, he stared into the amber liquid, letting the colors swirl around inside the glass. Finally, he put the glass to his lips, inhaled, and downed the contents. The burn numbed him pleasantly, but it wasn't going to last.

"We freed a male. Young. Scared. Hasn't ever been outside the lab. He was afraid of the damned trees."

"Did you bring him here?"

"Yup. Straight to the Island of Misfit Toys." Suddenly exhausted, Riker scrubbed his hand over his face. "When Terese died . . . fuck, I assumed the baby was dead, too. He wasn't. The humans delivered him and raised him in that lab." Saying it out loud made the liquor sour in his gut.

Hunter wasn't one to go slack-jawed, but with his stunned stare and slightly parted lips, he came close. "Are you telling me that the male you rescued is your son?"

No one but Nicole knew the real story, that Terese had been impregnated by someone other than Riker. He'd always planned to raise the boy as his own, so there was never any point in telling anyone the truth when Terese was alive. Then, after she died, it seemed wrong to cast even more shadows on an already dark situation. No one needed to know what happened to Terese—she wouldn't welcome the pity.

"Riker? Buddy?" Hunter prompted, and Riker cleared his throat.

"Yeah," he croaked. "He's mine." Just because Terese was dead didn't mean that Riker's promise was no longer valid.

"How do you want to handle it?"

Great question. How did you deal with a twenty-year-old son you didn't know you had and who had clearly gone through a lifetime of cruelty and neglect? Bastien was like a puppy-mill dog that had never been outside its cage to play or socialize and knew nothing but the people who abused it.

"I'd like him to stay with me, but I don't think it's a good idea. I think it'll be too much for him. I was hoping he could stay in the nursery with Morena."

"The nursery? Isn't he an adult?"

"He's twenty, but I doubt he was given an education in either human or vampire life. All he knew was a cage inside a lab. He's going to need a slow, nonthreatening introduction to our world, like Morena did with Lucy. He seems to have bonded with Nicole, so she might be able to help him adjust."

"Nicole." Hunter said her name with a distinct wariness. "Do you really want her around your son? It was her company that did all of this to him."

"Nicole isn't the enemy." Riker ignored Hunter's dubious snort and poured himself another drink. "She saved my life, Hunt. She volunteered to be turned into a vampire in order to save Neriya's life—"

"Which didn't go so well, did it?"

"Not because of Nicole." Riker threw back the shot he'd poured and filled the glass again. "It was her idea to break into the lab to save Neriya, and it was her idea to destroy the lab. She turned against her brother and fought to free us all."

"So what are you saying? That you're fine with having a human running around loose in our home? That you're totally okay with everything she's done for Daedalus?" Hunter regarded Riker with shrewd eyes. "Are you thinking with your dick?"

Riker breathed deeply in an attempt to keep from

lashing out at his leader. "When have you ever known me to think with my dick?"

"Isn't that what you were doing in her quarters yesterday?"

If he'd been thinking with his dick, he'd have been able to finish what they'd started instead of backing off like some kind of traumatized idiot.

"What we were doing is none of your business."

As silent and fast as a serpent, Hunter uncoiled in a lethal blur, backing Riker against the wall with a hand around his throat. "Everything that happens inside these walls is my business. You get that, right?"

Oh, hey, he was still holding his glass all nice and proper. Didn't lose a drop. Very deliberately, he put the glass to his lips and drank, even though Hunter was so in his face that the bottom of the glass brushed his nose.

When Riker had downed the last drop, he ground out, "And *you* get that I have followed every order you've given me, without question, for the last twenty years, right? Have I ever screwed up or given you reason to doubt my judgment?"

Hunter idly tapped his thumb on Riker's throat. "How did we get from me asking the questions to you asking?"

"Maybe I didn't like your question." Brittle tension winged through the air between them, and yeah, this could go critical real fast.

"Maybe I don't like your attitude." Hunter paused, letting the tension stew a little before pushing away. "If this is what fucking a human does to you, then you need to get back to eating them instead."

"With Nicole, I can do both," Riker said, knowing it was stupid to poke a vampire with a stick but doing it anyway.

"I'm going to give you a day to cool off. Settle in with your son. And get your head out of your ass. We'll talk tomorrow."

"I'm not killing her." Riker locked gazes with Hunter as he opened the door. "And I won't let you do it, either."

He slammed the door behind him, shutting out the male who had picked up the pieces of Riker that had been broken after Terese died.

NICOLE HAD NEVER enjoyed a shower as much as she was loving the one she was taking right now.

For the first time in not just days but months, maybe even years, she was able to relax and just let the hot water sluice over her body, washing away dirt, blood, sweat, stress, and fear. All that remained was gratitude that she was alive and that Riker had gotten the son he'd been so desperate for.

There was something tragic in watching Bastien, so timid and afraid, jump at everything as she and Riker had walked him to Grant's lab. But the second he stepped inside, it was as if he had arrived home.

Riker had clearly been rattled, so she'd promised to watch after Bastien while he met with Hunter. Mostly, all she'd had to do was stay with Bastien while he wandered around the lab, touching equipment like they were old friends.

It had broken her heart.

Food had arrived a short time later, and she'd left

Bastien to eat while she and Grant went through the bag filled with files and meds, which included the drugs she needed to manage her medical condition. They'd also discussed both Bastien and her own experience at the Daedalus facility. Grant hadn't appeared concerned that the vaccine she'd been given would fail, but then, to him, turning into a vampire could only be a good thing. Nevertheless, he'd taken blood, saliva, and cell samples for study.

Nicole just tried not to think about it. She'd know within twenty-four hours if the vaccine didn't work, and at that point . . . she didn't know. Ever since Boris nearly ripped her throat out with his teeth, her second-greatest fear had always been that she'd be bitten by another vampire. Her greatest fear had been that she'd be turned into one.

She thought about Riker sinking his fangs into her. Thought about him doing it again. And crazily, the idea excited her instead of repulsing her. Would turning into a vampire truly be so bad? Especially now that she had no desire ever to see anyone involved with Daedalus again, let alone her brother? She had nothing to return to in the human world, so how bad would it be to turn into a completely different person? A different species?

She let herself digest the idea as she dried off and headed for the bedroom, but a knock on the door stopped her in her tracks.

"Nicole?" Riker's muffled voice came from the other side.

"Um, yeah . . . one second." She hastily wrapped the towel around herself and cracked the door open.

Riker stood on the other side, also freshly showered and changed into jeans and a black sweatshirt. His damp hair, darker blond than when it was dry, stood up in spiky chunks that made her want to smooth them with her fingers, if for no other reason than to have an excuse to touch him.

"Can I come in?"

His hesitation was a new thing, and it highlighted the change in their relationship. Before, he'd barged into the room as if he owned it, and now he was asking to come in. She wondered what he'd say if she refused.

"Please." She backed up, allowing him to enter. "There's only one guard outside now," she said as she closed the door behind him. "Guess I've earned a little leeway, huh?"

It was meant to be a joke, but Riker's expression grew serious. "You'll earn more," he said. "I'm not going to let anything happen to you."

"Oh." Apparently, it was time to discuss her future. "Should I be worried that someone wants something to happen to me?"

"No."

She fisted the towel more tightly around her. "That wasn't a very convincing answer."

"I don't want to talk about it."

Too bad, because her life was on the line. "What do you want—"

With a great surge, Riker backed her against the wall. He didn't touch her. He caged her in with one hand on either side of her head, holding his body away from hers. He might not have been doing anything sexual, but intense hunger burned in his eyes.

"I can feel you running through my veins," he said.

"I can taste you on my tongue and smell your sweet spice. But more than that, I can't stop thinking about you and the way you gave yourself over to me in the lab. The way you sacrificed yourself to save Neriya." He swallowed. "The way you handled my son."

She licked her lips, and his gaze dropped to her mouth. *Kiss me*, she thought. *Kiss me, and make me feel safe here.*

When he lowered his head in agonizingly slow motion, she nearly wept with both relief and impatience. Then his lips were on hers, warm and soft, and so very gentle. A wonderfully shivery sensation spread through her insides as he licked and nibbled, alternating light pressure with firm kisses.

Oh, but he was amazing at this. He blew away the memory of every man she'd ever kissed. Hell, no one could compare to him. Ever.

Moaning, she opened to him. His kiss grew fiercer in response, but he still remained tamely away from her, the space between them nothing but empty air.

"Riker," she said against his lips, "I don't want this to be like last time. I need you to be all in."

He lifted his head and pegged her with those silver blades he called eyes. The hesitation in them made her heart sink. "I'm sorry. I can't promise you anything."

She jerked, lanced by his words. Sudden anger helped soothe the cut, and she shoved him hard enough that he had to step back. "Of course you can't."

"Dammit, Nicole." He closed in on her again, but she ducked out of the cage he tried to trap her in. "I came here to thank you for everything you've done for me, my clan, and my son."

"Wait . . . so . . . this is about gratitude? You want to pay me back with sex?"

His cheeks reddened, and she knew she'd hit the nail on the head. "No."

"Too bad," she said, surprising even herself. But dammit, she was tired of having no control over her life and feeling like she was blowing in the wind. If he wanted to thank her with sex, who was she to refuse? "I want an orgasm."

His mouth fell open. Closed. When she dropped the towel and stood in front of him, buck naked, his mouth fell open again.

"Go ahead and thank me," she said.

"Nicole . . ." The warning in his tone should have been a clue, but she was beyond comprehending subtle signals. Or maybe she just didn't care anymore.

She coyly circled her belly button with a finger, loving how his gaze latched on as she trailed her hand upward. Heat scorched her where he looked, and she took a very long time stroking her way up her abdomen, to the full swell of her breast, and finally, to her nipple.

"Well?" She pinched and played, enjoying the way Riker's breaths came faster. But he still hadn't moved. "Fine." She sighed, dropping her hand to her side. "I guess you aren't all that thankful." Very deliberately, she turned around and bent to pick up the towel.

That was it. Suddenly, she was upright, her body pinned between Riker and the wall, her cheek kissing the wooden support beam built into the stone. His hand gripped a fistful of her hair as the other delved between her legs. Forcefully, he tilted her head back so he could kiss her. The position left her immobile, barely able to move, and wow, something about being restrained like this was a huge turn-on.

She ground her butt against his erection in time to the stroke of his fingers at her core. Long, light passes over her sex grew firmer, and when he worked a finger into her slit, she cried out.

"Thank you." His hot breath caressed her cheek, and his deep voice vibrated through her in an erotic wave. "Is this what you want?"

"Yes." She gasped.

He made a harsh, greedy male sound as he pushed his finger inside her. He didn't waste time with teasing. He worked her hard, stroking that place inside her that had her pushing into his hand. Liquid heat seeped into her center, and she wondered if he noticed how ready she was for him.

"Thank you," he repeated, his voice guttural. "Thank. You." He pulled his hand away, and she almost cried at the loss.

Until she heard the *zing* of his zipper and felt the prod of his shaft between her legs. "Thank *you*," she whispered.

He drove into her, burying himself in one smooth motion. They moved together, his hips slapping against her buttocks. He released her hair and gripped her hips, holding her for his powerful thrusts. His breathing grew ragged, joining hers, and she knew he was as close as she was.

Could he go all the way?

She sensed he was holding back, that part of him still hadn't come to grips with what had happened to

Terese and Nicole's family's role in it. But screw that, she wasn't going to let his past interfere anymore. He was hers now, and he was going to learn that, right here and now.

Hers? Vaguely, she was aware that there was an impossible number of reasons he couldn't be hers, but right now, none of them mattered. A fierce, primal instinct rose up in her, requiring that she stake a claim on the male she wanted.

"Stop," she snarled, and to her shock, he froze.

She pushed against him, forcing him free of her body. In the narrow, crushing space between them, she turned, smiled at the confused look on his face . . . and then scaled him like a tree.

"Jesus, Nicole—" He caught her waist as she lowered herself onto his erection. Ruthlessly, she dug her nails into his shoulders, and he hissed in pleasure. Once again, he braced her against the wall as he pumped his hips with an urgency she hadn't felt from him before.

Still, she felt his restraint, weaker than a moment ago but hanging on. No, no, *no*. Rocking her head, she bit him, sinking her teeth into the soft spot between his shoulder and his throat.

He shouted and bucked, drilling her savagely, sparing her nothing. She clawed harder, forcing him to think about her and her alone. The past wasn't allowed here. No other female was allowed here.

Oh . . . *yes*. Her body tightened as ecstasy engulfed her, sparking from nerve ending to nerve ending. She cried out, clenching around him, the orgasm going on and on. Riker's chest expanded on a huge, shuddering breath, and then his movements became jerky and erratic. A hot splash filled her, setting off another climax for her as he convulsed and shuddered.

Riker's forehead, damp with sweat, rested against hers as he continued to move inside her, wringing the last drops of pleasure from both of them.

"Thank you," he murmured, petting her hair with lazy, uneven strokes. "That was . . . amazing."

She couldn't agree more.

Too soon, he slipped out of her and lowered her to the ground. With tender care, he wrapped her in the towel and kissed her.

"I have to go," he said. Sated and exhausted in a way she'd never been, she nodded. "Get some rest." She let him carry her into the bedroom and tuck her into bed.

He left, and she was nearly asleep when she realized that they still hadn't discussed a single thing.

RIKER WAS PRETTY sure hash browns weren't supposed to taste like sawdust, but wood chips were all he tasted as he shoveled food into his mouth on the way to Grant's lab. He left a trail of potatoes behind him, because apparently, he couldn't eat and walk at the same time. Add thinking about Nicole to the mix, and he might as well put on a bib and drink out of a damned sippy cup.

He'd gone to check on her this morning, but she was still crashed, and there was no way he was waking her. If she wanted to sleep for a week, he'd let her.

Well, maybe he'd wake her up for sex. She'd seemed to like what they'd done last night.

His cheeks heated in remembrance, and his body hardened in anticipation.

Whoa, buddy. We're not going back to her chambers right now.

Holding the plate he'd swiped from the main kitchen in one hand, he rubbed the spot where Nicole had bitten him with the other. She'd been a wild thing, and though her bite and claw marks had healed, he still felt them like erotic whispers on his skin.

Sex with Terese had never been like that. No, Terese had viewed sex as a duty to be tolerated, and the only time she was ever even remotely interested was on the new moon, when her hormones and her need for blood took control. Even then, she'd never scratched him. Or climbed up him. Or reveled in being fucked against a wall.

The raunchy images played like a skin flick in his head, and he missed a step as he took the corner to the lab. Baddon, who was coming in the opposite direction, grinned.

"Smooth, man," Baddon said. "Can you do it again? I missed most of it."

Riker snorted. "How about I kick your ass?" He popped Baddon in the shoulder as they passed in the hall. "You won't miss any of that."

Baddon's laughter followed Riker until he entered the lab, where he wasn't surprised to find Grant hard at work. He was, however, surprised to find a teepee in one corner and Hunter talking to Bastien at a table near the bison-skin tent.

His stomach did a few flips. It was both strange and awesome to see the boy Riker had once dreamed of having. The circumstances weren't perfect, obviously, but he wasn't going to turn down this amazing second chance.

When Hunter saw Riker, he excused himself and crossed the room.

"It seems," Hunter said, "that your son is as stubborn as you are."

Riker peeled his eyes away from the boy. "Why's that?"

"He refuses to sleep anywhere but here. Morena had to pull an old teepee out of storage for him. The biggest problem is he won't leave the lab." Hunter shifted his weight with an awkwardness Riker had never seen from the rock-steady male. "Grant thinks Nicole might be able to persuade Sebastian to get out of here. Seems Bastien trusts her."

"I seem to recall telling you that." Riker smiled. "Looks like she might be useful after all."

"We'll see." Hunter's mouth became a forbidding slash. "I met with the warriors last night—"

"Without me?" Riker broke in.

"You were . . . busy," Hunter said, leaving no doubt that he knew where Riker had been for part of the night. "But we didn't make any decisions without you."

"I'm guessing you discussed what we're going to do about ShadowSpawn?"

Hunter nodded. "We think it'll be best to wait until our deadline to tell ShadowSpawn that Neriya's dead. We can use the time to develop a battle plan."

"We're going to need to outline several strategies. I assume we're going to attempt to negotiate first? With Lucy's life on the line, I don't want to antagonize them with a forceful opening salvo." God, he hoped she was okay and that they were treating her well. Somehow he doubted it.

"Agreed." Hunter's expression said he didn't have high hopes for negotiation. "We have to try. We can't afford a war."

Riker glanced over at Bastien, who was sucking on

a glass of what looked like chocolate milk. Terese had loved the stuff. "Let's meet again this afternoon and storm some brains."

"How's Nicole?" Hunter asked, and hey, it had to mean something that he didn't say her name the way he might say "Ebola" anymore. "Any signs of the turn?"

Riker tried to keep disappointment out of his voice. "She should be in the clear."

"Keep me updated." Hunter gestured to Bastien. "Ditto with him. If you need help, everyone is here for you."

They clasped hands, friendship secured, and then Hunter left Riker with Grant and Bastien.

Riker approached Bastien slowly, letting the boy control their encounter. As Riker got closer to the table Bastien was sitting at with a deck of cards, Bastien gave him a timid smile.

"Hi, Bastien."

"Hi," Bastien said. "It's Riker, right?"

"Yeah." He tapped the back of a chair. "Mind if I sit?"

"No." Bastien looked down at the cards, each of which had an image of an animal or object. "Morena told me to make two piles. One of the images I recognize, and one pile for things I don't know."

One pile was twice as large as the other, but Riker didn't know which was which. "Did the humans teach you things?"

Bastien nodded, still not meeting Riker's gaze. "Every night, I got to watch movies and stuff on the TV across from my kennel. I can read, too. Some of the lab people taught me, but I don't think they were supposed to. They gave me books."

"Like what?"

"I'm halfway through *The Hobbit*." He finally peered through his long, shaggy hair at Riker, although he kept his head down. So like Terese. "Do you have books here?"

"We do. We have an entire chamber dedicated to them."

The boy's crystal eyes lit up. "I—I'd like to see that."

"I can take you."

Man, you'd have thought Riker had offered to beat him instead of show him the library. Bastien shrank back, his skinny fingers trembling over the cards. "That's all right. I like it here."

"How about if Nicole takes you?"

He gave a barely discernible nod. "That might be okay. She'll bring me back here, right?"

"If that's what you want," Riker said, but the dubious expression on Bastien's face said he didn't believe Riker. "Bastien . . . you said you don't know who your father is. Did anyone tell you anything about him at all? Or anything about your mother?"

"They said I look like her."

"You do. Very much." Riker just hoped no one questioned Bastien's dark hair and mocha skin that was a little too tan for someone who had never seen the sun, because neither Riker nor Terese bore that coloring.

The insane breeder male at the lab had.

"How did you know her?" Bastien asked. "You told Nicole about my name."

Now Riker needed to proceed carefully, dole out the information in small doses and see if Bastien would reach the logical conclusion himself. "That's because your mother was my mate, Bastien."

"Oh." He frowned. "Did you serve humans, too?"

"No." Riker used a finger to straighten the largest pile of cards, the one with a rabbit on top. "Humans captured her. They stole her away from me and turned her into a slave. Do you know what a slave is?"

He nodded, but his gaze had turned wary. "They said she liked working for the Martin family. It's an honor to work for humans—"

"No," Riker snapped. "It's not."

Bastien scrambled backward, knocking over his chair and scattering the cards. And for a split second, Riker could have sworn the kid vanished. Then he was there again, crouched in the corner, eyes wild, panting like he'd run a marathon.

"Jesus." Riker swallowed. So much for proceeding carefully. He'd just scared the boy half to death. "I'm sorry, Bastien. I didn't mean to frighten you." He righted the chair and held out his hand, inviting Bastien to come back. "I'm just very angry with the humans."

"Why?" Bastien crept toward the table, but when he sat, he did so a little farther away from Riker than he'd been before.

Riker struggled to keep in mind that Bastien had been raised by humans, had relied on them for his very survival. Like an abused dog that wouldn't run away because it didn't know any better, Bastien hadn't yet realized that the people he'd spent twenty years with were the enemy.

"They've lied to you, son." Riker kept his voice low and level and his hands folded tamely in front of him. "They're a cruel, selfish race that enslaves and abuses animals and people. That's what they did to your mother. That's what they did to you. You should have been born here and raised by vampires who love you instead of being kept in a cage and poked with needles."

Bastien appeared to consider what Riker had said. "Why do you care?"

"Because I made a promise to your mother twenty years ago. I promised that I would raise you and love you. I couldn't raise you, but I can love you." He inhaled deeply and blew out the breath in a rush. "You're my son, Bastien."

"You're my . . . father?"

Riker nodded. Bastien stared, his big eyes swimming in confusion and disbelief.

And then everything went to hell in a handbasket.

The table exploded upward, scattering cards and knocking Riker onto the floor. Bastien disappeared again. *What the fuck?*

"Bastien?" Riker leaped to his feet as Grant ran over. "What happened?"

"I have no idea." Riker swallowed. "Did you see him . . ."

"Disappear?" Grant nodded. "Amazing. Never seen anything like it."

A scuffling sound came from inside the teepee. Very slowly, Riker approached the tent and peeked through the flap. Bastien was huddled against a wooden support, curled into a ball under a blanket.

"Maybe you should go," Grant suggested. "Give him time to get himself together. I'll have him help me around the lab. He listened to everything they said in the Daedalus facility . . . he's got a surprisingly competent grasp of what I do in here, and he's very curious."

Dammit. Riker had, after twenty years, been given an opportunity to make a wrong right, and instead, he'd fucked it up. And what in the ever-living hell was the disappearing-act thing? He'd never even heard of a vampire who could do that.

"Rike?" Grant tapped him on the shoulder. "Anyone home?"

"Yeah." Riker nodded, but the question remained. Had Daedalus done something to Bastien? "Yeah," he repeated. "I'm fine. I'll send Nicole. See if she can get him to the library." Mind churning, he headed toward the door but paused as he reached for the handle. "And Grant? Don't stick him with any needles. He's had enough of that at Daedalus."

Bastien had been through way too much at that horror show, and somehow Riker was going to make it up to him.

The Martins would not destroy Bastien the way they'd destroyed Terese.

FOR THE SEVENTH day in a row, Nicole was sitting in the library with Bastien. She'd only seen Riker once, when he'd come to her chambers to check on Bastien's progress, which, with one exception, had been amazing.

The boy had come out of his shell enough to speak with everyone who spoke to him first, although he was noticeably more reserved with males. He still loved hanging out at the lab, but he eagerly went with Nicole to the library, and Morena had been able to get him to tour the entire compound. He'd been especially interested in the game room, and he seemed to have a particular talent for darts and an unholy love for Xbox games.

The exception to his progress had been Riker.

Bastien hadn't wanted to talk about him, let alone see him. Morena, used to working with children, had made a suggestion that Nicole was going to put to use today. She just hoped Bastien would be open to talk. And that he wouldn't disappear under stress, which, he said, was the only time it happened.

And what a bizarre thing that was. Nicole had never heard of a vampire who could make himself invisible, and no one else Nicole had spoken to had, either. No one but Myne.

There are legends, he'd said. *Legends of the first vampires, who had different gifts from those the rest of us have. Some are rare, like the midwife gift. Others are only alive in stories. Like traveling through portals or turning invisible.*

Looked like that one wasn't a legend, and if *that* didn't stick in her science-minded craw. Riker said that Terese hadn't possessed the ability, and what little they knew about the male who had sired Bastien came only from the files she'd stolen, and they didn't mention a tendency to disappear into thin air.

Daedalus had known about Bastien's talent, though, which explained why they'd kept him for as long as they had. When she'd gone through the files, she'd learned that over the last twenty-two years, the insane breeder vampire had sired thirty offspring with twenty different females, including one child by his own daughter from a previous breeding.

With the exception of Bastien, the children had been raised in human households and were occasionally brought into labs for testing. Two had been "euthanized" and dissected. Apparently, Daedalus had been trying to build a breeding program for years, which would allow them to genetically engineer vampires who would be docile yet efficient in human service.

It would also allow them to breed their own endless supply of test subjects, donors for medical applications, and whatever else their sick minds decided to do with them. No more quotas, no more millions spent to purchase vampires on the legal auction market or to pay poachers to procure wild vampires illegally.

The whole thing nauseated her. How could she have let all of that happen? How could she have taken the reins of a company before she learned the ins and outs of every single project?

You thought you had time. You trusted your parents to found a reputable company, and you trusted your brother to run it until you were ready.

Okay, so maybe all of that was true, and maybe she could actually make herself believe it. But where she really stumbled was the absolutely mind-numbing idea that if she hadn't met Riker, she either wouldn't have learned about all of this or she wouldn't have been as horrified as she was now.

She definitely would have stopped Daedalus, at least to the extent that she could. No doubt the board would have done exactly what they—Chuck, in particular—had already done, by finding an excuse to both discredit and get rid of her.

She felt a tap on her shoulder and looked up to see Bastien join her at the table after his foray into the small library's history section.

"I found a book about vampires and Native Americans," he said. "Morena and Grant told me the first vampires were from Native American tribes."

"It's true," she said. "All of the oldest born vampires have Native American blood running through their veins. MoonBound's chief is full-blooded Cherokee, and Myne is full-blooded Nez Perce."

"Do I have Native American blood?"

Yes, he did. According to his file, the male who sired him was a mix of two of the twelve tribes that had been affected by the virus first: Crow and Nez Perce. But obviously, the truth wasn't an option, at least, not right now. Someday Riker might tell Bastien about his real father, but it definitely wasn't her place to do it.

"I don't know about your mother."

He looked down at the book. "Oh."

"But you know, you can ask Riker about it."

His eyes flew wide open. "I can't." He shook his head. "I don't want to. Don't let him—"

"Hey." She took his hand. "It's okay. You don't have to see him if you don't want to. But he's a really good guy, and he loves you."

"Someone else did, too," he whispered.

"Someone . . . loved you?"

"He said he did."

Nicole's forehead broke out in a fevered sweat. She

had a very, very bad feeling about what was coming next. "What . . . um . . . what did he say to you?"

"He said I look like my mother. He said she was pretty." Bastien's hands clenched into fists. "He said since she was dead and I didn't have any parents, he'd be my father." His fists started to tremble. "He hit me if I didn't tell him I loved him, too. He broke my arm once."

Nicole struggled to keep from hyperventilating. She wanted to scream. To cry. To burn down the lab again, but this time with Bastien's abuser inside it.

Unless his abuser was already dead. Chuck had said Roland was involved with the breeding program. Suddenly, she was glad Myne had killed him.

"Listen to me, Bastien," she said, concentrating on keeping her voice calm. "Good fathers don't beat their children. Riker would *never* harm you. I promise. He's thoughtful, honorable, and loyal . . . and he loves you." Bastien didn't look convinced, so she tried again. "Do you trust me?"

Bastien leaned across the table, the slightest quirk on his lips. "Just because I trust you doesn't mean I trust your judgment."

She laughed, surprised by his common sense and candor. This was a strong, smart kid, and she had a feeling that with the help of the clan, he'd be healthy, mentally and physically, very soon.

"Busted," she said. "But you'll see for yourself that I'm right. Will you at least give him a chance?"

Cocking his head, Bastien studied her. "Do you love him? My father?"

The question caught her off guard. She looked up at

the ceiling, trying to marshal her thoughts and emotions, but she might as well have been herding cats. What it came down to was that she'd grown close to Riker, and she'd do anything to protect him. She wanted to heal his wounds, help him deal with his losses, and somehow make up to him what her family had done not only to Riker, Terese, and Bastien but to his entire clan.

Then there was the insane physical draw between them, the erotic pulse that throbbed in the air whenever he was near. When he wasn't around, there was a distinct emptiness in her chest and a flutter in her belly when she thought of him. She'd never felt this way before.

Did that mean she loved him?

"I guess I do," she finally said, and the most amazing sense of liberation practically lifted her out of her chair.

All this time, she'd been lost in both the human world and the vampire one, unsure of her future and, at times, unsure of her survival. And while she was between those worlds, she didn't feel stuck anymore. She was a human among vampires, but she felt far less alone than she had as a human among humans.

Bastien gave a decisive nod. "Then I'll give him a chance."

Grinning, Nicole leaned over and pulled Bastien into a big, squishy hug. "You'll love him. You'll see."

For a long moment, Bastien remained rigid in her arms, so stiff she wasn't sure if he breathed. But as she stroked his hair and just held him, he relaxed, and his arms went around her. She smiled when he snuggled closer, burying his forehead against her neck.

"Nicole?" His voice was tentative, barely audible.

"Yes?"

"He won't hurt me again, will he?" he whispered. "Chuck can't find me here, right?"

Nicole's heart stopped. *Chuck?* Dear God, it was Chuck who had beaten the boy? With all the strength she could muster, she found her voice.

"No," she croaked. "He can't. I promise."

NICOLE." RIKER'S HEART jackhammered in his chest at the sight of her outside his door.

He allowed himself the luxury of a slow visual ride down her body, taking in the worn jeans that hugged her softly rounded hips, the fluffy green sweater that matched her eyes and outlined her perfect breasts. She'd slicked her hair back in a barrette, and his fingers twitched with the desire to let her hair down and make it messy.

"I'm sorry I haven't been around much." He gestured for her to enter. "We're working twenty-four/seven on the ShadowSpawn problem."

He'd spent three full days on the edges of their territory with the clan's mystic-keeper, Sabre, while they set new wards and traps. ShadowSpawn would have their own mystic-keeper to identify and neutralize their setups, but they'd be slowed, and they'd take injuries.

Nicole stepped inside, bringing her fresh pear-ginger scent with her. "Have you come up with any solutions?"

"No." He didn't even wait for the door to shut before he gathered her against him and nuzzled her throat. He'd missed this. It had been far too long since they'd had a private moment together. "How's Bastien?" It had been killing Riker to not visit the boy, although he'd spied on him from afar when he could.

"He's doing great," she said. "He's so curious. He'll read anything you put in front of him, and he's trying really hard to help Grant in the lab. He's even in his own quarters now. And Myne's been working out with him in the training room."

Riker had wanted to be the one teaching Bastien about vampire life, about being a warrior, and a twinge of jealousy shot through him even though he'd asked for Myne's assistance. Riker had also had to suck it up and apologize to Myne for his behavior the night of the full moon, but like the male he was, Myne had shrugged it off with no more than a clasp of hands and a pat on the back.

"Does he seem happy?"

"Mostly," she said. "But he needs a father."

Riker's chest cramped. "I wish I knew how to be there for him." Immediately, he sensed a change in Nicole, and when she pulled away, he went on alert. "What is it?"

A shiver wracked her, but he wasn't sure how that was possible, because it suddenly felt like it was a million degrees in the room. "I know why he freaked out when you told him you were his father."

"I'm listening."

She shifted her weight. Glanced around the room. Stalled until he was ready to shake the words out of her. But as impatient as he was to hear what she had to say, he owed her a lifetime of patience. She had been instrumental in bringing Bastien out of his shell. Hell, if not for her, Bastien wouldn't be here in the first place.

"I'm not even sure where to start," she finally said.

He brushed his knuckles over her silky cheek. "Take your time." *But, you know, hurry.*

"Promise me you'll stay calm," she said, and shit, this couldn't be good, but he inclined his head in solemn agreement. "Okay." She inhaled and exhaled. Did it again. "When I was little, Chuck hung out with me a lot. I thought it was because he loved me and wanted to spend time with me. Now when I think back, I realize he was usually only around when Terese was there. When she wasn't there, he always asked about her. I figured he asked because he was uncomfortable around vampires. He didn't grow up with them the way I did."

The mere mention of Chuck made Riker's teeth clench. "Go on."

"Remember in the lab when he got so angry when he talked about you killing Terese?" All Riker could do was nod. "I think it's because he was obsessed with her. Maybe even in love with her."

Riker's skin grew clammy, and he felt sick to his stomach. "If this is some sort of joke . . ."

"It's not." She shifted her weight again, fidgeted with her hair, swallowed repeatedly. And she kept looking at the papers on his desk. Origami withdrawals, he was sure. "I think he transferred his obsession to Bastien. Chuck told him he'd be like a father to him, but when Bastien didn't return his feelings the way

Chuck probably thought he should, he beat him." She closed her eyes. "I asked Grant to look him over, and he found a number of healed injuries, including some broken bones."

Nicole's revelation hit Riker with the force of an avalanche, literally knocking him back a step. A black, indescribable rage carved out his chest, turning it into a fathomless cavern of frost. Even his heart, which had been beating obsessively fast for Nicole, seemed to have iced over.

"Riker?" Nicole reached out, but he dodged her touch, not ready to be consoled by the sister of the bastard who had tortured an innocent boy. "I convinced Bastien that you weren't a . . . father . . . like that. I told him he could trust you and that you'd never hurt him. Please don't go to him like this. He's timid around males as it is, and he associates the word *father* with what Chuck did to him."

Father. The word he'd always wanted to hear a child call him was now associated with terror and pain. Just when he thought the Martins couldn't fuck with his life any more . . .

He concentrated on breathing. Breathing was good. It would keep him from bolting out of headquarters and leaving the entire city of Seattle bleeding behind him as he tore the city apart in the search for Nicole's brother.

Inhale. Exhale. Inhale. Exhale.

He had to see Bastien. He glanced at Nicole, which should have comforted him, but right now, all he saw was a Martin.

"I need to go." His voice was utterly shredded.

He didn't even sound like himself. Fitting, he supposed, because right now, he didn't feel like himself, either.

Nicole held out her hand to him. "Can we talk about this?"

Dismissing her offer, he went to the door. "Later," he said, although deep down, he suspected that what he really meant was *never*.

RIKER SEARCHED THE compound for Bastien, using the time to calm down. By the time he decided to check Bastien's room, his desire to level Seattle had eased enough that he'd settle for only killing everyone Charles Martin had ever known. Then he'd spend a year breaking the man, piece by piece.

He forced himself to walk slowly up to Bastien's door. The boy was skittish as it was; if he sensed Riker's anger, every bit of progress Bastien had made could be reversed.

Bastien's door opened as he approached, and Morena emerged, her curly brown hair piled on top of her head in a messy knot.

"Good to see you," she said. "Bastien just had breakfast. Myne should be coming by in a little while to take him to the training room." She smiled. "He's going to teach him to shoot a crossbow today."

If that wasn't a punch to the gut. Yes, Riker had asked Myne to engage Bastien with physical activity, but Riker should be the one to do it. He should be teaching his son to shoot and fight and hunt. "Thanks, Morena."

He knocked lightly and entered. Bastien was curled

up on the couch with his nose in a book, but when he saw Riker, he froze.

"Hey," Riker said. "Do you mind if I come in?"

There was a heartbeat of hesitation and then a shy "Okay."

"I brought you something." He moved to Bastien, going slowly, slowing even more when the boy tensed. Riker silently cursed Chuck to an eternity in hell. And Riker planned to send him there.

"You're angry." Bastien inched toward the far end of the couch, and Riker's throat constricted with disappointment and self-loathing.

"I'm sorry, son," Riker said. "I'm not angry with you. I'm angry about what happened to you. You never should have grown up the way you did." He paused. "Do you want me to leave?"

Several agonizing seconds later, Bastien shook his head. Relief practically made Riker light-headed. He crouched next to the couch and held out Terese's ring.

"This was your mother's. Nicole kept it safe for a long time, and I think you should have it."

Bastien took it as if it were made of the most delicate glass. "What was she like?"

"She was beautiful." Riker smiled, recalling her fine features. "She was very quiet and shy, even with me."

"You were the wild vampire who killed her, weren't you?" Bastien asked, and Riker broke out in an *oh, shit* sweat. "Chuck said that if Nicole hadn't raised the alarm that day, you would have killed everyone."

Wait . . . Nicole? The crystal-clear recollection of that day shattered into a million pieces, each shard of memory sharper than the next. He'd been on the verge of talking Terese out of her suicide attempt when the siren went off, and she'd plunged the blade into her throat.

Nicole had been responsible for the alert?

The world fell away as his rage from earlier roared back, and Bastien, who was apparently as sensitive to negativity as his mother, shrank into the couch cushions.

Get it together, dumbass. Riker cursed silently and forced himself to relax.

"I swear I didn't kill her, Bastien. Humans killed her." Now wasn't the time to tell the boy that she'd killed herself. Hell, there might never be a time or need to tell him that. "They drove her to her death. You can't believe anything they said to you."

Very precisely, Bastien placed a bookmark in his book and set it aside. "But Nicole is human."

"And it was her family who killed your mother and who kept you in a cage for twenty years." He probably shouldn't have said that, but at least he'd said it very calmly. Progress.

Bastien frowned. "Then why is she here?"

Well, shit. Riker had stepped in that one, hadn't he? He didn't want to vilify Nicole, and he certainly didn't want to destroy her relationship with Bastien. No matter what her family had done to him, she'd helped the boy more than anyone else. More important, Bastien was still working on trusting his instincts and trusting people. He trusted and cared about Nicole, and to make him second-guess his own judgment could be damaging.

"We needed her help to rescue a vampire her company kidnapped," Riker said.

"Did you rescue the vampire?"

"Unfortunately, no."

"But Nicole helped, right?" There was so much hope in Bastien's voice that Riker had to smile.

"She helped a lot."

Bastien smoothed his thumb over the ring's smooth surface. "She loves you."

"Well, I wouldn't say *that*, but she might like me sometimes."

"*She* said that," Bastien insisted.

Riker's gut plunged to his feet. *Love?* Nicole had told Bastien that she loved Riker? Bastien must have misunderstood. Surely Nicole wouldn't do that to him, wouldn't expect him to give himself to not only a human but a Martin.

The door swung open, saving Riker from thoughts he wasn't ready to explore. Myne strode in, ready to hit the gym in sweats and a T-shirt that was stretched to the limits on his muscular upper body. The duffel in his hand had a crossbow handle poking out the unzipped top.

"Hey, man," he said to Riker before turning his attention to Bastien. "You ready to put on some muscle and then blow a few holes through some melons?"

"Ready." Bastien's shy smile reminded Riker so much of Terese that fresh anger reared its ugly head again.

Myne, always on top of things, gestured to the duffel. "Rike, you wanna come?"

As tempting as it was, Riker sensed that he'd done enough with Bastien for now. Time to let the boy absorb the visit and end it on a good note.

"Thanks, but I need to see Hunter." Riker came to his feet and shot Bastien a wink. "I'll see you later, okay? Have you ever had a root-beer float?"

Bastien shook his head.

"Ah, dude," Myne said, "you're in for a treat. Riker makes the best root-beer floats ever."

"Really?" Bastien asked.

Myne nodded. "Really."

Riker had never made Myne a root-beer float, and seriously, how did anyone screw one up? But he appreciated the male's help.

"I'll come get you later, Bastien," Riker promised. "I'll show you how to get in and out of the kitchen without Syrena the Wooden Spoon Tyrant catching you."

Bastien's grin spread from ear to ear, and for the first time, Riker felt like he had a chance to truly be a parent. To live the life Terese had been denied.

NICOLE SPENT TWO hours making origami animals and pacing around Riker's quarters, waiting for him to come back. He'd been so angry and distraught when he left, and God, she hoped he was okay. One thing was for sure, she wasn't leaving until he came back.

She wandered into his bedroom for the eighth time today, but there were no new pictures on the wall or trinkets on his bare dresser since the last time she came in. Well, his dresser *used* to be bare. Now it was home to a menagerie of paper animals and one paper vampire . . . her first. Taking the little vampire in her hand, she sank down on the bed, wishing he'd come back. Wishing he'd climb onto the bed with her and relax. Or ravish her.

She'd take either.

What she really needed right now, though, was a purpose. And a future. She flopped back onto a pillow and stared at the ceiling. At this point, she was certain she wasn't going to turn into a vampire, so the challenge became a question of how she fit in at MoonBound.

For the most part, the clan members had warmed up to her, and some, like Grant, treated her like she was no longer an outsider but a colleague. She especially liked that she'd *earned* some respect here, rather than it being given by Daedalus personnel simply because of who she was.

Maybe she could work with Grant in the lab. She'd spent her entire adult life working to make human life better. Could she not do the same for vampires? At least, she could until her disease progressed to the point where she could no longer function. Or until she ran out of meds.

She heard the front door open, and she clutched the paper vampire harder, her pulse picking up with excitement. "I made you something," she called out.

Riker's boots struck the floor with heavy thuds, and then he was in the doorway, his expression as dark and stormy as she'd ever seen it.

"Get out."

She sat up, baffled by his anger. "Excuse me?"

"Out." His guttural voice was as deep as thunder and just as loud. "Out of the bedroom." He stalked over to pull her off the bed, and then he escorted her into the living room. "I told you it was off-limits. You are never to go in there, do you understand?"

She blinked, startled by his behavior. "No, I don't understand. What is your problem?"

"Nothing." He yanked open the fridge. "Just stay out of there."

The image of him with Benet came back to her, of him holding her against the wall. The *living-room* wall. He'd said he hadn't been with any female since Terese died. So . . . he hadn't had a woman in the bedroom, had he?

"The bedroom reminds you of Terese, doesn't it?"

Shrugging, he peered into the fridge. "Want a beer?"

A beer? He'd dragged her out of the bedroom like she was contaminating it with her presence, and now he wanted to play polite host?

"No, thank you." She tapped her foot on the wooden floorboards. "Are you going to answer the question?"

"No."

"Dammit, Riker. You owe me that, at least."

"Fine." He reached for a bottle from a local microbrewery. "Yeah. That's the only place we ever had sex. She was extremely vanilla and conservative. She didn't let me go down on her or fuck her up against a wall like you did. Is that what you wanted to hear?"

Heat infused Nicole's cheeks at both the memories and the crude reply he'd made sound like an insult, and she had to clear her throat before she spoke.

"Okay, so what are you saying? We can have sex but only on your couch? Or against your wall? Maybe on your kitchen table?"

He fisted the bottle and popped off the cap with a violent twist of his wrist. He still wasn't facing her. That fridge must be extremely interesting.

"I'm saying you've outdone her in every way possible. Sex, strength, brains. Hell, you've even made sure her son cares about you. And now you want to take her bedroom, too?"

"What?" Nicole felt like she'd crossed into the twilight zone. "Where is this coming from?" When he didn't answer, she laid it out for him, plain as day, because hell if she was going to be his punching bag for whatever had triggered his asshole switch. "Your mate is gone, Riker."

He rounded on her, his lip curled into a sneer. "You think I don't know that?"

"Apparently, you don't," she shot back. "It's been twenty years. You need to let her go."

"Since when did you become the expert on dead mates?"

Maybe she should have taken that beer. "I'm not an expert on that, but I know what it's like to lose someone you loved." She stepped closer to him, instinctively wanting to comfort him somehow. "And I promise, life is so much better when you decide it's time to move on and forgive yourself."

"I can't." He took a swig from the bottle. "I won't, and you have no right to ask me to forget her. She was a part of my life that I won't get back."

Stubborn man. "I'm not asking you to forget her or even to replace her. I'm asking you to move on." *Move on with me.*

"You ask too much," he snapped.

Her chest constricted painfully. Yes, she was human, a human who hadn't even figured out her own place in the world yet, but the one thing she did know was that she wanted to find that place with Riker. She'd hoped he'd want to take that journey with her, but now doubt hung like a black cloud over her head.

She stared at him, searching for a crack in the hard shell he'd put up around himself for no reason she could discern. But there was nothing to find. Maybe she'd contaminated more than just his bedroom. Maybe she'd fouled his world, too.

"I guess there's nothing left to say." Hoping he couldn't sense how much she was hurting, she turned to leave.

Riker cursed, and in a heartbeat, she found herself pushed up against the door, his hands on her shoulders.

"You aren't leaving," he growled. Funny, not long ago she'd have been frightened out of her skull by his fierceness, but now she knew he wouldn't harm her. At least, not physically.

"Yes, I am," she said, meeting his hard stare with one of her own. "You can't have us both, Riker. I won't be the other woman."

His hand slipped around to the back of her neck in a gentle yet possessive grip she wished she could believe he meant. "You're not."

Anger flared, bright and hot. "Then what am I? A stand-in? A consolation prize?" Her eyes started to burn, and she prayed she wouldn't cry. She needed to be strong. Stronger than she'd ever been, perhaps. "Maybe it's selfish of me, but I need to be number one. I won't take a backseat to a mate who left you."

His upper lip curled, baring his fangs. "She didn't leave me. She died."

"She killed herself!" she shouted, desperate to get her point across. "She made a choice to leave you."

Riker recoiled at Nicole's harsh words, but she couldn't let herself regret saying them. God help her, she wasn't judging Terese, couldn't imagine what the poor female had gone through. But Riker needed to let go of his guilt over how she'd lived and forgive himself for her death.

"Your family killed her!" he yelled back. He pushed away and, in a great sweep of his arm, sent the bottle of beer flying across the room and crashing into the wall. "Your family drove her to it. They *raped* and *murdered* her, and then they took an innocent child and abused him, too." He jabbed his finger at her, and his voice went low, dark, like something straight out of hell. "And if you hadn't raised the alarm that day—"

The pain in her chest became a searing agony. How had he found out about that? "And that's what it comes down to, doesn't it?" she croaked. "No matter what I do, you'll never get past what my family did, and you'll never forgive me for being born a Martin."

Not that he didn't have reason to hate her family. Hell, *she* had reason. But she wasn't a part of that family anymore, and if Riker couldn't see that, there was nothing she could do to change his mind.

"I'm sorry for everything that's happened to you, Terese, and Bastien. I'm sorry for everything Daedalus has done to your entire race, and I wish I could do more." She opened the door. "I don't know what Hunter has planned for my future, but I hope you'll stand up for me. I like it here, and I think I can contribute to the clan."

She got out of there as fast as she could, and she wasn't at all surprised that Riker didn't come after her.

SON OF A bitch!

Riker banged his head against the door and stood

there, forehead to the wood, hand on the doorknob. What was wrong with him?

He shoved away from the door and stared at the broken glass scattered around his quarters. *Shit.* He'd never had a hair trigger, had prided himself on his control. But ever since he met Nicole, his emotions had been erratic, and he couldn't seem to get it together. He thought he could deal with Nicole's family background, but Bastien's revelation that Nicole had been the one to raise the alarm that ended in Terese's death was the tipping point.

And then he'd come home to find her in the bedroom. Terese had been the only female ever in the room, and having Nicole there felt like a betrayal. How could Nicole ask him to move on, and not only move on but do it with the very person responsible for Terese's death?

Logically, he knew it was stupid to blame Nicole for everything her family had done. But dammit, he'd wanted to strike back at the Martins for so long, and now one of them was right here . . . and he'd slept with her. He'd kissed her, fed from her, and been intimate with her.

The one person on the planet he should have stayed as far away from as possible.

A crumpled wad of paper lay on the floor near the door. He swiped it up, and his heart jerked violently when he realized what it was.

I made you something. Nicole had called to him from the bedroom, her singsong voice so full of eagerness. She'd fashioned an origami vampire for him as a gift.

And he'd not only dashed her happiness, which he knew she'd had far too little of, but he'd compounded his idiocy by once again blaming her for everything bad under the sun.

You fucking asshole. You took the best thing that's happened to you in years and turned it into a bag of dicks.

He had to make it up to her. He had to pull his head out of his ass and make things right.

Riker started after her, but as he reached for the doorknob, his phone beeped, an urgent text from Hunter.

ShadowSpawn knows Neriya is dead. They're on their way with a war party.

Riker hit the hallway at a dead run. He didn't think his boots even hit the floor as he charged to Hunter's chamber, where the other senior warriors were gathering, along with the two dozen lieutenants who operated under them. Hunter was standing at the head of the oblong table, his posture unyielding, his expression grave.

"Sit," Hunter commanded as soon as the last senior, Baddon, entered. "Where's Myne?" He shot a pointed look at Riker, and Riker gave him the usual response.

"He's with Bastien. If he got your text, he'll be here as soon as he can." Myne had a tendency to ignore Hunter, but even he wouldn't shrug this off.

Hunter remained standing while everyone else took a seat. "As I said in my message, ShadowSpawn is on the way. One of our scouting parties spotted them before being engaged by ShadowSpawn forward scouts. They killed Wolfgang, and Tena barely made it back. She's in the infirmary, but her injuries are serious. Grant's doing all he can."

The fuckers had killed Wolf? *Shit.* The warrior had been one of their best archers, and his loss would be felt for a long time. Tena wasn't a physically powerful fighter, but she was wiry and fast, with an uncanny ability to navigate tree branches like a lemur. The two of them had partnered for patrols for three years, and while they hadn't been romantically involved, they'd been close. Tena was going to be devastated by Wolfgang's death.

"Send Nicole to help Grant," Riker said. "Her knowledge of our physiology could be an asset."

Hunter jerked his head at Takis, who was seated next to his partner, Aiden. "Message Grant with Riker's suggestion." As Takis whipped out his cell from his jacket pocket, Hunter addressed the room once more. "Before Tena passed out, she said one of the ShadowSpawn warriors taunted her with the coming deaths or capture of our entire clan as punishment for letting Neriya die."

"Wait," Riker cut in. "How did they know about Neriya?"

"That's what I want to know," Hunter growled. "They either have a friend inside Daedalus, which seems unlikely, or they have a friend inside MoonBound." He raked his gaze over each warrior. "If the spy is within our clan, his head will grace the center of our table for a year and a day, and his body will be fed to the animals."

Everyone nodded. If anything, Hunter's punishment for a traitor sounded light.

"What about Lucy?" Riker asked. "Is she with the war party?"

"Unknown," Hunter replied. "But what *is* known is that we're out of time. We all put up dozens of options for how to deal with ShadowSpawn, but we're down to the wire. We have to arm everyone of fighting age and get the children to our secondary location."

"If we have a member sympathetic to ShadowSpawn, they could know where our secondary location is," Riker said. "Hell, they could have an ambush waiting there."

"If you have a better idea, I'm all ears."

Aiden stood. "I have an idea. We fight to the end. We can't let them take any of us alive, or they'll make slavery in a human household look like a vacation."

An uncomfortable silence fell as the reality of the situation sank in. Yes, they would fight. And they might even believe they could win. But even if they did win, it would inevitably cost them lives. So much death and blood between vampire clans when it should be the humans they were battling.

Takis tugged Aiden's arm until he sat. "We can send the children and those who can't fight on the run. Even if the location of our vehicles is compromised by a spy, they can flee—"

"To where?" Jaggar said. "The forest is full of hunters and VAST, and even if they get past the humans, they'll be out in the open until they can make it to a friendly clan."

"And there's no guarantee any clan will take them in," Hunter said, echoing Riker's thoughts. Any of the plans they'd come up with over the last few days would have at least given them a chance, no matter how minute. But if the clan had been compromised, all bets were off.

Katina cursed. "We should never have borrowed Neriya. Things were already tense between our clans. This was the excuse they needed to engage us."

Tense was an understatement. Riker's mating to Terese had been the spark that ignited the smoldering fire. And once again, because of him, because he'd failed to save Neriya, another spark had started a firestorm.

This was his fault. He'd been so full of anger since the day he'd turned into a vampire that nothing mattered but sticking it to the enemy. Any enemy, human or vampire. He'd been reckless with not only his life but the lives of everyone around him. Nicole had said something similar, and she'd been right.

And now, MoonBound was going to end up like the clan depicted in the bloody battle scene in the painting behind Hunter. Extinct.

Riker inhaled sharply as a thought whacked him upside the head. If he'd started all of this, he could end it.

Hunter turned to Riker. "What is it?"

Damn him. How did he do that? "I know how to end this. It sucks, but it's probably the only shot we have to prevent war." He stood, meeting his chief's steady gaze with one of his own. "Kars has been gunning for me since the day I mated Terese and humiliated him. I'll offer my life as payment for Neriya's."

The room exploded in curses and "Screw that"s and "No way"s. Only Hunter kept silent, and Riker knew the male was searching his brain for a counterargument.

But Riker knew there wasn't one. Hunter had to know that, too.

"And if Kars doesn't take you in trade?"

"He will."

"You do this," Baddon said, his voice as bleak as a graveyard at midnight, "and you're a dead man."

"If I don't do this, then we're all dead." Riker turned back to Hunter. "I'm going to need your word that Bastien will be taken care of."

"Of course," Hunter said.

"And no one harms Nicole." He locked his sights on every warrior in the room, one by one. "You will all treat her like a clan mate. Can I count on you?"

Everyone nodded. Including Hunter.

"Then let's get this over with."

Jaggar grabbed his arm. "There's got to be another way."

Riker clapped Jag on the shoulder. "If there is, you can get me out of there. I'll try to stay alive until you do."

"That's not funny, man," Baddon growled. "Not fucking funny."

All eyes latched onto Riker, and too many of them were red-rimmed. A few guys were shaking their heads, cursing. He had to get out of here.

"Let's rethink—"

Riker cut Hunter off. "I'm ready. Alpha Mike Foxtrot." *Adios, Mother Fuckers*, as his sniper buddies used to say. Said to friends, it meant good luck, but Riker figured his luck had run out. Best to go before anyone got sappy.

Which was why there was no way Riker could say good-bye to anyone, let alone Bastien and Nicole. He liked to think he was strong, but if one or both of them asked him to stay, he'd lose it. He'd fucking *lose* it. And if he'd learned anything in his life, it was that the last time you saw someone, you didn't want it to be ugly. Better that Bastien remembered Riker as trying to put together a relationship with him. Nicole . . . she'd remember him angry and being an asshole.

But it was far better than remembering him as an emotionally compromised male who ignored her pleas to stay.

Or worse, for him to remember her telling him to go.

WHAT IN THE hell was going on? Nicole had stepped out of her chambers to visit Bastien and had nearly been flattened by a group of males and females charging through the hall. The guard at her door was gone, but Katina skidded around a corner, her silver eyes bloodshot and rimmed with red.

"Come on," Katina shouted as she ran past. "Bastien is already in the lab."

"What's happening?"

"We're getting children and . . . ah . . . humans to safety."

"Safety?"

"ShadowSpawn is coming."

Oh, God. She let Katina guide her to Grant's lab, where children and a few adults with obvious injuries or illnesses that would prevent them from fighting had gathered. Bastien appeared to be occupied by something under a microscope, and Morena was pacing nervously around the lab, practically wringing her hands.

Grant looked up from the pallet in the corner, where he was smoothing ointment on a badly wounded female. He uttered a few whispered words to the injured vampire and then hurried over to join them.

"I want to go," he said. "I can fight."

"Sorry, man." Katina threw one booted foot up on a chair and tugged the laces tight. It didn't escape Nicole's notice that Katina's hands trembled. "We need you to take everyone to safety."

"Do I look like a babysitter?" Grant made a sweeping gesture at the lab equipment. "Maybe I can give the kids flasks of acid and Petri dishes of bacteria to play with?"

"Are you deranged?" Katina straightened. "I'd save those for snacks."

"Funny," Grant muttered.

"You're the closest thing we have to a doctor," Katina said. "Hunter needs you here. Nicole, too."

At the invocation of Hunter's name, Grant cursed but stopped arguing. "Are we going to the alternate site?"

Katina shook her head. "It's possible the site has been compromised. Plan B."

"Hide everyone in the secret passage? That'll be comfortable."

"You don't have to go yet. Not until you know the compound has been breached." Katina touched her finger to the hilt of the dagger at her hip. "We hope it won't come to that. If Riker's plan works, we'll be spared."

At the mention of Riker, Nicole's heart skipped a beat. Apparently, it hadn't gotten the same message her brain did, that he didn't want anything to do with any part of her body. "Riker's plan?"

"He's giving himself up in exchange for Lucy and as payment for Neriya's death."

Nicole couldn't speak. She could barely breathe. Riker was giving himself up? "He can't. They'll kill him!"

"Probably."

"He can't do that. Did anyone try to talk him out of it?"

Frustration and sadness drifted from Katina . . . and wait, how did Nicole sense that? But it wasn't so much a feeling as it was a smell. Like burning sugar and stagnant water.

Nicole sniffed the air, taking in other odors, most of them identifiable as both specific fragrances and emotions. Had she been living in such close proximity to vampires that she'd learned to read them by scent? It was a question for Grant but later. Like when they weren't on the brink of war.

"Trust me," Katina said softly, "none of us are happy about this. Riker is one of our best fighters, worth any two of most of us. We'll work on a way to get him back, but right now, this is all we have."

"What, you'll work on getting his *body* back?" Nicole's harsh words weren't fair, and she knew it. Katina wasn't responsible for any of this, but dammit, Nicole had hoped that they could talk after Riker cooled off from their fight.

No, she didn't see a future for them, not if he couldn't let go of his anger and guilt over Terese's death and her family's role in it. But Nicole wanted to be in Bastien's life, to make amends for her family's sins, which meant that she and Riker would have to learn to work together.

And she couldn't deny her love for Riker. No matter how he felt about her, she didn't want him to die.

"We're going to do everything we can to get him back alive. I swear." Bastien looked over and waved, and Katina lowered her voice. "It's probably best to not let Bastien know what's going on."

"Of course."

"You're cool for a human," Katina said solemnly. "And don't worry. Riker made sure we would treat you like any other clan member for as long as you're with us."

Nicole's mouth went dry. He'd done what she'd asked and made sure she was safe.

"For the record," Katina added, "it wasn't a hard sell. We appreciate the help you've been to Grant and Bastien, and we're grateful for how you tried to rescue Neriya." She pivoted toward the door.

Nicole's mind raced. She had to stop Riker from doing this. But how?

First things first. She had to get to him. "Grant." The vampire looked over at her from where he was trying to comfort a mother holding a newborn infant. The one Neriya had delivered before she was taken, perhaps? "I'm going to grab something from my quarters," she lied. "I'll be back in a little while."

She doubted he believed her, but, overwhelmed with a lab full of people, he didn't bother arguing. "The secret passage is behind the back wall in the chem closet." He pointed to the door on the far side of the lab. "If you tip the bottle marked *fermented guano*, the wall will slide open."

"Fermented guano?"

He shrugged. "I figured no one would randomly pick up anything they thought was full of superstinky bat shit."

Crazy smart thinking . . . exactly what she'd expect from a mad scientist.

"I'll be back in a little while." She hurried over to Bastien, who was now pacing in front of the wash station. "How are you doing?"

Bastien swallowed. "Too many people."

She looked up at him, thinking he'd grown since he arrived. He seemed a little taller. He'd definitely put on some weight. "It's okay to be afraid, you know that, right?"

"I'm not afraid," he said. "But I don't know what to do." He thrust his hands into his jeans pockets. "Where's my . . . um . . . Riker?"

Ah, damn. She should have seen that question coming. "I'm not sure," she said, and that, at least, was the truth. "But I promise he's doing everything in his power to keep you and the entire clan safe." She glanced over at the group of people milling nervously about. "And do you know what you can do? See all those kids? I'll bet that if you take them your picture cards, they'll love to guess the shapes. And I'm sure they'd love it even more if you read them a book."

Bastien's eyes grew bright. "Really?"

"Yep. That would help Grant a lot."

Grinning, he swiped the deck of cards off the table. And then, in a surprising move, he hugged her. It was a fleeting embrace, and he blushed shyly as he broke it off, but it was nice to see him getting comfortable enough to show affection. He'd come a long way in just a few days.

She waited until he was too busy with the kids to notice her exit, and then she hurried to her chamber, grabbed a coat someone had loaned to her until the clan placed its next supply order with their human contact, and went in search of a way out of headquarters. She just hoped no one would stop her, and fortunately, everyone was too focused on the coming danger to pay attention.

She fell in behind a group of young males who were so preoccupied with anxious boasting about how badass they were going to be in battle that they didn't notice—or care—that she was following. Apparently, vampire youths were as full of swagger as human teens.

The group moved swiftly through the forest, and she had to struggle to keep up.

She knew the moment they got close to the front line. The forest animals became silent, and raised voices vibrated the very branches on the trees. Tension hung heavy in the air, an invisible fog that seemed to squeeze the breath from her lungs. As she topped a ridge, she came upon MoonBound's warriors, and between them in a clearing, in perhaps a fifty-yard span, were easily three times as many ShadowSpawn fighters.

Where was Riker?

She pushed desperately through the forest of vampires and weapons toward the front of the crowd. Hunter's angry voice rose above the others, followed by another equally loud voice, and she wondered if he was talking with the other clan's leader. She was almost at the front when a hand came down on her wrist and yanked her aside.

"Don't." Myne's voice was a low growl in her ear. "You'll only make it worse for him."

She opened her mouth to ask what he was talking about, when two people shifted, creating a gap through which she saw what Myne was trying to hide from her.

Riker was kneeling with his head bowed in front of a massive ShadowSpawn male carrying a bloodstained club, wrists bound behind his back, a chain looped around his neck, and blood streaming down his face.

"No," she croaked. "No."

Riker lifted his head, and her heart stopped. Had he heard her? The two vampires closed the gap. She struggled against Myne's grip, but she might as well have been as chained as Riker. Myne held her against his big body, his hold bruisingly firm.

She heard a noise, the sickening thud of something hard and blunt striking flesh. A chorus of angry growls and curses stirred through MoonBound's ranks. Myne's bloodcurdling snarl drowned them all out.

"What's going on?"

Myne held her tight, ignoring her, as a new sound rose up, as if a herd of horses was circling. Standing on her toes, she looked out at the enemy, who were doing exactly what it sounded like. The entire clan was surrounding MoonBound.

Suddenly, the enemy disappeared, melting into the forest. The last thing she saw was Riker, being dragged by his feet into the brush.

"*Riker!*" Her hoarse cry was cut short by Myne's hand over her mouth. She kicked, screamed deep in her throat, beat at him with her fists, but he only held her more securely against him to quell her struggles.

"He's gone." Myne's shredded voice sounded like it had been dragged over sharp stones with Riker.

"We have to do something. We have to—"

"There's nothing you can do." Myne released her, but he hovered close, prepared to grab her again. "But I'm going to make those fuckers pay, Nicole. I promise."

Rage, unlike anything Nicole had ever felt before, welled up. She'd spent her entire life drifting, passionate about the scientific field she'd chosen but knowing she'd be forced into a company position she didn't want. Since being captured by Riker, she'd learned to hate that company, to wish for its destruction.

But now she wasn't going to let her entire life go to waste. Daedalus was going to do something good for once.

Daedalus was going to save Riker's life.

NICOLE DIDN'T SLEEP at all that night.

She'd fought Myne until exhaustion left her so numb and worn out that by the time they made it back to clan headquarters, she could barely think, let alone move. She'd let one of the females, Alina, take her to her room, where a pounding headache and nausea joined the exhaustion as she pored over the files she'd stolen from Daedalus. Surely she'd find *something* to take to ShadowSpawn, perhaps information on where to find clan members snatched by the company.

So far, nothing.

She'd come across a lot of fascinating research but nothing of potential use in getting Riker back.

At six A.M., as she was fighting to keep her blurry eyes open, a thumb drive fell out of one of the files. Hoping the walk to the lab would help wake her, she shuffled down desolate halls that should be bustling with vampires coming in from night hunts. Instead, there was only silence. The clan had been spared a horrific battle, but Riker's loss had hit them hard.

It had hit *her* hard.

Spurred on by renewed desperation, she sprinted the rest of the way to the lab, where she found Grant entering data into a computer.

"You look like shit." He peered at her from over the computer screen as she took a seat in front of the laptop across the table from him. "Are you okay?"

No, she wasn't. And she wouldn't be until Riker was back. "I'm fine." She jacked the thumb drive into the computer.

"You sound like shit, too," Grant added. So helpful. "Did you get any sleep?"

Several dozen files popped up on her screen. "Slept like a baby."

The files all appeared to be related to the breeding program. She steeled herself for a lot of disturbing data.

Grant's chair squeaked as he started to stand. "I'll get you some coffee."

"Thanks," she muttered, "but my stomach isn't playing nice today." As if to bring her words home, a wave of nausea hit her hard enough to make her sway.

Grant scowled at her. "Have you eaten?"

"I don't think I can." Was she coming down with

something? She couldn't afford to be sick. Not now. Not when Riker could be dying.

"I'm going to get you something." Grant headed toward the door. "And don't argue," he added, when she opened her mouth to do exactly that.

Sighing with resignation, she refocused on the computer screen and clicked on a file labeled *Fraser's Notes*. Dr. Fraser was a colleague, a vampire physiologist whose work in the field had led to major advancements in human medicine, including a cure for type 1 diabetes. But even among the ranks of his fellow scientists, his methods were considered questionable, and he'd recently come under fire by vampire-rights groups who claimed he was killing and torturing vampires unnecessarily.

Nicole rubbed her aching eyes as she scanned the documents in the file. Fraser had collated the medical stats of every female who had conceived in the lab and then compared the data against those who hadn't become pregnant. Interestingly, the rate of conception in the lab was higher than that among vampires in the wild.

Fraser had concluded that being bound and forced to copulate increased the chances of conception, but he didn't know exactly why that was.

Fraser was a fucking idiot.

A sharp, stabbing throb started up inside her head, and oh, yeah, she was on her way to Flu-ville. Maybe when Grant got back, he could get her some aspirin.

Nicole massaged her temples as she jotted down notes on a pad of paper. Only the females who had been fed blood taken from males on the night of the new moon had gotten pregnant, but not all who drank the blood had conceived.

Sweat bloomed on her forehead. Why was it so hot in here?

She wiped her brow and went back to the research, finding it curious that the females who got pregnant had also fought the hardest when they were taken into the breeding chamber. Fraser's conclusion was that in their natural state, the females battled the males, causing a rise in hormones.

Nicole threw down the bullshit flag on that one. It didn't make sense. Rough play . . . perhaps dominance play might happen among animal species when the females were receptive to males, but the females in the lab weren't "playing." They were fighting for their lives. That wouldn't happen in normal vampire society.

But then, normal vampire society saw a sadly pathetic birthrate.

Dammit. She was missing something important here. But her head was spinning, and the lights were dimming to the point where she was having a hard time seeing the screen.

"Nicole?" Bastien's voice came from somewhere behind her. "*Nicole.*"

Something hit her like a full-body slam by a bus. The floor. The floor had jumped up and struck her. She couldn't see, and suddenly, she could barely breathe.

"Help! Someone help!" Bastien was closer, maybe even touching her shoulder.

She heard more raised voices, running footsteps, curses, and then someone picked her up. Words buzzed in her ear. She heard them but couldn't comprehend them.

"It's too late. Is it too late?" Grant's voice, she thought.

"Shit." Myne for sure.

"Hurry, dammit," Grant insisted. "She's dying."

"Don't let her die!" That, she was sure, was Bastien.

A massive explosion of pain blew every cell apart. Dear God, it was as if every bone was breaking and every muscle fiber was stretching to its limit and then snapping. Agony such as she'd never known became her entire world, until mercifully, life as she knew it . . . ended.

MYNE RUSHED THROUGH the compound, the unconscious female limp in his arms. Grant had to hold Bastien back; the boy had gone nuts, full-blown, rabid, fangs-bared nuts, when Myne tried to take Nicole from the lab. Nothing Myne had said convinced Bastien that he wasn't going to hurt Nicole. The kid had been too far gone with protective instinct, like a dog standing near the body of its owner, defending even against the paramedics who had come to help.

Myne just hoped he *could* help. The silver flecks forming in Nicole's eyes were a clear sign that she was in the middle of the change from human to vampire, but he'd never seen it happen so suddenly, and definitely not after a full week of no symptoms. Usually, humans showed signs within hours after being introduced to the virus, and they were sick for weeks as their bodies changed over. Hell, it could take up to a month for the full transition.

Nicole appeared to be halfway there, and as far as he knew, she'd only been sick for hours. This could be bad. Real fucking bad.

His first instinct was to deliver her to Hunter, but before Riker had offered himself up to ShadowSpawn's leader, he'd asked Myne to take care of Nicole. Myne would have refused, but how could he refuse a guy who had saved his life?

And who was on his way to certain death.

Shit.

He headed toward his quarters, but when he reached the door, he changed his mind. She needed the best shot at survival he could give her, and keeping her someplace strange was a piss-poor idea. Right now, she needed Riker, so he'd give her the next best thing.

He burst into Riker's apartment and laid her carefully on the bed. She groaned and rolled onto her side, curling into a fetal position. She was burning up, her skin so hot that she wasn't even sweating.

Sinking down onto the bed, he thumbed her upper lip and exposed her canines. Gently, he touched the tip of his finger to one. It jiggled under his touch, loosening as the vampire fang behind it grew in to replace the human tooth.

"Nicole? Can you hear me?"

She let out another groan, and her eyes flickered open. The green irises had clouded over, and the whites had turned red as the blood vessels inside them burst.

It was at this point that infected humans would, if left on their own, either die or rally enough to attack anything that moved in order to drink its blood. Few would survive if they found only animals. More would survive if they drank from humans. The best chance at survival was to drink from a vampire, and best of all was a born vampire's powerful platelets.

This wasn't something Myne was comfortable with. If Nicole survived, he'd forever be linked to her, when he'd never been linked to anyone but his brother. If she died, he'd have failed Riker, the only person he'd ever considered a friend.

Exhaling on a curse, he stripped her down to her bra and underwear, partly to help cool her down and partly because her body would change, and the clothing could restrict blood flow. Naked would be best, but he figured he could go that route later if needed.

He just hoped it wouldn't come to that. If Nicole survived, she didn't need to spend the rest of her life knowing he'd seen her naked. Although he wasn't sure seeing her like this was any better. Her black bra cupped breasts made to fit into a male's palm, and her blue panties, while not the sexiest things he'd ever seen, covered a rounded bottom he'd admit to admiring every time he saw her in the jeans with the hole under the back pocket.

He'd always been an ass man, and Nicole had a spectacular one.

Myne tore his gaze away with another foul curse. He wasn't especially noble, didn't even have to pretend to respect her modesty, but Riker was his friend, and Myne wasn't going to ogle his only friend's helpless female.

"Riker, you lucky bastard," he muttered as he put his wrist to his mouth and then ripped open the vein with his titanium teeth, cradled Nicole's head in one hand, and put the wound to her mouth.

She reared back, swatting at him.

"Come on," he urged her, but her struggles only got fiercer. She kneed him in the groin, and son of a bitch, that hurt.

He was done trying to be hands-off. No more Mr. Gentleman. He'd never been good at it anyway.

With a grunt, he fell on top of her and rolled them both so he was behind her, his legs clamped around her thighs, his arms pinning hers securely while he forced his wrist against her mouth.

Suddenly, she jerked and stopped fighting. Thank the spirit-gods. Her lips closed on his wrist, and she began to take dainty draws.

Excellent. Now he had to stay with her, feeding her when she needed blood, holding her when she went through agonizing changes. He just had to hope she wouldn't demand his body as well as his blood. She was beautiful, passionate, intelligent . . . everything he'd ever wanted in a female.

She was also Riker's. It didn't matter that Riker wasn't here. It wouldn't matter if they never saw him again.

This was Riker's female, whether he'd claimed her or not, and Myne would treat her that way.

And that meant keeping her alive and untouched.

"Drink," he murmured into her ear.

Moaning, she wriggled closer to him, tucking herself into the curve of his body. He cursed as his body hardened, reacting to the awareness of a gorgeous female rubbing herself against him, and he cursed harder when his chest tightened with an even worse sensation: loneliness.

He shouldn't be enjoying the feeling of closeness, of holding someone who didn't belong to him, but damn, this felt good. He didn't get to be with females often, not when his bite caused excruciating pain, and he definitely didn't get to save a life . . . ever. Nicole was depending on him in order to survive, and he began to shake with the magnitude of it all.

Rike, he whispered to himself. *If you come back and don't mate this female before the next daybreak, I'll kill you myself.*

Of course, that was if Riker didn't kill him first for getting a raging erection for his female.

NICOLE WAS *STARVING.*

She rolled over, groaning at the aches and pains in her body. Geez, had she gone a few rounds in a boxing ring? If so, she'd lost the fight.

Riker's earthy leather scent surrounded her, both comforting her and making her even hungrier. Her stomach growled, and deep inside, another hunger throbbed, a sexual one that pulsed hottest between her thighs.

The two needs tangled together, becoming one monstrous entity that demanded satisfaction. It was as if nine-tenths of her brain was operating only on instinct, and she had to struggle to get the remaining tenth to focus on rational thought.

Through a haze of hunger and lust, she reached for Riker, found him next to her. She opened her eyes but saw only pitch blackness. She should probably be afraid, but the rational sliver of brain was rapidly being swallowed by primitive compulsions. She wanted to climb on top of Riker, close her mouth over his throat, and—

"Ouch!" A needlelike stab of pain pricked her in the lip. She dabbed at the spot with her finger, felt the distinct warm stickiness of blood. She licked the puncture before touching the tip of her tongue to the sharp, pointed end of her canine tooth. Then the other.

Were those . . . oh, God, yes, they were.

She had fangs.

Her breath snagged in her throat. Her heart, which would have nearly doubled in size during her transformation, pounded erratically against a rib cage she knew had also expanded and grown an extra set of bones.

Holy shit, *she was a vampire*.

A confusing mix of emotions crashed over her in a violent wave: fear of the unknown, relief that she'd survived the transformation, and sorrow at severing the last link to humanity she had left. It didn't matter that she'd had her eyes opened to the vampire world. She'd been born a human, but she'd die a vampire, and that was a difficult concept to grasp, especially as a fresh swell of hunger crushed her ability to think.

Need became a wicked jolt of pain that streaked from her belly to her teeth. Crying out, she curled in on herself. Hands came down on her, and suddenly, it was as if she knew exactly what to do.

She dived for Riker's throat, clawing her way up his body. A guttural growl echoed in her ears. Hers? Was she actually *growling*?

"Your tongue," he rasped. "Touch your tongue to the backs of your fangs."

What was he babbling about? She didn't care. She

needed food. Hissing, she opened her mouth, ready to punch her fangs into anything that came within striking distance.

Fingers closed on her jaw, forcing her face up and squeezing hard enough to make her eyes sting.

"Your tongue," he repeated sternly. "Do it, or you don't eat."

Food. She had to have food. Okay, wait, the tongue thing. Hastily, she probed the backs of her fangs, and there, just behind each, was a soft spot. She pressed inward and moaned as an erotic tingle spread along her teeth.

"Good girl," he murmured, lying back and allowing her to pounce.

As if she'd been feeding like this her entire life, she struck, biting deep into flesh. The warm, heady rush of liquid filled her mouth and slid down her throat like silk. Her body jolted as if she'd plugged herself into an electric socket, and as her blood hunger began to ease, the other hunger swamped her.

It didn't matter that Riker didn't want her. Right now, all that mattered was satisfying the insane urges twisting up her insides.

Reaching between their bodies, she palmed the thick bulge behind his fly. He sucked air and arched up, pressing himself into her touch. A heartbeat later, he snarled a vile curse and shackled her wrist with his fingers.

"No."

No? She whimpered, not understanding why he would deny her something she needed so badly that she couldn't stop rocking her sex against his. The shifting, restless energy inside her demanded release. Demanded a merging of bodies and blood.

Frantically, she writhed, seeking relief that was only two thin barriers of clothing away. He groaned as she ground on top of him, and then, suddenly, she was on her back, and he was gone.

"Riker?" Her voice sounded like it had been dragged behind a car on a gravel road. Sitting up, she inhaled, but alongside Riker's earthy scent was the distinct tang of meadow grass and warm, musky skin. "M-Myne?"

"Yeah." He was panting, and she could smell both lust and anguish coming off him in alternating waves. "Riker isn't here."

Confused, she sat there, trying to put the pieces of this bizarre puzzle together. Why would she be in a dark bedroom—Riker's bedroom, she was sure—with Myne? And . . . was she in her underwear? She touched herself, confirmed the bra and granny panties, and was flooded with mortification.

"What's going on?" she finally managed.

She heard the distinct sound of boots scuffing the wooden floor. "You passed out in the lab. You've been out of it for four days."

She frowned. "But . . . Riker?"

"ShadowSpawn, remember?"

Everything came back in a dizzying, nauseating rush. Riker was in trouble, and she needed to help him. That was why she'd been in the lab. And shit, four days had passed? So much time . . . he could be dead by now.

She flailed around on the mattress in an uncoordinated scramble, feeling for her clothes. Where were they? She needed to find them, needed to help Riker—

"Hey." Myne's arms came around her. "Settle down. You can't move too fast until you've gotten used to your new body."

New body. She froze up as her new reality sank in. She really was a vampire, and this was the beginning of a new life. A new set of rules.

Overwhelmed by everything closing in on her, she forced herself to relax but only a little. She needed to find her bearings if she was going to both recover quickly and save Riker.

"How did this happen?" she croaked. "I was symptom-free for days."

Myne eased away from her, and a moment later, he settled a wool blanket over her shoulders. "Grant thinks Chuck's immunization delayed the symptoms but accelerated the turn. Either that, or whatever made you react so badly to the original vaccine you received as a child also reacted to the recent one." His voice lowered, almost to a whisper. "There were a couple of times we thought we were going to lose you."

She swallowed dryly, still tasting him on her tongue. "You were with me the entire time?"

"Yeah." His breathing was still labored, and now she understood why.

She'd practically attacked him. Groaning, she flopped back on the mattress and covered her eyes with her arm. "I'm sorry," she murmured.

"S'okay." She heard him shuffle around the room. "Can you see yet?"

"It's not dark in here?" Propping herself up on one elbow, she peered into the blackness. A tinge of gray teased the edges of her vision, and gradually, she could make out his shadowy form standing near the dresser. "I can see shapes now."

"Good. Your vision will come fully online soon, within half an hour or so." He moved to the doorway. "I had food brought for you. It's in the kitchen. I'll go if you want me to. I'll leave my cell number on the counter. You're going to need someone to help you through these next weeks. If you need a female for . . . female things, Katina will help you out."

She knew he was desperate to get away from her, and she didn't blame him. "Thank you, Myne. Right now, I just want a shower."

Dead silence. Then a raspy "Do you want help? You're going to be as clumsy as a newborn foal for a while."

Heat blasted her face at the thought of Myne helping her into the shower. "I'll manage. But, Myne? Thank you for everything you've done."

"I did it for Riker," he said roughly. "It should have been him."

She agreed. But she wondered if Riker would feel the same way.

29

BEING A VAMPIRE was taking a lot of getting used to. Mainly because, as far as Nicole could tell, there weren't a lot of downsides, and that bothered her. She wasn't sure what she'd expected.

Fangs were awesome. So was the extra energy, speed, and strength that came with turning into a vampire. Nicole still wasn't used to the silver eyes or having to drink human blood, but she supposed that would come in time.

She hoped. She was having a hard time accepting the fact that the mere sight of blood made her mouth water. It was one thing not to be bothered by it; it was quite another to attack a packet of food blood like a starving wolverine.

She was now the very thing she'd despised for so long, and what did it say about her that she didn't care? For the most part, the clan members had accepted her, but she realized it would take time to earn their complete trust. No one was outwardly malicious, but a few weren't letting her off the hook for her role as Daedalus's CEO. Their questions and comments were blunt but not unfair. She answered with straightforward honesty no matter how difficult it was.

How many vampires did you kill?

None.

How many did you dissect?

Dozens.

How many slaves did you own?

None.

Did you sleep well at night, knowing what your company was doing?

Except for a few nightmares, yes.

What will you do if we take your brother? Will you speak up for him?

I won't watch him die, but I won't stand in anyone's way.

Do you have any regrets?

Yes.

Are you proud of yourself?

Actually, yes. I cured cancer. I developed treatments that saved a lot of human lives. And now I plan to use what I learned at Daedalus to help vampires. So bite me.

Bite you? Now or on the next full moon?

Okay, so she'd have to learn that vampires took things like "bite me" very literally, and she'd have to watch what she said. But otherwise, no one could say she was shrinking away from either the good or the bad that she'd done. Everyone in the clan was welcome to grill her about her past, and the sooner the better. She wanted the air cleared so everyone, including her, could move on.

But moving on might not be so easy with Myne.

She hadn't been able to face him since he'd left her alone at Riker's place two days ago. He hadn't made an effort to see her, either. At least, Katina had been an invaluable help with navigating the new world Nicole had just joined.

Tomorrow, Katina planned to teach Nicole how to hunt humans.

With any luck, Nicole wouldn't be around to learn. At least, not anytime soon.

She stood before Hunter in his chamber, wondering how the guy was going to react to her announcement. He hadn't really liked her when she was human, and she still couldn't get a read off him. Especially because at the moment, he was sprawled on his fat leather couch, video-game controller in hand, cursing at the purple dragon flying around the TV screen. Strangely, even though he was immersed in a cartoon game, the vibrant aura of power and leadership that always surrounded him wasn't diminished in the least.

"Spyro is flying like he's drunk," he muttered. "What the fuck, dude. *Through* the rings, not over them."

She eyed the screen. "Is that a children's game?"

"It's rated *All* Ages," he said defensively. "Why are you here?"

Right to it, then. "I want to go to ShadowSpawn."

Hunter's head came up, making his black hair drape like silk over his broad shoulders. "You what? You can't just move from one clan to another like humans move from city to city. And if this is to be with Riker, trust me, you won't be *with* him."

No, it wasn't to be with him. He'd made it crystal

clear that he didn't want to be with her. But that didn't mean she didn't want to help him. God help her, she loved him. "It's to save them both. Riker and Lucy."

She couldn't believe ShadowSpawn had refused to give up the girl. What could they possibly want with her?

"Fuck. Now I'm dead." He dropped the game controller. "I'm working on a way to get them out of there."

"Really? Because it looks like you're playing video games while Riker and Lucy could be hurt, suffering, or dying."

A vein in Hunter's temple pulsed, and when he spoke, his tone was glacial. "I'm going to let that pass, since you're a baby in our world. But you should know that I think best when I'm playing video games." He stood, forcing her to crane her neck to look up at him. "Now, what makes you think you can help Riker?"

The way he said it, as if he were humoring a child who wanted to heal the world with a tea party, pissed her off. A lot. "What's the one thing troubling your race?" she asked, a little too impatiently, if his withering stare was any indication. "Besides humans killing and enslaving you, anyway."

"It's your race, too, now," he pointed out.

How long would it take to get that through her head? She had to start thinking like a vampire if she wanted to survive. And if she wanted to prove herself to everyone who would have a hard time seeing beyond her Daedalus roots.

"Okay, *our* race. What problem plagues it?"

"Low birthrate," he said.

"Exactly. What do you think babies would be worth to ShadowSpawn?"

Hunter narrowed his ebony eyes at her. "What are you getting at?"

"Grant and I have been poring over the files I took from the lab . . . There's so much more, but I believe Daedalus has discovered why vampires have difficulty conceiving and giving birth. That's what the breeding experiments have been about."

"They *want* vampires to conceive?" His skepticism rang clear as a bell.

"No. Well, yes, because the goal is to fully domesticate vampires. Engineer them into docile, harmless creatures and then breed them like cattle." She watched his hands open and close into fists over and over, and she wondered if he was imagining squeezing any particular human—or recently turned vampire—between them. "It's too much work and too expensive to catch wild vampires and enslave them. Too much risk when things go bad. And only the wealthy can afford vampire slaves."

"But if they bred their own mindless, spineless drones, they could mass-produce them and make a fortune selling to the average citizen."

"Exactly."

Hunter snarled. "I hate humans."

Not long ago, she'd have been insulted. Now she was right there with him.

"So what's your plan?" Hunter asked, all business and impatience.

"I'll promise ShadowSpawn as many pregnancies as they want in exchange for Riker and Lucy. And don't worry, I'll make sure Grant has all of the information he needs to help MoonBound make babies, too, just in case anything goes wrong with ShadowSpawn and I'm, well . . . not able to come back."

"No."

She uttered an exasperated curse. "How can you say no? This is the best shot we have of getting Riker out of there alive, and you know it."

"He wouldn't want this, Nicole."

"I don't care what he wants. He's not here to make the decision, is he?" She wheeled around, paced a few steps, and came back, more determined than ever. "This is *my* choice. If you don't agree, I'll find a way to do it. I'm nothing if not resourceful, Hunter. I got out of here before, and I can do it again. So either I do this with your backing, or I go alone. Which is it?"

Hunter thought about that for a long time, his shrewd gaze never leaving her. Finally, he said quietly, "When do you want to go?"

"I need a day to get everything together."

There was a knock at the door, and Hunter barked, "Enter."

Myne appeared in the doorway. He didn't meet her gaze. "Nicole left me a message to meet you both here."

Hunter crossed his arms over his chest and shot her an accusatory look. "Did she?"

She nodded. "I want Myne to take me." For some reason, Myne jerked like he'd been stuck with a cattle prod.

"Take you?" Myne's voice sounded strangled.

"To ShadowSpawn," Hunter said, and Myne blew out a relieved breath before he squared his stance, as if preparing for danger. "But you're not going alone. I'm going with you."

"Is this about Riker and Lucy?" Myne asked.

Nicole closed her eyes, relieved and happy to be able to help. "I think I can save them." She opened her eyes to find that Myne was finally looking at her, but his cheeks were flushed pink. "I also have something I think you can use." She gave herself five seconds to change her mind, and then she said very deliberately, "Chuck is always at the Daedalus Ridge Golf Course on Thursdays."

COLD. PAIN. HUNGER. Riker was close personal friends with all of them. Most people would have called them enemies, but Riker knew what an enemy was, and in comparison with ShadowSpawn vampires, even starvation seemed friendly enough.

Shackles bit into his raw wrists as he shifted from his knees to sitting against the rock wall with his legs stretched out in front of him. Those were the only two positions available to him, and neither was comfortable, given that his arms had been bound behind his back. He'd been stripped and beaten, but on the second day of his captivity, one of the chief's daughters, the one with the limp, had brought him a pair of flannel pajama bottoms. They were too short, but he'd been grateful nevertheless.

Of course, he'd also been suspicious as hell, but no matter how many times he asked the female, Aylin, why she was giving him clothes, she didn't respond.

Her twin sister, however, had left him bleeding and nearly blinded just two hours earlier.

Rasha was a royal bitch.

He wondered how Bastien and Nicole were doing. He regretted not having more time to spend with the boy, but maybe those few hours they'd spent together before this all went down would leave Bastien with positive memories. The idea that all he'd ever known of fathers was pain and abuse was too horrible to bear.

And Nicole . . . *Jesus.*

He closed his eyes and rocked his head back against the wall. She'd been at the gathering of the two clans. She'd seen him chained and dragged away. He'd heard her. Sensed her. And all he could think of was how he'd left things between them.

He'd yelled at her for making herself at home in a place where she should have been welcome. Instead, he'd freaked the fuck out. He'd been so full of guilt over how Terese had lived and died that he hadn't been able to let anyone else in.

What if he couldn't love someone the way she deserved to be loved? What if he didn't imprint on the female he wanted? What if she died thinking she was nothing but a burden to him? An obligation?

Nicole had been a burden at first. Definitely an obligation—nothing more than part of his mission gone awry. And he'd treated her as exactly that.

But at some point, his feelings toward her had changed. He'd discovered that she wasn't the evil Daedalus bigwig he'd believed her to be, and if anything, she had a bigger heart than many vampires he knew.

ShadowSpawn vampires, most notably.

Assholes. They couldn't just kill him and be done with it, could they? No, they were going to drag out his humiliation and death for as long as possible. Not an hour went by when someone wasn't coming into the dungeon to torture him. And every night, they hauled him to the common room, where they chained him to a whipping post for some wholesome family entertainment. While the entire clan looked on, he was beaten, cut, stabbed, whipped, pissed on—yeah, it was all great fun. He especially liked it when they threw rotten food at him and tried to force him to eat it.

Aylin always came into the dungeon after the family fun night events to clean him up, but she never spoke. Not that he was in the mood to chat by that point. Usually, he couldn't see, let alone speak, through the blood and swelling.

The chamber door creaked open. Squinting at the bright light streaming through the opening, he braced himself for whatever was coming next.

A squat male who was built like a brick filled the doorway. "You have five minutes," Brick said, speaking to someone outside.

Riker smelled Nicole before he saw her, and his heart screeched to a halt so fast it must have left skid marks on his ribs. Gripped by shock, he could only gape as she entered the dungeon.

"Oh, my God." She ran to him and knelt at his side, taking his face in her hands. "What have they done to you?"

His injuries weren't important. The fact that she was here and was staring at him with silver eyes was.

"Holy shit, Nicole . . . you're a vampire." His voice

was as trashed as his body. His mind seemed to be equally trashed, because he couldn't focus his questions or his thoughts. And like a dolt, he'd also just told her something she already knew. "Why are you here? How?" He swallowed. "When did you turn?"

"Shh. First things first." She stroked her thumbs over his cheeks, her touch extremely light and gentle on his bruises. "I'm here to free you and Lucy." He wrenched his fists futilely behind his back, wishing he could touch her. "They're letting you go. Lucy is already with Hunter and Myne."

Thank God, Lucy was safe. But his situation was a little more serious. "That's not possible," he said. "Kars wants to wring every drop of life out of me."

"I have something he wants more than he wants you dead." She smiled, revealing her new pristine white fangs. "Oh, and obviously, the vaccine Chuck gave me didn't work."

Riker couldn't stop staring at her mouth and the way the tips of her fangs peeked from between her parted lips.

"Are you okay?" he rasped. "I know you didn't want this—"

She pressed her finger against his lips. "I'm fine, I swear. I'm still getting used to it, but I'm really okay. And if nothing else, it cured my lip-biting habit." She gave him a sheepish smile. "At the end of the first day, I had a super-swollen lip, and if I'd had quarters, I'd have had a full swear jar."

He strained against his chains, desperate to get closer. Mere inches separated them, and he could barely move. He needed to touch her, needed to feel for himself that she was healthy and whole. Kars thought he was being so clever with his torture methods, but this . . . this was by far the worst thing Riker had been put through.

"You look amazing," he said, loving the dusky blush that spread over her cheeks.

He'd thought she was gorgeous before, but the dental makeover, along with the new sensual energy that vibrated the very air between them, had transformed her from a sleek, elegant housecat to a muscular, powerful tiger. He wished he could hug her. Wished he could whisk her away, strip her, and make love to her until she swore to never leave him.

"Wow," she whispered. "I can feel your desire." She licked her lips, and his body, abused as it was, fired up like the trusty engine in the old Land Rover he'd bought after graduating from Army basic training. "I can actually smell it. This vampire thing is . . . incredible." A dark, crafty gleam sparked in her eyes a split second before she captured his mouth with hers.

A moan of pleasure and a frustrated growl that he couldn't touch her mixed in his throat. He leaned into her as best he could, meeting her passionate kiss with equal enthusiasm. He danced the tip of his tongue over her fangs, testing the sharpness, fantasizing about how they'd feel as they sank into his neck.

He breathed her in, reveling in the new Nicole. He'd sell his soul to be able to ravish her right here in the cell. Stretching his restraints to the limit, he kissed her harder, stroking his tongue up and down her fangs in a blatantly sexual tempo. He was rewarded with a groan that vibrated him all the way to his groin.

"Oh, my," she gasped into his mouth. "Fangs are . . ."

"Sex," he finished.

"I want—"

"I know."

She shuddered and pulled back, panting as hard as he was. He wondered if arousal had turned his eyes blue the way hers had gone to glowing green. "They're going to be back for me in a minute. I just wanted to see you before I started work."

"Tell me what's going on. What do you have that they want?"

"Babies." She brushed her finger over a laceration on his cheek—given to him courtesy of Fane an hour ago. "I know how vampires get pregnant. I can help them conceive."

Damn, that was huge. Now he understood why Kars might deal. He'd been waiting twenty-five years to get his hands on Riker, so he could wait another twenty-five if he had to. Ensuring the survival of his clan and the entire vampire race was worth it.

But . . . "What's the catch?"

"I have to stay here until five females are pregnant," she said, as if it was no big deal to be held by ShadowSpawn for God knew how long. "Tonight is the new moon, so if I can get the formula put together in the next six hours, it's possible that we could know tomorrow. Pregnancy in vampires is detectable within hours after intercourse. "

"It's too risky," he said. "I can't let you do this."

"It's definitely risky," she said, and he wondered if she'd honed her brisk, businesslike tone in Daedalus boardrooms. "But I don't know what gave you the impression that you have any say in it."

Fair enough. But this was too dangerous for someone who had been a vampire for hundreds of years, let alone for a brand-new vampire.

"Nicole, what if the conceptions don't happen? You could be here for years."

"It'll happen," she assured him. "As Hunter so kindly pointed out, I'm a baby in your world, but when it comes to this, I'm an expert. I know what I'm doing. By this time tomorrow, if five females pop a positive, I'll be free."

He leaned back against the wall, getting comfortable. "I'm not leaving until you do. I'm definitely not letting you feed from any of these Neanderthals."

"*Letting* me?" She jabbed her finger into his sternum. "You gave up the right to have any input into my life when you chose a dead woman over me, so let's stop with the he-man act. Besides, I don't plan to feed from any of them. Vampires can skip a moon feeding or two."

He shook his head. "It's not good for you, especially during the first months after you turn."

"This isn't negotiable," she said. "Think about Bastien. He needs you. You need to go home."

"So do you."

She smiled, a bitter upturn of her lips. "My home isn't yours. You made that very clear."

"Nicole—"

She poked him again. "Now isn't the time for this."

"Now is maybe the *only* time for this."

The door slammed open, and Nicole, bless her

heart, crouched in front of him like a fierce guard dog. Rasha stood in the entry, a deceptively attractive demon outlined by light. All she was missing were horns and hooves. Maybe the hooves were concealed by her knee-high boots.

"Time to go, female," she said.

Nicole swung back around to him. "Don't volunteer to stay. Let them take you to Hunter."

All he could think about was Nicole, stuck here during moon fever, her new body craving male blood, and his inner he-man started pounding his chest. "You're not feeding from another male tonight."

She stood, all grace and elegance that went hand in hand with her snooty "I'll feed from anyone I want to feed from."

Possessive rage turned his vision red. "Who fed you during the turning?"

"Myne."

Darkness swallowed him at the sudden, unbidden image of Nicole lying with Myne in her bed, her teeth in his throat, his expression etched in pleasure. That was bad enough, but had things gone even further?

Territorial jealousy seared his veins. Myne had now been there for *both* Bastien and Nicole. It should have been Riker's privilege to help his son integrate into the clan and help Nicole survive her transformation. He should be grateful; he knew that. But he didn't think he'd ever get past the fact that Nicole and Myne would be connected forever in a way Riker never would be.

"Hurry up," Rasha snapped. "You have babies to make."

Nicole started toward the door, but Riker wasn't ready for her to leave. He doubted he'd ever be ready.

"Wait." He lunged against his restraints, and fresh blood streamed down his wrists as the shackles dug into his skin. "Did you do more with him? When he fed you?" He hated himself for asking that. And for sounding like the wrong answer would destroy him.

Nicole pivoted, her body taut as a bowstring. "Again, none of your business. But screw you, Riker, for thinking I'd kiss you after leaving his bed." She disappeared, leaving him with his regrets, his bad attitude, and the ShadowSpawn bitch.

Rasha entered, her seemingly permanent scowl etching deep grooves in her face. "I have to take you to your chief."

"I'm staying."

"For the female?" She snorted. "You're a fool." Her to-the-knee fuck-me boots *clack*ed on the pavings as she sauntered over. "I'll give you until tomorrow." She stomped on the chain connecting his wrists to the wall, wrenching his shoulders so hard he saw lights behind his eyelids. "And you stay in chains."

30

IT TURNED OUT that while being a vampire was generally awesome, what wasn't awesome was that vampire emotions seemed to be a lot more intense than those of a human. Things that might have been only mildly irritating before now had Nicole struggling not to break objects against the wall. Grant and Katina both had warned her that the adjustment wouldn't be easy, and if anything, they'd understated the problem.

Because between Riker's ridiculous show of jealousy and her current situation, Nicole was ready to rip some heads off.

And as a vampire, she had the strength to do it.

"I can't believe I'm trying to manufacture a fertility treatment with sticks and rocks in a lab that's little more than a supply closet," she muttered.

The vampire assigned to assist Nicole, Aylin, shrugged apologetically. "We don't have much use for science here. My father says science is for weaklings who can't survive in the real world."

Nicole shot a glance at the blond female, who, except for her pronounced limp, was nearly identical to her tall, blue-eyed twin sister, Rasha. The similarities ended at their appearance, however. Aylin was quiet and reserved, where Rasha was arrogant, loud, and crude. And she dressed like a streetwalker.

After meeting Kars, the twins' father and Shadow-Spawn's leader, Nicole understood Rasha's personality and where it came from. Aylin, on the other hand, was a mystery.

"Do you believe what your father says?" Nicole glanced at Aylin from across the makeshift table constructed of a sheet of plywood lying atop two sawhorses and held steady by massive stones.

Sticks. And. Rocks.

"No." Aylin fiddled with the buttons on her shirt—red, to match her sneakers. "I think surviving isn't all about being physically strong. If it was, I would have died a long time ago."

Nicole couldn't imagine Aylin being considered weak in any way. She appeared fit and healthy, and she was definitely smart.

"What happened to your leg?" Nicole dumped a tablespoon of habanero pepper powder into the liquid base she'd prepared from items taken from Moon-Bound's kitchen, lab, and infirmary. Well, the last two were one and the same, really. "Were you injured?"

"I was born this way."

Odd. Nicole had never heard of any vampire suffering from a birth defect. In fact, the utter absence of birth defects was under study at several universities worldwide. "Where's your mother?"

Aylin pushed a bowl of pulverized aspirin to Nicole. "She died during childbirth."

"I'm sorry," Nicole said, knowing how inadequate the words were.

Aylin shrugged. "I never knew her. My father doesn't talk about her much." Aylin lowered her voice, even though they were alone. "It was kind of a scandal. She was human when he took her from a railroad camp way back in the late 1800s. She was intended to be food, but I guess he became obsessed with her. He turned her into a vampire, and the next time they had sex, he imprinted on her."

Idly, Nicole reached out and brushed a lock of blond hair away from the flawless porcelain skin of her face. "You must take after her. You look nothing like your father."

She nodded. "He's a second-generation vampire from a Comanche tribe. According to him, my great-grandfather was one of the chiefs the raven and crow fought over."

Nicole barely restrained an eye roll at that. Not only was the legend ridiculous, but Kars's assertion that he was descended from said legend was beyond ludicrous and brimming with egotism.

"I think he's full of shit," Aylin said, and Nicole laughed. She liked this vampire.

Nicole added a teaspoon of the aspirin powder to the fertility concoction. "Your father's name is odd. What's it mean?"

"Apparently, my mother couldn't pronounce his Comanche name, Karshawnewuti, so she shortened it. He won't let anyone call him anything else now."

Sounded like Kars had cared about Aylin's mother in his own sick way.

Aylin craned her neck to peer at the mixture Nicole was stirring. "Is it almost done?"

"I think so." She just hoped it worked. Her confidence with Riker had been solely for his benefit. Inside, she was so nervous that her intestines were rattling.

If this failed, either Kars would force her to stay until she made good on her promise, or he'd kill her.

She'd kept quiet to Hunter and Myne about Kars threatening her life. And she was definitely not letting Riker in on that little gem.

Aylin fanned herself. "Can you feel it?"

"Feel what?"

"The moon." An erotic undercurrent infused Aylin's husky voice. "It's almost time to feed."

Nicole had tried not to think about it. When she'd first arrived with Hunter, Rasha had assured them that a suitable male would be available for her to feed from. At the time, Nicole hadn't let herself stress over the idea of feeding from a ShadowSpawn male who, no doubt, would be chosen from the vilest of the clan's warriors.

Now she was starting to stress.

The heat that had been building all day intensified under her skin, and her fangs tingled. Was that part of the moon need? Probably, since her stomach was growling, but she had no desire for food. What she did desire was Riker.

Idiot.

She watched Aylin pace and fidget, and finally, she couldn't take it anymore. She snatched a sheet of paper from the random scattered piles lying around the room.

"Let me show you something." She waved Aylin over. "It's called origami." Although she scarcely had time for this, she showed Aylin how to make a basic flower and a bird.

Aylin's broad smile made the time-suck worthwhile. Nicole got the impression that smiles were rare around here.

"They're beautiful," Aylin said. "Can I try?"

"Go for it."

Aylin was a quick study. She folded out the bird without any help at all. As Aylin started on a flower, Nicole's thoughts shifted back to Riker. Had he gone like he was supposed to? The ShadowSpawn bastards had better not have beaten him before they escorted him to Hunter. What they'd already done to him was horrific enough. Nicole had tried to hide her shock at the extent of his injuries, but inside, she'd been fuming.

Even now, just thinking about it, sweat beaded on her forehead, and she couldn't stop her hand from shaking as she mixed and measured twenty equal doses of the liquid medicine into shot glasses.

Nicole wiped her brow and looked over at Aylin. "Will you make sure these are given to the participating females? They should take it fifteen minutes before feeding and intercourse." She sniffed one of the glasses' contents and grimaced. "It's going to taste horrible. And it'll burn like hell. You guys really need a pill-filling machine."

Aylin put the finishing touches on her paper flower. It was perfect. Nicole had needed several tries to get that flower right when she'd first learned. "I'll put in an order."

Nicole blinked in surprise. "Seriously?"

"No." One corner of Aylin's full mouth tipped up in an impish smirk. "My father believes that if we can't kill it, make it, or steal it, it isn't worth having. And that includes a sense of humor." She smirked. "Welcome to life in a clan that follows the way of the raven."

"The raven?" Nicole frowned. "As in, the crow and the raven story you were talking about?"

"You must be newly turned." Aylin bumped against the plywood table top, nearly knocking over the shot glasses of pregnancy concoction. "Dammit," she breathed. "And yes, most clans identify with either the raven or the crow. It's all total bullshit." She cast a covert glance at the door. "Not that I'd say that too loudly."

"What's the difference?"

"You know the basic story, right? Two chiefs fought, and then a raven and a crow fought over their dying bodies, and their blood mingled, creating the first vampires?" When Nicole nodded, Aylin continued. "Supposedly, the crow betrayed the raven, and when they battled over the chiefs, the raven had to fight dirty. So those who identify with the raven make survival and war against crows a priority over all else. To fight hard, you must live hard. They view followers of the crow to be inferior and soft." She straightened all the shot glasses into neat rows on the tray. "Some clans have stricter interpretations of the legend than others. ShadowSpawn is what I like to call *ravengelical*."

Nicole laughed, although truly, it was no laughing matter. With the apparent exception of Aylin, ShadowSpawn vamps were exactly the kind of vampires that humans were afraid of and that gave the others a bad name.

"I'm guessing that's another thing you don't say too loudly?"

"Hell no. As a rule, I try to avoid the whipping post."

A knot formed in the pit of Nicole's belly. "Is the whipping post where Riker was . . ." She couldn't say it. Didn't need to. Aylin knew, and she nodded.

"He was very brave," Aylin said. "No matter what they did to him, he didn't scream."

Bastards. Desperate to change the subject, she pushed the tray of shot glasses toward Aylin. "Are you going to be taking one?"

"Even if I was allowed to breed," Aylin said, "I wouldn't. No child should grow up in this clan."

"You aren't *allowed* to?"

"I'm defective. I was born second, and I have this." She tapped her right leg. "Only the strongest females and males are allowed to breed."

Born second? What kind of stupidity was that? Nicole would love to introduce a stake to ShadowSpawn's leader's heart. "Can you leave the clan? Go somewhere else?"

"I tried once." She shuddered as she picked up the tray, making the glasses rattle and clink. "I'm stuck here until my sister is mated. Then I'll be sent to NightShade's clan leader."

"To be his mate?"

"One of many." Aylin's disgusted tone told Nicole what the other female thought of the situation.

And Nicole had thought it was bad that *her* destiny had been planned out. "I'm guessing it's not by choice?"

"Choice isn't something a leader's offspring gets a lot of."

Nicole understood that more than she wanted to. "What about Rasha? Is she supposed to mate with someone?"

"Since she's considered to be a valuable prize, my father is being very selective about who he wants her to mate with."

Rasha was a *prize*? Nicole felt sorry for whatever poor jackass was going to have to put up with her for the rest of his life.

Aylin inched a little closer. "So . . . what's your special ability?"

Strange, Nicole had been so busy since becoming a vampire that she hadn't noticed. "I haven't found mine yet. What about you?"

Footsteps sounded outside the room, soft sounds Nicole wouldn't have heard when she was human. Aylin's voice dropped conspiratorially low.

"I don't have one, either," she whispered. "Not really."

Not really? Nicole didn't have time to ask more, because the rickety wooden door creaked open, and the leader of the group of males Nicole and Riker had run into in the forest stalked into the room. With the exception of the fur mantle around his shoulders, he didn't look any different from when she'd seen him before. His clothes were still bloodstained, and he looked like he could use a shower.

"You're out of time," Fane said. "Feeding needs to

start." His gaze raked her, and she had to struggle not to gag. No way was she drinking from him.

Her fangs tingled at the thought, because clearly, they didn't care where the blood came from. Even a shadowy corner of her brain was telling her that food was food and a male was a male. Fortunately, clearer thoughts overrode the others. But how long would that last? As moon fever kicked in, she could be driven to take whatever was available.

"The meds are finished," she told him. "Aylin was just going to distribute them."

Fane took one of the shot glasses off the tray and held it out to her. "Drink."

She couldn't help recoiling from his filthy hands. What in God's name was under his long fingernails, anyway? "I don't need it—"

"Drink," he repeated, less politely this time. "Do it, or I'll do it for you." He bared his pearly white fangs. Figured they'd be the only clean thing on his body. "I want to make sure you aren't trying to poison anyone."

"You people are seriously paranoid." Cursing, she swiped it out of his hand and knocked it back. And yep, it burned. Holy cow, it was as if she'd swallowed a hot lump of coal.

After she finished wheezing, the hunger returned tenfold. The warmth in her throat and belly spread through her entire body, concentrating in her breasts and pelvis.

"Oh, wow," she whispered. "I don't know if anyone will get pregnant, but this stuff is going to make them want to try."

"I'm not servicing a female tonight." Fane reached

out and cupped the back of her neck. "I'll volunteer my vein and my cock."

His touch was horrifyingly electric on her nerve endings, sparking all along the fibers like little bursts of ecstasy. But she wasn't that desperate. She'd never be that desperate.

Please, never be that desperate.

"Release her," Aylin barked, and although Fane gave her a glare of utter contempt, he obeyed. Obviously, being the chief's daughter came with perks. "We have a male for her."

Nicole's gut clenched. "Who?"

"Your MoonBound male." Aylin shoved Fane aside, earning another glare. "He refused to leave."

Nicole's knees went rubbery with both relief that she wouldn't be forced to feed from a brutish, unwashed male like Fane and irritation that Riker had remained instead of leaving with Hunter and Myne.

So . . . now what? Oh, she had no problem feeding from Riker, but sex? Sex wouldn't be a good idea if she *hadn't* just taken something that could make her pregnant. Still, her body vibrated with need, and she had serious doubts about how in control she was going to be while feeding. If Fane's touch had set her off, and she despised him, what would Riker's do?

"Nicole?" Aylin's hand came down on her shoulder. "Do you want to go to him? You don't have to." She squeezed gently. "But you should know that Rasha has her eye on him."

"She *what*?"

"Not because she wants him," Aylin said in a rush. "She wants to humiliate him."

A possessive growl rose from deep inside Nicole, from a place she hadn't even known existed. "And what better way to humiliate an enemy than to take something from him while he's helpless?"

"Exactly."

Now she got it. Now she understood why Riker had gotten so jealous at the idea of Nicole feeding from another male. Because right now, jealousy like she'd never experienced before seared her from the inside out. Jealousy, fury, hunger, and lust made for one hell of a potent cocktail, and with a guttural snarl, she rounded on Fane.

"Take me to Riker. Now."

THE HEADY ODORS of blood and sex reached Riker, even inside the dank chamber where he was still chained. The air hummed with the familiar thrill of an erotic storm as the moon fever took hold of the clan. Riker gritted his teeth, fighting the urges taking over his body and cursing his errant cock. Usually, after he fed Benet, he spent the rest of the night alone, with a bottle of liquor, or out hunting.

Riker was alone, but sans alcohol, and both hands were bound behind his back. *Excellent.* Another form of ShadowSpawn torture.

And where the hell was Nicole? He knew how difficult the first new moon was on newly turned females, how they couldn't control their need for blood, how hard it was for them to differentiate between blood hunger and sexual hunger. New vampires were often mindless, feeling as if starvation for both had set in.

The idea that Nicole might be slaking her thirst with a ShadowSpawn male ate into his brain like corrosive acid. He had no one to blame but himself for chasing her away, but he swore he'd find that male and dismantle him. Slowly.

The door opened, and he threw himself against the chains, hoping against hope that they'd break, but nope, the suckers held, and—

His heart skipped a beat. Maybe a hundred.

Nicole stood in the doorway, bathed in light like an angel. An angel with fangs and glittering silver eyes. Wordlessly, she slammed the door shut and came at him with a growl. She hit him full force, knocking him from his knees onto his ass. His spine hit the wall, and the force against his shoulders wrenched them in their sockets.

He didn't give a shit. Not when Nicole straddled his thighs and sank her fangs into his neck. He shouted at the searing bliss, and somewhere in his lust-soaked brain, he remembered to be thankful that she'd remembered to activate the pleasure glands.

Awkwardly, he shifted his legs out from under him. She moaned as he moved, rubbing her sex against his erection. The decent thing to do, given their last argument, would be to tell Nicole to relax, to take the blood but ignore the lust.

But he'd never been decent, so when she reached under the waistband of his pajamas and took his cock in her palm, he gasped. "Oh, fuck, yeah."

She writhed on his lap as she stroked him in her tight fist to the rhythm of her mouth sucking on his vein. *So good. So. Damned. Good.*

An urgent whimper broke from her chest as she picked up the pace, grinding hard against him.

"Nicole," he moaned. "You have to take off your pants. Stop feeding—"

She growled, a basic, primitive sound he'd heard from wolves whose food was threatened.

"It'll only be for a second," he assured her. "You can take my vein again as soon as you're naked."

With a pure animal snarl, she pulled back and tore at her jeans. Damn, she was beautiful in her frenzy, as wild as the wolf he'd compared her to. As she shimmied out of her jeans, her hair fell in untamed waves around her shoulders, and her lips, swollen and red, were parted just enough to reveal a tantalizing glimpse of snow-white fangs.

He strained at his chains, knowing that if he were free, he'd be on her and in her in about half a heartbeat.

"Stand up." He met her fevered gaze. "Straddle my thighs. Let me put my mouth on you."

"Yes," she rasped as she shoved to her feet.

Her long, toned legs gave way to a delicate, plump mound covered by pale strawberry curls. She planted one foot on either side of his thighs, putting her core right where he wanted it.

"Closer," he murmured, tilting his face up to meet her flesh as she scooted forward. His mouth watered for her, his body ached for her, and the moment his tongue slipped between her pillowed folds, they both groaned.

With the fervent appetite of a male who had gone far too long without a female to love, he licked at her, swirling his tongue around her swollen nub and then sucking, drinking in her sweet juices. He swallowed and licked, working her into a fit of impassioned mewls that made his blood pound in his ears.

"There," she said on a strangled gasp.

She pumped against his mouth, taking what she wanted, and damn, he'd never seen anything so sexy in his life. Suddenly, she went rigid and let out a strangled cry. He dragged the flat of his tongue through her slit slowly, wanting to make this last, but she would have none of it. She dropped to her knees, sank her teeth into his vein, and sat down hard on his cock.

"Christ!" he shouted. Her slick heat surrounded him, hotter than the times they'd made love before. Her new vampire body was stronger, faster, more flexible, and she was using all of it.

Her fingers dug into his shoulders as she rose up until the tip of his cock nearly broke free of her body, and then plunged down, driving him deep inside her. Taking long, hard pulls on his vein, she did it again, faster, then faster still, until her hips were hammering into his. She let out a throaty moan that undid him.

His balls tightened and pulsed, and his molten rush pumped into her. He roared her name over and over as the endless waves of euphoria poured over him. She bucked, her entire body clenched around his, and her climax took her.

"Nicole," he whispered. "That's it, baby." He arched his back as best he could, meeting her brutal thrusts.

She jerked, biting down hard. He bore the pain with pride, thinking he'd be happy to go through that every day.

Gradually, she eased up, pulling her teeth free. He

smiled at the soothing stroke of her tongue over the bite wound. Either Myne had taught her well, or the instinct was strong in her. He'd made a dozen mistakes before his healing instinct kicked in.

She slumped against him with a sigh. He wished he could wrap his arms around her.

"I'm sorry," she muttered against his chest.

"For what?" Man, his voice was shot to shit.

She shifted, and his cock slipped from her warmth. "Attacking you. Using you like that."

"Are you kidding?" He inhaled a choppy breath, wondering how long it would take to recover. She'd *used* him well. "That's pretty normal."

What wasn't normal was how powerful his orgasm had been. Or how many emotions she'd stirred up. And wait, had the word *love* actually gone through his head? Yes, he thought it had.

He waited for the remorse over Terese's life and death to descend like a wet shroud. Nothing. For some reason, the absence of the guilt bothered him. He'd been so filled by it for so long that he felt almost . . . bereft. As if the guilt had been a limb. A cancerous limb, maybe, but something that was useful nonetheless.

It had kept him primed for revenge. It had ensured he kept his mind focused and his fighting skills sharp, because the only thing he had to live for was making things right for Terese.

"Normal?" Nicole nuzzled the curve between his neck and shoulder. "Wow."

Well, not completely normal, at least, not for him. Sex with Nicole the last time had easily been the most amazing sex he'd ever had. But this . . . this blew the last encounter away. "Welcome to the new world."

Lazily, as if she was ready for a nap, she pushed back to look at him with heavy-lidded eyes. "It won't happen again. When I get back to MoonBound, I'll arrange for a moon partner."

So much for the warm fuzzy feeling. "Like hell you will."

"We're not doing this again, are we?" She sighed. "I can't be with you like this."

"This," he growled, "was pretty damned great."

"And it would be great in your chambers. In your bed. Right?"

He hesitated, once again waiting for the insane guilt to take him in its jaws and shred him to pieces. The brief delay cost him.

"That's what I thought," she said coldly. "You should probably know that I stayed in your chambers during my transformation. With Myne. In your bed."

A white-hot poker of fury impaled him from the top of his head to the base of his spine. "Why are you telling me this?"

"Because the world didn't end, Riker. Terese's ghost didn't come slay either one of us." She put her hand directly over his heart. "I know you don't want to hear this, but I love you. I'm not sure I would have made it through the turn if I hadn't been surrounded by your scent. When I was hurting and delirious, I thought you were there with me, and I fought to stay." She locked her gaze with his. "So yes, I love you, but I've lived my entire life connected to a company that didn't want or need me. I won't do that again. We'll always be connected because you turned me. But what you and I want are two different things."

The anger drained abruptly, leaving in its place a feeling of dread and a strange burn near his hip bone. "Nicole, I want you."

"You want *parts* of me. You want what's in my veins and between my legs," she said, and he kicked himself for making her believe that. "I'm not judging you, and believe me, it's tempting to settle for what you're willing to give. But I'm worth more than that. I've thrown off the Daedalus shackles, but if you can't do the same with Terese, if you can't look at me without seeing a Martin who destroyed your life, we have nowhere to go but our separate ways." Standing, she shoved her feet into her jeans, and he was helpless to stop her. "I'd better go. The females I dosed will be starting to come into the supply-closet-slash-lab for some tests. You're going to be taken to Hunter now."

"I'm not leaving. Not until you do. We need to talk, Nicole." The burn at his hip intensified, and he shifted to get comfortable.

"We just did, and we've been through this," she said, sounding tired. "I need you to go. If I'm worried about you, I can't work." Reaching up, she pinched the bridge of her nose as if trying to stave off a headache. "Please."

As much as he hated the idea of leaving her here alone, he didn't want to jeopardize her work or her chances of getting out of here as soon as possible.

"I'll leave the compound," he agreed. "But I won't go far."

"I'd rather you went back to MoonBound."

"I don't know what gave you the impression that you have any say in it," he said, throwing her words from earlier back at her.

She cocked an eyebrow. "Touché." Pivoting, she headed toward the door.

A stabbing sensation joined the burn, and seriously, what the fuck? He glanced down, sure someone had jammed a red-hot needle into his lower abdomen. But no, there was some sort of reddish marking. He craned his neck a little more, and . . . *oh, damn.*

A feather had been carved into his skin. The Mark of the Crow. Or the Mark of the Raven, if the individual subscribed to that particular canon. Riker had never truly believed in the vampire superstitions, legends, and hokum so many of his kind—especially the oldest and born vampires—subscribed to, but now that he was experiencing this, he might have to reconsider his stance.

Because as he stared at the glyph setting into his skin, its lines growing darker and more distinct, there was no mistaking the fact that *he* hadn't put it there. There was definitely no mistaking what it was: the mating mark all males both feared and wanted.

Nicole paused at the doorway, but she didn't turn to look at him. "Please don't worry. I'll be okay."

He jerked, the mark forgotten. He'd heard those words before.

Riker couldn't help but feel that this was Terese all over again. He was leaving Nicole with the enemy, just like he'd left Terese, who had also assured him she'd be okay.

The difference was that this time, he not only loved the female he was about to lose . . . he'd imprinted on her.

OF ALL THE things ShadowSpawn had done to Riker, being blindfolded and dragged from his cell to Hunter's camp several miles away sucked the most. Having his skin scraped off during the drag wasn't even the worst of it. No, what Riker hated was being blind.

The way the other senses became overly acute made him too reactive and combative, so by the time the ShadowSpawn goons dumped him at Hunter's feet, he was a mass of lacerations, abrasions, and contusions, and he was pretty sure his nose had been broken by a couple of different fists.

After a brief wait that included a lot of harsh words and kick in the ribs, someone unlocked the chains around his ankles and wrists. He bounded to his feet and ripped the blindfold from his eyes.

They were at the edge of a moonlit clearing, with MoonBound's warriors flanking the meadow, weapons drawn, bows trained on ShadowSpawn's males. Whatever confrontation had taken place while Riker was blindfolded and on the ground was over, and as he rolled his shoulders to ease the aches, the enemy clan disappeared into the shadows that gave them their name.

Hunter, wearing only camo pants and boots despite the fact that the scent of coming snow was in the air, pulled Riker into a rare, and awkward, embrace. "Good to have you back and in one piece." Stepping back, he revised his initial impression. "*Mostly* one piece. I think you left some bits of yourself behind."

"Always good to see you, too, Hunt," Riker muttered. He lifted his hand in greeting to the warriors and their mystic-keeper standing silently in the forest. "Where's Myne?"

Riker owed the guy a lot of thanks and a lifetime of debt. Riker might have lost his shit to jealousy a few times, but he'd always known Myne had his back.

"Your guess is as good as mine." Hunter gestured for Riker to walk with him toward camp. "He came with us, but . . . you know."

Yeah, Riker knew. Myne wasn't one to hang out with Hunter, and he definitely didn't like to spend any amount of time with a group. No doubt he was nearby, but he wouldn't be trading ghost stories and making s'mores around a campfire anytime soon.

Or anytime ever.

Hunter adjusted the weapon belt that crossed over his bare chest. The guy had always been more comfortable in battle when he felt unrestricted. Riker was surprised he wasn't barefoot, too. "Did you see Nicole?"

Riker nodded. "Why did you let her make that idiotic trade?"

"Have you even met her?" Hunter said wryly. "She

was going to do it whether I *let* her or not." That was probably true. The stubborn female. For some reason, that thought made him smile. "And I hate to say it, but it was a good idea with little risk. If she pulls it off, her company will have actually done some good. Accidentally, but I'll take it."

Right now, Riker didn't give a shit about what Nicole was doing for the sake of the vampire population. He just wanted her back. "I can't leave her with them."

Closing his eyes, Hunter turned his face up to the stars. "I was afraid you were going to say that." He lowered his head and pegged Riker with eyes as black as the sky. "You always were loyal to a fault."

"It's more than that." Riker pushed down the waistband of the shredded pajama pants and exposed the crimson wing above his pelvic bone.

"Oh . . . damn." An owl hooted in the distance, distracting Hunter for a heartbeat. "Is that a good thing?"

Good? It could be, but given their last encounter, it could also be a disaster. "I love her."

"But?" Hunter asked. Riker must have made "I love her" sound like a total downer.

"She doesn't know." Riker jammed his hand through his hair. "Fuck me, I didn't know until today. All this time, I've been so hung up on Terese and everything that happened to her." An ache pounded inside his chest, right behind his sternum. "I thought I was getting over it, but when Bastien came, the hell he went through brought up all that shit again."

"Let me guess." Hunter paused to signal Jaggar and Baddon, and the two melted into the forest for a routine patrol. The mystic-keeper, Sabre, rubbed herbs together in his hands and began to reinforce the defensive wards he would have set up around the camp. "You wanted Nicole but couldn't commit because of who her family is, what they did to Terese and Bastien, and because she was human. How am I doing so far?"

Right on target. "Like an arrowhead between the eyes," Riker admitted.

"So you finally got over yourself and decided you can commit, but now that she's a vampire and you've imprinted on her, if you tell her you love her, she'll think you only want her because she's no longer human and because of the imprint."

Clearly, Hunter had a better grasp on the situation than Riker did, and he nodded sullenly. "After the way I treated her before she turned, she's not going to believe I'd have wanted her even if things hadn't changed."

Hunter considered that. Finally, he shrugged. "Dude, you're screwed."

"Thank you, Chief," Riker said flatly, "for stating the fucking obvious."

Hunter shrugged. "I should have been a relationship therapist or some shit."

Sarcasm aside, Hunter did have a point. Riker was screwed. There was no way Nicole was going to look past the imprint and think he'd want her if he weren't biologically linked to her. He'd kicked her out of his bedroom, for fuck's sake.

Maybe he could beg for her forgiveness. He considered the idea but rejected it almost immediately. Even if she forgave him for his idiocy, she would always in the back of her mind wonder if the imprint was the reason for his apology and attention.

Somehow he had to convince her that he loved her and that it had nothing to do with the fact that she was no longer human and he was imprinted.

The answer struck him like one of Hunter's uppercuts, leaving him stunned and a little shaken. In order to win Nicole, he was going to have to take a huge risk, and while he'd always been comfortable gambling with his life, this was different. This time, he wasn't just putting his life on the line; he was jeopardizing his sanity and his heart.

NICOLE SPENT THE next twenty-four hours in hell. ShadowSpawn's massive complex was filthy and dark, and those who lived in it were suspicious and brutish. The males had little respect for females, and while the females didn't appear to be abused and they certainly didn't shrink away from confrontation, they were definitely treated like second-class citizens.

She couldn't wait to get back to MoonBound, but first, she had to analyze the remaining fifteen pregnancy tests from the nineteen females who had taken the conception mixture she'd created.

Well, nineteen . . . plus herself.

Anxiety fluttered through her at the unlikely possibility that she could be carrying Riker's child. So far, of the five tests she'd checked, only one popped positive. Yes, a 20 percent success rate, especially in a race that rarely conceived, was fabulous, but it also meant that the chances that she *wasn't* pregnant were pretty good.

Her hand shook as she used a clean syringe to draw blood from a vial she'd taken from a pureblooded female named White Fox and injected it just under the skin on Fane's broad back. Daedalus had determined that the males' bodies reacted to female pregnancy hormones, which made sense, since even before the end of the first trimester, males could taste it in the blood.

Instantly, a silvery patch bloomed in a circle around the injection site. "Positive," she announced, and Kars, lurking with some of his minions near the door, let out a grunt of satisfaction, as if he was responsible for knocking up White Fox.

With Aylin's help, she repeated the tests over and over. Negative. Negative. Negative. Positive. Negative. Test number nineteen was the fourth positive. Only one was left.

Stomach churning, she injected the sample into Fane's skin. Throat so tight she could barely breathe, she waited. Had the others taken this long to reveal a positive or a negative? She was torn about what she wanted to see. A negative meant she wasn't pregnant and that she'd failed to get the five pregnancies needed to get herself out of here. A positive meant freedom.

And a baby that would tie her to a male who clearly didn't want to be bound to her in any way.

She'd be happy, though. She'd always wanted children, even if she hadn't thought it would really happen. Not with her work schedule. Not when the only men she ever met were Daedalus employees.

Fane's skin at the injection site darkened . . . and turned silver.

"Positive," she rasped, and then cut off Kars's shout of jubilation by adding, "I'm pregnant."

In the sudden silence, she gave herself a moment to recover, but she wasn't going to freak out. There was time for that later. Right now, she had to push ahead and get the hell out of here.

"That's five." She eyed the door. "I kept my end of the bargain. Now it's time for you to keep yours."

Kars came at her like a bull, backing her against the table holding the equipment and supplies she'd brought with her.

"You aren't going anywhere."

Anxiety and despair formed a lump in her throat and left her barely able to speak. "The deal was for five pregnant females. Five are pregnant."

"Not five of *our* females," he roared. "The deal is off. We're keeping you and your child."

"What?" She shoved against him. "You can't do that!"

"I can do whatever I want." His hand clamped around her throat. "You're ours now." His nasty sneer radiated malevolence. "Aylin, why don't you help our newest clan member make herself comfortable in her new home?"

THERE WAS NO freaking way Nicole was staying in this hellhole. No way she was going through pregnancy and childbirth in what amounted to a den of wild animals. Of course, childbirth would be dangerous whether she was here or at MoonBound, but the thought of these creatures providing care was unacceptable. And what if she died but the baby survived?

She shuddered at the idea of her child growing up all alone with these monsters.

The second Kars and his merry band of assholes left, she started to plot. By the time she and Aylin were halfway to the cell Fane had assigned her to, she'd formulated a plan to escape. Unfortunately, it involved tricking Aylin, the one person who had been kind to Nicole.

But she had to get out of here. She'd do anything to protect her child, even if that meant betraying Aylin.

"Are you okay?" Aylin asked as they approached the row of cells that unmated females called home. They were nicer than the "guest" quarters Nicole had been assigned to before, but that wasn't saying much.

A cot, a blanket, a pillow, and a wooden box for belongings didn't make for a homey environment.

"I'll be fine." Her stomach growled, and the sound vibrated through the dank, tight passage.

"You should visit the feeding room," Aylin said, and Nicole grew nauseated.

The feeding room was full of humans who volunteered to live at the compound to feed anyone who came to them, but Nicole had no desire to feed from anyone but Riker. She'd have to learn to feed from humans eventually, but for now, she was fine with packaged blood.

"I'll pass." She planned to be out of here in about five minutes, anyway.

Aylin pushed open Nicole's cell door. "I don't blame you. If I could hunt, I would."

"Your father doesn't let you?"

Aylin's blond hair swooshed around her waist as she shook her head. "I'm not strong enough. He's afraid I could be captured by another clan and held for ransom or something."

"Forgive me, but your father is an ass."

Aylin laughed. "That's the general consensus."

Nicole wondered why, if everyone disliked Kars, the clan didn't overthrow him. Not that it was any of her business. She liked Aylin, though, and hated not only what she was about to do, but that she had to leave her here with her bastard of a father.

"I'm sorry, Aylin," Nicole said softly.

She frowned. "For what?"

Nicole took a deep, bracing breath. "For this." She shoved Aylin into the cell and slammed the door shut, engaging the lock. The disappointment in the female's expression devastated her. "I had to.. I'm so sorry, but I have to get out of here."

"I know." Aylin's tone was sad, but she smiled. "I'd hoped you wouldn't do it, but I expected it." Her smile grew mischievous. "I also expect you to let me out and let me help."

Taken aback, Nicole blurted, "Why would you want to help me?"

A muscle ticked in Aylin's jaw, and her eyes glinted with defiance. "I might not be a warrior or a hunter, but that doesn't mean I'm useless. I can do more than mend clothes and wash ale mugs." She reached through the bars, lightning quick, and took Nicole's hand. Her nails bit into her skin but didn't break it. "I don't get the chance to do anything important very often, so I take opportunities as they come. I can get you out of here."

Breaking out of Aylin's grip, Nicole weighed her answer, which seemed genuine. But could Nicole bet not just her life but that of her unborn baby on a Shadow-Spawn female's word? "I like you, Aylin, but—"

"But I'm the enemy, and you can't trust me," Aylin finished. "I know. But if you don't, you won't get out of here. I promise you that. And once you're caught, I guarantee you'll never get another chance to get out." She wrapped her hands around the iron bars and leaned in. "I understand why you don't trust me, but we're not all bad people."

Not long ago, Nicole had said something similar to Riker about humans. And she'd learned the same about his people.

She looked around at the cells that doubled as private quarters and weighed the risks of living here permanently versus escape. There was no question. She had to get out of here, and if Aylin could help, she had to take that risk. After all, even if this was a trick, how much worse could her treatment get?

An image of Riker, beaten and bleeding in the dungeon, popped into her head, and okay, it could get worse. But babies were precious to this clan—any clan, really—and while she didn't doubt she'd be treated badly, she doubted they'd actually harm her.

At least, not until the baby was born.

Freshly spurred more by the fear of what would become of her child than what would become of her, she flipped open the locking mechanism on the cell door.

"Okay," she said to Aylin. "Let's get out of here."

RIKER COULDN'T STAND this. He'd been hanging out in the MoonBound camp for a full day, and now, with the afternoon sun starting to duck behind the mountains, they still hadn't heard if Nicole's pregnancy plan had been successful. Shouldn't ShadowSpawn have brought a message by now?

He'd suggested that everyone else head back to headquarters, but every warrior, including Hunter, looked at him like he was a fucking idiot.

"One of ours is in trouble," Hunter said. "Until we know her status, we stay."

For the first couple of years after being turned, Riker had missed the military. Oh, he hadn't missed being human or being betrayed by the very military he'd dedicated his life to, but he'd definitely missed the camaraderie, the brotherhood that had tied his squad together.

He'd gotten that brotherhood back when he'd accepted his place with MoonBound. Hunter's words just now reminded him of what he had. And what he stood to lose if something happened to Nicole.

After twenty years of feeling empty, Riker had started to feel whole again, and it was all thanks to her. Even if they couldn't work out a relationship, he needed her in his life. He needed her to be back at MoonBound, safe, and to be there for Bastien.

He looked down at the crude map he'd drawn with a stick into the damp forest floor near the fire pit. Shallow holes indicated low-lying areas between MoonBound's camp and ShadowSpawn's headquarters. Small stones represented trees or bluffs where MoonBound's archers had been stationed. High ground favorable to MoonBound in a battle was marked by an *X*, and scout positions were assigned an *O*.

There were too few of everything.

"I'm going to patrol," Riker said, to no one in particular. Hunter, Takis, and Aiden were out hunting, Myne was MIA, and Jaggar was checking on the scouts he'd assigned to monitor the area to the southeast, where ShadowSpawn was located. Only Baddon, Katina, and half a dozen of their warriors were hanging around camp, and none of them was paying attention to him.

Their poker game was apparently a life-or-death situation.

He took off toward the southeast and made it about half a mile before Myne appeared, dressed from head to toe in black and silent as an owl dropping from a tree.

"How the fuck do you do that?" Riker asked.

Myne remained in the crouch he'd landed in. "I was born awesome."

"You were born a dick." Riker glared. "Where have you been?"

"I've been around." He stood slowly, but he didn't stop staring toward the east. "Didn't feel like listening to Hunter's bullshit."

"What happened between you two, anyway?" Riker asked him the same question every so often, always got the same answer.

Weapons clinked as Myne shrugged. "Just don't like him."

Yep, same answer. There was more to the story, Riker was sure, but as usual, the guy didn't want to talk about it. "Hey, ah . . . I wanted to thank you." His face heated. There really was nothing more uncomfortable than two dudes getting sappy.

"For what?"

"For taking care of Bastien." He forced his jaw to unlock for the rest, because as grateful as Riker was to Myne, he couldn't completely get rid of his envy over Myne being there for Nicole. In Riker's bed. "And for helping Nicole through her change."

Finally, Myne's gaze met Riker's. "Nothing happened."

"I know."

"Yeah? Do you also know you're a fucking idiot?"

Okaaay. "Is that a trick question?"

Myne blew out a frustrated breath and turned away again. "You need to mate her."

"That decision is up to her."

"Then make her choose you, because if you don't make her yours, someone else will."

Riker went taut. "Meaning?"

"Dumbass," Myne snapped. "Not me. I'll never see her as anything but yours. But there are a lot of unmated males in the clan, and she's . . ."

"Special. I know."

Myne pivoted, very slowly. "Do you also know someone's coming? Two people. Females or young males."

Shit. Riker reached for a dagger as Myne palmed his twin swords out of the sheaths on his back. He heard the sound of two sets of feet pounding on the forest floor, and then, coming up fast, the rumble of dozens more feet.

He saw Nicole before she saw him. She was running, but the female with her, Aylin, he was sure, was slowing her down. He and Myne bolted toward them at a dead run. Nicole finally saw him, but as she screamed his name, she and Aylin were swarmed by Shadow-Spawn warriors.

Rage shattered Riker's ability to think about anything but protecting Nicole. Bellowing with fury, he launched a blade, catching one of the enemy warriors in the throat. The guy went down hard, but three more replaced him. An arrow shot past Riker's head. He ducked another as he raced toward the enemy line.

In the space of five seconds, he and Myne were engaged in battle, outnumbered, and balls-deep in trouble.

Nicole shouted his name, but it was barely out of her mouth when Aylin's scream rang out. He couldn't see the females, couldn't help them, not when he was fighting five guys at once. He dodged and spun between the enemies, burying a dagger in one belly and then spinning and slashing chests and throats on the return. Blood spurted, some of it his as he took more than his share of damage.

A blow to the head made him see double, and as he wobbled on his axis, something sliced open his shoulder and sent him spinning into a tree. As a hatchet came at his head, he hit the ground and rolled. He hunched down behind a stump to avoid another blow, and the hatchet sank into the tree with a dull thud that could have belonged to Riker's skull.

As the hatchet wielder yanked the blade free of the wood, Riker exploded to his feet and threw a double tap to the male's face, followed by a roundhouse kick to his gut. The guy dropped, but there were ten more warriors to take his place.

Suddenly, war cries filled the air, and in an instant, all but two of the ShadowSpawn males scattered, their focus on fresh targets.

Hunter and the rest of MoonBound's warriors had arrived.

New energy hummed through Riker's bones. He welcomed the adrenaline rush, welcomed the smell of blood, pain, and fear that fueled his desire to rip apart the males who were manhandling Nicole. Battle lust reduced him to a weapon of pure power as he fought his way toward the last place he'd seen Nicole, cutting through ShadowSpawn's warriors with a dagger and throwing stars.

He caught sight of Nicole as she struggled against two males who were dragging her away from the battle. He roared her name and hurtled over a fallen Shadow-

Spawn warrior, but as he landed, he took a blunt-force blow to his kidney. The impact made him stagger, and pain made him grunt in agony, but he kept going, never taking his eyes off Nicole.

She cursed viciously and sank her fangs deep into one of the warriors' biceps. He yelled as she shook her head like a dog with a rabbit, ripping his flesh from his bone. The other male with them brought his arm back, hand balled into a fist. Before it landed on Nicole's jaw, Riker hit the guy from behind and brought him down in a tangle of limbs.

Riker took a solid punch to the face, but the other male was no match for Riker's fangs. He sank them deep into the guy's throat, clamped down hard, and tore the bastard's carotid artery out of his neck.

"Rike—!"

At Nicole's cutoff scream, Riker half scrambled, half spun off the spasming body of the dying vampire in time to see Kars, his fist tangled in Nicole's hair.

ShadowSpawn's unholy leader shoved her to her knees and jammed a dagger against her throat. "Lay down your weapons!" he shouted. "Or the bitch dies."

NICOLE SWALLOWED AGAINST the feel of the cold blade pressed into the soft spot that bisected her jaw and her jugular vein. The sting told her it had cut into her skin, and the hatred in Riker's eyes told her he knew it as well.

Hunter stalked toward them, his bare upper body a mass of cuts, his knuckles shredded. As his boots crunched dead leaves and fallen branches, she wondered how hard it was for him to avoid looking at the dead and wounded lying in pools of blood on the ground as he passed. She hadn't even known most of them, but the sight tore at her. She couldn't imagine what it must be doing to him.

"What the fuck is the meaning of this?" Hunter's voice was distorted, warped with something disturbing. Malevolent, even. Crimson streaks cut through the black in his eyes, and Nicole shrank back, somehow more afraid of whatever was inside Hunter than of the knife at her throat. "We had a deal."

Kars snarled. "And we kept our end of the bargain." He yanked on Nicole's hair, hauling her to her feet next to him. "This bitch did not."

Face twisted in an expression that promised pain, Riker lunged at Kars. Fane intercepted, tackling Riker from the flank and slamming them both to the ground. Fantasies of dropping a boric-acid bomb on top of the ShadowSpawn bastard went through Nicole's head.

Please don't fight them, Riker. She caught his eye as he struggled with Fane. *Please.* If he got hurt—or worse—while trying to save her, she'd never forgive herself.

He read her, thank God, and eased his palm off the dagger he'd been about to draw from the leg pocket of his military fatigue pants. As he raised his hands, she watched to make sure he didn't go for one of the weapons he'd have concealed under his black sweater.

"She gave us only four pregnancies, and then she used my daughter to help her escape." Kars tugged again, this time so viciously that her eyes watered. Where was Aylin, anyway? Aylin had kept her word, and Nicole owed her more than she could possibly repay. "Nicole brought this war down on you. Not me." He signaled to his men. "Kill them all."

Oh, Jesus. "Wait!" she screamed. "We know the treatment works. I'll give you more next month—"

"Yes, you will." He signaled again, but this time, Hunter shouted for a halt to the killing.

"Stop!" He raised both hands, fingers splayed in a gesture she didn't recognize but was of clear importance to Kars. "*Nuh-hun esu . . . vedi.*"

Silence fell on the forest. Even the insects and

birds held to an eerie truce, and all eyes went to Hunter. But Kars alone seemed to understand what Hunter had said. Tension crackled in the air like the moment before lightning struck, and Nicole swore she smelled ozone.

Kars spoke, his voice low but threaded with an electric undercurrent. "*Estaltias en flori esu. Vedi ak'nya.*"

Nicole glanced at Riker, but his barely discernible shrug told her he had no idea what was going on, either. Hunter didn't make a move. Not for a long time. When he finally did, it was to incline his head in a slow nod of acceptance. But acceptance of what?

The two clan leaders spoke more in the language only they seemed to know. The tone of their conversation varied from calm to angry, and twice she thought battle would break out again. After what seemed like forever, the red streaks faded from Hunter's eyes, and Kars stepped away from her. Both chiefs signaled to their warriors.

As the two parties sheathed their weapons, she grabbed Kars's thick arm. "Where's Aylin? What have you done to her?"

His smile was chilling as he shoved her away. "She's not your concern."

Riker reached her as Kars stormed off, leaving his warriors to collect their injured and dead.

"Nicole." Riker choked out her name as he folded her into his arms and crushed her against him so hard she *oof*ed. "Thank God. Oh, thank God."

She hugged him tight, never so glad to see anyone in her life. "I'm sorry," she whispered. "I'm so sorry."

"For what?"

"For this." She squeezed her eyes closed against

all the blood, death, and misery. How many had died today? How many would suffer in agony as they healed? "It's all my fault. If I hadn't tried to escape—"

He cut her off with a kiss so passionate it took her breath. By the time he broke off the kiss, she was dazed. "You're safe, and that's all that matters."

She looked over at Hunter, who was kneeling, head bowed, next to a dead MoonBound male she recognized but didn't know. All around, the surviving clan members were patching up the severely injured or gathering those who hadn't made it. The clan had taken a hard hit, and it would be a long time before they recovered.

"What language were Kars and Hunter speaking? What were they talking about?"

"Fuck if I know. I've never heard that language before. And I've never seen him like that." Riker sounded as shaken as she was as his hands roamed her face, her neck, her arms, as if he couldn't believe she was alive and in one piece. She knew the feeling, because she couldn't keep her hands off him, either. "It sounded like a negotiation, but whatever it was, I get the feeling we didn't exactly win the battle."

She got that feeling, too. And it had nothing to do with the fact that so many had been injured or killed. Whatever Hunter had done, the consequences were going to be with them for a long time.

Hunter came over to them, his expression grave. "Are you okay?"

She nodded. "I'm sorry," she said. "What Kars said about me breaking the deal . . . it wasn't that simple. It was—"

Hunter silenced her with a gesture. "I know. He's a bastard with no sense of honor. He shouldn't have tried to keep you . . . or anything that belongs to you." He gave her a look charged with meaning, and she knew he was aware of the life she carried in her belly.

Riker tucked her into the curve of his arm, and she settled against him as if everything was right with the world. It wasn't, but for now, she needed this, even if it only lasted a few minutes.

"What did you do to end the battle?" Riker asked.

"What I had to do," Hunter said in a clipped voice that dripped with a *drop it* vibe.

Nicole had never been very good at dropping anything, but in this case, there were more pressing matters. "Did you bring first-aid supplies? I can help with the injured."

Hunter shook his head. "Jag's handling medic duty. I want you out of the way." He shot a pointed look at Riker. "Take Nicole back to the clan, and have Grant see to your wounds. I'm sending some warriors with you."

Riker's wounds would be mostly healed by the time they got back, but Nicole kept her mouth shut. Hunter was trying to get her pregnant butt to safety, and she knew it.

"Hunt—" Riker started, but the clan chief rounded on him with a hiss.

"It wasn't a suggestion."

Riker popped a sarcastic salute. "Heading home as ordered, sir. Moving out now." As Hunter strode away, Riker uttered a curse. "Whatever went down between him and Kars is going to come back to bite us in the ass."

"I'm thinking the same thing." She glanced in the direction she and Aylin had come from, hoping the ShadowSpawn female was okay. How much had Aylin risked to get Nicole back to MoonBound? Nicole doubted that Kars would let his daughter's actions go unpunished. The question was, how severe would the punishment be?

"Let's go." Riker took Nicole's hand and started toward MoonBound's headquarters.

Instantly, several clan members fell in with them. Most of the warriors kept to the rear, but a few scouted out ahead and to the sides in a well-coordinated tactical maneuver. Nicole didn't miss the way Riker watched them all, nodding his approval and, once, barking out an order to one male who fell back a little too far.

For a long time, no one said anything, and the farther they got from the site of the battle, the more distance came between Nicole and Riker. The things they'd left unfinished were like an invisible crowbar prying them apart, until they weren't holding hands anymore.

"Did they treat you well?" Riker finally asked, although he kept his attention focused everywhere but on her, even as he spoke.

"They didn't hurt me, if that's what you're asking." A squirrel scolded her as she stepped over a gully, waving away Riker's offer to help. "Have you seen Bastien?"

"Not since I left ShadowSpawn."

She hopped another stream, loving how effortless these things were with her new vampire body. Even at an easy jog they covered almost twice the amount of ground a human could at a run. "I've missed him."

"Me, too," Riker admitted. "I have a lot of time to make up to him."

"I'm sure you'll develop an amazing relationship with him."

"I hope so." He slowed as they approached a giant, moss-covered boulder she recognized. They were close to headquarters. By her estimation, they'd traveled a hundred fifty miles in just over three hours, and they hadn't been moving at full speed. "Who knows what kind of damage was done to him, though."

She hoped Myne had used her intel to make Chuck pay for what he'd done. She wasn't going to apologize to Riker, though. Not again. If he didn't know how deep her regret ran by now, he never would.

A low, steady hum vibrated through her bones as they approached headquarters, and she realized the buzz had been there all along, like a signal from a homing beacon that grew stronger the closer she got to MoonBound.

"I can feel the clan," she murmured. "Wow."

Riker grinned, a stunner that made her heart flip. "It means you associate the clan with home. Helps you find your way back."

Emotion gripped her so tightly she forgot to breathe. She hadn't had a home since she was a child. She'd had houses, but not homes. Now she had something worth finding her way back to.

Speaking of finding her way back . . . "How is Lucy doing?" Nicole asked. "ShadowSpawn didn't hurt her, did they?"

"Not as far as we know," Riker said darkly. "She won't talk about it." Nicole's thoughts went to really bad places. Riker seemed to know, and he came to a stop outside headquarters. He waved everyone off, leaving them alone under the light of the rising moon. "She's okay. But I'm not sure you are. Hell, I'm not sure I am."

Something *was* different about Riker, but she couldn't put her finger on it. What she did know for certain was that she wanted to tell him about her pregnancy and beg him to take her to bed. But a child wasn't going to change anything. Oh, she knew he'd be an incredible father, and there was no doubt whatsoever that he'd be by her side. But if he wasn't over Terese, he wasn't getting Nicole in a two-for-one with the baby.

"If you're talking about my health, I'm fine."

"And if I'm talking about your emotions?"

"Not so fine." She sighed. "Nothing has changed, has it?"

"A lot has changed. You were right about my guilt over Terese." He shoved his hands into his pants pockets and spoke quickly, as if he was afraid he'd forget what he had to say if he didn't get it out. "I was blaming you, and it wasn't fair, because none of it was your fault. I blamed myself but didn't want to, and you were an easy target. I never felt like Terese had the life or the mate she deserved while she was alive, because no matter how hard I tried, I couldn't love her. Not like I love you."

On the heels of that admission, Nicole could barely form a coherent thought. "You . . . what?"

"You heard me," he said gruffly.

She thought back to the day he'd kicked her out

of his bedroom. He'd been so full of festering poison. Something must have lanced the wound. "What changed?"

A breeze filtered through the tree branches, and a single snowflake drifted to the ground between them. Riker turned his face into the wind, and she had a feeling he was looking for an excuse not to meet her gaze. "I realized I was a fucking idiot."

"When?" she asked, suddenly suspicious. "After I turned?"

"Before."

She didn't see how that was possible. He'd kicked her out of his bedroom, and the next time he saw her, she was a vampire. "Bullshit."

"It's true."

"Then why didn't you say anything?"

He turned back to her, his sandy hair mussed from the breeze, and her fingers itched to comb through it. "The thing with Bastien and Chuck. The bedroom. It all came down on me at once, and I freaked out. Instead of giving in to my need for you, I pushed you away. I was a huge jerk. A total bastard. I'm not proud of it, but there it is."

What he was saying made sense, but there was something more going on here. Nicole wasn't sure how she knew that, but her new vampire senses were tingling. "Ah."

"You don't believe me?"

She wanted to. God, she wanted to. How easy it would be to say yes, to take Riker at his word. She wouldn't even feel foolish about doing it, since he'd been nothing but honest with her from the beginning.

But if she'd learned anything at all over the course of the last two weeks, it was that she should never ignore her instincts. She'd disregarded her gut feelings about Daedalus, had trusted others far too easily, and the results had been disastrous.

"Nicole?" Riker prompted, and she winced at the slight crack in his voice. He sensed her doubt, and she hated that her hesitation hurt him.

"I want to believe you," she croaked.

"But you don't." His expression shuttered so completely that he looked like a different person. A stranger. "Then there's nothing left to say."

Throwing her words from the day he'd kicked her out of the bedroom back at her—he was good at that—he stalked off, leaving her standing at the entrance to headquarters.

Heart aching, grief leaving her frozen to the cold ground, she waited a long time before she went inside . . . but to what, she had no idea.

AFTER MAKING SURE his surviving warriors were being cared for, Hunter made a beeline for his quarters. He hit the wet bar before his door even gave the soft *whoosh* of air that signaled it was halfway closed. In a single, fluid motion, he grabbed a bottle of vodka and a glass in one hand and then sank down onto the couch.

Blindly, he splashed liquor into the highball and knocked back three huge gulps. The powerful burn didn't even come close to scouring away the echoes of the dead.

He'd lost six warriors today. Six more were seriously wounded. More than a dozen would spend a couple of miserable days recovering.

Then there was the conversation he'd had with ShadowSpawn's leader as he bargained to get Nicole back.

Hunter had made a deal with the devil, and payment would be due soon.

Fitting, he supposed, since a pact with a demon was what had led to the creation of vampires in the first place.

Hunter sprawled against the cushions, legs spread, eyes closed. He hadn't spoken the ancient language of the Elders in almost a century, since the last time he'd traveled through mystical vortexes to Boynton Canyon to meet with said Elders. Every time he spoke the inherent language that he, and every first- and second-generation vampire, had been born with, it rattled him. Drained him. Reminded him that he was very different from everyone else in the clan.

He wondered if Kars was right now feeling the same way. Not that Hunter gave a rat's ass if Kars was as drained as he was. It would just be cool to know Hunter wasn't alone.

There were times when Hunter liked being one of the special few who knew the true history of vampires, but this wasn't one of them. How lucky those like Grant, Riker, and Myne were, to attribute the vampire curse to a scientifically explained virus or two tribal chiefs who were bled on by a raven and a crow.

Very few vampires knew the truth, thanks to carefully crafted legends and half-truths fabricated by the first- and second-generation vampires, all of whom had sworn an oath of silence to the demon that had bestowed the gift of vampirism on them.

As a second-gen, Hunter was sworn to secrecy, but every time he drank, he wondered why he bothered. Why anyone bothered. All but two of the Originals were dead, and more than half of the first-generation vampires were gone. At this point, no one would believe the truth, anyway.

Demons? Even Hunter wasn't convinced. At least, he wasn't convinced that they still existed. Maybe the demons of the Native American beliefs had faded away, victims of a lack of education of the old ways and gods. If no one believed, how could demons exist?

He started to pour more vodka into the glass, but screw it. A bottle was glass, right?

Tossing the glass aside, he put the bottle to his lips and chugged. Ancient curses and oaths, demons and devils, none of it was important. What was important was the deal he'd made today. A deal that saved Riker from going mad with need for the female he'd imprinted on and that might have saved the life of Nicole and her unborn child.

But it was also a deal that would tie MoonBound and ShadowSpawn together forever. Kars was finally getting what he'd wanted, what he'd been pressuring Hunter to do for decades.

Nuh-hun esu . . . vedi.

I'll mate your daughter.

SOMETHING WAS WRONG. Nicole didn't know what it was, exactly, but something was making her chest hurt. She'd gone to Grant for a checkup, but he was useless. He could perform advanced first aid, but when it came to examining the female body, he got all flustered and fidgety. He could barely listen to her heart through a stethoscope without hyperventilating. And it only got worse after she told him she was pregnant.

He'd finally fetched Katina, but all Nicole and the other female had done was drink Grant's Kool-Aid concoctions. Nicole decided she liked whatever flavor blue and purple made.

"So." Katina sat back in the rolling desk chair she'd planted herself in. "You broke up with Riker, and your chest hurts." She shrugged. "I'm no rocket scientist, but even I can see that those two things are related."

Nicole huffed. "It's not a broken heart." Yes, she had that, too, but the ache in her chest was physical. "There's something . . . weird. Maybe it's the pregnancy?"

Katina's placating smile had Nicole bracing for the

other female's sarcasm. "Honey, I know you're some sort of vampire physiologist, but you must have missed the class about babies growing in your belly, not your chest."

Nicole glared at Katina before doing the same to Grant, who sat at a nearby computer and snickered. "You two are no help. I could be dying."

"And I could be sleeping." Katina yawned. "Is your crisis over yet?"

"No." Nicole nudged Katina with her foot. "Wake up. This is payback for wanting to eat me."

"You used to be food," Katina pointed out, without an ounce of contrition.

Nicole threw her head back and let out a sound of frustration. She wasn't truly upset with Katina and Grant; she was upset with herself. She was pregnant, her chest hurt, and she'd probably ruined her relationship with Riker. He'd tried to tell her he loved her, and she'd doubted him. No wonder every time he saw her, he'd turn and walk the other way. Or even worse, he'd pass her by with nothing more than a polite nod. A polite freaking *nod*.

They'd kissed. They'd fed from each other. They'd had sex against a wall. And in a dungeon. He'd used his tongue on her in ways that gave her hot flashes just thinking about.

And he was *politely nodding* at her.

"You know," Grant said, "Riker's pretty miserable, too."

"Could have fooled me," she muttered.

"It's true." Katina downed a test tube filled with orange liquid. "That one's nasty." She plunked the tube into an empty wooden holder. "I sparred with him this morning. He's all sullen and broody, like one of those emo TV vampires that were popular a while back. So lame."

"Well, he's never been a load of laughs," Grant chimed in. "But yes, he's even less mirthful than usual."

Mirthful? Who used that word? "He said he loved me even before I turned into a vampire, and I wasn't sure if I should believe him or not."

Katina thought about that for a second. "Yeah, you know, I'd be skeptical, too. He had a lot of reason to hate the human you."

"I think you should have believed him," Grant said.

Both Katina and Nicole turned to him. "Why?" Nicole asked.

Grant went back to whatever he was doing on the computer. "Because males don't say sappy things like that unless they mean it."

"Then why was he so quick to walk away from me?"

There was a loud sigh, and then Grant pushed away from the table. "Okay, let's say you accepted him at his word, even though you had some niggling doubt. Then later down the road, humans do something stupid and heinous to vampires, the way they always do, and he gets angry. Starts railing about how awful humans are. How self-conscious are you going to be? Are you going to wonder if, deep down, he still thinks of you that way? Even if you don't worry about it, he will. He needs you to know he's past it and that he loves you for who you are. Not *what* you are."

Nicole stared at the scientist, floored that he was

so in tune with relationships when he was so out of tune with pretty much everything else.

"Damn," Katina said as she eyed him up and down. "Sometimes you actually make sense."

"I always make sense." Grant stood, yanking the bottom of his jacket to straighten it. "Everyone else needs to listen better."

Nicole watched him gather up empty test tubes. People accused Grant of not playing with a full deck, but she was starting to suspect that his deck was full—he was just playing a different game.

"Does he know about the baby?" Katina asked.

"I haven't told him."

Katina *tsk*ed. "You need to. And if you believe what he said, you need to tell him that, too." She leaned forward and patted Nicole on the knee. "It'll make your chest feel better."

So many emotions brewed close to the surface, leaving Nicole on the verge of breaking into a loud, sloppy bawl. Love for Riker. Sorrow for hurting him. Anger that he'd taken so long to come around. And joy that he'd given her the chance to find a real home among the least likely people she could ever have imagined.

She owed him. Not because of all the horrible things her family did to him and his race. But because her family had done all those horrible things and he loved her in spite of it.

Now she just had to hope it wasn't too late.

RIKER HADN'T SEEN Nicole, except in passing, for four days.

It was killing him. He'd left the ball in her court, letting her decide if she could believe he'd fallen for her when she was still human.

Apparently, she didn't believe him.

He kept playing with the little origami animals she'd made, smiling at how they reminded him of her, delicate and complex, beautiful and yet capable of cutting deep. The dragon figure had cut his thumb, but she'd slashed his heart.

"Nicole showed me how to make birds." Seated at the kitchen counter, Bastien touched his finger to the wing of a paper butterfly Nicole had left near the toaster.

Today was the third day in a row he'd come to Riker's quarters after they sparred in the exercise room. Myne had taught Bastien well—the kid was a fast learner, and he was starting to gain control of his ability to briefly turn invisible. Once he mastered that, the power to flash invisibly out of the way of an incoming strike would make up for his lack of fighting experience. Bastien was going to be one hell of an asset to the clan someday.

"I'd like it if you made me a bird sometime," Riker said.

"I'll *carve* you one out of wood. Baddon showed me." Riker had to smother a grin as Bastien swung off the bar stool. The boy had grown, not just physically but emotionally. "I'm going to shower and help Grant in the lab. Are you going to teach me how to read the wind tomorrow?"

"You bet. You'll be hitting the bullseye with arrows in gale-force winds before you know it."

There was a single knock on the door, and then Myne strolled in with a six-pack of beer. "Swiped it from a hunter's camp." He gestured to Bastien. "If you guys are busy, I can come back."

"I was just leaving." Bastien started out the door but turned to Riker at the threshold. "Later, Dad."

Bastien disappeared, leaving Riker's mouth dry and his heart pounding. "Did you hear that?" he asked Myne, hoping his buddy had heard it, too, and it wasn't all in his head.

Grinning, Myne tossed him a beer. "Yeah. Pretty cool. Guess he's over his daddy issues."

Riker didn't raise his hopes that much, but it was a good start. "I heard you haven't found Chuck."

"Fucker is practically on lockdown since Nicole was taken." Myne sank into the overstuffed chair kitty-corner from the couch. "It's going to be a while before we can do the world a favor by removing his head."

Riker looked down at his beer, wondering how Nicole was going to feel about that. It was one thing to say you didn't care what happened to your brother and another to experience it.

"And Bastien? Have you felt him out about this?"

"He says he doesn't care what happens to Chuck." Myne *clink*ed his bottle against Riker's. "Personally, I think we should catch the bastard, toss him into the prey room, and let Bastien have him. We'll call it alternative therapy."

Riker had always believed in alternative therapy. Even when he'd been human, he'd known that a well-placed bullet in a terrorist's chest could heal the mind and spirit.

"How's Lucy?" He planted his ass on the couch, figuring they were stuck talking for a while. "I haven't seen her since I got back."

"She's been making friends with Bastien. He reads to her like a big brother." Myne leaned back in his chair, cradling his beer like a lover. Myne's therapists had always had names like Henry Weinhard and Captain Morgan. "Now, what's up with Hunter? No one has seen him in days. He's been shut up in his chambers. Won't even let in any females."

"No females?" Riker frowned. "That's disturbing." Almost as disturbing as seeing the change in Hunter when he spoke to Kars. Both chiefs had radiated a certain sinister energy that had raised the hairs on the back of Riker's neck. Then there had been the crimson lighting in their eyes. It was almost as if they'd been tapping into a well of power so strong their bodies couldn't contain it.

Myne twitched one shoulder in a half shrug. "I'm happy enough not seeing him every day." He took a swig from his beer. "Have you talked to Nicole?"

Her name was a blade to the chest. "I was hoping she'd want to talk by now. Guess I underestimated how she felt about me."

"So you want to see her?"

Riker inhaled raggedly. "I'd sell my soul if she'd walk through my door."

"Huh." Myne chugged his beer and slammed the bottle down on the coffee table. "Gotta go." All Riker could do was stare as his friend popped to his feet and took off. Before Riker could even process the fact that

Myne was gone, he was back, pulling Nicole inside with him.

"What the hell are you doing?" The feather mark tingling, Riker stood, unsure if Nicole needed help or if she was completely cool with being dragged into Riker's quarters.

"She's been waiting in the hall." Myne shoved her forward. "She didn't want to come in if you weren't willing to talk to her. Since you said you'd sell your soul, I took that as a good sign. Now, if you two will excuse me, I'm outta here."

"Well," she said, after the door closed, "that wasn't how I imagined this would go down."

"I'm pretty sure Myne has a disorder that makes him completely oblivious to social etiquette."

"Hmm." Nicole smiled wryly. "I noticed that when we first met. I didn't think it was polite of him to kill Mr. Altrough after knowing him just sixty seconds."

Riker nearly groaned. This conversation wasn't going well. At all. "Ah, yeah. There are some things in both our pasts we should probably move beyond."

"I agree." Nicole glanced at the bedroom door. "But if you're not ready to let go of *everything*, I can leave—"

"No!" He cut her off, unwilling to let her go now that she was here. Screw it, he wasn't going to waste another minute while he waited for her to come around. Letting her go was a stupid mistake, and he was going to rectify it. He wanted to grab her. Haul her against him and never let her go.

"You really mean that?"

He grabbed her. Hauled her against him. Wasn't going to let her go until she forced him to. "God, Nicole," he murmured into her hair, "I've been wanting to see you for days. I haven't eaten. Haven't slept."

He inhaled deeply, taking comfort in her scent, which seemed stronger, spicier than before. The imprint, maybe? Whatever it was, as her feminine fragrance penetrated his lungs, a warm sense of calm came over him, like everything was right in the world.

Arms tight around him, she buried her face in his chest. "I'm sorry, Riker. I'm so sorry."

"For what?"

The tremor in her voice broke his heart. "For not believing you."

He pulled back to look her in the eye. "What are you saying?"

"I'm saying I believe you love me, and I don't want to be apart anymore." She cleared her throat. "And it only took twenty shots of Kool-Aid flavors that should never be mixed, imaginary chest pain, and girl talk with a female vampire and a male vampire who plays Go Fish when everyone else is playing Five-Card Stud."

"I don't understand any of that, but if it got you here, that's all that matters." He slid one hand around to the back of her neck to caress the warm, satin skin there, only to freeze as something she'd said rang in his ears. "And wait . . . chest pain?"

"Imaginary," she muttered. "But it did feel real."

"When did it go away?"

She shrugged. "A few minutes ago, I guess. Why?"

He wasn't ready to share his theory yet, so he took

a page from his favorite tactics manual and went for a distract-and-evade maneuver.

Framing her face in his hands, he kissed her deeply. It took a whopping two seconds for his body to harden and heat, and with a low growl, he swept her up and carried her to the bedroom.

In his arms, she tensed. "Are you really okay with this?" she whispered.

"You belong here. You belong in my bed and in my life. Every aspect of it." He placed her gently on the mattress. "But I have a confession."

She smiled shyly. "So do I."

He sank down onto the bed with her and carefully laid her on her back. "You first."

He tucked a pillow under her head and stretched out beside her. What he really wanted to do was stretch out on *top* of her, but they were at a critical junction in their relationship, and he didn't want to mess it up by moving too fast.

Anxiety all but bled from her pores, and he got real fucking nervous, real fast. "Nicole? What is it?"

"I'm pregnant," she blurted.

Every muscle in Riker's body vapor-locked. "You're . . ." He swallowed. Cleared his throat. Remembered to breathe. Couldn't think. "When?"

"At ShadowSpawn."

ShadowSpawn? Darkness closed in around him, and he started to pant. *Nicole . . . oh, Jesus . . .*

She shoved herself up on one elbow. "No, oh, Riker," she rasped. "It's not what you're thinking. No one touched me. I swear." Reaching for him, she cupped his cheek in her warm palm. "It was the night I went to your cell. Fane made me take the fertility drug. Apparently, it works."

"We're having a baby?" His heart went crazy, tapping spastically against his rib cage. Excitement and fear sucked the air out of his lungs. There was nothing he wanted more than a family, but childbirth was extremely dangerous, and with no midwife to help, he could lose both Nicole and the baby.

"I can feel your fear." She kissed him lightly on the lips. "But please don't worry. When I researched the fertility treatment, I found that Daedalus hadn't lost a single female or child during birth. I believe fertility and childbirth are related. I have nine months to get it figured out. It's not the ideal timing, but—" He crushed her in a bear hug. "Okay, okay," she said on a laugh. "What's your confession?"

Slowly, he eased himself out of her grip. The curiosity etched in her expression made him squirm. She was here because she loved him, but would she believe he loved her after he told her about the imprint? He hesitated, wanting to stretch this out, because it might just be the last intimate, happy moment they had.

"Well?" she prompted, and pressure built in his chest.

He cleared his throat, stalling for more time. Finally, when she started tapping her foot on the mattress, he asked, "You believe I fell for you before you turned, right?"

"I do."

"You're sure?"

She scooted back, eyeing him warily, and he hated that he'd done that to her. "What's this about?"

Gripping the hem of his shirt, he peeled it off over his head. Her gaze immediately dropped to his chest, and he had to admit he enjoyed the way her eyes grew hungry. He tore open his fly and pushed one flap aside to reveal the new feather glyph pulsing on his skin.

Frowning, Nicole leaned forward, and then she straightened so fast she nearly fell off the bed. Might have if he hadn't grabbed her.

"Oh, my God . . ." Her mouth worked soundlessly for a moment. "Is that . . . an imprint mark?"

"It was the night you got pregnant," he said in a rush, stupidly, because when else would it have happened? They'd only had sex once since she'd turned into a vampire. Trying to sound a little less addled, he added, "I think it's why you felt chest pain. Vampires can sense emotions in others through scent or physical manifestations, but they have to be in close proximity . . . unless the male is imprinted. It's rare, but sometimes the female can actually feel the male's strong emotions even when they're miles apart."

"So you're saying I was feeling . . ."

"My pain," he finished.

Her long sable lashes flew up as her eyes shot wide open. "Oh, my God. If I'd known earlier how much you were hurting, I'd have come sooner."

He leaned over and kissed her, going again for the tried-and-true distract-and-evade strategy. "I guess we just have more time to make up, then."

"I'm being manipulated, aren't I?" she murmured against his lips.

Laughing, he eased them both back down on the mattress, eager to get her out of her clothes. She seemed on board with that plan, reaching for his fly. But instead of going where he thought she was going, her fingers found the raised crimson lines that defined his imprint. An intense, almost orgasmic shock shot straight to his groin, and he hissed with pleasure. An impish smile twitched at the corner of her mouth.

"I do believe I could have fun with that," she murmured.

He thought she could, too. "As often as you want."

She nipped his bottom lip as she traced the glyph, each feather-light stroke of her finger making him breathe faster. Between his legs, his erection ached, wanting the same attention.

"I also believe," she said, in a husky, intimate rasp, "that I'll take the timing of your imprint and my pregnancy as a sign."

"A good one?"

She slid her hand to his cock, and he groaned. "What do you think?"

Think? That ability had just gone AWOL. Drawing air into lungs so tight they felt like fists, he relieved her of her sweatshirt. She was gloriously braless, and he showered kisses on each breast before blazing a trail with his lips and tongue to her abdomen, where his child was growing.

"I'm so glad I found you," he said against the soft expanse of skin between her hip bones. "I gave up on life when Terese died, but you gave it back to me. You also gave me a son, and now you're going to give me another son or a daughter. I can't thank you enough."

"This again?" she teased. She shoved her fingers through his hair and forced his head up so their gazes met and held. "I'll let you thank me over and over, several times a day." Her smile grew wicked. "Maybe I'll demand it."

"Yeah?"

"Yeah."

It was his turn to get naughty, and he ripped open her jeans. She wasn't wearing underwear.

"I got tired of the granny panties," she said. "I didn't think you'd mind."

He let out a purr of approval and tugged her pants down her legs. "Are you ready for some serious thanks?" he asked as he prowled up her body from the foot of the bed.

"Oh, yes," she breathed. "Thank me. Thank me hard and fast. And then hard and slow."

He did. Over and over. And afterward, as they lay together in a tangle of arms and legs, he knew without a doubt that he could never thank her enough.

But he'd sure as hell try.

Epilogue

Hunter stood outside the ceremonial teepee he'd erected near clan headquarters decades ago, his heart racing. Every year on his birthday he came to this rocky cove to seek guidance from the demon that had started all this. And every year he came out of the buffalo hide tent with no answers. He'd never once seen the legendary demon, and bit by bit, doubt chipped away at his beliefs.

This time had to be different. It wasn't his birthday. And this wasn't about answers or proving the demon's existence. It was about a curse that was going to activate the moment he took a mate. A curse he knew he wasn't strong enough to survive.

Baddon and Myne flanked him, daggers drawn, waiting for his signal. Myne was the most bullheaded, disobedient son of a bitch on the planet, but even he didn't shirk ceremonial duty. He was a born vampire through and through, and Nez Perce honor flowed thick through his veins. He respected tradition and ritual.

He also liked making Hunter bleed. So yeah, this

was always great fun for him and the only time Hunter could count on him to show up when ordered to.

Fresh from Riker and Nicole's mating ceremony, Hunter squared his shoulders and let the ceremonial robe pool at his feet, leaving him naked in the biting cold night. Signal given, Baddon swung around in front of him. His silver blade flashed in the moonlight as he slashed a shallow cut across Hunter's chest. The sting from Baddon's knife was fleeting, but Myne's wouldn't be.

Baddon stepped aside, and Myne took his place, an eager smirk curving his lips as he jabbed the tip of his dagger into Hunter's sternum. Pain made Hunter clench his teeth as Myne took his time carving a deep gash all the way to Hunter's navel.

Myne was such an asshole.

Satisfied that Hunter was bleeding enough, Myne stepped back. "May your spirit quest bring you good fortune," he murmured, the genuine sentiment behind the words leaving Hunter slightly astonished.

Baddon bowed his head. "Spirits be with you."

Hunter acknowledged them both with nods. But he wasn't here to talk to his totem animal or to contact any spirits. As third-generation born vampires, they wouldn't know about the demon, and Hunter couldn't tell them. They probably wouldn't believe it anyway.

Sometimes even Hunter wasn't sure what to believe.

He strode inside the teepee, his bare feet coming down on the soft animal pelts that lined the floor. In the center of the tent, the small fire Baddon had prepared crackled, its flames beckoning him closer.

Nervous energy made Hunter's hand shake as he dragged his palm across his bloody chest and then gathered a handful of herbs and grasses from the plain wooden box placed near the fire.

Kneeling, he tossed the herbs, coated in his blood, into the flames. Almost instantly, the tent filled with a fragrant fog that teased his nostrils. Hunter closed his eyes and breathed deep, taking the smoke into his lungs.

"Come to me," he whispered.

A grayish mist clouded his mind, and the ground fell away beneath him. Pressure built in his chest, a crushing, squeezing sensation that turned every breath into a searing whip of agony. At the same time, an intense buzz vibrated every cell in his body. He felt as if he could come apart at any moment. He hated this part of the ritual, when he was torn between wanting to throw up and wanting to scream with the ecstasy of it. This was the point where his totem animal, a grizzly bear, would often appear to him, but that wasn't what he'd come for, and through a thickening haze of swirling colors in his head, he called out again.

"Samnult. Show yourself."

Damn you, demon, if you exist, now's the time to prove it.

Through a hum in his ears, he heard a voice. He called to it, and then he cried out as a tidal surge of euphoria washed over him. It was as if he were floating, cradled by warmth while a million hands caressed him both inside and out. He was sex. The air touching him was sex. The smoke he breathed was sex.

"Hunter." The impossibly deep voice rolled through him like an orgasm, and he moaned with the pleasure of it. "Open your eyes."

Hunter obeyed, found himself standing across the tent from a man draped in plush furs. Iron rings circled the rich reddish-brown skin of his arms. Crimson paint streaked his face from the corners of his mouth to where it disappeared into hair so black it absorbed the light from the fire, leaving the man surrounded in a swirling, pulsing shadow.

The world around Hunter lurched.

Demon. And not just any demon. This was *the* demon.

As if a secret door inside Hunter's head had been unlocked, hundreds of years of history flipped through his brain like a movie on fast-forward. The very origins of the vampire race came to vibrant life in his mind. Everything he'd learned about the twelve original chiefs was exactly as he'd been told.

The chiefs, guided by visions of war between tribes and an invasion of white men, had summoned a demon they'd believed to be a god. Samnult had promised them unmatched strength, speed, and immortality in exchange for allegiance, obedience, and the firstborn child of every mated first- and second-generation vampire.

Flames flickered in the demon's ebony eyes. *Actual* flames that singed everything they touched. Including Hunter's skin. "You summoned me." It wasn't a question.

In the dim recesses of Hunter's mind, he knew he should be more shocked and terrified than he was. Should be agonizing over whether this was real. But as the herbal smoke swirled around him, nothing seemed out of the ordinary.

"I summoned you," Hunter said, inclining his head

a fraction of an inch. "As I've attempted to do every year since my twentieth birthday, Samnult."

"Call me Sam." Sam bared a mouthful of teeth that would be better suited to an orca. "And don't try to shame me again. Not if you enjoy having your organs on the inside of your body."

Right. Sam. And yep, Hunter would rather not be turned inside out. "Noted. I summoned you because I'm taking a mate—"

Sam cut him off with a sharp gesture. "I'm aware. A union with ShadowSpawn. The eldest of Karshawnewuti's twin daughters." He yawned, as if this was all too boring to be bothered with. "You know the deal."

The first stirrings of fear and anger broke through the agony/ecstasy haze of the ritual. "I'm not handing my firstborn child over to you."

Hunter would sooner slit his own throat than deliver a baby into the hands of a demon.

Sam's voice degenerated into a serrated growl. "Then you and your mate will watch your child suffer before it dies a horrible, miserable death."

Hunter really wanted to give Sam a *horrible, miserable death*. "Not if you lift the curse."

"Few make that request." Sam folded his arms across his chest. The furs, some of which didn't look like they'd come from any animal Hunter had ever seen, parted, revealing a patch of black scales overlapping his rib cage. "Why do you think that is?"

"It's because anyone who doesn't ask you to lift the curse is an asshole who doesn't deserve to have children." Hunter moved closer, determined to make the demon understand how serious he was about this. "I'll do anything."

Sam's maniacal, sharp-toothed grin was like something straight out of an alien movie, and Hunter was the dumbass character who thought negotiating would be a good idea.

"So," Sam said in a voice that made Hunter's hair stand up, "if I asked you to kneel before me and take my cock in your mouth, you'd do it?"

Hunter dropped to his knees. He'd have to drown himself in vodka later, but he hadn't been lying when he said he'd do whatever it took to save the life of his child.

Sam's smile faded as he shifted his gaze to the fire, which flared as if he'd thrown gasoline on it.

"If you want to be released from the bargain I made with the twelve chiefs, you must first negotiate a series of tests." Sam gestured for Hunter to rise. "And one of them isn't to suck my cock."

Thank the spirits. Hunter wouldn't be nursing a grizzly-sized vodka–blow job hangover later. He rose. "I accept."

"Fool." The shadow surrounding the demon seethed like a living thing, and Hunter wondered if it was a measure of Sam's irritation. "You don't even know what the tests involve."

"I don't give a shit what they involve."

Sam reached out and dragged one hideously long, black-lacquered nail down the gash Myne had made. Hunter sucked air as fresh blood streamed from the newly opened laceration.

"Before your trial can begin, you must choose one

of the twins to accompany you. You can't pass through the membrane into my realm without either your intended mate or her sister. It doesn't matter which, since their veins run with the same blood. But consider this." He paused his finger's downward path just above Hunter's navel. "No matter who you choose, you will die."

Hunter recoiled, wrenching away from the demon. Die? His choice was to either never have children with his mate or *die*?

"If I'm going to die on this fucking quest of yours, what's the point of taking these tests?"

The fire roared to ten times its original size. Flames licked the wooden tent supports. Heat slammed into Hunter, blistering his skin and charring his hair. The stench of burned flesh filled the air, but Hunter held his ground, suffering through the searing agony with clenched teeth.

"The point is that even if you don't go on this quest, you will die." Sam's hand snapped out to take Hunter by the throat. Drool dripped from the demon's orca teeth, which looked a lot larger than they had a moment ago. "Before the winter ends, you will be dead."

"Again," Hunter ground out, "why should I go on your stupid quest?"

The demon cackled, a sinister, resonant sound that turned Hunter's marrow to ice. "Because going with one of the ShadowSpawn females is your only hope of survival. Both twins would be the death of you." In a *whoosh* of air, he turned to mist, his form twisting with the smoke from the fire. As the flames snuffed out and the smoke dissipated, the demon's voice echoed in Hunter's head. "*But only one of them will choose to bring you back.*"

ACKNOWLEDGMENTS

THERE ARE ALWAYS so many people to thank after a book is written, and *Bound by Night* is no exception. Huge thanks to my awesome editor, Lauren McKenna, whose brilliance and faith made this book such fun to write. And thank you to the entire Pocket Books team, not just for the fabulous cover, but for the support and hard work. Thanks, too, to Kimberly Whalen . . . everything fell together perfectly for us, didn't it? I also need to send big hugs to Michelle Willingham and Stephanie Tyler, because I swear, without you ladies, I'd never get anything done. This book should have your names on it, too! Love you!